P9-AOB-393

THE
Five-Minute Marriage

THE
Five-Minute Marriage

JOAN AIKEN

1978
DOUBLEDAY & COMPANY, INC.
GARDEN CITY, NEW YORK

Library of Congress Cataloging in Publication Data

Aiken, Joan, 1924–
The Five-Minute marriage.

I. Title.
PZ4.A289Fi3 [PR6051.135] 823'.9'14
ISBN: 0-385-12990-4
Library of Congress Catalog Card Number 77-72443

PRINTED IN THE UNITED STATES OF AMERICA
FIRST EDITION IN THE UNITED STATES OF AMERICA

THE

Five-Minute Marriage

1

"Pa, may we all go too?" sang the pupil on an ascending scale and then, coming down again with more assurance if less intelligibility, "La, pray, see, raw dough's blue!"

"Thank you, Miss Smith; you are showing great improvement in your upper notes. And," said Philadelphia, glancing at the ancient carriage-clock on the mantel, "that will be all we have time for today, I fear." She looked out through the first-floor window into Greek Street. "Yes—I see your mother coming."

Showing considerable relief that the termination of an exacting half-hour had arrived, the pupil quickly gathered her music together and donned her pelisse.

"Next Thursday, then, Miss Smith, as ever; and do not, this time, forget to practice your aria," added Philadelphia, casting the pupil into guilty confusion, but then assuaging this by a smile which lightened her rather serious countenance with a sudden transforming flash of gaiety.

"When I hear you next, I shall expect to feel myself translated to a box at Covent Garden."

"Good day, Miss Carteret. I shall not forget again, I promise." And with a worshiping glance the pupil, who was only three years younger than the instructor, took her departure, congratulating herself on having escaped the trimming she had expected and indeed deserved. But Miss Carteret seemed unusually preoccupied today, and contrived to greet the pupil's mother, and get rid of the pair, without the lengthy discussion of her daughter's abilities and progress which Mrs. Smith generally exacted.

When they were gone, Philadelphia walked swiftly through a communicating door from the room which did duty as combined music room, sleeping chamber, and parlor, into her mother's room.

Mrs. Carteret lay resignedly in bed against a pile of pillows. Her gold-gray hair was braided up into neat bands and covered with a cap. The cap, and the peignoir which she had wrapped around her shoulders were trimmed with lace of the very plainest quality, but exquisitely white; likewise the furnishings of the room, though simple, were carefully arranged and most scrupulously clean. A bunch of primroses stood in a blue pot on the bedside table, and the bed-curtains, though faded, were of excellent quality damask, and looked as if they might, perhaps, have descended from some superior establishment.

"I have to go out, now, Mamma, to give the Browty girls their lesson in Russell Square," Philadelphia said, leaning over to kiss her mother's smooth pink cheek. "Shall you be able to manage without me for an hour? Have you all that you require?"

"Russell Square? Why do you have to go *there?*" returned her mother with a certain petulance. "In *my* young days, nobody who was anybody lived in such a neighborhood. Some jumped-up tradesman or cit's daughters, I apprehend?"

"The Browtys pay a handsome fee," answered Philadelphia calmly, taking a bonnet from a drawer and fitting it with care over her smooth nut-brown locks. A pair of large and unusually beautiful almond-shaped gray eyes dispassionately regarded the result in a mirror; the plain bonnet was neither new nor fashionable, and its straw-colored Lyons silk lining showed decided signs of wear; but still it set off her eyes and framed her thin oval face agreeably enough.

"Why the deuce can't they come here?" inquired Mrs. Carteret. "Think themselves too good to set foot in the streets of Soho, I suppose?"

Wisely avoiding a discussion on this irrelevant issue, Philadelphia said, "Now, Mamma, it is only for a little over an hour! I will not dawdle, I promise. And I will bring back some neck of mutton and barley to make a good supporting broth for you—and a few of those little almond cakes of Mme. Lumière's that you always enjoy," she added coaxingly, but Mrs. Carteret was not to be placated, and only remarked in a grumbling manner,

"Mutton broth! Why must it be *that?* Why not a nice roast chicken? I am sick to death of mutton broth!"

"Dr. Button thinks mutton broth is better for you." Philadelphia refrained from pointing out that in any case they could not afford roast chicken and that her own dinner would probably consist of a boiled egg. "Now, Mamma, while I am gone, *please* do not you be getting out of bed and playing the piano—or—polishing the silver cream-jug or trying to trim your mantle—or anything else! You are not well enough yet. Will you promise me that?"

Mrs. Carteret's pretty pink-and-white face assumed an expression of martyred discontent.

"*Why* may I not? I could at least do some needlework in bed, Delphie! If you bought me a small quantity of cambric I could be making myself a new cap and jacket; these ones are so old and worn I am ashamed to face the doctor in them; I declare I have been wearing them forever!"

"Well, I will bring you back some cambric, Mamma, but you are not to be making it up yourself; you know Dr. Button said you should not undergo the least exertion, because of your heart. But I will try to find time to make you a new jacket this evening, when I have finished my last lesson."

"*You* do it? A sad botched job you would make of it," sniffed Mrs. Carteret. "You know you have no more notion of fine needlework than a July cuckoo!"

"Well then I will get Jenny Baggott to help me—shall I?"

"*That* vulgar creature—oh, very well! Stay, while I think of it—a piece of jaconet might be better than cambric."

"What color?"

"Humph; I am tired of white; what say you to pearl gray?"

"I think you would look charming in pearl gray, Mamma."

"Or no—I believe I prefer lavender. I think I will ask you to procure me a piece of lavender jaconet; or do you think that might fade? Perhaps it had better be rose pink—"

Concealing her impatience to be gone, Philadelphia encouraged her mother to settle for the original pearl gray.

"Now, shall I ask Jenny Baggott to step up and play a hand or two of cribbage with you while I am gone? She is the most good-natured creature in the world; I am sure she would contrive to find the time if you wish it?"

"Certainly not! Her voice is so loud that it goes through my head like a brass gong. I shall just lie here," said Mrs. Carteret in a melancholy voice, "I shall just lie here and entertain myself by recollecting the better times that are passed away forever."

"Would you care to read?" suggested Philadelphia. "Here is *Rasselas*; or the *Spectator*; or the poems of Pope—"

"No, thank you, dear; I do not have the energy to be holding a book; besides, my head aches too badly to be able to concentrate on those works. If it were something by Mrs. Radcliffe, now—something a little more entertaining—"

"I will try to get you *Sir Charles Grandison* or *Udolpho* from the circulating library," offered Philadelphia. "So you will have something to look forward to. Now I must run, or I shall be late. Mind you stay snug in bed, Mamma, for the wind blows cold today, though it is nearly May."

An expression compounded of rebellion and cunning appeared on the elder lady's face at this request, but she only replied,

"Pile up the fire, then, child."

"The fire is well enough," said Philadelphia, glancing at the modest pile of coal as she put on her shawl.

"Do not you be *walking* to Russell Square, now, Philadelphia!" said Mrs. Carteret. "It is not at all the thing for you to be arriving on foot to give your lessons. What will the servants at the house think of you? You must take a chair, Delphie—you must indeed—otherwise you will be quite blowsy and blown about—you will look like a kitchenmaid and will be directed to the back door!"

"Do not exercise yourself on that head, Mamma; the manservant at the Browtys' house knows me well, and I am always treated with the most distinguishing civility," Delphie answered calmly, and she escaped from the room before her mother could think up any further reasons for arguing and delaying her departure.

The stairs from their apartments led down through a millinery shop which occupied the ground floor of the premises, and here Delphie stopped to speak to the aforementioned Miss Jenny Baggott, who stood serving behind the counter. She was a black-eyed, bright-complexioned, good-humored-looking personage in her early thirties, whose yellow-spotted lilac gown was very gorgeous, and whose glossy black hair was arranged in a row of small curls like snails across her forehead.

"Well there, Miss Delphie! I was meaning to step up and say good day to your Ma this two hours agone, but we have been that busy this morning, you can't think! I have been obliged to help Sister ever since we opened the shop, and she has just slipped out for a morsel of ham and a pint of porter. But if you would like me to run up and sit with your poor dear Ma when Anne comes back, only say the word and I'll do it in a moment, for you know I am always happy to oblige."

"You are the best good creature in the world, Jenny—but Mamma is inclined to rest today, and I believe we need not trouble you," Philadelphia said with real gratitude.

"Why, it's no trouble, my dearie! You know I am always happy to sit with her. Even when she goes on a bit twitty and cantankerous, it's such an education to listen to her lovely ladylike way of speaking! I often say to Sis, 'Anne, you ought to pay more heed to Mrs. Carteret, then you wouldn't speak out so rough, the way you do.' Well, I'll just pop up presently with a cup of tea or a little bowl of bread-jelly for her, shall I?"

"I am sure she would be very much obliged—but you do too much for us, Jenny."

"*Nothing* would be too much trouble after all those beautiful lessons you've given me, and not charged a penny. My gentleman friend Mr. Swannup is used to say you've taught me to sing like a nightingale—and you with two things to do every blessed minute of the day," said Jenny vehemently. "The very instant Sis comes back I'll just step up and ask if there's anything the old lady would like."

"Pray don't trouble to do more than just peep in—I am in hopes she may doze off. She was in one of her quirky moods, and that generally means she is tired," Delphie said. "But I would be *very* much obliged, Jenny, if you would make certain that she does not try to get out of doors. You know how independent she is! And, I fear, since her illness, not *wholly* reasonable; she will not be brought to understand that there are some things she cannot do any more."

"*I'll* keep an eye on the poor dear lady," promised Jenny. "She shan't go out! Nor I won't let her buy twenty yards of violet satin from Sis, like she tried to the other week, nor order half a dozen ducklings from the poulterer, nor send for a hackney carriage to take her to Allardyce's library or the Pantheon. I'm up to all her tricks, Miss Delphie, believe me, and she shan't get away so long as I'm in the shop."

"Thank you—that is a great weight off my mind!" said Delphie, with her sudden flashing smile, which revealed two wholly unexpected dimples in her thin oval cheek.

Jenny beamed back at her and turned to measure a breadth of muslin for a waiting customer.

As soon as she was out on the pavement the smile left Philadelphia's face, to be replaced by a look of anxious preoccupation. She knew her mother's willful ways; and she also knew that, good-hearted and well-meaning though Jenny was, watchful though she intended to be, she was also the most impulsive creature in the world, easily tempted into the street by any interesting commotion or sound outside; during which periods, if her sister Anne was not at hand, customers were free to help themselves to caps or shawls, gloves or laces, should they choose to do so.

It occurred to Philadelphia, whose intelligence was of a humorous turn, and who dearly loved such absurdities and anomalies, that during the last half-hour she had received three earnest promises: from Miss Smith, to practice her aria; from Mrs. Carteret, to stay in bed; and from Jenny, to keep an eye on her mother. It seemed to her that all three promises had about as much chance of fulfillment as that lilies should spring up through the cobbles of Greek Street, along which lively and crowded thoroughfare she was now making her rapid way in a northerly direction toward St. Giles' Circus.

She would have been even more certain of this hypothesis could she have seen her mother at that moment. For Mrs. Carteret had not waited more than two minutes after she heard her daughter reach the foot of the stair to jump quietly out of bed and pull aside the curtain in the corner behind which her clothes were kept; having got herself into her stockings and petticoat, she was now deliberating between a dove-colored velvet dress with a worn breadth in it, and one of tabby-striped silk, rather finer, but not nearly warm enough for the sharp spring day. After a short period of consideration, Mrs. Carteret decided on the silk, and replaced the velvet dress behind the curtain, from which a strong smell of Tonkin beans emanated.

Then she began carefully and expertly doing her hair.

The fifteen-year-old Miss Lydia Browty had no great talent for music, but she was a painstaking child, and devoted to her teacher; Delphie was pleased to find how assiduously she had been practicing, and the lesson went well. It was always a pleasure, too, for Delphie to have a chance to play the Browtys' pianoforte, which was an extremely handsome and brand-new instrument from Broadwoods with a most excellent tone. Mr. Browty, a nabob who had acquired a very comfortable fortune during twenty years in Calcutta, had recently returned home to establish himself in town and enjoy the fruits of his labors. He was a widower, his wife having succumbed to the adverse climate of the East, but had two daughters in their teens who were delighted to be removed from the young ladies' seminary to which they had been dispatched at an early age, and to provide the necessary feminine element in their Papa's London establishment.

At the end of Lydia's lesson (Miss Charlotte being confined to bed with a cold) Mr. Browty himself came surging into the large and elegantly appointed music room, as if he had been waiting impatiently for the sounds of singing to die away.

"Hey-day, Miss Carteret! How d'ye do! Good day to ye! (No need, indeed, to ask how you do, eyes sparkling like diamonds as usual!) How's my Lyddy coming along, now? Learning to tirra-lirra like a regular operatic signorina, is she, hey?"

Delphie truthfully replied that Miss Lydia was taking great pains with her music and making excellent progress, at which the fond father beamed affably on pupil and teacher alike. Delphie smiled back at him. She had a great liking for Mr. Browty, who, in spite of his large fortune and impressive City connections, was a plain, unassuming man. His complexion was somewhat yellow, due to his years in the East, and his thick hair was grizzled to a salt-and-pepper color. He was not handsome, but his eyes were clear and direct, and his expression both shrewd and good-natured. He was far from fashionable: today he wore a full-skirted coat of drab-colored broadcloth, drab knee breeches, and old-fashioned squre buckled shoes, with a white neckcloth and a mustard-colored waistcoat, whereas his daughter's French cambric dress was in the height of the current mode.

"Hark-ee, Miss Philadelphia—hey, hey, shouldn't call you that, should I—to tell the truth I caught the trick from Puss here—"

Delphia said calmly that nothing could give her greater pleasure and it made her feel quite like one of the family.

"Just what *I* feel too," he said, beaming, "and what I had in mind when I took the notion to approach you with this plan—"

"It was *my* idea, Pa!" interjected Miss Lydia.

"Hush, Puss, and let me make all plain to Miss Carteret without any roundaboutation. The gals and I, Miss Carteret, have taken a notion to run over to Paris next Tuesday, for a few weeks, now the war's over and we can all get about again with Boney safe under hatches. And what we are hoping is that you might see your way to come along with us, so the girls need not miss their lessons. Not only that—we'd value your company, for I'm but a creaky old stick when it comes to escorting the young misses around, and know little of museums and milliners and such feminine fripperies. Whereas you are quite the lady and can tell my pusses how to go on in every kind of way.

"Besides which, Lyddy tells me you speak capital French, while I can't parleyvoo to save my life, and I don't believe Lyddy and Charlie are much better, despite all those years at Miss Minchin's! So how about it, hey? Will you give us the benefit of your presence, Miss Philadelphia? We'd dearly like to have you with us. I'd guarantee to treat you as one of my own, and," Mr. Browty said emphatically, "you'd not lose on it, for I'd reimburse you on any lessons you'd be obliged to miss over here. I'm very certain you deserve a little holiday, so hardworking as you are!"

Philadelphia was extremely touched, and said everything that was proper. She would have loved to visit Paris, which in 1815, was the gayest city in Europe. But with considerable regret she informed Mr. Browty that it was quite out of her power to leave London at present, since her mother, who had had a sharp illness during February and March, was still far from well, much pulled-down, and in no condition to be left.

Both Lydia's and Mr. Browty's faces fell very much at this information.

"You are quite sure, Miss Carteret? You couldn't leave her, even for a couple of weeks?"

"I am deeply sensible of your kindness, Mr. Browty, and more sorry than I can say to be obliged to forgo such a treat. But indeed, I cannot leave my mother. It is not only that she is ill and weak. But, since her illness, her—her good sense has been somewhat affected, so that she cannot be relied upon not to do exceedingly odd and awkward, not to say even downright dangerous things. Last week, for instance, while I was away giving a lesson in Hampstead, she somehow contrived to slip out, went to Fordham's Stores, and ordered enough provisions for an Assembly Ball, which she seemed to be under the impression that she was about to hold! Fortunately she had neglected to give them our direction, so when I learned what she had done, I was able to countermand the order before they had discovered where to send the things."

Mr. Browty laughed heartily at this disclosure, and said,

"But could you not hire some reliable person to look after your mother, Miss Carteret? It is too bad that you must be burdened with such an anxiety while you are teaching as well."

"I am afraid that would not be possible," Philadelphia replied in a dispirited manner. "You see, for a start, my mother will mind no one but me—though indeed, she does not always mind me either."

She had been about to explain, also, that their circumstances did not permit of such an expense, but, glancing at Mr. Browty, she decided to remain silent on that head. He was so good-natured that it was quite possible he might offer to assist them, and Delphie, who had inherited considerable family pride, as well as her distinguished good looks, from her mother, could not bear the idea of accepting charity.

"Excuse my asking this question, Miss Carteret, but have you no friends—no relatives—who could give you assistance during your mother's illness?"

"No," Delphie answered firmly. "We have not, sir. My mother and I are alone, and are supported solely by what I can earn from giving music and singing lessons. That has hitherto been quite sufficient—but—but my savings were somewhat depleted by her illness. Now she is recovered, matters will soon be in a better train, however."

"Your father, I take it, is no more?"

"No, sir; he was a captain in the Navy, and died in the Battle of St. Vincent, when I was only four years old. I do not remember him very well."

"He had no kinsfolk—no parents or relations?"

"No; he was an orphan, making his own way in the world. That is why when—when my mother fell in love with him, her family forbade the match. It was a runaway affair—an elopement. And in consequence of *that*, my mother's family quite cut her off, and have refused to have anything to do with her, ever since."

"Can you believe it!" exclaimed Mr. Browty. "What a currish set of hardhearted skinflints they must be! There's your aristocracy for you!—for I'll be bound, from the cut of your jib, that they are aristocracy, amn't I right, my child?"

"Yes, sir," she replied, somewhat reluctantly.

"What was your mother's maiden name, if I may make so bold, Miss Carteret?"

"*Papa!*" exclaimed Lydia, blushing. "You are distressing Miss Carteret. It is the outside of enough! She may not wish to tell you these things!"

"Fiddlestick, Puss! Hold your tongue! Miss Carteret knows I only mean well by her, don't you, my dear? I'm just wishful to find some way to assist her, that's all. Nor I'm not going to thrust alms down her throat unwanted, she knows that too! Miss Philadelphia's got a head on her shoulders worth two of yours, Lyddy!"

Encouraged by this statement, Philadelphia said,

"My mother's name was Penistone, Mr. Browty. My grandfather was the Fifth Viscount Bollington, and had estates in the Peak district, and in Kent, which was where my mother was brought up. But of course I never met my grandfather. He died when my mother was quite young, and was succeeded by his brother, the Sixth Viscount, who, I understand, was of a very arbitrary and tyrannical disposition. He also quarreled with my uncle, my mother's brother, who went into the Navy and was killed in the same action as my father; they were great friends, which was how my mother happened to meet my father, when he came to stay at the family home."

"Indeed? There were no other sons, besides your mother's brother?"

"No, sir; as I said, the title passed to my great-uncle. I presume he is still living. I do not know if he has children of his own. My mother has always been very reluctant to talk about her family. She felt it so deeply when they cut her off that she would sooner die than be beholden to them."

"Do you, also, feel as deeply as that?"

"N-no, not quite," admitted Delphie. "It did seem to me—since my mother would, in the natural order of things, have been able to expect a handsome competence at her majority—that it was monstrously unjust and unnatural that her family would not assist her in her illness; and so—and so when she was in very bad case I did venture to write off—"

"Aha, you wrote off?"

"But only received the briefest of curt notes back, rejecting my appeal as a piece of imposture. So I resolved to demean myself no more in that direction."

"I dare swear I'd have done the same," nodded Mr. Browty. "But—there's a wicked, hardhearted, clutch-fisted set of penny pinchers for you! What did you say the name was, again?"

"The family name is Penistone, and my uncle is Lord Bollington, the Sixth Viscount."

"Bollington—the name is familiar," mused Mr. Browty. "Didn't we meet a Lord Bollington—somewhere abroad, Puss? It sticks in my nodbox that we did—where would that have been, now?"

"Was it at the baths, Papa? At Bad Reichenbach?"

"Ay—that's it—that's where it was! I mind him now—a queer, sad old stick, full of odd freaks and fancies, like a cudgel with a hank of white hair atop, forever with some odd notion in his attic, and set on maudling his innards with every kind of medicine, always fancying himself at death's door. I mind him well. Right, and I was able to do him a good turn that he needed sore, for his bankers' drafts hadn't come through, and *my* name on a bill's as good as gold from here to Constantinople."

"I'm sure it is," Delphie said politely, glancing at the clock on the marble mantel. "But—excuse me, Mr. Browty—I promised to return to my mother as soon as might be, and I am somewhat anxious about her—"

"In course you are! But, listen, my dear; write again, and this time, give *my* name as reference. *I* know you are no imposter, and Browty's word is as good as his bond. Or no—better still—where does the old cull keep himself?"

"I beg your pardon, sir?"

"Your uncle, child—great-uncle—whatever he be?"

"Oh, Lord Bollington? He has several estates; but I believe that his main residence is in Kent, where my mother was brought up, at Chase Place."

"Ay, Chase—that is it. I mind him referring to it now. To be sure, Chase—that was it. Ay, he and I grew to be close as birds of a feather, lying in those mud baths together—he'll recall the name of Josiah Browty. Chase Place—very good! My sixteen-mile-an-hour grays can spank down there in four hours, or I'm a Dutchman. I'll give you a note to the old curmudgeon that will make him sing to a different tune, I'll warrant you!"

"But—" said Delphie, taken aback, "I beg your pardon, my dear sir, but what are you proposing?"

"Why, that I lend you my posting-chariot, supply you with a note of recommendation, and that you drive down to Chase yourself and beard the old put in his den! Take the bull by the horns, that's my motto, and always has been, and a fair pile of feathers it's fetched me!"

"But, sir!"

Although this plan did have considerable appeal to Delphie, who was herself of a forthright and enterprising character, always apt to act rather than repine, she could see many objections to it.

"In the first place—I cannot be so beholden to you! What have I ever done to deserve such distinguished—?"

"Pish, my dear! The chariot will be here, and the grays eating their heads off, for I'll take the bays and the bigger coach to France with all the gals' gear—I was about to offer the use of the chariot, in any case, for you to take your Mama for an airing, now and again. And as to *deserve*—I'm well aware of the pains you've spent on Lyddy and Charlie, who've neither of them a note of music in their brainboxes—besides all the other things they've picked up from you in the course—all your ladylike ways and elegancies of behavior—"

"Nonsense, my dear sir—certainly not enough to earn the use of your carriage for at least two days!" said Delphie, blushing and laughing.

"Say no more, Miss Philadelphia—my mind's made up to this plan and I'll hear no argufication! Why would that old skinflint loll there on his millions—ay, now I recall, he owns the coal under half Derbyshire—besides a hundred and fifty thousand in the Funds—he's one of the warmest men in the country, my dear! Why should he sit there while you and your mother can hardly scrape ten guineas together?"

"Yes, it is the injustice of the situation that really puts me in a rage!" Delphie could not help bursting out, and Mr. Browty said approvingly,

"Ah, I knew you was a lass of spirit! Now we'll say no more at this present, for I know you're itching to be off to your Mama, but I'll write a note to his ludship and have it sent around to you in Greek Street, and I'll tell Bodkin, my under-coachman (who is as steady a man as you need hope to find), and the postilions to be ready to wait on you whenever you say the word. And think nothing of coaching-inn fees or any other such expenses, my dear"—as she opened her mouth—"that will all be found, I promise you."

"But, sir, how can I ever repay you?"

"Why, as to that, my dear—if you and your Mama come into your rights, you will be able to repay me with the greatest ease! If it weighs on your mind, as it certainly does not on mine."

"But if I don't come into my rights?" Delphie could not help saying.

"We'll concern ourselves with that another time!"

Delphie endeavored to render suitable thanks—her head was somewhat in a whirl with the suddenness of all these plans—but Mr. Browty indulgently told her to run along and save her breath for arguing with Lord Bollington.

Lydia bade good-by to her preceptress with a warm hug and a little skip of excitement, crying,

"Oh, it is the most romantical plan imaginable! I wish I might go along."

"Much help you would be, Puss!"

"I wish we might be here to learn what comes of it! Can we not stay in England another fortnight, Pa, till Miss Carteret has been to see her great-uncle?"

"Nonsense, Puss! We have all our hotel reservations, and my man of business in Paris waiting on my arrival—we shall hear soon enough how Miss Carteret has sped. I daresay she will be good enough to write us a note about it."

"Indeed I shall!" said Philadelphia. "And I am *very* much obliged to you."

With that she collected up her music and left, for she had already overstayed her time by more than a quarter of an hour, and she was becoming momentarily more anxious to return to her mother.

"Ah, there goes a lass in a million," said Mr. Browty, gazing after her with unmixed respect. "Strong-minded—clever—and real high-class looks into the bargain! You'd have to beat over half England to find her equal. It was a lucky day for our family, Lyddy, when I picked Miss Carteret to be your singing teacher."

"Yes, Papa," said Lydia.

Philadelphia hurried home, stopping in Brewer Street market to buy the promised neck of lamb, and again at Mme. Lumière's for the almond cakes. Mme. Lumière, like many of the residents of Soho, was an émigré Frenchwoman who had left Paris during the Terror, and had prospered so well with her pastrycook's business during the following twenty-odd years that she had long since abandoned any thought of returning to her native land. It was from Madame's brother, Christophe Lumière, that Delphie had learned her music; he was a distinguished composer and conductor who, since he stood in high favor at the court of Louis XVI, had been obliged to escape with his sister. For many years he had been the lodger of Mrs. Carteret, whose husband had left her just sufficient money to buy a small house in Soho and rent out most of its rooms to support herself and her child. The rents had also sufficed to send Philadelphia for a period to an Academy for Young Ladies in Chiswick. But M. Lumière had died and misfortunes had then overtaken the Carterets; debts had piled up, and Mrs. Carteret had, in the end, been obliged to sell the house and move to their present accommodation. The money from the sale, which would, in the normal course, probably have provided for the mother and daughter's needs for several years, had been almost entirely consumed by the expenses of Mrs. Carteret's illness, and a frighteningly small sum now stood between them and complete destitution.

Philadelphia sometimes trembled, waking in the night, at the thought of what would become of them should she herself, through any mischance, lose her capacity to earn. Suppose she too were to fall ill? Or be run over by a carriage or abducted in the streets of London—such occurrences were not unknown. What would Mrs. Carteret do then? Even before her illness she had been somewhat feckless, and wholly lacking in any qualification to earn her own living; her only accomplishment was the cutting out of very beautiful paper spills, but the sale of such articles would barely suffice to keep the pair in candles.

Mrs. Carteret herself had never been troubled by anxieties as to the future.

"My dear child, pray do not be forever fussing and fretting and spoiling your looks over these trifling considerations! Of course you will presently make an eligible match, and then all our troubles will be over. For I will say this—although you have unfortunately inherited your father's cautious, prosy, down-to-earth, pinchpenny temperament, you have luckily taken from *me* the Penistone family looks, and *those* are not to be sneezed at; you must be worthy of the first consideration in any circles in the land!"

"But, dearest Mamma—we don't move in any circles in the land! We don't even move in a segment of a circle!" said Delphie, who had learned a little Geometry as well as the Use of the Globes at Miss Pinkerton's Academy in Chiswick.

"Never mind that, child! It is true—if only you could be presented at Court—how advantageous that would be. But still, I do not despair of some gentleman of breeding and discrimination observing you as you pass by in the street. So do not let me see those desponding looks, any more—but hold your head up straight, and walk with elegance. You will see, all those hours that I made you spend on the backboard will presently bring their reward! In fact it would do no harm if you were to lie down *now* upon the backboard for half an hour!"

"Never mind the backboard, Mamma. I am more likely soon to be upon the shelf! Do not forget that I am three and twenty!"

"No, impossible, how *can* you be? I am sure you must be mistaken. Though it is true," sighed Mrs. Carteret, "that I was only sixteen when I eloped with your dearest Papa. In any case, Philadelphia, your looks are in the bone, and not such as will fade in your twenties; I by no means despair of your forming an eligible connection, even now."

Philadelphia herself had no such certainty; nor was she even sure that she wished to marry. Certainly she had never, among the respectable tradesmen, exiled French, and down-at-heels gentry who formed the Carterets' principal acquaintance, encountered the man whom she felt she would be able to love. Her main ambition was centered on saving enough to start a small music school by which she could keep herself and her mother in modest comfort. But with Mrs. Carteret's frail health and awkward propensity for disbursing money and running into debt, such hopes were slender indeed.

Passing swiftly through the Baggotts' millinery establishment, Delphie stopped to make the promised purchase of pale-gray jaconet from Jenny, who greeted her with a beaming smile.

"There you are back then, Miss Delphie! I just stepped upstairs, half an hour agone, with a bowl of bread-jelly, and peeked through the crack, like you said, but she was fast; I could just see her blessed head on the pillow; so I didn't disturb her, but came right down again. She hasn't stirred once, not all the while you've been out; not a whisper have we heard from her."

Much relieved at this news, Delphie thanked Miss Baggott, paid for the jaconet with some of her fee from Mr. Browty (who always settled on the nail), and ran upstairs. Opening the door softly, she laid her purchases on a small table which did duty as both kitchen and dining table, then stole into the farther room to see how her mother did.

For a moment she, too, was deceived and thought Mrs. Carteret lay sleeping on the bed; then, approaching closer, she saw with deep dismay that the lace nightcap had been cunningly drawn over a rolled-up nightgown, and the bedclothes pulled together to make it appear as if a sleeping person lay under them. But the bed was empty; and also cold; it must have been unoccupied for at least an hour.

With speed born of experience, Delphie scanned her mother's wardrobe, and her anxiety was greatly aggravated by the discovery that Mrs. Carteret must have gone out in her tabby silk and an embroidered India-muslin shawl—very insufficient covering for a barely convalescent invalid on a cold April day.

Trying to quell her agitation, Delphie ran down the stairs again. Both Miss Baggotts were now in the shop, and, addressing them in somewhat desperate accents, Delphie informed them that her mother had gone out.

The sisters were aghast.

"She's not run out *again?* Are you certain, Miss Delphie? Have you looked behind the curtain—behind the sopha? I'd be ready to swear I'd not taken my eyes off the stair the whole blessed afternoon!" Jenny declared agitatedly.

"You forget, Sister, the time the funeral passed by and you was so anxious to run out and discover whose it was!" Miss Anne tartly reminded her sister. "And it was just then that I was obliged to go to the stock room for a new bale of sprig-muslin—depend on it, that must have been when Missus must ha' cut and run for it!"

Despairingly, Philadelphia remembered that she had passed a funeral procession herself, at the top of Greek Street, very shortly after leaving home. If her mother had managed to slip out while the cortege was passing the Baggott establishment, she must have been gone for a very long time, and there would be little use in hunting for her among the streets close at hand. There were a dozen places she might have reached by this time—the Pantheon Bazaar in Grafton House, where she might take it into her head to order a hundred yards of Irish poplin for housemaids' dresses—or Mudie's library, where she might bespeak the most expensive new publications—or Bond Street, which offered a terrifying range of temptations to a lady who seemed to have completely forgotten her penurious situation. Or there was another Mecca, more dangerous still. To this resort of enterprising and disengaged females, Philadelphia first turned her steps. It was in Orchard Street, and was known as Heiresses' Haven, though in fact its proper appellation was Duvivier's Tea and Domino Salon. Here ladies of somewhat doubtful respectability and others with too much time on their hands repaired to drink Bohea and play écarté and preference, and here it was that Mrs. Carteret, during the previous year, had contrived to expend a larger and larger proportion of their slender resources.

So it was with a failing heart that Delphie climbed the familiar narrow stairs, and looked around the somewhat shabbily furnished rooms.

"Has my mother been here?" she inquired of Mme. Duvivier, who was presiding at the table nearest the entrance. Madame was a formidable-looking lady in a sky-blue turban, enough diamonds to buy up Kensington Palace, if they had been real, and a highly powdered countenance. She gave Delphie a very sharp look.

"No—Mrs. Carteret has *not* been here, Miss—not this afternoon. If she had, it would have been my painful duty to remind her that she is owing five guineas on account of—"

"Thank you! I cannot give it you at the moment," said Philadelphia hastily. "But I will see that you are paid within the week."

"Stop, Miss—stop!" exclaimed Mme. Duvivier as she turned to leave.

"I cannot stop; my mother is at this instant somewhere in the streets and likely to catch her death from chills," Delphie called back, and ran down the stairs.

Next she went to Bond Street, and investigated all its jewelers and hat shops, incurring the various coarse remarks and incivilities to which an unescorted lady in London was liable; these, however, she turned off with such a practiced air of haughty, cool reserve that none of the accosting males dared pursue their advances any further.

But she did not find Mrs. Carteret. One or two of the jewelers were known to her, for it was in their emporiums that she had been obliged to dispose of some of her mother's few last good pieces; but they all denied having set eyes on her mother.

Nor, apparently, had Mrs. Carteret ordered any provisions at Fordham's, in Piccadilly—which was something of a relief—nor had she been to Hatchard's bookshop nor to Allardyce's library.

Delphie began to fear that she must have taken the opposite direction; once or twice in the delirium of her illness she had been heard to murmur that she "must very soon pay a visit to my brokers in the City"; no such brokers, to the best of Delphie's knowledge, existed; certainly Mrs. Carteret had had dealings with none in the last fifteen years, but if she had taken it into her head to proceed in the direction of Threadneedle Street or Petty Cury, the hope of discovering her was scanty indeed, for the older part of London was such a warren of small thoroughfares that a person might be lost within them for weeks on end.

To add to Delphie's despair, a thin rain was beginning to fall.

"Perhaps she may take a hackney cab home," Delphie thought. The expense would be a crippling addition to their strained exchequer, but better that than the poor lady should be soaked through in her flimsy silk and muslin.

Delphie herself was insufficiently equipped for a wetting, and she turned homeward, somewhat hopelessly scanning the Oxford Street shops and the stalls of Brewer Street market again as she passed. Most of the stall-holders knew her, but none of them were able to give her tidings of her quarry.

At last, very despondent, she arrived back at the rooms in Greek Street and saw at once, from Miss Anne's downcast look and Miss Jenny's expression of guilty despair, that her mother had not returned while she herself had been out.

"Should we inform the constables?" quavered Jenny. "She has not been out for so long since her illness! Indeed and indeed I'm sorry, Miss Delphie—I could beat my head in the dust for shame —but there! What good would that do?"

"Not the least bit of good in the world!" snapped Miss Anne. "You had better by far brew Miss Delphie a cup of Bohea; she looks worn to a thread-paper."

"I do not like to call in the constables unless the case seems desperate," said Delphie, gratefully accepting the proffered beverage, which was indeed welcome, for she had had nothing since her scanty breakfast of one piece of bread and butter. "I know Mamma would be dreadfully ashamed and overset to think we had taken such a step. I will wait a little longer. When I have drunk my tea I shall put on a pelisse and search around Seven Dials and Drury Lane; I have not yet looked in that direction, knowing Mamma's preference for the more fashionable part of London."

"Oh, no, Miss Delphie, you didn't ought to think of going out again!" scolded Jenny. "Why, you are quite fagged out already—white as cheesecloth, ain't she, Sister, and your bonnet all soaked. That straw will never be good for anything after this!"

"But I must go out," said Delphie. "I cannot bear to think of her, perhaps lost, somewhere in this downpour"—for the rain had come on more heavily and was turning to a real spring deluge.

Out, despite all their remonstrances, she went, clad in a worn old tartan pelisse, and wearily made a reconnaissance of Charing Cross, Covent Garden, and Drury Lane, even going so far east as Holborn and Chancery Lane. Once or twice she thought what a fortunate occurrence it was that many of the families whose children were her pupils had at present gone out of town for the Easter Holiday; at least it meant that lessons were few and far between. Her income, in consequence, was sadly depleted, but no indignant pupils were being deprived of their tuition while she scoured the streets for her straying parent.

Presently dusk began to fall, early because of the rain, and Delphie was forced to acknowledge to herself that it was quite useless for her to continue the search; a few of London's streets were now gaslit, but the majority were not; and in general the illumination was dim, flickering, and inadequate; there was no possible chance any longer of spotting the lost lady. Delphie herself, by this time, was soaked and shivering; all she could do was turn homeward once more.

There, the Baggott sisters received her with distressed and contrite looks; urged her to come into the back parlor, where they had built up a roaring fire, and revived her with what Miss Jenny called "a little drop of summat 'ot"—a very little brandy and a great deal of lemon, sugar, and hot water, which in the circumstances was highly welcome, for with all the hurrying and calling, searching and inquiring, Delphie's throat had become very hoarse and sore.

"If only you haven't took cold your pore self!" said Jenny anxiously. "You didn't ought to be running about in the rain, Miss Delphie, indeed you oughtn't, for if you was to take a putrid sore throat, what's to become of you? You can't teach them blessed lambs to sing!"—a fear which Delphie herself entertained but did not dare acknowledge.

"Oh, it is nothing—I am very strong," she said, sneezing, "but poor Mama! I am worried to death about her. Now, I am afraid, I shall really have to inform the constabulary."

The sisters had shut up shop, in consideration of the wet weather, and the emergency, but just at this moment a faint tap was heard on the outer door.

"Run, quick, Jenny!" said Miss Baggott. "Somebody's out there —only think, perhaps some kind person has took Missus up!"

Jenny flew to the door, and, opening it, cried out in a tone of ecstacy, "Lord, if it ain't Missus herself, but oh! what a pickle she's in! Lord bless us, ma'am, where *have* you been all this time, here's Miss Delphie and all of us in such a pucker and a pelter over you—and you come in looking as if you've been drug backwards down the Fleet River!"

"Quick, bring the poor lady to the fire, Jenny, don't stand there a-gabbling," cried her sister.

Mrs. Carteret certainly was in a deplorable condition, the feathers on her bonnet hanging limply down her back, her hair all out of curl with wet, and her soaked clothes clinging to her "for all the world like a drowned rat's fur," as Miss Jenny said. She tottered to the fireplace, hardly seeming to know where she was, and sat down abruptly on an upright chair as if her stiff legs would hold her up no longer.

Sipping a hot toddy which Miss Anne quickly mixed for her, she gazed at her daughter and the Miss Baggotts vacantly over the rim of her cup. Her eyes were strangely bright, and there was a hectic flush on her cheekbones. Kettles for a mustard bath, Delphie thought rapidly, a hot brick for her bed, warm flannel to wrap round her chest . . . Will she survive this? Will the congestion return to her?

"Mamma dear, where were you?" Delphie asked gently, as the spirit began to take its effect and a faint spark of understanding returned to Mrs. Carteret's eyes. "Don't you remember I implored you *not* to go out, because you are not well enough? What did you have to do that was so important, that I could not have done for you?"

"Where did I have to go?" quavered Mrs. Carteret at last. "Why—of course—need you ask?—of course I went to St. Paul's!"

"*St. Paul's?* But that is over two miles from here—nearer three! You mean to say that you walked all that way? But why?"

"My dear Mamma would *always* go to evensong in St. Paul's when she was in town—or so I understand," said Mrs. Carteret firmly.

"You walked all the way there? And all the way back?"

"In course I did! When I was young we thought nothing of a six- or seven-mile walk. It is not right in you to nag and reproach me, Philadelphia," said her mother, with more spirit. "Particularly since it was you that I had in mind when I made the expedition."

"Me, Mamma? What can you possibly mean?"

"I cannot tell you that in front of these strangers," said Mrs. Carteret with dignity.

"*Strangers?* Lawk, and she's known us any time these twelve years!" exclaimed Jenny indignantly, but Anne whispered,

"Hush, Sister, can't you see Missus is not herself! Come, Ma'am, let me and Miss Delphie help you up the stairs, the best thing you can do is get into a hot bath directly, and I've a pair of kettles on a-boiling this minute. Indeed you should not have run out like that, Mrs. Carteret, frightening your poor daughter so dreadfully, and putting us all in a tweak!"

Somehow, very slowly, poor Mrs. Carteret, now trembling with weakness, was helped up the stairs, and the Baggott sisters then tactfully left her alone with her daughter, but promising to run up directly if required. When they were alone Mrs. Carteret fairly burst into tears.

"Why do you all *scold* me so," she sobbed, "when I only did it for the best?"

"Did *what*, Mamma? *What* did you do?"

"Why, went to St. Paul's to pray for a husband for you, naturally!"

Delphie hardly knew whether to laugh or weep. What a hopeless quest! What a piteous pilgrimage! At least it had not involved Mrs. Carteret in any outrageous, wild expense, but it seemed highly probable that she might have caught her death from wet and exhaustion.

"That was a very kind, thoughtful thing to do," Delphie said, giving her parent a warm and loving embrace, and then proceeding to whisk off the sodden shawl, "but, you know, I don't want a husband, I would rather by far remain with you."

"Of *course* you want a husband," said Mrs. Carteret, shivering miserably as the draggled silk was peeled away from her shoulders. "For if you had a good one, we could all live together and *he* would support us!"

And she beamed into her daughter's face as Delphie guided her faltering steps toward the mustard bath Miss Anne had made ready, which stood steaming in front of the fire.

2

It was hardly to be expected that Mrs. Carteret's expedition to St. Paul's, though undertaken from the highest of motives, should not lead to a recurrence of her lung trouble; in fact she was laid upon her bed for more than a week with a sharp attack, complicated by pleurisy, and for many hours her life was despaired of. But by one means or another, partly due to some innate strength in her, partly through Philadelphia's careful tireless, tender nursing (though herself afflicted with a heavy cold), Mrs. Carteret scraped through.

"She will not achieve full health for a long time yet, though," said the doctor, on the fourth day, when she had passed the crisis. He glanced about him. "These rooms are not at all suitable for her—no sun, no healthful circulation of air. She should be in the country—preferably in a warm climate. Rome would be excellent —or the South of France."

Delphie looked at him in exhausted silence. How could she possibly achieve such a removal? His own bill was still owing, and likely to remain so for some time.

"Well—well—do what you can for her," he said in a kind tone, understanding the situation. "An airing in the park, as often as possible, in a week or so, when it is warmer. And perhaps she might go to stay on some farm? Do not be worrying too much, Miss Carteret—or we shall have *you* falling sick. And don't fret about my bill—that can wait."

Delphie, with her usual resilience, had recovered from her cold, but she was pale and heavy-eyed from long watching at night, and considerably thinner than she had been before her mother's illness.

"You must get into the fresh air too," said the doctor. "Take a walk in Kensington Gardens twice a week at least. Don't trouble your head about your mother—she will do now. I shall return in four or five days, to see how she goes on."

And he picked up his hat and cane and went down to his barouche.

When he had gone Delphie lifted the lid of the pianoforte and removed from inside it an envelope which had arrived from Mr. Browty some five days previously. In it was a note, written hastily in large unformed characters:

Dear Miss Carteret, Here is the recommendation to Lord Bollington that I promised you. Mind you use it, now, or I shall be uncommon vexed! I am also enclosing 10 Guineas to pay any expenses, besides some good professional Woman to mind your Mother while you are out of town, for I know otherwise you will not stir a Step, out of anxiety for the poor lady. Now do not be troubling your head about post-fees or the servants' accomodation—I have told Bodkin he is to arrange all that. The village of Cow Green is not a stone's throw from Chase, and the servants can rack up at the Inn there.

I believe you shd take some Female Person as companion when you go—Ld.B was a very twitty old Chaw-Bacon & wd not countenance a young Lady gallivanting about the countryside unescorted.

Write us a Note to the Hotel Creçy to tell how you go on—the girls and I will be Agog for news.

Yr sincere well-wisher,
Jos. Browty

Enclosed were the ten guineas and an open envelope which had another note in it:

My dear Lord Bollington,

You will recall me as had the Honour to do you a small Service when we was both convalessing from the megrims at Bad Risenback. This is to introduce to your Notise a young Connection of yours, Miss Carteret. Miss C is the best, most scrupulously honest young Lady of my acquaintance & wd no more conduct on Imposture than she wd commit Murder. Her Morals are Unblemish'd, her Character direct & Sinsere, her Mind of a Purity the most Unecsepshionable & Limpid. Any that says she is capable of falsehood commits a most Gross Injustise, & in my Opinion she & her Ma has been treated with very Scandalous Inequity, whch I Hope will now be righted.

Inquiries as to my Credentials may be directed to any Bank in the City of London, but most especial the City Cotton & Woollen Bank in Lombard St.

I have the Honour to Subscribe Myself,

Yr Obdt. Srvt.

Alderman Josiah Browty.

Delphie glanced at her mother, who was sleeping peacefully after the exertion of receiving the doctor. Then she slipped downstairs to consult with the Miss Baggotts.

"For sure you must go!" said Anne Baggott when the situation had been explained to her. "Why, Miss Delphie, it might be the making of you, if your Great cousins would be brought to receive you. Lord bless me, if I had rich kin, I'd ha' been a-knocking at their gates years agone! And the gentleman offering his coach to take you, too—I call that real bang-up behavior."

Delphie then cautiously opened to the sisters a proposal she had been turning over in her mind—that Miss Jenny might care to accompany her as a kind of chaperone.

"For Mr. Browty says—and I fear he is right—that my uncle will think but slightingly of me if I travel unescorted."

"Me?" cried Jenny. "Me travel in a coach—to a castle—to visit a lord? Lawks, Miss Delphie, I should just about think I *would!* Why, that'd be better than a play at the Pantheon—better than a visit to Vauxhall Gardens—better than anything! Oh, wait till I tell Maria!"

"Shall you be able to manage without Jenny in the shop for a couple of days, though, Miss Anne?" inquired Delphie, smiling at Jenny's enthusiasm.

"Why, bless you, yes, miss. To tell truth, she's no more use half the time than a wet hen, so harum-scarum and shatter-brained as she is, always running into the street if a hurdy-gurdy or a funeral goes by—and it's only right she should bear you company, seeing as 'twas her totty-headedness got you into this fix in the first place."

So that was settled. Then came the question of some reliable person to watch over Mrs. Carteret for two days.

"At least, poor lady, she's not like to get out of bed and run off to St. Paul's now," sighed Miss Anne.

This was true, and though Delphie grieved to see her mother so quiet, docile, and biddable, it did mean that Mrs. Carteret could be left without apprehension of any more disastrous excursions at the present time.

"Can you suggest any kind, reliable woman with nursing experience who would take charge of her?" Delphie inquired.

"Say, Sister," exclaimed Jenny, "how about Aunt Andrews from Edmonton? 'Tis about time for her town visit, any road, and the old lady might as well make herself useful while she is here. By the same token, she dotes on cosseting folk and coddling 'em—she's never happier than when she had some poor soul in bed and can make them up all her Panaceas and Elixatives."

"For once, Sister, you have struck on a sensible notion," said Miss Anne, and she assured Delphie that Aunt Andrews would be the most kindly and capable person in the world to look after an invalid. So a note was dispatched to the old lady (who lived with a married son) and at the same time Delphie wrote to Mr. Browty's coachman in Russell Square, bidding him be in readiness to drive her to Kent on the third day from then.

"Ah, you poor dear, and you can do with an outing yourself," said Miss Anne sympathetically, "so tired and hagged-looking as you've been ever since your Ma took sick."

"Indeed if my relatives accept me, it certainly won't be for my looks," agreed Delphie, whose mirror told her that her face had become as thin and pale as an almond and that her gray eyes appeared overlarge in their shadowed sockets.

But she still could hardly regard the journey to Kent as a restorative outing or an excursion of pleasure. Too much hung on its outcome.

"Tell you what," proposed Miss Anne, looking her up and down. "What you need is a new gown (asking your pardon for the liberty, Miss Delphie), for every stitch on your back you've had since I dunno when, and, when all's said and done, there's nowt like new clothes for making a body feel more the thing."

"Lor, yes, Sister, what a famous notion!" struck in Jenny. "Let's rig up Miss as fine as fivepence! It's a downright shame she should be going about all the time in threadbare bombazine and linsey-woolsey when she's a figure as would set off the finest silks and velvets."

Delphie demurred very much at this.

"My relations must take me as they find me," she said. "Besides, if I were rigged out very fine, they would hardly believe in the necessity of my application."

"Ay; very true," said Anne. "But there's a difference (asking your pardon again, miss) betwixt being too fine, and being barely decent, and the back breadth of that gown you have on, Miss Delphie, is so rubbed I can just about see my face in it."

Reluctantly, Delphie was brought to agree that if she were too shabby her grand relatives might take her in scorn; and, as Aunt Andrews, when she arrived, proved to be a cheerful, friendly old countrywoman with a white-covered basket, who was astonished that she should be offered *payment* for looking after a sick person, since this was a most particular treat to her, and could with the utmost difficulty be brought to accept a fee of two guineas, the sisters managed to persuade Delphie to lay out a couple more of Mr. Browty's guineas on clothes. They escorted her to the Pantheon Bazaar, where the most amazing bargains were to be found, and gave her the benefit of their experience in selecting some lengths of French cambric in a very pretty dark blue shade, for a carriage dress, and a piece of upholstery velvet in French gray which, said Miss Anne, "will make up into as fine a pelisse as you please and I daresay Miss's kin will never notice the difference if it's properly trimmed." Buttons, thread, and a plain bonnet of basket willow completed their purchases, for Delphie already possessed a very respectable pair of navy-blue jean half boots (good footwear she regarded as a practical economy since she had to spend so much of her time walking to lessons) and a plain white crape dress for holidays or evening occasions, very little worn.

Next ensued a frenzy of dressmaking. Aunt Andrews was fetched into this, and proved to be an exquisite needlewoman, setting stitches so tiny "that they could hardly be seen except through a quizzing glass," as Jenny said. In twenty-four hours the dress and the pelisse were made, more plainly than the sisters would have wished, but Delphie was adamant on this point.

"It would not be suitable for someone circumstanced as I am to be laying out money on French floss, or silk fringe," she pointed out.

"Ay, very likely that's so," sighed Anne, "though it's a shame not to use that beautiful beading, only three farthings the yard! Still, Miss has very choice taste, and always looks the lady, no matter what, so I daresay she's right. *You* could take a lesson or two from her, Jenny!"

So the gray velvet pelisse was trimmed merely with French braid of a darker gray, and the cambric dress (which was made regrettably high to the neck in Jenny's view), with deep frills of its own material. And the bonnet was adorned with one curled black ostrich plume which Miss Anne "had had by her this age, and never could seem to find a use for, somehow."

Thus equipped, and with a small carpetbag of needments for the night, Delphie was ready to set off on the Thursday morning when Mr. Browty's carriage rolled around to the door.

She bade a tender good-by to her mother, who was under the impression that Delphie was merely going into the country for a night to recruit her strength after so much nursing.

"I hate to deceive her so," Delphie said to Mrs. Andrews, "but she becomes so very excited and distressed at the least mention of her family that I do not dare run the risk of upsetting her by speaking of them, particularly when it may be all for nothing!"

"Quite right, Miss. He that lives in hope danceth to an ill tune," remarked Mrs. Andrews, who was full of proverbs. "Best not tell the lady anything unless you can give her fair news. Call me not an apple till you see me gathered. Sickness of the body is cured by health of the soul. Don't you worrit your Ma with possibles; she's happy as a lark to think you're a-jauntering into the country, and I'll have her so tended with panadas and my toast-gruel that she'll be a new person by the time you come home."

Thus encouraged, Delphie ran down to the carriage, where Jenny was already impatiently waiting for her, rigged up in a stunning outfit of bright green cloth with velvet sleeves and gold buttons and a floss fringe, an enormous green velvet bonnet, a parasol, and a cloak to match. Anne waved from the doorway, Mrs. Andrews fluttered a handkerchief from the window upstairs, the coachman cracked his whip, and they were off.

"Off to seek your fortune," sighed Jenny ecstatically. "Lor, Miss Delphie, ain't it romantical!"

Delphie laughed. She could not help feeling many apprehensions as to the outcome of her expedition, but, insensibly, from the fineness of the morning and the smooth motion of the carriage, her spirits had taken an upward turn. Mr. Browty's carriage was so very comfortable! It was deeply upholstered, a thick sheepskin rug muffled any possible drafts on the floor, and besides that there was a fur carriage-rug, which was hardly needed on a bright May morning.

"But so grand!" sighed Jenny. "My stars! I feel as if I was a duchess."

They took their way along the Kent Road, and then through Maidstone and Charing. At Delphie's request Bodkin drove the horses at an easy pace; she by no means wished to exhaust Mr. Browty's team by unnecessary fast work, for Bodkin had given her to understand that they could comfortably reach Chase by late afternoon. So they paused here and there to breathe the horses, and took a nuncheon at the inn of a small village called Hollingbourne; Jenny would have preferred a grander place, perhaps the Angel at Maidstone, which had greatly taken her fancy by its handsome appearance, but Delphie, always practical, wished to conserve as much as possible of Mr. Browty's money, in case her relations were unwilling or unable to receive them, and they were obliged to spend the night at an inn. Besides, she felt that she herself would greatly prefer the humbler, more unassuming establishment. She was not at all used to going about and dining in public places. In fact, to Delphie, who had been obliged to keep steadily at work in London, day in, day out, ever since she had left school, the country was a complete and delightful novelty: every object interested her; she exclaimed over the beauty of the green thorn hedges, still pearled and spangled with white; she was enchanted by the birdsong, the burgeoning woods, the late primroses and early bluebells along the banks of the highway, the white roads of Kent, and the neat thatched and timbered villages through which they passed.

"Pho, pho!" said the traveled Jenny. "This is *nothing*, let me tell you! You ought to see South End, where Sister and I went for a few days last August. *There's* a place for you! There's bands—and donkeys—and a promenade—and a Kiosk—why this is just fields and fields full of sheep—there's nothing to it."

But Delphie could not imagine anything prettier than the green and flowery Kentish landscape.

However, when they passed a signpost that said, "Cow Green 7 miles," and presently came to another pointing sideways off the highway along what was evidently a private roadway through parkland, which simply said, "Chase," her good spirits abated and her courage began to falter.

"Never mind, dearie," said Miss Baggott, observing that the bright color whipped into Delphie's cheeks by fresh air and interest in the things about her had vanished again, leaving them uncommonly pale. "Ne'mind! Perhaps your great kinsfolk are from home, and there will be nowt to worry about. Didn't you say that Lord Bollington had a mort of other houses? He might be at any of 'em. Then," she added hopefully, "we could go back to Maidstone and stop at the Angel!"

But when the narrow white road took a turn, elbowing past a stand of oak woods all misty with bluebells, and brought them in sight of Chase Place, she changed her tune.

"A *moat!* A real moat! Battlements! A tower! Why, it's better than Hampton Court. Lor bless me, only think that I should be coming to stop in such a bang-up place!"

Chase Place was not precisely a castle, but it had some of a castle's adjuncts; it was certainly much more than a mere house. Big, rambling, many-chimneyed, and gray, it lay inside an indubitable moat; there was a keep, with turrets, evidently left over from a Norman residence on the same spot; the main part of the building looked to be sixteenth-century, however. It sat snugly in a hollow, facing southward, and the approach road had to describe a half-circle to reach the front entrance. The surrounding green land was studded all over with sheep and half-grown lambs, and their bleating filled the air. The gardens of Chase, if gardens there were, must, Delphie surmised, be on the western or northern side of the house; from this aspect the green pastureland swept right to the moat.

At length Bodkin, slowing down, pulled his team to a halt on this side of the bridge over the moat.

"Begging your pardon, ma'am," he said, turning and touching his hat to Delphie, "but this 'ere carriage is too wide to pass over that 'ere bridge."

Delphie stepped down into the road and agreed. The bridge (not, to Jenny's disappointment, a drawbridge, merely a plain stone arch) was certainly too narrow for Mr. Browty's coach, which was extremely wide. Moreover there were no railings at the sides of the bridge.

Mr. Bodkin was very apologetic. "Mr. Browty did say as 'ow I was to drive you right up to the door and wait to see how you got on, miss," he said, "but, seeing I can't do that, I'll send Jem Postilion to bang on the knocker, shall I, and I'll walk the hosses here, till you find out if your folks are home? I'm right sorry not to take you up to the door in style, miss, but I don't see what's to be done about it."

"Thank you, Bodkin, but pray don't distress yourself," Delphie said with a friendly smile. (She had a shrewd suspicion, from the encouraging expressions on their faces, that both Bodkin and the postilions had somehow learned the nature of her journey, and wished her well.) "The fault is certainly not yours, but that of this very narrow bridge, and Mr. Browty's very stylish carriage! Do you walk the horses here; that will serve admirably, for anyone looking through the arch will be able to see what a handsome equipage I have come in. And Miss Baggott and I will send word back to you in a very few minutes, either that we should like our baggage brought in because we are staying here, or that we intend to continue with you, and find accommodation at an inn in Cow Green."

Jenny had jumped out of the carriage in time to hear this last, and her face fell considerably. To stay in a castle, or at the Angel in Maidstone, was one thing; to be putting up at some village hostelry in a place called Cow Green was quite another, and not at all the kind of evening's entertainment that she had proposed for herself.

"Look—there's folk about—I daresay his lordship *is* in residence," she said hopefully, nudging Delphie's arm. "I can see a gig standing in the courtyard through that arch. And I just noticed a couple of dogs run across."

"So did I. There is certainly somebody in the place. But of course Lord Bollington may keep it staffed with servants even when he is from home. In any case, let us go forward and see! We shall not be long, Bodkin."

Delphie walked swiftly across the narrow stone bridge, glancing about her, in spite of her growing nervousness, with considerable interest. A high stone wall rose on the far side of the moat, which did not look to be very deep, but might be about twenty feet wide. It was full of water-lily pads, with the flowers just coming into bloom, among which ducklings and moorhens swam and paddled and splashed.

Through a stone arch at the far end of the bridge could be seen a wide, grassy inner courtyard, on the distant side of which wide stone steps led up to an imposingly massive wooden door under a Gothic arch. This door, encouragingly, stood open, and a black-clad man, who appeared to have alighted from the stationary gig, was just passing through it. Delphie had only a brief glimpse of him but decided that he did not look like a lord (not that she had any very clear notion of what a lord should look like); she thought he might be a lawyer, clergyman, bailiff, or some other person from the professional classes.

Having crossed the bridge she was just about to pass under the stone arch when she was arrested by the sound of a loud splash, followed by a series of ear-piercing shrieks, from just behind her.

Spinning around she saw with the utmost astonishment and consternation that Jenny, through some unimaginable mischance—perhaps from staring about her and not looking where she set her feet—had fallen off the bridge and landed plump in the water.

There she was, bobbing about among the lily leaves, thrashing the water with her velvet-clad arms, and shrieking at the top of a pair of exceptionally powerful lungs:

"Help! Help! I shall be drowned. I shall die for certain. Help, help! Oh, why does nobody save me? Help! Help! Will no kind soul come to my aid?"

Bodkin and the postilions were gazing at Jenny in stupefaction. All seemed reluctant to take action. Then Bodkin, evidently unwilling to ruin his livery by jumping into the water, if it could be avoided, ran to the carriage boot, and pulled out the rope which was always carried there in case of an overturn.

"Here, miss! Try if you can catch hold of the rope's end!" he shouted, and hurled the rope so accurately that it knocked off Miss Baggott's green velvet Waterloo hat.

"Oh, help—bubble bubble—my hat, my hat! Oh help me—I can't reach the rope!"

Amid Jenny's deafening cries, Bodkin drew back the rope, recoiled it, and threw it again; but the sufferer in the moat, either out of anxiety not to lose her hat, which she now grasped with one hand, or because her eyes were full of water, seemed very unhandy at catching the end of the rope; she missed it a second time and then a third. Meanwhile she continued to splash and flounder among the lily pads, sometimes submerged and silent, sometimes half out of the water and shrieking, insensibly all the time drawing nearer to the inner margin of the moat and the archway that gave onto the courtyard.

At this juncture reinforcements arrived in the shape of three men running over the grass, evidently alerted by all the cries and commotion.

"Merciful heavens! What in the devil's name is going on?" demanded one of them. "Is somebody being murdered? Or is a pig being killed?"

At the instant when they came through the archway and emerged onto the bridge, Jenny had finally just succeeded in catching hold of the rope's end, and had suffered herself to be towed through the lilies to the outer bank, and then drawn slowly up it.

She stood then, dripping, gasping, hysterically laughing, crying, and exclaiming on the bridge, ruefully regarding her draggled plumage and streaming apparel.

"Oh, my feathers! Oh, my fringe! Oh, my dear, dear Miss Carteret, I thought I was a goner! I thought I should be drowned for sure! Oh, Mr. Bodkin, my preserver! How can I ever thank you for saving me from a watery death?"

"I scarcely think you could have achieved a watery death in three feet of moat," dryly observed one of the three men who had come through the archway.

Miss Baggott gazed at him reproachfully, and Delphie turned to look at him.

He was unusually tall, a strongly built individual with a profusion of jet-black hair, somewhat carelessly arranged, and a decidedly sardonic expression on his long face. He wore a riding costume of drab buckskins, a plain but well-cut jacket, highly polished top boots, and a neckcloth of dazzling whiteness. He was much too young to be Lord Bollington—in his middle thirties at the outside. Perhaps Lord Bollington had a son? speculated Delphie, and realized how little she knew about her hypothetical cousins.

"Nay, but consider the stems of the lilies!" remonstrated Jenny, in answer to his remark. "You can have no idea how dreadfully I found myself entangled among them—my arms and limbs all tied up, quite powerless!—and my head being slowly pulled under by the current—I had begun to despair and feared every moment would be my last!—But it is no matter now; 'twas but a trifle!" she added heroically, fetching up an absolutely graveyard cough from the region of her diaphragm. "Ahem, ahem! Now that I am on dry land again, I think nothing of it at all; 'tis not of the slightest consequence, after all! Pray let us not refine upon it any longer. Only, I think perhaps I had best get afore a fire, and replace these sopping things by dry ones—or I might easily take one of my inflammations—my lungs are so delicate, so wretchedly delicate—they give me Old Scratch at the least hint of a chill. Alas, I fear I am a sad invalid!"

Since Jenny was as robust as a shire horse and had never, to Delphie's knowledge, suffered a day's illness in her life, the latter gazed at her wide-eyed after this statement, and received a very innocent look in return.

The second of the three men remarked calmly,

"Certainly you should change your garments, ma'am, and that without delay. Even on a mild day like this, some harm might accrue. Fidd, see to it, will you? Direct one of the maidservants to make ready a suitable bedchamber; lead these ladies to it, and make sure that a fire is lit, hot water brought up, and suitable refreshment is offered to them."

"Certainly, Mr. Fitzjohn," said the third man, who was elderly, white-haired, and wore the uniform of an upper servant. "Would you care to follow me, ma'am?" he said to Jenny.

"Oh yes—but I need my bag from the coach" uttered Jenny in failing accents, "for all my dry things are in it. Could you get it out, Bodkin?"

"Surely, miss," said Bodkin, wooden-faced. "I'll just carry it in, shall I?"

"Yes—and you had best bring Miss Carteret's too—in case there is anything I lack. You do not object, dear Miss Carteret, do you?"

"Of course not," said Delphie, but her response was lost in the bustle, as Mr. Fitzjohn, remarking, "I had better take your arm, ma'am," escorted Jenny carefully across the bridge, she clinging to him, looking fearfully down at the water, and letting out little nervous cries at every step.

Mr. Fitzjohn seemed completely at home in Chase, and Delphie, following thoughtfully behind the pair, at the side of the dark-haired man, wondered if he were a member of the family—as seemed possible from the assured tone of his orders to the servant—or merely a member of the household. He was a stocky, thickset personage, of considerable height, but appearing shorter because of his broad shoulders. His countenance was square and somewhat taciturn-looking, though not unhandsome; his eyes were light blue and extremely piercing, his complexion both freckled and lightly tanned, his thick hair of a sandy hue.

While they were crossing the grass, Delphie murmured some awkward commonplaces as to her gratitude—the unfortunate accident—their regret for the imposition they were causing—but these were received with such dour grunts by her black-browed companion that she set him down as a churlish boor and abandoned her attempts at conciliation.

The party ascended the steps to the front door and entered a large, cold, stone-paved entrance hall, adorned with a diversity of stags' antlers and foxes' masks along its walls, but hardly furnished at all. Five or six large, melancholy, molting hounds lay about on the paving stones, as if they had nothing to do, and greatly regretted the circumstance.

"Here we will leave you in Fidd's charge," remarked Mr. Fitzjohn, removing his hand, with some relief, Delphie thought, from Jenny's damp velvet arm. "Fidd, look after the ladies as well as you can. Pray send word, ma'am, should there be anything further you require, or think we could supply."

"Thank you; you are extremely kind," said Philadelphia, immensely embarrassed by this whole sequence of events. "I cannot say how much I regret—I am sure we need nothing—"

"Perhaps a doctor?" faltered Miss Baggott in dying accents. "After such a prolonged immersion I am afraid my lungs—" She coughed again several times, and then gasped, "My poor mother would wish me to see a doctor, I am sure."

As Mrs. Baggott had lain in Highgate Cemetery for the past twelve years this seemed a doubtful assumption, but Mr. Fitzjohn rejoined impassively,

"By all means, ma'am. There will not be the least difficulty about that. A doctor is in the house at present, and I make no doubt he will be able to wait on you when he has finished attendance upon his other patient. It may be a matter of some little time yet, however."

Philadelphia pricked up her ears at this. Who could the other patient be? Perhaps it was Lord Bollington? Her heart sank at the thought. If her great-uncle were ill, then this was a most inauspicious time for an unheralded visit.

She longed to put questions to Fidd, but scrupled at interrogating a servant. He was leading the way at a rapid pace up a wide flight of polished (and villainously slippery) stairs; Delphie took Jenny's arm and assisted her to follow.

At the top, where the stairs led into another wide hallway with numerous passages leading off it, the manservant selected a rather narrow passage turning sharp to the left, past a long row of windows, and took them down it for what seemed an excessively long distance.

"Pray don't take trouble fixing a chamber especial for me," panted Miss Baggott after a while, as they went farther and farther. "The housekeeper's room would do well enough!"

"There's no housekeeper at Chase, ma'am," said Fidd. He added, with what sounded like grim approval, "His lordship can't abide wimmen getting their fambles on things."

"Good gracious. Are there no women servants at all?" inquired Philadelphia, with mixed curiosity and disapproval.

"Oh, yes, miss. There's maids, but they're only under-servants, and has to keep in their place. They dassn't be seen in the passageways or rooms where his lordship might come—if he should set eyes on them, they're turned off directly. And they has to do their work while he's still abed. Now, here we are, miss."

He opened the door of a large, pleasant chamber, agreeably illuminated by the rays of the westering sun, and furnished with a few handsome pieces which were, however, both dusty and in bad order. The bed-curtains, Delphie noticed, were half eaten away by moth, the chairs seats were threadbare, and the carpet had a great faded patch where the afternoon sun lay across it.

Fidd vigorously tugged on a beaded bell rope, and then left them. Bodkin deposited their bags, glanced about him, and then said, rather doubtfully,

"Shall you be all right here, Miss Carteret? It seems a hem queer set-out—axing your pardon, miss!—if no women's allowed to be seen in the place? Say the word, and I'll fetch you away, soon as Miss has changed her things."

"I think we shall do, thank you, Bodkin," Delphie replied, with rather more firmness than she in fact felt. "Do you go onto Cow Green and make arrangements for yourself and the outriders to spend the night there. If I do not send you word to the contrary, come and pick us up here at ten o'clock tomorrow morning."

"Yes, miss. Very good, miss. I—I'm sure I hope you manage to get what you came for—and I wish you good fortune, miss." Touching his forelock, Bodkin left them to themselves.

Directly he had done so, Jenny, who had sunk onto a straight-backed chair as if utterly exhausted and shocked, raised a round face brimful of glee and self-congratulation.

"Well!" she said to Philadelphia. "Wasn't I clever? Warn't I artful? Didn't I play them a famous turn? Wasn't it as good as a box at Covent Garden? Now we're fixed here for as long as we like. They *dursn't* turn us out while my lungs is inflamed!"

"Do you mean to say, you wretched girl," exclaimed Delphie, aghast—though in fact she had half suspected as much—"Are you telling me, Jenny, that you fell into the moat *on purpose?*"

"Sure's you're born, I did!" said Jenny triumphantly. "Wasn't it just the nackiest thing? Didn't I do it as it might 'a been done in Drury Lane? But I had the hardest trouble in the world not to bust out laughing when I saw the look on all your faces!"

"But your dress—your hat—they are ruined!"

"Lor, what's a few bits of clothes?" said Jenny largely, "I dare swear, when you come into your rights, that you'll buy me some others! (And to tell truth, I never cared for this dress above half —it's well enough, but has no *dash,* to my mind. I prefer something that's trimmed up a bit more. I've always fancied a cherry-red . . .) But didn't it fall out handsomely? 'Is somebody being murdered?' the tall fellow calls out as he comes a-running—oh, I could have died laughing, it was all I could do to keep a straight face. And come, now, ain't they a fine pair? I never saw two prettier-looking fellows! With any luck, my dearie, you and me has fixed ourselves up with as handsome a couple of beaux as any young lady could wish for! (Seeing Mr. S., my gentleman friend, isn't calling any more.) Who do you think they are? Is any of your kinsfolk named Fitzjohn?"

Delphie was obliged to reply that she did not know, and Miss Baggott's further remarks were cut short by the arrival of a pair of maids, who proceeded respectively to kindle and light a fire in the hearth, and to pour hot water into a hip bath.

The warmth of the flames was decidedly grateful, for the room had been as chill as a tomb, and Delphie was beginning to be anxious for Miss Baggott in good earnest.

One of the maids (who both seemed young, timid country

girls) then shyly offered to stay and assist Miss with her undressing and bath.

"Ay, I'll be glad of that!" said Jenny. "And do you," she said to the other one, "do you make up the bed—plenty of covers, mind! —and thrust a warming pan atwixt the sheets; then you can bring me up a nice mug of hot negus with a twist of lemon peel in it!"

Delphie was astonished. Here was Jenny Baggott, whose father had run a laundry, whose mother was a sempstress, conducting herself in this mansion with all the confidence and aplomb of one born to it; while she, Delphie, who had some right to be there, whose mother actually *had* been born in the house, felt nothing but diffidence, embarrassment, and awkwardness.

However, seeing Jenny so thoroughly prepared to take care of herself, or rather, see that care was taken of her, Delphie said,

"If you will not dislike it, I think perhaps I should go down now—if you can spare me, Jenny dear? I feel I ought to say everything that is proper to those gentlemen."

"Ay, do that!" approved Jenny, who, stripped of her sodden green cloth, was just in the act of stepping into the hip bath like a large pink seal. "Ah!" She sank into its steaming depths with a sigh of gratification. "Now's your chance, I reckon, to grab the bull by the horns. So you keep your pluck up, dearie, and don't let yourself be choused out of your rightful due! Never fret your head about me, I'll be as snug as a bee in bugloss!"

With which parting salutation, she closed her right eye and contorted her face in a violent wink, unseen by the maid, who had turned to put more wood on the fire.

Delphie, while in the bedroom, had seized the opportunity to tidy her hair and remove her pelisse, but as she threaded her way back along the endless corridor she regretted the pelisse, for the house was excessively cold. However, all this region seemed uninhabited; she hoped that the occupied rooms might be warmer.

After carefully descending the slippery stairs, she paused at the foot, undecided in which direction to proceed. There were no servants about; and even the aged hounds seemed to have vanished. As she stood hesitating, she heard two voices issuing from an open doorway.

"How the devil the wench came to do such a totty-headed thing as to fall off a wide bridge into three feet of water passes comprehension!" said a cool male voice.

"My dear fellow, it was obviously a hoax!" replied another, equally cool, but with a faint hint of amusement in it. "What else could you expect from that type of female? They know nothing of a straightforward approach—it is all tricks and artifices and cunning. The hussy wanted access to this house—for some purpose of her own—and that was her means of achieving it."

"You think so?"

"My dear Mordred, I am sure of it."

"But the other girl—the pretty one—seemed quite a different kind; much more ladylike, and better bred altogether."

"She's sharper, that's all; has picked up a bit more of what passes for polish. My advice to you, Mordred, is to bundle them both out of doors as soon as the wet one has got dry clothes on her back. Think what my uncle would say if he knew they were here!"

Evidently the other shrugged, or grimaced, for the first voice spoke again.

"Well, to be sure, he is not likely to know—but in the circumstances it will hardly do to allow two strange females to remain. Consider his disgust for the whole sex!"

Delphie had heard enough to give her considerable food for thought. Acting with almost instinctive care, she retraced her steps across the wide hall, walking soundlessly on the dusty flagstones; she then returned toward the open door at a brisk pace, making as much noise as possible.

Now one of the voices was saying impatiently,

"I wish Elaine would come. When I met her during that month in Bath I thought she consulted her own wishes more than anything else in the world, but I thought also that she had reasonable sense. This is no time for some flighty quirk!"

"She'll come, Gareth, never doubt," the other said soothingly. "Probably stopped to assemble a suitable wardrobe. What a combination of events, after all—!"

There was a snort of laughter from the speaker addressed as Gareth; and then Delphie walked into the room, and the two men, who had been standing by the fireplace, turned, with a signal lack of enthusiasm, she thought, to greet her.

The room she had entered was a library, well furnished with leather-bound books, which lined three of the walls, and all of which looked to be of considerable antiquity. A fire burned under a black marble mantelpiece, a businesslike desk, covered with papers, occupied one corner, and a large table, leather-covered, gold-embossed, and badly in need of repair, stood in the middle of the room. A clutter of armchairs surrounded the fire, which Delphie approached with shivering gratitude. It was impossible to come very close to it, however, because of the aged dogs now huddled around the warmth.

"May I have the honor of procuring you some refreshment, ma'am?" said the man called Fitzjohn, after a short, awkward pause. "What shall it be? I fear we are somewhat at sixes and sevens at present for we have illness in the house—Fidd has been called off—would you care for a glass of Madeira? I am afraid the household may not be supplied with tea, or any such ladies' drink."

Delphie replied equably that Madeira would do very well, and he went quickly away. She was left with the dark-haired man, who appeared to be taking calmly hostile stock of her. Delphie's spirits always rose to such a challenge—she had bested enough antagonistic and recalcitrant pupils to be unmoved by dislike; she met his regard with an equally cool appraisement, and remarked, since he had not inquired,

"My friend is going on well, thanks to the prompt and practical attention of your servants, for which I thank you; I am in hopes she may suffer no ill effects from her unfortunate mishap."

His eyes were very handsome, she thought (at least they would have been if they had held a pleasanter expression): almost black, and well set under level dark brows; his face was rather too long and thin, certainly, but his mouth, if it had not been folded into such an unaccommodating line, ought to have been redeemingly wide; and he had a good nose, straight, but not too narrow in the nostrils. His face seemed faintly familiar; could she perhaps have seen a sketch of him in one of Jenny's illustrated magazines?

"I must thank you also for coming to the rescue of my poor

friend, sir," she continued in her clear, musical voice, for she felt the awkwardness of remaining with him in silence. "I must, also, apologize for your being troubled by such a tiresome incident when, as I gather, you have sickness in the house?"

She paused inquiringly, but he said nothing, and she went on, "I deeply regret—but it is no use talking—"

"No use whatsoever!" he agreed in the dryest possible tone. "But since it is by speech that we must communicate, and only by speech that we are able to learn, may I inquire to whom I have the honor of speaking? And who is your unfortunate friend? And what brought you here—not chance, I infer? My name, by the by, is Gareth Penistone—at your service."

"Gareth Penistone?" she exclaimed. "Why then you must be my cousin! No wonder your face appeared so familiar! I see now that you have a strong resemblance to my grandfather's miniature."

His dark brows shot up at this, and she explained,

"I should have told you at the outset that my name is Carteret—Philadelphia Elaine Carteret. I am the daughter of Elaine and Captain Richard Carteret. Are you the son of Lord Bollington?"

At this moment Fitzjohn reappeared, carrying a decanter of wine and three glasses, which he set on the table.

"Only think, Mordred," remarked Mr. Penistone, turning to Fitzjohn, still with his brows very high, and an expression of total skepticism on his countenance, "we have here a new cousin! This lady has just favored me with the surprising information that she is Miss Carteret, daughter of my deceased cousin, Elaine Penistone Carteret. Is not that a remarkable piece of news?"

Mr. Fitzjohn's hands paused, momentarily, in their task of pouring Madeira into a glass; then he filled the glass up and handed it to Delphie, who received it with a nod of thanks and, since no one invited her to do so, sat down uninvited in one of the armchairs, pushing her way past a large snoring hound. She took a sip of the wine, and it fortified her courage.

"You say this information is surprising," she remarked levelly to Mr. Penistone. "But I fail to understand why that should be. Were you not aware of my existence?"

"My dear ma'am—"

"I am supplied with plenty of documents to prove who I am," she continued, opening her reticule. "Here is my mother's wedding certificate—my own certificate of baptism—a letter from the Navy Office regarding the death of my father, Captain Carteret—some letters from my grandfather to my mother—and—and my own Certificate of Proficiency in Singing and the Musical Arts. If you find that these suffice to establish my identity, I hope that you may presently be good enough to conduct me to my uncle—for I have a letter of recommendation addressed to him personally."

She took another gulp of her Madeira. Both men, having exchanged rapid glances, were regarding her in fascinated silence, Mr. Penistone with eyes very much narrowed. Mr. Fitzjohn seemed almost to have ceased breathing, as if too many urgent matters were crowding for precedence in his mind.

Since neither of them spoke, Delphie remarked after a moment, "Well? You seem to have nothing to say?"

"Your credentials seem commendably complete, Miss—Carteret," said Mr. Penistone, with a slight pause after the *Miss*. He glanced without much interest at the papers she proffered. "However I do, in fact, have two things to say. Firstly—your own birth certificate seems to be missing from these documents; Miss Elaine Penistone was doubtless married to Captain Carteret, but how are we to be sure—forgive me if I speak bluntly—that you are the product of the union? Do you not regard a birth certificate as a necessary proof of identity?"

"Hardly, in view of all the rest, I should have thought." Philadelphia replied, raising her own brows. "However, if you think it necessary, I am sure a copy can readily be obtained from the Record Office. I had not been aware that it was missing until I set out to come here. My mother, of—of late years—has become somewhat absentminded and scatterbrained—she tends to lose articles."

"*Has?*" Mr. Penistone's brows shot even higher, if possible. "You are telling us, ma'am, that your mother is *still alive?*"

"She was when I left London—no thanks to any help or kindness she has received from this family!" Philadelphia retorted bitterly. "It is on her account that I came hither. Permit me to say that if it were only for myself, I would have bitten my tongue off at the roots, sooner than make application—"

Mr. Penistone's lips silently formed a word that would have been interpreted as *Humbug!* But he only said,

"And, pray, why did your mother not come with you? I assume that the lady who fell into the moat is *not* your mother?"

"Certainly not—I should think you could see that!" Delphie said angrily. "She is Miss Baggott—a—a friend who has been so good as to bear me company on the journey. My mother was unable to come because she has been extremely ill, Mr. Penistone, at death's door, in fact. Moreover, she holds this family in detestation. I have come without her knowledge."

"I am sorry to hear it," he replied coldly, and fell silent, sipping his wine, studying her over the rim of his glass. She could not help being aware that Mr. Fitzjohn was doing likewise, and a flush crept into her pale cheeks.

"Am I right in assuming that my great-uncle—that Lord Bollington is here in the house?" she asked. "May I inquire whether it will be possible for me to see him presently?"

"No. It will not be possible, Miss—Carteret," Penistone replied with harsh finality.

Delphie's flush turned to a burning spot on either cheekbone at this flat rebuff. However, controlling herself, she inquired in a level tone,

"Oh? May I ask why not?"

Mr. Penistone's lips parted as if he were about to make some derogatory remark about impudent imposters. But Fitzjohn restrained him with a murmured word, and a hand on his arm; he said shortly,

"You cannot see my uncle because at this moment he is dying."

"*Oh!*"

After one soft, gasping sigh, Delphie was silent, turning over this utterly unforeseen situation in her mind. She found it hard to withstand a deep sense of chagrin and exasperation at her own dilatoriness. Had she but thought of taking this journey six months ago—even *one* month ago—or at any time during the last five years! But, she reminded herself, there would still have been no guarantee of a favorable outcome—though it could hardly have been *less* favorable than her chances appeared at present.

The elderly manservant, Fidd, appeared in the doorway and stood, urgently signaling to Mr. Fitzjohn with his eyes.

"Begging your pardon, Mr. Fitz," he murmured, "Dr. Bowles has left master now, and Mr. Wylye is with him, and he wishes you to step up to his chamber. Also master's been asking for the last hour if Miss Elaine is come yet. What shall I say?"

"Thank you, Fidd—I will come up myself, directly. Where is Dr. Bowles?"

"He's a-gone to the young lady what fell in the water, sir."

"Ah—yes. Ask if he will be so good as to come to the library before he takes his departure, will you? And serve him with some refreshment."

"Yes, sir."

Both men went out; Mr. Penistone and Miss Carteret were once more left alone together.

"Tell me, sir," she began, since he showed no disposition to speak, "why are you so rigidly disposed to put no credence in my story?"

"Why?" He raised his gray eyes to hers, laughed shortly, and took another sip of his wine. "For a very simple reason, my dear ma'am. Because the *real* Miss Carteret has been supported and provided for by my great-uncle for the past twenty years—sixteen of them at the Queen's Square Academy for Young Ladies in Bath. She was presented at Court two years ago under the sponsorship of Lady Bablock-Hythe, who was a friend of her mother's. Her identity is established beyond question. And—I myself am engaged to be married to her."

"Oh!" said Philadelphia, rather blankly.

3

After about ten minutes, Mr. Fitzjohn returned to the library. He walked in with a somewhat hasty, uncertain step and, ignoring the constraint in which the other two were sitting, ignoring Delphie altogether, said to Penistone,

"My uncle wishes to see you. And—and a letter has just arrived from Bath—from Cousin Elaine."

"A *letter*—?"

"—I have it here."

Without another word, Mr. Penistone took the white oblong, broke the seal, and read the few lines written inside. Then he gave a brief, grim laugh, and tossed the paper over to Fitzjohn.

"Can't see her way to leave Bath until after the Assembly—"

"Oh, my God!" With unsteady hands, Fitzjohn spread out the missive, and read it. The two men stared at one another.

"What now?"

"You had best come to him—he has been asking for you repeatedly."

They hurried out, taking no notice of Delphie, who remained absently gazing at the deplorably aged dogs huddled shivering about the fire. Was somebody *fond* of them? she wondered.

During her previous silent interval alone with Mr. Penistone, she had been reviewing her situation with greater and greater amazement and indignation. On her first entrance into Chase, she had felt awkward, guilty, intrusive, embarrassed, wholly *de trop*; but now that she was mistress of some of the facts of the case, both her sense of outrage, and her spirit, grew rapidly.

Some imposter had usurped her place! An imposter it must be, since she knew herself to be her mother's true daughter, and had not the faintest doubt of her mother's innocence and probity. But this imposter, this *snake*, reared and supported by Lord Bollington for so long, was without doubt the reason why her previous application had been so rudely rejected.

But—given such a state of affairs—how would it be possible to prove her own and her mother's claims? It must, Delphie supposed, mean having recourse to a lawyer—for there was plainly no help or sympathy to be obtained from any person at Chase—and lawyers cost money . . . unless one could be found who considered their chances of success sufficiently good to be worth his risk.

Moving restlessly under the anxieties aroused by these ideas, she glanced toward the window and realized with dismay that dusk was beginning to fall; consulting her mother's watch (another proof of identity—as if anybody cared—for it had the Penistone crest, a hand grasping a battle-ax, engraved on its back) she discovered that the evening was well advanced. And they still had made no arrangements for the night! She decided that it was her duty to return at once and see how Jenny did.

Not a soul did she meet as she retraced her steps to the West Wing. Either this establishment was remarkably deficient in servants, or, which was more probably, they were all assembled in a distant region, performing services for their dying master.

Delphie had taken the precaution of counting doors along the west passageway on her previous return journey and so was spared any trouble in relocating the chamber where Jenny lay—which by now, illuminated both by the fire and a sufficiency of candles, had attained quite a cheerful aspect.

What was Delphie's surprise to discover that Miss Baggott, far from reclining in bed, was up and nearly dressed, hard at work fastening the innumerable buttons of an azure-blue brocade evening gown with a demi-train and adorned with a great quantity of false pearls.

"Ah, there you are, dearie; what a mercy you are come back, I was just commencing to think that I must ring for Meg or Jill again," observed Jenny, desisting in her struggles with relief. "Well-meaning gals, both of them, but that clumsy you wouldn't believe! Be so kind as to do up the middle button, love—I have managed all the rest."

"But—do you intend to come downstairs, then?" Delphie said in astonishment. "What about your inflammation of the lungs?"

"To be sure I must come down! Since the gals told me his old lordship's lying a-dying, I couldn't be so thoughtless as to leave you to eat your supper all alone with two young men (for that's all the company there is in the house, they tell me)—could I now? *Unchaperoned?* Why, it would be enough to sink your reputation forever; my conscience would be nagging at me for the rest of my days," Miss Baggott said virtuously. "O' course after my being so nigh drownded, I had *ought* to lay down on the bed, I know that, but there! I was never one to desert a friend in time of need!"

And she favored Delphie with another large wink.

"Come, bustle about, my love! The maids told me they keep country hours, here, dine at three, sup at eight—you had best get yourself changed. And you need not be troubling your head about our quarters tonight—I have bid the servants fetch another bed into this chamber, so there can be no quizzing talk about our visit —all's right and proper if we share the same room, nothing havey-cavey about that!"

Delphie doubted if there would be such talk, but thanked Jenny for the prudent forethought. She herself, since Mr. Penistone's revelation, had doubted the propriety of their remaining at Chase at all—so unwelcome as they must be—but Jenny's firmness dispelled any hesitations on that score.

"The sawbones said I must on no account stir out of doors until daybreak, or it might be the death of me," announced Jenny firmly.

"Do you really think it needful to change our dress? You are so very fine! It is more than likely that we shall be served with a tray of soup in the library," Delphie said doubtfully.

Not if Miss Baggott had any say in the matter, proclaimed the gleam in her eye, but she merely replied,

"Certainly it is needful! We want them to see that we know what's proper. If there is trouble in the house, we should pay all due respect. Make haste; I'll curl your hair in ringlets."

Delphie, however, preferred to keep it in her plain bands, which her companion sniffed at, as the most unmodish style possible—but she did admit that in Delphie's position, since it was her great-uncle who was dying, a plain style might be more suitable.

While Delphie swiftly donned her white crape gown, Jenny, who appeared to have a positive genius for extracting information from the servants, imparted what she had learned of the family situation.

"Mr. Fitzjohn is the son of the natural son of your grandpa, the Fifth Viscount Bollington—did you know that? What does that make him to you, then?"

"His father would be my mother's half brother," said Delphie, working it out. "We are therefore cousins, or half cousins."

"His father was the agent here, and so is he, now," Jenny went on. "I think it monstrous unjust, do not you, that he don't come in to the title, just because his Pa was a bastard? La, my dear, your grandpa seems to have been a sad old rip, from what I learn! Did you know that he died in a duel?"

No, Delphie certainly had not.

"A *duel?* Are you *sure?*"

"Sure as sartin! In this very house, too. With his own brother, what's more! Over a girl, into the bargain—a dairymaid, will you believe it! Plenty of the older servants remember it still, Meg said. It was a most shocking scandal. But since the actual death was an accident, Accidental Death was the verdict brought in at the Crowner's Quest—otherwise brother Mark would ha' been charged with manslaughter and couldn't ha' come in to the title. But he did both—he took the title (for his brother's son had died at sea) *and* he married the girl, Prissy Privett, that all the ruckus had been about! She'd had two children already, bastards both, by his brother—only think! And then married t'other one, but had no more. There's a portrait of her in the dining room, Meg says. I'd be curious to see her—the bold-faced thing!"

"How did the death take place—my grandfather's death?"

"They was both of them drunk, a-dueling on the roof about Priss Privett: Lord Bollington, your granda—Lancelot, his name was—and this one that's dying now, his brother Mark. Lancelot missed his footing and fell off into the moat. Just like me, only fancy! Only he fell from higher, and was killed."

"Good God!" said Delphie. "My mother's father died in such a way? What a thing! I wonder Mamma never mentioned it."

"Like as not," pointed out Jenny, "it happened after she'd left home? Or maybe 'twas all hushed up—as much as they could, that is. The gals said this one got the place, but little good it did him, for the ill talk and slights from neighbors soured his nature. And though he married the gal, Priss Privett, he used her so badly that *she* died not long after, and he never wed again. Put off the whole female sect by what had gone before, seemingly. Maybe she played him false too."

Unraveling and assimilating this tangled and gloomy tale, Delphie began to feel less surprise at the callous abandonment of her mother. After the rather scandalous death of the father, it was no wonder that the runaway daughter should be neglected and out of mind. Mrs. Carteret's father, presumably, had made no provision for her in his will, and the guilty (by intent if not by deed) brother who succeeded him would have even less reason to do so.

"And where does Mr. Penistone come in?" Delphie inquired.

"Aha! He's the one for you to fix on, dearie! (Though for my own part, I prefer t'other fellow; he has a better pair of shoulders on him, to my mind, and is more like my Mr. S. what's gone; besides which, I never could abide those brusque, bony, bracket-faced fellows.) But Mr. Gareth is the Heir, now—since your great-uncle Mark has none of his own, and Mr. Fitz is the son of a bastard and can't succeed. Mr. P. don't live here—has a manor of his own at Horsmonden—he just rid over for the death."

"Whose son is he, then?" inquired Delphie, draping a plain scarf of white crape over her shoulders.

"It seems there was yet another brother to your grandpa, a good bit younger than the other pair—Gareth, his name was, the Honorable Gareth Penistone (he's dead now) and he had a son who was this Mr. Gareth's father."

"I see. Perhaps he is my cousin once removed."

"Too bad he ain't removed altogether," said Miss Baggott roundly. "For I don't fancy his haughty airs above half—and besides—think of it—if it weren't for him *you'd* be the Heir, you'd be Lady Bollington, lovie—for poor Mr. Fitz don't count."

Philadelphia felt some pity for poor Mr. Fitzjohn, unreasonably debarred from the succession by the accident of his father's base birth, but said, laughing,

"Girls cannot inherit, in any case, Jenny! If there were no other heir, I believe the title would die out."

"What a hem shame! Well, in that case, love, you'd best marry him," Jenny said matter-of-factly.

"Even that is out of my power, I fear! He is already betrothed."

And betrothed to *whom?* Delphie wondered. She did not immediately disclose to Jenny that there was another claimant for her place. The intelligence was too new, and too upsetting. It made her feel thoroughly uncomfortable. She wished to go on digesting it in the privacy of her own mind for a while.

But she found herself unexpectedly impressed by Jenny's shrewd, clear grasp of a family situation not, after all, her own, or at all the kind to which she was used; Miss Baggott was showing qualities hitherto quite unsuspected, and her company was decidedly welcome.

"Are you ready to come down, Jenny?"

"Not on your Oliphant—nor I shan't be for another twenty minutes sartain," cheerfully replied Jenny, who had pulled a pair of curling tongs out of her portmanteau, heated them over the fire, and was building her shiny black hair into an amazingly elaborate arrangment. "But do you go on ahead, if you wish, love—and tell 'em I'm clemmed after my ducking! None of your trifles on trays for me—I want a proper bang-up supper—after all, we *are* staying under a lord's roof! And in the dining room, *not* the library," she added as Delphie, chuckling, started for the door.

"Shall you be able to find your way alone, though, Jenny?"

"Bless you, yes. I'll ring for Jill or Fidd to guide me."

Satisfied as to Jenny's being able to look after herself, Philadelphia made her way back to the library, where she found Mr. Penistone impatiently walking up and down.

His eyes widened at sight of her, and he looked quite startled; he still had on his riding clothes, and she wondered if he thought it a piece of impertinence that, in her somewhat doubtful circumstances, she had behaved herself so familiarly as to change her dress for the evening.

But he said only,

"How does your friend do?"

"Well enough, thank you. The doctor told her there was no danger to be apprehended if she stays indoors for another twelve hours. So I believe we must burden you with our presence overnight. I regret the necessity."

"So I had gathered. It is of no consequence," he said in such neutral tone that she had no clue as to his feelings. She therefore merely inclined her head in acknowledgment, and sat herself down in one of the armchairs.

"I have bespoken supper," Mr. Penistone said presently. "But it will not be ready for an hour yet. A tray will be sent up to your friend—perhaps you would prefer to sup with her in your chamber?"

"Thank you, but that will not be necessary. She is getting up. She—she did not wish to be an extra charge on the household. She will be down by and by."

Another of their long silences ensued; looking up, questioningly, she saw that his cool measuring gaze appeared to be making a complete survey of her, inch by inch.

Delphie saw no cause to engage in polite and meaningless chitchat; she therefore returned her gaze to the fire and sat quietly meditating.

After a short time Fitzjohn returned, looking both distressed and exasperated.

He said at once to Penistone:

"Have you spoken to her yet?"

"No," Mr. Penistone replied after a pause. "I confess that I found it hard to make a beginning."

Delphie raised her brows inquiringly, looking up at the two men, who were both now regarding her—Fitzjohn with what seemed surprise and undisguised admiration.

"Miss Carteret," he said in a brisk, direct manner. "We have a proposition to make to you."

Delphie began to feel a decided oddness about the atmosphere; as if the two men were calculating on her in some way. With considerable caution in her voice, she replied,

"Oh? Of what nature?"

"You have never met my uncle?" Fitzjohn inquired, with seeming irrelevance. It seemed to be put in the form of a question, so Delphie shook her head. He went on, "May I ask—are you acquainted with the family history?"

"A portion of it," Delphie answered circumspectly.

"You had heard of the duel between my grandfather and his brother?"

"On the roof? Yes," Delphie answered.

"You knew, perhaps, that Great-uncle Mark succeeded to the title—but has lately been much troubled by remorse and regret."

"So I understand."

"My uncle is a singular—somewhat superstitious—character," Mr. Fitzjohn pursued, in a level, expository tone. "All his life he has been beset by a feeling that he is—in some sense—a usurper—in consequence of which he has always exercised the most stringent economy—"

"Parsimony," remarked Mr. Penistone in a dispassionate manner.

"Parsimony, if you will; he is of an austere, puritanical turn of mind. As he has grown older, his dearest wish has been that his heir—my cousin Gareth here—should be united in marriage with the sole legitimate issue of his deceased brother—so as to make a kind of reparation for his brother's death."

"Yes?" said Delphie. "That issue being—"

"Ah—Miss Elaine Carteret."

"My supplanter, you mean?" Delphie said dryly. It occurred to her to wonder whether Mr. Fitzjohn did not also, like herself, suffer from some sense of grievance at seeing such careful plans made for a reparation which certainly would not benefit *him;* but perhaps a financial settlement had been made in his favor; that would alter the case, of course. Certainly he seemed quite detached about it all.

"Where, then, is your problem?" Delphie inquired. "I understand that Mr. Penistone *is* affianced to his—to the *soi-disant* Miss Carteret—so my great-uncle must surely be satisfied? All his hopes are fulfilled."

"Ay, but you see, he wanted them united in matrimony before his death!"

"It appears then that he is likely to be disappointed," Delphie remarked coolly.

She now began to understand Mr. Penistone's dismay at his affianced bride's curt note announcing the postponement of her arrival. "You think Miss Carteret will not arrive in time? It is a pity she is not more considerate of her friends."

Glancing down at her white skirts, Delphie fastidiously removed a dog hair which was adhering to the hem.

Mr. Penistone remarked in his dry tone.

"Unfortunately my uncle is of a valetudinarian turn, and has frequently been prone to imagine that he has fallen into his last sickness. In point of fact we have been summoned to his deathbed on half a dozen occasions in the course of the last five years—and each time he has sent a message when we were halfway here, to say that we need not come after all; so it is to be feared that Miss Carteret believed this to be yet another cry of Wolf, Wolf!"

"Whereas it is more serious this time?"

"We fear so," said Fitzjohn.

"I am sorry to hear it. Just the same—forgive me—I do not quite see how this can affect *me*—except that it must preclude any chance I have of becoming acquainted with my uncle and pleading my mother's case."

"On the contrary," said Fitzjohn, as his cousin seemed unwilling to speak. "We wish to enlist your help, Miss—er, miss, in return for which we are prepared to make a bargain with you. My uncle's lawyer Mr. Wylye is in the house—attending to some last testamentary dispositions my uncle wished to make—and it would be a matter of no difficulty to see that a respectable annuity—say three hundred pounds a year—is, or, in certain circumstances, would be—settled on your mother—such as she would have been entitled to by her father's will if—if matters had fallen out differently."

Delphie was thunderstruck. She felt her head almost commence to spin. Here—offered quite simply, and, as it seemed, without the least difficulty, as a kind of minimum exchange, was all that she had ever meant to ask; for she had intended to make no extravagant claims on the estate, out of respect for her mother's antagonistic feelings toward the family.

Concealing her surprise, however, she replied carefully,

"How could that be? If my uncle does not believe that my mother is—who she says she is—he would hardly be likely to make provision for her in his will?"

"There would not be the least difficulty about it," said Mr. Fitzjohn calmly. "My uncle has dictated a series of legacies and annuities to various old servants and dependants of the family; your mother's name could be slipped in there without any trouble whatsoever."

Suppressing a natural resentment at the low status thrust on her mother by this suggestion, Delphie inquired,

"If this is so simple, where is the need for any bargain?"

"Because, ma'am, *we* have *no* reason to believe in your mother's claim to such a provision."

"But what is your own problem then? It must be quite acute," Delphie said shrewdly, "if you are willing to collaborate in what you regard as an unjustified measure in order to secure my co-operation? What is to be *my* side of the bargain, pray? Silence as to Miss Carteret's false declarations?"

The two men looked at each other again. Mr. Fitzjohn, Delphie noted, seemed calm enough, but Penistone looked both angry and troubled; a line creased his brow, a flush had risen on his lean, sardonic countenance.

"I must explain a little further, ma'am," said Fitzjohn. "My uncle is so set on the marriage between my two cousins, that he intends to disinherit them both if the wedding does not take place before his death. He will leave his entire fortune to provide for the upkeep of his pack of hounds."

He looked morosely at the moth-eaten animals snoring on the floor.

"*Oh,* indeed?" said Philadelphia slowly. She recalled Mr. Browty's hushed voice: ". . . a hundred and fifty thousand in the Funds . . . one o' the warmest men in England . . . owns the coal under half Derbyshire . . ."

She inquired rather dryly, "And what about you, Mr. Fitzjohn? Shall you also be visited by my uncle's displeasure in this contingency?"

"No, madam," he said. "My uncle has made—has made what

he considers a suitable testamentary disposition for me—which would not be affected—but his displeasure would certainly be a heavy misfortune for my two cousins, who, in the event of their marriage, would otherwise be his main inheritors."

"So I am to assist a person whom I know to be a false pretender to a handsome fortune, in return for a meager annuity to be paid to my mother, paid on *sufferance*, as if *she* were the wrongful claimant?"

Mr. Penistone's eyes flashed; he gave Delphie a furious glance and said in a low voice to Fitzjohn,

"I told you how it would be! She is hard—hard and calculating to the tips of her nails—"

Ignoring him, Fitzjohn said calmly, "Nonsense, madam. You know, as I do, that your pretensions are false; you may think yourself lucky to receive this offer, which will not be held open for long, let me tell you!"

She chose not to reply to this, but asked again, "And what is to be my side of the bargain?"

The two men glanced at one another again. Then Mr. Fitzjohn said,

"We should like you to go through a pretended form of marriage with my cousin at my uncle's bedside."

"*What?*"

She gazed at them, completely dumbfounded. They looked impassively back at her.

After a moment she said weakly,

"You cannot be serious?"

"Perfectly serious, I assure you," replied Mr. Fitzjohn.

"But—I never heard such an outrageous proposal—every feeling must be offended—"

Mr. Fitzjohn lifted an interrupting hand.

"Please! No time should be lost in idle exclamation."

"Idle exclamation! It was not idle, I assure you."

"And I assure you, ma'am, that we are both men of probity; that our proposition was made in perfect seriousness. There are more, and weightier considerations dependent on this issue than the mere disposition of a fortune, are there not, Penistone?"

Mr. Penistone, who was now looking somewhat haggard, inclined his head at this. Delphie, giving him a penetrating glance, recollected that his cousin had so far done all the arguing, and he had said very little; she asked him,

"Are you really agreeable to this plan, sir?"

Reluctantly, it seemed, he said, "Yes; in the circumstances I see no alternative." But he sounded as if he had numerous and strong reservations.

"But there must be many practical objections!" Delphie exclaimed. "The first and obvious one being that my uncle, unless he is raving delirious, must recognize that I am not the—person Mr. Penistone is affianced to."

"No, ma'am; that is not the case. My uncle has never laid eyes on the young lady in his life."

"What?" exclaimed Delphie again. "His own ward—for whom he has provided—and he has never even seen her?"

"He preferred not to," said Penistone shortly. "He has a disgust for the whole female sex." He sounded as if he shared his uncle's prejudice.

"Good heavens," said Delphie slowly. "I begin to see . . ."

Fitzjohn continued. "And it is certainly true, ma'am, that you —that you have a certain resemblance to the family physiognomy and could pass for a Penistone—"

"Thank you," she said with irony.

She began to wish that Jenny would make her appearance. What would Jenny have to say to this amazing proposition? Delphie could imagine her friend's robust urging—"Go on, dearie; what have you got to lose? Besides which, I never heard such a prime lark!"

"But you—but—even for a pretended ceremony—you would need someone dressed as a clergyman—something that resembled a license—"

"Madam," said Fitzjohn patiently, "in preparation for the *real* marriage which we hoped would take place this evening, we are already provided with a special license and with a clergyman."

"But you do not *want* a real marriage," Delphie objected. "Mr. Penistone for sure does not wish to be married to me. And I am very certain that I do not wish to marry *him*."

Mr. Penistone cast her an inimical look, and observed,

"All that needs is for some other piece of paper to be substituted for the license, and for some other person to borrow the clerical robes. Deuce take it, ma'am—the whole affair will only take five minutes!"

"But the clergyman himself cannot approve of such a scheme?"

"On the contrary," said Fitzjohn. "He thinks it essential for my uncle's peace of mind—otherwise he is like to die in a wretched state of agitation and useless repining, without having properly made his peace with God."

"He sounds a most singular creature . . . But if that is really so—" said Delphie slowly. It had occurred to her that here, at least, by agreeing to this bedside ceremony, she must achieve a chance, which would not otherwise be granted, of getting to see her great-uncle. She might have an opportunity to mention her mother—

"Come, miss," said Fitzjohn. "We have—I promise you—no time to waste in arguing. Lord Bollington's state is critical. Even now it may be too late. Is it to be yes, or no?"

Delphie looked at him. His square face was impassive; he did not seem as if he personally were greatly interested in the outcome of her deliberations, but merely wished a tiresome problem to be resolved; he gave her a brief, encouraging smile, however. Penistone seemed much more agitated; he slightly loosened his carefully tied neckcloth, and drew a short, weary breath.

"Very well," said Delphie. "I do not approve—I do not at all condone your scheme—but—in the circumstances—and if it is truly for the welfare of a dying man—I am prepared to co-operate with you."

"In that case," said Fitzjohn, "be so good as to come with us. There is no time to be lost."

He led the way out of the room and, after an instant's hesitation, Philadelphia followed him, with Mr. Penistone close behind her.

4

The distance from the library to Lord Bollington's chamber was by no means so great as the way that Delphie had been taken to the West Wing; within a very few minutes they were standing in a broad carpeted anteroom, while Mr. Fitzjohn tapped on a paneled door; then they passed through another antechamber, in which a thin man in a close snuff-colored suit and an old-fashioned wig—presumably the lawyer—sat writing busily at a table in a corner, while two others—the elderly Fidd, and a black-clad man, no doubt the doctor—conferred in low voices. Fitzjohn stopped to say a word to them and they glanced at Delphie with a kind of apathetic, gloomy curiosity; then Fitzjohn passed through yet another door and led them into the room beyond.

This was an enormous chamber; it had mullioned windows, a high ceiling with elaborate moldings, and bosses suspended from its plasterwork, a thick carpet, and a few massive pieces of furniture at large distances from each other. An immense pile of coal on the hearth had burned down to a hot red glow; two oil lamps supplied a shadowy and insufficient light. Fitzjohn, with a nod of his head, signaled Delphie to approach the roomy four-poster bed which stood on the far side of the hearth.

For a few moments she found it difficult to distinguish the man who lay on the bed from the shadows surrrounding him; then as her eyes by degrees became accustomed to the somber light, she slowly began to take in his apprearance.

Her great-uncle lay propped against a pile of pillows; despite the pains that had evidently been taken to ease his position, he drew each breath with a harsh rattle, as if the effort gave him severe pain. He looked to be about seventy years of age; his face was much lined, and all the color and blood seemed to have been drained away from it. His hair was a shock of coarse white, like a thistle head; his eyebrows, too, bristled white above the closed eyes, deep sunk in their hollows. He looked all skin and bone; the hands that lay inertly before him on the counterpane might have been carved from grainy, weather-beaten wood.

It was hot and close in his chamber; a smell of burnt paper and Russia leather hung in the air, and the lingering aromatic fumes of some vinegary medicament; Delphie began to wish herself elsewhere; she felt it very oppressive in there, as she stood silently waiting for the man in the bed to open his eyes.

"Ahem!" said Fitzjohn, quite loudly. "I have brought my cousin, sir—my cousin Miss Carteret."

The small eyes under the frosty brows flew open. Delphie was uncomfortably reminded of a spider, couched motionless in a shadowy corner, waiting for its prey, as the head slightly moved, and the sparks in the deep-socketed caverns traveled slowly around toward her. She fancied that there was an expression of considerable malice in them.

"Found your way here at last, then miss, have you? A moneyless mare trots fast to the market! Heh, heh, heh!" He spoke in a kind of whispering rattle, but his laugh was disagreeably loud and shrill.

Delphie opened her lips to reply, but he gestured her to silence with one of the gray, bony hands. "Quiet, miss! I want no parleying! *I* do the talking here. Silence is a woman's best garment." His face wrinkled into a scowl; his lower lip thrust out. She thought that he looked a most evil old scarecrow.

"Ay," he muttered, "they're all alike; bright eyes and hard grasping hands, lying tongues and mouths that will suck the life's blood out of you. Hearts like stones; she-hyenas who would eat their own children if no other food offered."

Delphie wondered if Lord Bollington's mother had been unkind to him—or had his wife, the former Prissy Privett, played him false? Or was he raving in delirium? His spiteful glance moved round to Gareth Penistone, who was standing with no very submissive expression on his dark features, at a slighty farther remove from the bedside.

"Well, Gareth," croaked the old man. "Are you prepared to have the knot tied—hey? Are you ready for the noose?"

"Yes, sir; I have already expressed my willingness," replied Gareth shortly.

"Wise man!" Lord Bollington gave his disagreeable chuckle. "Knows which side his bread is buttered on! To be sure, she's a handsome wench enough—the outside of the platter, hah! Favors the family, too. I daresay the inside's as black as the rest of her species. Well, fetch in the parson! Let's get it done with!"

Mr. Fitzjohn walked rapidly and noiselessly from the room. Penistone made a hasty movement, of impatience or despair, as if minded to call his cousin back; then desisted, and, turning, stood by the mantel with a slightly bent head, staring down into the red coals.

Delphie stood calmly regarding the old man, and he looked back at her.

"Spirit, too," he muttered. "Put that white thing over your head, girl—no, *no*, not right over!—ay, that will do"—as she draped the white scarf, framing her face. "Ay, ay, so she looked—it must be fifty years agone."

"Who looked, Uncle Mark?" said Gareth, but not as if he had any particular interest in the answer.

"Why, Mary—your Great-uncle Lancelot's first wife—this girl's grandmother." He added, as if to himself, "A Howard, *she* was."

At this moment the old man's mutterings were drowned by a strange noise—a kind of loud, staccato rattling, which was audible somewhere high up in the room, above the bed valance. The wind had got up, and was probably disturbing some loose board or piece of lath in the ancient structure of the house.

"Hush! Hush!" gasped Lord Bollington. Even in that dim light it could be seen that his face had blanched to a paler, more leaden hue; his fingers worked convulsively on the cover. "Do you hear them? They are impatient! They are waiting for me!"

"It is nothing, uncle!" said Penistone irritably. "Rats in the timbers perhaps! Or just the joists creaking."

"Nay! It is the spirits telling me to make haste. My brother is angry. He that dieth in the water shall never lie quiet; and he that lacketh burial shall be for ever unappeased; his voice crieth in the wind! It is my brother and his son Tristram."

For a moment Delphie wondered where nephew Tristram fitted into the family pattern; then she recollected that he was her own uncle, her mother's brother, who had died at the Battle of St. Vincent; presumably that was why his aged relation felt that his restless spirit wandered in the wind.

"It is nothing, sir," she murmured. "My cousin was right—it was the timbers creaking, I daresay. It has stopped again."

"Quiet, girl! I tell you, the spirits are angry with me!"

And it was true that, in a moment or two, the rattling began again. Delphie looked upward, but could see nothing above the shadowed bed valance. Then the sound died away again.

Shortly afterward, Fitzjohn returned with a tall, balding man in clerical robes, who moved swiftly, with a rustle of his gown, to Lord Bollington's bedside.

Jenny accompanied them, looking both amazed and subdued.

"We needed a witness," Fitzjohn explained to Philadelphia in a low tone. "I thought you might like your friend to assist you at the ceremony." She was somewhat surprised at this consideration, but thanked him with a nod, and smiled at Jenny's look of round-eyed amazement, laying a finger on her lips.

"Uncle Mark," murmured Fitzjohn, "here is His Grace, the Bishop of Bengal, who has expressed his willingness to perform the marriage ceremony for my cousins."

"Why the devil need you fetch a *bishop* into the business?" demanded the old man testily. "What's wrong with Bragg from the rectory, pray?"

"Mr. Bragg is attending a diocesan conference, sir."

"Got no right to slope off without my permission," grumbled Lord Bollington.

Delphie had been wondering to herself what reason Mr. Fitzjohn would give for having some stranger perform the mock ceremony; she was impressed by his power of invention, for up till now she had put Fitzjohn down as a decidedly sober and prosaic person. The Bishop of Bengal—good heavens! And no doubt, once the ceremony was over, he would conveniently return to Bengal again.

Mr. Fitzjohn now turned and made the introductions between the clergyman, herself, and Mr. Penistone.

"How do you do, Your Grace?" said Delphie with a slight curtsy. "I hope you are enjoying your visit to this country?"

"Thank you, my child. Unfortunately this chilly spell has given me a severe cold," the apparent bishop replied, blowing his nose and sneezing several times. "I am afraid it is but a hoarse blessing that I shall be able to pronounce over you. And I think it as well if we perform the ceremony without delay. I have no wish to add to his lordship's troubles by giving him my cold."

"No indeed," agreed Delphie. "That would be the outside of enough."

Mr. Penistone threw her a sardonic glance, but said nothing.

"Have you the license, Mr. Fitzjohn?" inquired the bishop.

"Certainly, sir; here it is."

The bishop scanned the paper that Fitzjohn handed him, apparently found it in order, and handed it back.

He then, without more ado, pulled a prayer book out of a pocket in his robe and proceeded to read the marriage service.

Delphie listened in a kind of wondering calm. When the priest reached that formidable adjuration: If any man can show just cause why they may not lawfully be joined together, she felt both sadness and guilt. How do we dare fool that poor old sinner on the bed with such a mockery as this? she thought. And when the final exhortation came: Let him now speak, or else hereafter forever hold his peace, she half expected some voice, perhaps from above the bed valance, to cry, *I* do! It is all a false deceit. *I* do!

But no such interruption occurred.

At the point where the ring was called for, she wondered fleetingly if this necessity had been remembered; but apparently it had; Mr. Penistone produced a gold ring from his waistcoat pocket and handed it to the pretended bishop, who gave it an approving glance and passed it back. Next moment it was on Delphie's finger.

"I now pronounce you man and wife," said His Grace, and added, "You may kiss your bride."

Philadelphia coolly inclined her cheek; Mr. Penistone slightly touched it with his lips; their eyes met for a brief moment.

Lord Bollington's chamber was now in profound silence; the rapping in the shadows had died away during the short ceremony.

"Are they tied up?" demanded the old man, opening his eyes, which had been shut while the service was going on. "Are they properly shackled?"

"They are, sir; tight as holy church can make them," replied the bishop.

Jenny stepped forward, threw her arms round Delphie in a warm hug, and gave her a smacking kiss. Her eyes sparkled, but she still did not dare speak.

"Very good! Then get out of my room, the whole pack of you!" declared Lord Bollington when the witnesses had signed their names, Mr. Fitzjohn acting as the second. "I do not wish to see any of you again. But let Fidd come in with a decanter of brandy, and send that lawyer fellow the very minute he has finished his scratching and scribing. I'll need witnesses for my will, too," he added, recollecting. "The servants won't do—they are all mentioned in the will. The doctor's assistant can be one. And you, sir"—to the pretended bishop—"you can be the other."

"Indeed, Lord Bollington, I think it best—considering my cold —that I do not remain in your presence, if you will be so good as to excuse me," said the bishop.

Lord Bollington muttered some words, among which "devilish awkward disobliging shovel-faced fellow" could be distinguished, but said, "Oh, very well! Let the wench remain, then," indicating Jenny with a look of loathing. "The rest of you—clear out! Yes— you as well," to Fitzjohn, who seemed as if he wished to say something to his uncle. "I will see you later!"

The instant they were all outside Lord Bollington's chamber, Mr. Fitzjohn took the bishop's arm and led him away, calling back some brief explanation over his shoulder as he did so.

"Allow me to escort you back to the library, Miss Carteret," said Mr. Penistone.

Delphie cast a quick nervous look backward, in case the old man might have caught the name *Miss Carteret,* but the door was already closed.

"Thank you," she said absently, "you are very good," and was silent for the rest of the short walk downstairs. Something about the artificiality of the brief, odd constrained ceremony had moved her very strangely: the bitter old man, churlish in his loneliness and guilt, beset by superstitious terrors; the hot, close, dim room; the total lack of any sympathy or affection for the dying man in his last illness; the two cousins, impassively practicing their deceit by means of this elaborate pretense; these things had affected her deeply, and gave her a feeling of inexpressible sadness. But she could hardly expect that the same impression had been made on Mr. Penistone. When they reached the library, therefore, rather than remain with him, alone in another uncomfortable silence, she said,

"Pray, sir, do not feel that you need be at the trouble of keeping me company. No doubt, now that you have achieved the end for which you came to Chase, you have many things that you will wish to be doing—"

Without immediately answering her, he turned and tugged at the bellpull. Then he said, with some difficulty, it seemed,

"Miss Carteret—I cannot express to you how much I disliked the—the necessity of—of going through the performance which has just been concluded. Believe me, if I could have seen any means of avoiding it, I would have done so. But one kind of unreasonable behavior leads to another. My uncle brought it on himself."

"Pray do not concern yourself, sir," she answered coolly. "In order to achieve posession of a fortune, I believe it is occasionally necessary to do things which one may dislike."

His eyes flashed. "You do not understand how matters are in the very least! It was not only my own interests which were at stake—you do not realize how I am circumstanced—I was not the only party who would have been struck out of my uncle's will—other, innocent persons would also have suffered—"

"Do not be at the trouble of explaining, sir. I perfectly comprehend the case. There was also the—ah—the other Miss Carteret to be taken into consideration! Little did she realize, when electing to remain in Bath for that tempting Assembly, that she ran the risk of being disinherited—all for the sake of a waltz or two and a few quadrilles."

"She had nothing to do with the matter!" snapped Mr. Penistone. "If it were only for *her* sake—but I cannot explain to you!"

"No, and I beg that you will be at no further pains to do so. It is not of the smallest consequence, after all!"

A young nervous footman came into the room, and said,

"Axing your pardon, Mr. Gareth, but Mr. Fidd's upstairs with his lordship."

"That's all right, Cowley—bring us a couple of bottles of champagne, will you?"

Evidently trying for a lighter note, Penistone said, as Cowley left the room,

"The servants know a marriage has been performed, and they will be expecting some health-drinking!"

"But I do not quite understand," Delphie said, wrinkling her forehead, "how it is to be accounted for in the household that you have apparently been married to the wrong lady."

"Oh, there is no trouble about that. Elaine has never been here; nobody but my cousin and myself can be aware of the substitution. When I have seen her, it has always been in Bath. I was about, Miss Carteret, to express my gratitude to you for what must—what must without doubt have been a bizarre, if not a most distressing, most repugnant affair. I beg that you will now do your best to put it completely out of your mind and memory."

"I am quite sure you do!" she answered rather tartly. "Has it occurred to you, Mr. Penistone, that in your anxiety to pull the wool over your uncle's eyes, you have now placed yourself in a somewhat perilous position in regard to *me*?"

"How do you mean, ma'am?" he said stiffly.

"Why, suppose I were of extortionate turn of mind? Suppose I were not to be content with a mere pittance of an annuity to my mother, but were to demand, on her behalf, a fairer share of the family fortune? Suppose I threatened to make this business public? Or even to inform your uncle—should he not immediately die?"

His face, which had begun to appear more relaxed, and even show some traces of friendliness, now stiffened into its former mask of cold dislike.

"I might have known it!" he muttered to himself, and to her.

"How can I tell *what* you will be at, madam? When one is in straits, one employs such tools as come to hand. But may I point out that the story will hardly redound to your own credit, if you choose to let it out. Do your worst, however; we shall fight you with what weapons we may."

"Oh, do not put yourself about, sir," she replied lightly and coldly. "I was only funning, I assure you! Like you, being in straits, I did what I could to secure my poor parent a small competence. I shall be entirely satisfied and shall not, I daresay, ever have the least wish to recollect the disagreeable means that we were forced to adopt in order to achieve the desired end. I only wondered at the risks you were prepared to run without, apparently, considering them. Set your mind at rest, however, Mr. Penistone! You are by far more likely to do *me* harm. Suppose it should get about to the parents of my pupils that I had compromised myself by suffering myself to be employed in such a masquerade—how many people do you imagine would then continue to employ me as a music teacher?"

"A music teacher?" he said. "Is that what you are?"

He sounded so astonished that she raised her brows.

"Why, what had you taken me to be, Mr. Penistone?"

"I—I do not know; I had not given the matter much thought," he was beginning rather confusedly, when Cowley came back into the room with champagne, glasses, and an ice bucket. At the same moment Jenny came running in, followed more slowly by Mr. Fitzjohn. Jenny bounded up to Philadelphia and gave her another warm embrace.

"Mrs. Penistone!" she said, laughing, "Well, did you ever? Isn't this famous! I was never so ready to burst in all my life as when Mr. Fitz here asked if I'd be so good as to step upstairs to witness a wedding! Lord, Lord, if I'd ever a guessed that was how the day would end! You could have knocked me down with a feather! A wedding? says I. Pray *whose* wedding did you have in mind? Little thinking—"

As Cowley handed her a glass, Philadelphia gave her an anxious glance, and murmured in her ear, "Hush, now, Jenny! I will explain all to you later!"

"Well, no matter!" said Jenny, raising her glass. "A long life to you both, and a gallon of happiness to every dram of trouble!"

"I second that wish," said Mr. Fitzjohn quietly, raising his glass. "My felicitations, Gareth! Madam, your health!"

"Thank you!" said Philadelphia coolly. "Sir!" She raised her glass to Mr. Penistone, who met her look with one so impassive that she could only infer that it concealed a very great many inner preoccupations. Fleetingly, she wondered what occupied his thoughts.

"Supper is ready whenever you want it," announced Fitzjohn, who had been conferring with Cowley. "I am sure, ladies, that you must be both hungry and tired and will doubtless wish to retire fairly soon. Miss—er, Miss—?"

"Baggott," suppled Jenny obligingly.

"Miss Baggott has had a wetting—you have both had a journey—suppose we adjourn to the dining room?"

He gave his arm to Jenny. She threw a mischievous, triumphant glance at Delphie, who, taking the arm of Mr. Penistone, allowed herself to be led across the entrance hall to a large and lofty room, rather chill, despite a handsome fire which had evidently not long been lit. Here Delphie was interested to observe a number of family portraits hanging on the walls. She would have liked to inspect them at close quarters; unfortunately in this room, as elsewhere in Chase Place, the lighting left very much to be desired, and most of the pictures were veiled in obscurity.

Jenny was obviously somewhat disappointed by the repast, which was by no means elaborate: a capon, a pigeon pie, various dishes of fish, a ragout of mutton, a blackberry syllabub, and some jellied quinces.

"We pride ourselves on our salt-marsh mutton hereabouts," remarked Mr. Fitzjohn, helping Delphie to the ragout. "But I was forgetting—your mother was born here, was she not? Doubtless you have heard all about it?"

His glance at Delphie was full of irony, but she merely replied, "Yes, sir."

She was beginning to feel inexpressibly weary, and longed for solitude and privacy. Helpful though Jenny had been, the thought of sharing a chamber with her was not a welcome one. Vaguely she was aware of a stilted conversation conducted between Jenny and Mr. Penistone about London entertainments. Mr. Penistone, it seemed, spent a considerable proportion of his time in London, despite the manor at Horsmonden. No wonder he has need of money, Philadelphia thought. Perhaps he is a gambler—like Mamma.

She and Mr. Fitzjohn had little to say to one another.

"What became of the bishop?" she bethought herself to ask him at one point when the servants were out of the room.

"His Grace had been on the point of setting out for Canterbury, and has now done so; he wished to leave as soon as might be," Fitzjohn replied with a wary glance at his cousin.

"Oh? Despite his cold? Was that not rather rash?" Delphie said, raising her brows.

"What a piece of luck that he was at hand!" broke in Jenny. "I call being wed by a bishop really bang-up stylish! It was the most romantical wedding I ever did see, and I was ready to cry my eyes out, I can tell you. You looked a picture, Miss Delphie, with your veil and all. What a lucky thing you brought your white!"

Mr. Penistone's somber countenance was lightened by a faint smile.

"Are you finished, Jenny?" Philadelphia inquired rather hastily. "Then I think we should leave the gentlemen to their wine."

"Oh—very well!" said Jenny with evident reluctance.

The two men rose and bowed.

"Cowley will bring a tea tray into the parlor, unless you wish to return to the library?" said Fitzjohn.

"Oh, the library, by all means," said Philadelphia, who had noticed an ancient pianoforte in one corner of that room. "Let nobody be at the trouble of warming another chamber for us. We shall retire very soon, in any case."

"Lor', Miss Delphie!" exclaimed Jenny when they were alone in the library and Cowley had brought the tray of tea. "You won't want to be sharing *my* chamber now! I had but just thought of it! I should hope as how they've got a room more fit for a bride and groom than one where half the bed-curtains has been et by moths!"

Philadelphia had given no thought to this aspect of her situation.

"Oh—well—as to that," she said hastily. "There are considerations why—circumstanced as we are at present—I will explain all later, Jenny, when we leave here—but in the meantime Mr. Penistone and I do not intend—"

"*What?*" cried Jenny in amazement when she understood what Philadelphia meant. "Good Lord! No wedding night? Is that acos o' the old lord lying a-dying? Well I never heard of such delicate scruples! Sure I honor you for them—for I know you're all that's ladylike, Miss Delphie—but I must say I don't think *nothing* of a fellow as will allow his new bride to lie chill and lonesome on her bridal night! Sulky and black-browed though he be, I'd ha thought better of your gentleman than *that!* Why, there's been chaps as come a-courting *me*— When I think me of my poor dear Sam—"

Made voluble by the champagne and the wine she had drunk during supper, Jenny would have proceeded to expatiate on this theme, but Delphie, to discourage her, for she did not wish to embark on tricky explanations while the gentlemen might at any moment be expected to walk in, went over to the pianoforte. In a tattered pile of music she found a sonata by Mozart, and began to play it, very softly, out of respect for her uncle's condition.

She was soon lost in the music, which both soothed and cheered her, and she forgot her surroundings entirely until, halfway through the adagio movement, she was aware of a presence at her elbow, and turned her head to see Mr. Penistone standing beside her, wearing a many-caped greatcoat.

"I am come to say good-by, ma'am," he said as Delphie, surprised, lifted her hands from the keys. "Ah—urgent private affairs render it essential for me to leave for London immediately. "I—" He hesitated. "I would like once more to express the sense of obligation toward you under which I stand—"

"Think nothing of it," Delphie said calmly. "We have each gained a little, and lost a little. I daresay we shall not be meeting again, so I will take this opportunity of wishing you well. I hope—I hope that matters transpire favorably for you. Good-by!"

She held out her hand frankly.

He seemed surprised by her calm demeanor, but impressed.

"I thank you, madam. And I, too, wish you every good fortune; I hope that on your return you discover your mother in better health. I—" He stopped again, glanced at the pianoforte as if seeking words, and said, "I shall always remember you. Adieu!"

He took her hand, carried it to his lips, and then, saluting Miss Baggott, turned and left the room.

A few moments later Mr. Fitzjohn came to wish them good night.

"How is Lord Bollington?" Philadelphia inquired.

"He is very weak, ma'am, and low; shortly after signing his will he underwent a Spasm, and then slipped into a kind of swoon; he still lies in that condition, and Dr. Bowles has bled him; the doctor remains with him at present, and I purpose sitting up all night in his antechamber."

"Ah well," said Philadelphia, "in that case, as we are very weary, I think that we had best retire. I wish you as good a night as possible, sir." She added with some irony, "I am glad that, at all events, the object of the performance has been achieved. Mr. Penistone must have gone off with feelings of considerable satisfaction."

"I believe so, ma'am," said Mr. Fitzjohn stiffly, and left them.

"Now tell me," cried Jenny, wild with curiosity, when they had regained their chamber, "what was all *that* about? Where is Mr. Penistone gone? There is something havey-cavey here, or my name is not Jenny Baggott!"

But the two little maids, Meg and Jill, were there, with cans of hot water and warming pans, waiting to assist the grand London ladies undo their laces and curl their hair. A second bed had been introduced into the room and made up with sheets and pillows.

"I will explain all in the carriage, Jenny, on the way back to London," Delphie promised, slipping gratefully into the hot hollow left by the warming pan. "For indeed I am tired to death now, and can hardly keep my eyes open."

"Ay, to be sure, you do look pale and fagged," Jenny acknowledged. "Your eyes are as big as filberts and you've got no more color to you than a clout. Very well—but tomorrow I shall expect a round tale, mind!"

"A round tale you shall have!" Delphie drew the ancient and frail, but lavender-scented, sheet up to her chin and shut her eyes. The little maids extinguished all but one of the dimly burning lamps, and tiptoed away.

For a moment, Delphie thought that she would *not* sleep; the day had been so full of extraordinary and unlooked-for occurrences that her thoughts were in a race, faces and voices jumbled together: Jenny falling in the moat; Jenny's voice saying, "They was both of them drunk, a-dueling on the roof about a dairymaid called Prissy Privett"; Mr. Penistone's voice saying, "She is hard and calculating to the tips of her nails"; Mr. Fitzjohn saying, "There is no time to be lost—my uncle's state is critical."

Had she allowed herself to be pressed into a piece of disastrous folly? Would she have cause to regret this day for the rest of her life? Or would it all be forgotten—a strange, dreamlike episode, with no bearing on anything that followed after, save that her mother had now been secured of a competence to support her in comfort during her old age? Very likely I am refining upon it too much, thought Delphie and moved into a more comfortable position on the soft feather-mattress.

A gust of rain slapped against the casement—for the night had set in wet and stormy—and she thought, Mr. Penistone will have a disagreeable ride back to London in this. For a moment his face swam in front of her closed eyes, with its mocking, satiric look; odd to remember that he had kissed her. Twice, she thought floatingly, my hand too . . .

Then she was asleep.

Breakfast next morning was served with much formality in the chilly dining room. There *was* a breakfast parlor, Fidd explained apologetically, but the furniture was all sheeted up and not in good nick; if Mrs. Penistone had no objection, since the household was all at odds . . .

Delphie had not the least objection in the world. Her only wish was to be gone, and she ate her bread-and-butter and drank her coffee at speed, hurrying the dilatory Jenny, who was not at her best of a morning, and yawned like a kitten all through the short meal. While Jenny was finishing, Delphie seized the opportunity to walk around the room, inspecting the family portraits by the light of the stormy, shining May morning.

She was amused to discover her own indubitable likeness in half a dozen of the faces along the wall; it was no wonder that both Fitzjohn and Penistone had been prepared to fob her off on Lord Bollington, even if they did not believe in her tale. Perhaps—she suddenly thought—they believed her to be some other bastard descendant of her grandfather; considering his other propensities this idea must be considered quite a likely contingency. The thought made her very uncomfortable.

Over the mantel was the picture of a curly-headed girl in a short dress and kerchief, who stood with ankles crossed, leaning against a tree. She was laughing. Beside her on the ground were two pails and a dairymaid's wooden yoke.

"That's Prissy Privett," said Jenny, noticing the direction of Philadelphia's gaze. "Wearing her dairymaid's dress, do you see? Meg told me it was painted by Mr. Romney; he did it for the lord as was your grandpa—*not* the one she married in the end. She's an impudent, forward-looking hussy, ain't she?"

"There is certainly something very arresting about her face!" Delphie remarked, standing in front of the portrait and looking up at it. "Taking, too! She looks so merry. She is pretty—not beautiful."

"Ay," Jenny agreed, nodding, and she said after a moment, through a mouthful of bread-and-butter, "It's queer, there's naught special about her face—yet you'd know her if you met her in China!"

It was a pert, pointed, laughing face, with rounded, blooming cheeks and bold brown eyes; the hair was drawn up into a pile of nut-brown curls under a tiny muslin cap with a cherry ribbon.

"She do look like one to get what she wanted," Jenny observed.

"But she didn't," said Delphie.

"Sure, she did! She married a lord."

"But then he was so unkind to her that she died—and her children were bastards. Poor girl—I truly pity her."

At this moment Fidd returned to the room, and glanced up at the portrait somewhat disapprovingly.

"How does my uncle do this morning, Fidd?" Delphie asked him.

"He is still very poorly, ma'am. Dr. Bowles is still with him, and so is Mr. Fitzjohn. He sends his respects and asks you to excuse him for not coming down to say good-by."

"Pray take mine back," said Delphie.

"I am come to tell you, ma'am, that your carriage is waiting beyond the bridge, and I have instructed Cowley to have your bags carried down."

"Thank you, Fidd," Delphie said, wondering how much it would be proper to lay out in vails to the various servants.

Anxieties on this score held her silent and preoccupied throughout the departure from Chase, and she was relieved when Fidd, bowing, said in what seemed quite a friendly manner,

"Good-by, ma'am. I hope we see you again in happier circumstances," and shut the carriage door on them.

"Well now!" cried Jenny, as the carriage rolled away from the bridge. "A round tale you promised me, and a round tale I am determined to have. Why would you not speak last night? Why did your bridegroom set off directly after the wedding and ride away through as wet a night as ever drowned ducks? Why would your uncle not speak to you? Why did you never mention him before? What about your Mamma? Why—?"

"Stop, stop!" cried Delphie, laughing—her spirits had risen mercurially as soon as they had left the gloomy silence of Chase Place behind them.

Already the whole of yesterday seemed like a page from another life.

"One question at a time, please! And, first and foremost, I must bind you to strict and absolute silence about the circumstances of last night, Jenny—please not to mention a word of *anything* that happened, not to a single soul—not even to your sister. Will you promise me that?"

"In course—if I must!" cried Jenny, round-eyed. "But why ever not, i' mercy's name?"

"Because, firstly, that was no real wedding, Jenny—it was all a piece of playacting!"

"*Playacting?*" exclaimed Jenny, thunderstruck. "How can that be? It *seemed* real enough—the ring was real, the parson was real—"

"No, he was not, Jenny—he was just some acquaintance of Mr. Fitzjohn's, dressed up in parson's clothes."

"What a take-in! Are you truly sure that it was all make-believe?" Jenny still seemed full of doubts.

"Sure as sure, Jenny."

"I don't believe it!" Jenny declared. "For, if it wasn't real, what's this I brought away in my pocket?"

And she pulled out a piece of paper which, unfolded, purported to be a special marriage license (and looked remarkably like one) recording the nuptials of Gareth Lancelot Penistone, bachelor, and Philadephia Elaine Carteret, spinster, as celebrated by Wm. Blackstone, Suffragan Bishop of Bengal and Southern India.

"I thought as how it should stay in *your* keeping, so I just pocketed it when no one was looking," Jenny explained with quiet satisfaction.

5

Mr. Browty's carriage made such excellent time up to London that Delphie concluded the coachman was eager to return to the peace and quiet in Russell Square attendant upon his master's absence in Paris. They were back in Greek Street by midafternoon; Delphie thanked the driver, and found herself ascending the familiar stairs with a most curious sensation of depression and flatness.

She had been received at Chase Place with no particular civility, and with a contemptuous disbelief in her story such as must affront every sensitive feeling; she had taken her great-uncle in immediate dislike, and the most she could wish for him was a true repentance of his various misdoings, and a reasonably peaceful conclusion to his sufferings; she had been dismayed by the scandalous nature of such portions of her family history as had been unfolded to her; she had been obliged to take part in a masquerade which offended her principles, infringed upon her dignity, and left her in a most invidious position; she had taken no particular liking to either of her two cousins; yet, despite all these evils, she felt that she had come back from the expedition with some positive gains—although she could not precisely define to herself the nature of these benefits.

She had bidden Jenny a swift good-by in the shop, thanked her warmly for her company, and again anxiously enjoined upon her the most absolute discretion (a quality in which she had cause to fear that Jenny was not too well endowed) regarding the events of the last twenty-four hours.

In her mother's apartment Delphie was relieved to discover a scene of the most orderly placidity. Mrs. Andrews was knitting in front of the hearth, where a small fire burned, and some delicate invalid mess was cooking in a pan on the hob; while Mrs. Carteret, exquisitely neat and tidy (wearing a new frilled peignoir made from the dove-gray jaconet, and a tatted cap of net over her gold-gray curls) reposed on the bed, and read Volume Two of a novel entitled *The Orphan of the Wilderness*, which Delphie had procured for her before setting off to Kent.

"There you are, dearest," said Mrs. Carteret tranquilly, as if Delphie had just stepped outside the door for a minute. "You cannot imagine what an affecting work this is! I quite long to know what will occur in Volume Three, and how it will all end! I have been reading this last three hours, I do believe. Mrs. Andrews said I might as well defer sending out the invitations for the ball until tomorrow, so that I may finish the book first. The poor Orphan! Her plight reminds me so much of your own, my darling."

Delphie gave her mother a kiss, and quite agreed that the invitations for the ball need not be sent out immediately. (Indeed she trusted that they need never be sent at all.) She was delighted to find her mother so wrapped up in the fictional adventures of the Orphan that there seemed no necessity to give a verbal account of her own activities; for it would have taxed her forthright and candid nature very considerably to give any version of the last day's doings which did not contain at least enough untruth to prevent her mother from suffering a Spasm, knowing the elder lady's dislike of anything connected with Chase. Complete silence would be much easier. Delphie therefore cordially thanked Mrs. Andrews for the evident care which she had taken of her patient, and was on the point of paying her and saying good night, when Mrs. Andrews remarked,

"There's a note for you on the mantel, Missie; a manservant brought it yesterday, two hours or so after you had left."

"I wish it will be an inquiry about lessons," Delphie said, breaking the seal. "So many of my pupils are gone out of town for the Easter Holidays that I find myself with too much time on my hands."

The note, inscribed in a small, ladylike hand on paper topped by a coronet, was not a request for lessons, but a polite and peremptory invitation from a Lady Dalrymple that Miss Carter (misspelled) should entertain the guests at an evening party Lady Dalrymple proposed holding on the following day; she was not aware if Miss Carter was in the habit of performing in this manner, but Lady Dalrymple's friend Mr. Browty had spoken so highly of Miss Carter's talents that Lady Dalrymple felt sure it would be well within her power and that she could not fail to please. A fee of five guineas for the evening was suggested, as well as refreshments, and she signed herself, Yrs, Letitia Dalrymple.

The date of the party was that very evening, Delphie realized with some alarm. She had better go: receiving no word to the contrary, Lady Dalrymple would no doubt be expecting her. She was not in the least accustomed to giving such performances, and felt decidedly nervous at the prospect; but the fee offered was more than she would normally charge for half a dozen lessons—not counting the refreshments! It would be folly to refuse, Delphie thought, for she and her mother were still drastically short of money. There had, after all, been no actual financial benefit from the visit to Chase—nor could any be expected until after Lord Bollington's death and the execution of his will—occurrences of which the imminence could only remain conjectural. At all events, they had not taken place yet.

Moreover, Delphie's performance at this party might lead to other such engagements—or, preferably, to the acquisition of new pupils.

Glancing at the clock on her mother's mantel, Delphie saw that there was little time to be lost if she were to be ready at the appointed hour.

She said,

"Should you have any objection, Mamma, if I were to go out again for—for an engagement? That is if you, Mrs. Andrews, would be able to remain with my mother during the evening?"

"Lord, bless you, yes, dearie," replied Mrs. Andrews comfortably. "That will give me nice time to finish this piece of tatting, and Mrs. C. can get on with her book, can't you, ma'am? We'll be as snug as sevenpence, don't you worrit your head about us, missie."

Mrs. Carteret was likewise acquiescent, only murmuring that

the lessons given by Delphie seemed to fall later and later in the day, did children nowadays never stop learning, poor little things? Delphie did not enlighten her mother, for she was not at all certain that Mrs. Carteret would approve of her daughter singing at an evening party, for pay. Singing as an accomplishment was of course very suitable for young ladies, and even the giving of singing lessons was sufficiently genteel—but a paid performance came dangerously close to acting, or performances in opera, which were of course not at all respectable; not for one moment to be considered by any properly brought up young person.

Delphie therefore retired to the other room to change into her white dress (which she imagined would be suitable enough for such an occasion, but which she knew would immediately arouse comment and inquiry if Mrs. Carteret observed that she had it on). Then she muffled herself from chin to toe in a very old brown velvet cloak, before going in to take her leave.

"You haven't had a bite to eat, Miss Delphie," scolded old Mrs. Andrews. "You didn't ought to go out giving lessons on an empty stummick."

Delphie was too nervous to eat.

"I—I had a nuncheon during the afternoon. I will have something to eat when I come back," she promised, picked up her music, and ran out swiftly.

She had over half an hour's walk, for Lady Dalrymple lived in Portman Square, and she felt both tired and hungry by the time she arrived, just at the appointed hour. A few carriages were already beginning to roll up to the door. A suspicious footman inquired Delphie's business, having observed that she arrived on foot. She was swiftly dispatched up a flight of back stairs. On the floor above she was received by another servant, who curtly and summarily indicated the corner of a large saloon which was furnished with a pianoforte and a potted palm. There Delphie established herself, reflecting, not without humor and a certain self-mockery how different had been the treatment at Chase—which earlier she had felt inclined to criticize as lacking civility. She had been shown nowhere to leave her cloak or do her hair; perforce, she bundled the cloak underneath the instrument, and smoothed her banded hair with her fingers, hoping that she would not be the object of any particular notice.

The promised refreshment did not appear.

Presently guests began to trickle through the main door in twos and threes. This, it seemed, was the newest fashion in evening parties: a beaufet laid out in one room, instead of a regular dinner. Mrs. Carteret had read aloud a paragraph about such parties from the *Ladies' Magazine*. "So much more sensible and economical, dearest!" had been her comment. "I think we should most certainly confine ourselves to that form of entertainment in future!"—a proposal with which Delphie most cordially agreed, though her smile as she did so was somewhat sad, since the Carterets neither gave nor attended parties of any kind at all.

Ladies in silk dresses with demi-trains, gentlemen in elegant evening black, or in knee breeches and striped silk stockings, if they proposed going on to Almacks, strolled about the room; the air filled with talk and laughter. Delphie was much exercised in her mind as to whether or not she should begin to sing; or should she wait for some instruction from her employer? But presently Lady Dalrymple, a fat little woman in tight pink silk and feathers, whom she remembered to have seen several times at Mr. Browty's house, came hasting over to exclaim,

"Sing, pray sing, Miss Carter, why do you not sing? Hawkins, bring up some more ices directly," and she hurried away again, as fast as she had come.

Thus adjured, Delphie assembled her courage by playing a vigorous prelude on the pianoforte (which proved to be villainously out of tune) and then bravely accompanied herself in one of her own favorite songs, an Irish ballad. A very few heads turned at the sound of the music when it began, but by the time she had reached the end, it seemed to Delphie that her performance had passed virtually unnoticed; she might as well have been a bullfrog croaking, or a hen cackling. Nobody clapped when she finished the song, so, after a few minutes, she sang another, which was received as indifferently as the first. There was no consecutive audience; guests kept arriving, and others leaving; footmen carried around small trays of refreshments (none of which were offered to Delphie); guests kept pressing into the second room, where the beaufet stood. Thus the evening wore on, and presently Delphie began to feel very tired indeed. She had slept badly and risen early, anxious not to keep Mr. Browty's coachman waiting; the journey home from Kent, punctuated by Jenny's amazed questions and comments, had been more of a penance than a pleasure.

But if she ceased her performance for even a few moments to rest, a message was sure to arrive from Lady Dalrymple, inquiring why she did not sing? Pray continue at once, Miss Carter. After a while, Delphie had reached the end of her repertoire; she merely began again at the beginning, feeling sure that none of the guests would notice or care; in which assumption she appeared to be correct. Somewhat despondingly, she wondered how long Lady Dalrymple's evening parties usually lasted; and did her best to divert herself by recalling that yesterday, at roughly this hour, she had been going through the marriage ceremony and having the ring placed on her finger by Gareth Penistone. How the people in this room would stare if they knew such a story about her! It occurred to her that the ring (rather a pretty old one, with the word *Forever* and the initials C.P. engraved inside it) was still on her finger. She had intended to return it to Mr. Penistone after the ceremony, but the swiftness of his departure had taken her by surprise and it had slipped her mind. She must remember to remove it from her finger before returning home, for Mrs. Carteret would be certain to notice it soon; it was a wonder she had not already done so.

Suddenly Delphie saw Gareth Penistone.

He was over on the far side of the room, talking somewhat urgently to an elderly, prosperous-looking man, who was shaking his head in a very decided manner. Gareth had not seen Delphie. That was some relief. She did her best to shrink down behind the music stand of her instrument, hoping that he would not look in her direction, and that if he did so, he would not recognize her among the crowd. To meet again so soon—in such contrasting circumstances—would, she thought, occasion almost unbearable embarrassment to them both—and to herself, especially, mortification, at being discovered so employed! It must be avoided if possible.

To her dismay, Mr. Penistone seemed to be moving slowly, almost involuntarily, in her direction, as the groups in the room swayed and shifted and broke and reformed. There was no doubt, Delphie thought, stealing a look at him past the music stand, that he was handsome, in his saturnine, hatchet-faced way, that evening clothes set off his well-shaped muscular figure—but he certainly did not look as if he were enjoying himself; having parted from the prosperous man he now wore an expression of harsh impatience, hardly suitable for a party. Now he was talking to Lady Dalrymple—or rather, she was talking, and he was listening; his nostril and lip slightly but unmistakably curled in scorn. Now he was moving farther away; suddenly animated, he was talking to an exceedingly pretty young lady, whose dark hair and diaphanous gauze robe were ornamented with large, almost ostentatious diamonds; thank goodness he is gone, thought Delphie, her fingers running over the keys in a minuet which she knew so well that she could play it without the least need for mental effort.

(She had stopped singing some ten minutes before, her throat being so tired and dry that the last ballad had come out in a kind of croak; nobody appeared to have noticed that either.)

Then she heard a silver-haired lady inquire of Lady Dalrymple, who chanced to be standing quite close to the pianoforte,

"Who was that delightfully fierce-looking young man that you were talking to just now, Letitia?"

"Flashing black eyes, and as swarthy as a pirate? Don't waste your time on him, my love," Lady Dalrymple replied with a tinkling laugh. "He hasn't a feather to fly with! That's Gareth Penistone; an excellent figure, I grant you, but they say the poor fellow has not two brass farthings to rub together."

"Indeed? No wonder he is making up to Laura Teasdale!"

"Nothing will come of that! They say she had a *tendre* for him years ago, but Teasdale was the better catch."

"Penistone? Penistone? Is there not money in the family, though? Is he not connected to Lord Bollington—who surely is sufficiently well-found?"

"Lord bless you, yes, the old ape is as rich as Croesus. Gareth *might* come into it some time—but then again he might not—they say the old man is very capricious—Gareth has nothing but a little manor in Kent."

The other lady asked some question.

"Gaming, they say!" Lady Dalrymple's artificial laugh rang out again. "They always say it is gaming when a young man has run through his fortune without any visible reason for it." She sank her voice to a malicious whisper. Delphie missed the next words. All she could catch was "—petticoat company, I fear! Hardly ever goes into polite society, any more! When he *does*, of course, hostesses are delighted to welcome him—I account it quite a triumph to have him here tonight—because he is delightfully clever and agreeable; his manners are such as cannot fail to please."

Can they not? thought Delphie tartly. Just let Lady Dalrymple see him in his ancestral home!

"But most certainly not the kind of husband you would want for dear Margaret or sweet Elizabeth—not at *all* a good parti," Lady Dalrymple concluded firmly, and then, again in her carrying whisper, added something that sounded like "perfectly shameless—understand—mistress—lives in a house on Curzon Street—have it on the best authority—brazen hussy!"

Delphie was somewhat sourly amused by the avid look of curiosity on the face of the silver-haired lady, as she listened to these revelations, and turned to gaze after the departing Mr. Penistone.

That, doubtless, was why he was in such a hurry to return to London, Delphie thought. He was impatient to get back to his charmer! No wonder he had to be practically dragooned into that bedside marriage.

And then she wondered about the girl referred to as Elaine, the other Miss Carteret, the girl to whom Mr. Penistone was supposed to be betrothed. How did *she* feel about this state of affairs? Not very pleasant for her to be aware that her affianced husband was openly flaunting a mistress in London—or, far away in Bath, was she *not* aware of it? Despite her indignation at the false substitution, Delphie was almost inclined to pity Elaine. Such a public slight could not fail to be sadly mortifying. What would happen when they were married? And why had Gareth agreed to the marriage in the first place?

Because of the money, presumably.

Lady Dalrymple, suddenly observing that her singer had ceased to perform, exclaimed,

"Miss Carter, Miss Carter, pray, what are you about? Continue singing at once, at *once*, if you please!"

"I am afraid, Lady Dalrymple, that I cannot sing any more. I have sung for the best part of three hours now, and my throat has become quite hoarse," Delphie replied.

"Really? How very singular—most inconvenient!" Lady Dalrymple commented with displeasure. "Oh, very well—in that case I suppose you had best continue merely playing. It is very provoking! Pray recommence singing as soon as possible, Miss Carter. It is what you are here for, after all!"

"If I could have something to drink it might help," said Delphie.

Lady Dalrymple gazed at her as if she had asked for a seven-course dinner.

"*Drink?* You want some *drink?* Well, you had best ask one of the footmen for that."

And she moved hastily away, before Delphie could formulate any other outrageous demands. She looked so ridiculously affronted, in her tight pink silk and pearls and feathers, with her high color and her bulging blue eyes—so like some high-stepping ornamental fowl with its crest indignantly raised—that Delphie could not help chuckling a little as she watched, forgetting that she had some right to indignation herself. Then she turned, with no great hopes, to try to attract a passing footman—and found herself staring straight into the astonished face of Gareth Penistone.

He seemed quite as taken aback as she was. His dark visage turned distinctly pale, and his knuckles, which were resting on the pianoforte, perceptibly whitened.

"*You!* But what—are *you* doing here?"

"I could ask the same question," Delphie said. "But I conclude that Lady Dalrymple is your friend. She can hardly be said to be mine, however!"

"I do not understand!" he said blankly.

"I have been employed to sing and play at her party." Delphie could not resist adding, "And you? What are you doing here? You do not appear to be enjoying yourself greatly?"

"I came here to meet someone," he said shortly. His expression conveyed, "And what business is it of yours, pray?"

Delphie told him with formality, since he had not asked,

"I am sorry to inform you that your uncle was no better this morning. But he was still—he was still battling. I did not see Mr. Fitzjohn, however. Fidd gave me the report on Lord Bollington."

As he was about to reply—

"Mr. Penistone!" said Lady Dalrymple, suddenly reappearing, and darting a needle-sharp glance at Delphie. "I should like to present you to a dear friend of mine, Louisa Carmichael." She gave Delphie another quelling look, and remarked, "You are not hired to *converse*, Miss Carter! If you can neither sing nor play, you may as well retire, perhaps! I shall tell Mr. Browty, when next I see him, that I consider your talents were highly misrepresented —*highly!*"

Inclining her head—she did not trust herself to speak—Delphie stood up. Her legs were trembling with hunger and fatigue, and for a moment she was obliged to lean on the pianoforte, to steady herself. She saw Lady Dalrymple and Mr. Penistone glance back, and caught Lady Dalrymple's voice:

"—do believe that girl has been drinking. She *asked* me, in the most brazen, barefaced way imaginable, for a glass of wine! Can you believe it!—Certainly shall not employ *her* again!"

Delphie dragged her cloak from under the instrument and edged her way toward the servants' entrance. Just before walking through the door she glanced across the room again—but Gareth Penistone was out of sight.

It was not until she had walked half the distance home that Delphie recollected she had not been paid her five guineas. Nor had she given Mr. Penistone back his ring.

6

No further invitations to sing at parties followed on from Delphie's engagement at Lady Dalrymple's house—presumably Lady Dalrymple had found herself unable to recommend Miss Carter to her friends—but in due course more pupils trickled back from their country holidays, and a number of new ones applied for lessons. Poverty seemed a little less threateningly imminent on the Carterets' horizon. Delphie managed to earn a few extra shillings in various ways—by writing out menu cards for Floris's restaurant around the corner, by translating some letters into French for Tellson's Bank, by reading aloud French memoirs for half an hour a day to an émigré marquise who could not afford to return to France even now that Napoleon was gone.

Better still, Mrs. Carteret's health was now improving every day. With the warmer weather, she was able, first, to get out of bed and sit on a chair, then to allow herself to be dressed, then to dress herself. Scrimping and saving, Delphie was just able to pay Mrs. Andrews for a couple of hours a day, and the kind old lady seemed inclined to stay on in London permanently. "For there's ever so much more to see here than in Edmonton—let alone not being trampled by grandchildren all day long!" Fortunately Mrs. Carteret had not resumed—as yet—any of her frantic and unpredictable activities; though she did, every now and then, threaten to send out the invitations for a ball, a soirée, or a rout party, or murmur,

"Next week Mrs. Andrews really must start making white soup; and I must write to Totterridges about carpeting for the stairs and pavement, and to Gunter's about the ices. Or do you think we should have Searcy's to do the catering, my dearest? I so particularly wish you not to be worried about anything except dancing with the right partners and keeping a good lookout for an eligible parti."

"Pray do not be troubling your head about that, Mamma," replied Delphie, wondering how great would be her mother's dismay if she knew that her daughter was already quite extra-legally and unofficially plighted to somebody who had been described by Lady Dalrymple as "not at *all* a good parti."

"What do you know about Gareth Penistone, Mamma?" she asked once, carelessly.

"My uncle Gareth? Why, how ever do you come to speak of him? He was a great deal younger than my Papa. He was interested in nothing but hunting—was killed by a fall from his horse," Mrs. Carteret replied with perfect calm. Evidently this branch of the family had no associations to agitate or distress her. "His son became an officer under Lord Wellesley in the Peninsula, and, I think, died at Badajos, but I lost touch with those cousins entirely, of course, after I broke away from the family. Whether the younger Gareth had children, I do not know."

I suppose his son would be this Gareth, Delphie thought. She would dearly have liked to continue asking questions about the ancient scandal involving her grandfather, the dairymaid Prissy Privett, and her great-uncle Mark, but did not dare take the risk of disturbing her mother's tranquillity. For, glancing at a copy of Debrett's Peerage in a great house where, one morning, she had been obliged to wait in the library for a dilatory pupil, she had realized that her grandfather's wife, the Miss Howard who had been her mother's mother, had died the year her mother was born, and her husband had followed her only three years later; from the age of three on, therefore, her mother must have been brought up by Great-uncle Mark and his unsuitable wife—who already had two base-born children of her own. What a childhood! No wonder Mrs. Carteret never referred to it, and had run off from home at the age of sixteen to marry Captain Carteret. She and her own brother, the Tristram who died at sea, must have been bitterly unhappy in such an atmosphere. Delphie thought how much she would have hated to be brought up by Great-uncle Mark, with his sharp voice, his malicious cackling laugh, and his detestation for the whole female sex. It was no wonder Mrs. Carteret hated any mention of Chase.

On the sixth day after Delphie's excursion into Kent, a note arrived from Russell Square.

"Dear Miss Carteret," wrote Mr. Browty, "the gals and I are Returned from the Frogs' Capital & very Wishful, they to resume their lessons, I to hear how you prospered at Chase, and all of us to see you again. So Pray let us have a Note by the Bearer, informing me when it will be Convenient for you to come around. Your Sincere Friend, Jos. Browty."

Delphie wrote that it would be convenient next day at noon, and kept the appointment punctually. She found the Browty family in high fettle, the girls rigged out in the first stare of the Parisian mode, and Mr. Browty cheerfully complaining that his full-skirted coats would no longer button around him because of all the fine French dinners they had consumed. They had brought Delphie a parasol from France, an elegant gray-and-white silk one with tassels and an ivory ferule, and she exclaimed at its prettiness and scolded them for bringing her such an expensive gift.

"Nay, nay!" said Mr. Browty, "'tis a nothing, a trifle, for we look on you quite as one of the family, Miss Philadelphia! *I* would have liked to fetch you back one of those fancy Paris bonnets from Phanie or some such place, but the girls were not just sure how your tastes ran, and there was no sense in saddling you with some oddity you'd never wear. But a parasol is neither here nor there!"

Delphie said it was the most charming gift she had ever received, and just what she needed for the summer.

Then she rather firmly dismissed Mr. Browty, and gave the girls their lessons, for she felt it incumbent upon her to make it plain that she wished to keep the relationship on a professional footing. Mr. Browty accepted his dismissal with good humor, but reappeared again the moment Miss Charlotte's last chord had been played, and, summoning Moses the footman with wine and cakes, ordered the girls to run off and find their governess, for he wished to ask Miss Carteret about her family affairs.

"Now let us have a comfortable coze, Miss Philadelphia, and

you tell me how matters went at Chase!" he exclaimed the instant the door had closed behind his daughters.

Delphie had been much exercised in her mind as to what she could tell Mr. Browty—who, as prime instigator and abettor of the excursion, certainly had a right to know at least some part of the whole. She could not tell him about the pretended marriage, for that was very much not her secret, but she did tell him that, in return for a promise that she was not allowed to divulge, she had been assured an annuity of three hundred pounds a year for her mother after Lord Bollington's death.

Mr. Browty's brows drew together as he heard this tale.

"If you ask me," he burst out, "it all sounds like a deuced havey-cavey business! Damme, I had a fear you'd make a mull of it, Miss Philadelphia! It's no use entrusting business matters to females—more particularly gently raised ones—they haven't the spunk for it. You've let them chouse you, my dear—that's the long and the short of it. I should have undertaken your business myself, I knew it!"

Delphie could not help a chuckle as she imagined Mr. Browty at Lord Bollington's bedside, being united in marriage to Mr. Penistone. She said hastily,

"No, no, my dear sir, it is very well as it is, and I am infinitely obliged to you for your part in the affair. I am quite satisfied with how it has all turned out. *Pray* do not be troubling your head about it any more."

Mr. Browty regarded her shrewdly.

"In other words, I'm to keep my nose out of what is none of my business—hey, Miss Philadelphia? Is that it? But tell me about your great-uncle—did he recognize you? Did he claim you as his niece? Did he seem to wish to make reparation for all those years of neglect of your poor mother?"

Delphie said truthfully that her uncle had appeared to recognize in her a likeness to his brother's wife; and that he had seemed very sorry for his misdeeds.

"Is he dead now?" inquired Mr. Browty. "Has his will been put into effect?"

"I have studied the *Gazette*, sir, on such days as I have seen it," said Delphie. "But I have not seen any notice of his death. Perhaps it escaped me—or perhaps he may still be lingering on."

Mr. Browty said he would make inquiries.

"Any of the fellows at my club will be sure to know."

Delphie would have liked to tell him about the false Miss Carteret, who had so successfully established her claim, but to do so must involve her in explanations which could not fail of revealing the bedside "marriage"—and she therefore felt obliged to remain silent. But she very much disliked having to practice this piece of *suppressio veri* toward such a good friend as Mr. Browty, who was so generous and well disposed toward her; and she resolved that she must somehow contrive to meet Mr. Penistone again, if only once, have a discussion with him about the whole affair, and tell him that she could not keep his secret forever. Meanwhile she was relieved when Mr. Browty turned the conversation to Mrs. Carteret and inquired how she did.

"Oh, she is going on famously now, I thank you, and has regained all the ground lost during her setback. In a few days I hope that it will be warm enough to take her for an airing."

Mr. Browty instantly offered his closed carriage, and would not take no for an answer; he overbore all Delphie's protests that he was far too kind, and arranged that the carriage should be sent around next Monday, if the day proved a fine one.

"I hear Letty Dalrymple asked you around to sing at her party?" he next remarked. "I was a bit put-about when I heard that! I may have mentioned your name—just dropped some remarks as to your high abilities and so on, you know—but Letty's as clutch-fisted as she is mean-minded. But how did it go, hey? Did they applaud as they should? And did Letty pay you a proper fee?"

Delphie hesitated. In fact, after several days had elapsed and no money had been sent, she had herself delivered a bill for five guineas at Lady Dalrymple's house—and had then been sent four guineas with a disagreeable note, explaining that as *she* had not fulfilled *her* part of the contract by singing for the whole evening, part of the fee had been deducted.

"You need not scruple to tell me the whole," remarked Mr. Browty, narrowly observing Delphie's face. "Letty Dalrymple is as sharp as a razor and cheeseparing as a sexton's tabby. She has been on the catch for me any time there three years—would be Mrs. Browty inside a week if I'd drop the handkerchief—but I'm not such a flat, no, no!"

Thus freed from constraint, Delphie was able to give him the history of the evening (excluding her conversation with Gareth Penistone); he laughed very heartily, apologized, said she had a real gift for telling a tale, and urged her to apply to him for advice before undertaking any more such engagements.

Then Delphie took her leave and returned to Greek Street.

In the shop she paused to speak to Jenny, who was minding the counter while Miss Anne went marketing.

"There, I've been on the lookout for you, Miss Delphie," exclaimed Jenny as soon as a small girl who had been buying three yards of spangled ribbon for her mother had trotted out of the shop. "Only think! I saw your—ahem!—Mum's the word!—I saw *you-know-who*, walking along, as large as you please, only yesterday afternoon, in Shepherd's Market! He didn't see me—and I'll tell you why! He had a young lady on his arm, and three children following behind. What do you say to *that?* Barefaced as you please! He's as bad as his uncle! If she warn't a bit of muslin, my name's not Jenny Baggott!"

"She could have been his sister," Delphie pointed out mildly.

"Sister? Pho, pho! They were as different as chalk from cherries: he so big and black and brawny, with a face as long as a shovel, and such a damn-your-eyes look about him—"

"And what was the lady like?" Delphie inquired. She was much interested in Jenny's tale, which certainly appeared to substantiate what Lady Dalrymple had said. But somehow she could not withstand a slight sinking of the spirits.

"*Lady?*" said Jenny scornfully. "She was no lady, I'll be bound. She was a little, puny thing, hobbling along, hanging on his arm as if she was scared to lose him—hardly up to his shoulder—with a pale peaky look and hair done all anyhow—shawl on crooked—muslin so faded you'd be ashamed to be seen out in it—darn on one elbow—toes of her slippers quite worn and stubbed—and a bonnet I'll swear I have seen on a second-hand stall in Berwick Market. You'd think he'd keep his Peculiar in a better style than that! Mean as his grand-uncle, he must be!"

What were the children like? Philadelphia wanted to know. But Jenny took little interest in children. Shabby-looking little things, was all she could say.

"Lor, Miss Delphie, I can't fathom you, not you, nor him neither! If I was *you,* I wouldn't let him slip through my fingers! And if I was him, I wouldn't hang onto that poor little dab of a thing, not when he has a chance of a handsome looker like you, dearie, that would be a proper credit to him."

But Delphie pointed out soberly that he was probably fond of the lady in question, and that, if so, he did right to stick by her.

"In that case," said Jenny, "he oughter look after her better, and keep her in better style!"

Next Monday proved fine and balmy, and, prompt to its time, Mr. Browty's carriage rolled up to the door in Greek Street. Mrs. Carteret, wrapped in shawls, was assisted into the carriage and departed, escorted by Mrs. Andrews, for Delphie had to give a lesson in Russell Square—not to the Browty girls, but to some friends of theirs on the north side of the square, who had been supplied with her name by the obliging Mr. Browty.

Walking back across the square afterward, and admiring the young blossoming trees which had been planted in the garden, she ran into Mr. Browty himself, who appeared to have been on the lookout for her.

"Ah, there, Miss Philadelphia!" he exclaimed. "I was hoping that I might run across you."

Delphie began some sentences of thanks about her mother, and the carriage, but he impatiently waved these aside. "No matter, no matter! Coachman and horses eating their heads off—happy they can be of use. Any time, any time. No, why I wished to see you, my dear, was to apprise you of the intelligence which I had at the club—namely that your grand-uncle is *not* dead, as you had supposed, but, on the contrary, he has made a most amazing recover, and is now expected to live out the year, at least! So is not *that* something to take you aback?"

"Well," Delphie said thoughtfully, "I suppose one must be glad for him, poor man, since he seemed in such a pitiable state. I hope this amelioration of his condition will afford him time to improve the tone of his spirits, to repent whatever misdeeds appeared to be troubling him so, and to put himself into a better frame of mind to meet his Maker."

"Yes, yes, yes!" exclaimed Mr. Browty, cutting short her periods. "*I* hope so too—but you do not appear to observe the bearing of this intelligence on your own affairs, Miss Carteret! If the old cove is still alive, and likely to remain so for some time yet, *you* are properly in the basket! Where's your annuity now? Do you not see? You have been fobbed off, Miss Philadelphia, by those as wishes to keep you from any part of the family inheritance."

Delphie thought this over.

"Yes—that may be so," she said at length. "But I cannot believe that his illness was not genuine, or that there was any *intent* to impose on me. Matters have merely turned out unexpectedly. It is of no use to repine about it. And indeed, it does not greatly signify. My mother's and my fortunes are improving—thanks in large part to your generous recommendations, Mr. Browty—and I now have the comfort of knowing that Mamma's future, at least, is provided for. Sooner or later, after all my uncle must die, and then she will come into the annuity."

"And when will *that* be?" exclaimed Mr. Browty with some acerbity. "His nabs is only sixty-eight—so they say—he could live to ninety and disappoint you all! For that matter, what's to prevent him from changing his will again?"

These were considerations that certainly had not yet occurred to Delphie, but she said philosphically that in such a case they would simply have to manage as best they could, in the same manner as they had done formerly.

At this point Mr. Browty astonished her very much by going down on one knee in front of her. She could not help wishing that they were on the grass, rather than on the gravel path, for she feared that the gravel must be cutting through his worsted stocking in the most painful way; but she was at least grateful that, for the moment, they appeared to have the Square garden to themselves.

"Miss Philadelphia," said Mr. Browty earnestly, "pray, pray, do me the honor of allowing me to take these cares and considerations off your shoulders! Only say that you will be Mrs. Browty, and you need never give that pinch-fisted old muckworm another thought! Let the old niggard starve himself to death in his castle. Let the miserly old screw leave his wad to whom he will. I beg your pardon!"—seeing her face of astonishment—"I meant this declaration to be far otherwise, Miss Carteret. But when I think of the lickpenny old skinflint, it makes me so mad! The thing is, I had hoped first to put you in the way of establishing a competence for yourself in your own right. Knowing the delicacy of your principles, I feared you might be too proud to accept—"

"Oh, sir, stop, stop!" exclaimed Delphie in distress. "Indeed, I am deeply sensible of the honor you do me, but you must not be saying these things to me!"

"Why not?" said Mr. Browty practically. Deciding, apparently, that it was not feasible to remain upon his knee on the gravel any longer, he stood up, but without any particular embarrassment. Indeed he appeared so wholly in earnest as to be lost to any sense of the ludicrous. She could not help admiring him for this. He clasped her hand between his two large ones.

"Miss Philadelphia, I am so concerned about you as you can't think!" he said with great feeling. "I cannot endure to know that you are living so, from hand to mouth, while I have enough to keep me and the girls three times over. And they doat on you, too, the pair of them! They will be so disappointed if you say no! (Not that I have mentioned this matter to them)," he added hastily. "But I had hoped so much that you would come to give us all the benefit of your pretty, ladylike ways. Now I see I've made a mull of it—shouldn't have hoped to profit by your gratitude. But pray, pray, do not immediately say no! Think it over—do! Take your time—take all the time in the world!"

Delphie murmured something about the disparity of their ages.

"Pish! What's thirty years? That does no more than give a man time to settle down. If *I* were a young girl I wouldn't give a fig for a husband in his twenties or thirties—always going off on some caper or freak—casting his eye over the hedge, changing his occupation, becoming castaway, giving her pain in any one of a dozen ways. Whereas I, a sober, healthy fellow in my prime, Miss Philadelphia, need never give you a day's uneasiness in your life. There's my hand on it!"

As he was holding her hand already, he shook it up and down vigorously.

Delphie allowed all this to be true, but still doubted if they would suit.

"Have I mistaken?" he then inquired. "I thought you heart-whole and fancy-free, Miss Philadelphia—so cheerful and even-spirited as you always appear—which is another thing I like about you, damme!—sure, you aren't bespoke already, are you?"

No, she said, no, there was nothing exactly of such a kind—indeed, nothing at all! Saying so, she was visited by a sudden image of that deathbed ceremony, the hot, hushed atmosphere of the room, and the dark, intent face of the bridegroom looking down at her hand as he fitted on the ring—what a different opinion would Mr. Browty entertain of her, could he have any inkling of the strange occurrence which had so recently drawn her into such a perplexing entanglement!

"Mr. Browty, I will, I promise I will think with care about your very flattering offer," she said quickly, to bring to an end this scene which was beginning to oppress her spirits. "I will not come to any scrambling, precipitate decision. And indeed I am truly grateful to you. But there are considerations which—which make it *impossible* for me to act precipitately. Now I must leave you. I have another lesson at one, and I shall be late for it, since it is in High Holborn."

"Lessons, lessons!" he exclaimed discontentedly. "I *hate* to see you wearing yourself to a bone, when it should all be otherwise, when you should be occupying yourself with naught but gaieties. I should like to see you free as a bird, singing for the joy of it."

Delphie was touched. She had not known that Mr. Browty could express himself so prettily.

"Now we shall still be friends, shall we not?" he continued, refusing to relinquish her hand, which he still grasped in both of his. "I hope that you know me too well for any of this missish, awkward constraint next time we meet? I'm a plain man, Miss Philadelphia, and can't be playacting or pretending that this hasn't happened, but it need make no difference between us, I hope, whichever decision you arrive at?"

His kind, large face looked so anxious and concerned that she firmly promised she would not allow her behavior toward him to be altered in the smallest degree.

"Come, that's capital!" he said more cheerfully. "I hope I shall bring you around in time, Miss Philadelphia! For indeed, I meant every word of it!"

And he stood looking after her wistfully as she finally disengaged her hand from his, and walked swiftly away across the sunny garden.

Her mind was in some turmoil. Mr. Browty's proposal had taken her quite by surprise, though she supposed, looking back, that she should have realized what was in the wind.

And she thought, also, how very completely her and her mother's fortunes would be altered, if she were to marry kind, generous Mr. Browty. No more anxieties about finding seventeen shillings a week for the rent, paying for the groceries, footwear, coals, candles, and the doctor's bill. No more trudging through wet, windy, or cold streets all over London, to give lessons to pupils who were sometimes rude, recalcitrant, lazy, untalented, or peevish. No more snubs from servants, or acts of meanness from such employers as Lady Dalrymple. There would be no more worries. But there would be no more hopes, either, she added honestly to herself. Mrs. Carteret's safety would be assured. And she, Delphie, what would she have left to look forward to? A comfortable middle age, giving loo-parties in Russell Square to Mr. Browty's friends, and leaving cards on acquaintances, paying calls in Mr. Browty's carriage.

She occupied the rest of the day in these reflections, failing to come to any resolution of her conflicting emotions. Luckily Mrs. Carteret had so much enjoyed her unaccustomed and delightful outing in Hyde Park, that, in relating all its details and remembering its pleasures, she quite failed to notice her daughter's pale face and troubled manner.

Presently excusing herself under pretext of a headache, Delphie retired to her own chamber, where, even when laid down upon the bed, she remained feverishly awake, tossing and turning herself about, staring into the darkness for upward of three hours, before at last crying herself to sleep.

7

Still shaken, next day, by her interview with Mr. Browty, Delphie was congratulating herself that at least they need not meet again for a week, during which time it was to be hoped that she would have collected her wits and spirits, and would be able to give him some kind of answer, when, looking out of the window into Greek Street, she saw the familiar carriage pull up, and Mr. Browty himself step out of it, adjuring the coachman to walk the horses if he should be more than ten minutes. With that, he disappeared inside the Baggotts' shop.

Startled, Delphie cast a swift surveying eye around their modest establishment. All, thanks to Mrs. Andrews, was noticeably neat. Mrs. Carteret was peacefully established before the fire in the next room, with a light shawl around her shoulders, occupying herself with one of her numerous lists. Delphie herself was awaiting the arrival of a pupil. She had nothing to blush for, and was able to receive Mr. Browty calmly, when, next minute, she heard him scratching on the outer door.

"May I come in, Miss Philadelphia? It's only I—Josiah Browty. Now, do not be putting yourself in a pelter!" he added, stepping inside. "I shan't stop above a moment if it is not convenient—but I just thought, seeing as it's such a fine day, and my gals gone out to the Botanic Gardens in Hans Town with their governess, why don't I step round to Greek Street and take your Mama for an airing? It seemed to me, so much as I've heard of the good lady, that it was high time she and I were acquainted, and, since she enjoyed the drive so much yesterday—Bodkin said she was fair beside herself with pleasure all through the park—why should not she have it again today? But only if she's quite up to snuff and feels the inclination, mind! I shan't constrain her to come out if she don't feel the thing."

"That is exceedingly kind and thoughtful of you, sir," said Delphie, quite startled by this unexpected departure. "Indeed, my mother feels in excellent spirits—the drive yesterday did her a world of good. But w-will you not step through and put the invitation to her yourself?"

Saying so, however, she glanced at him inquiringly, and he, correctly reading a hint of doubt in her look gave her an encouraging nod, and said,

"Now, you are not to be thinking, my dear, that I shall mention a word to her of—of what we was speaking about yesterday. That's between you and me, and will remain so, unless it should come into your mind to give me yes for an answer. But there's no harm in my getting acquainted with your Mama, now, is there?"

"Certainly there is none, sir," said Delphie, smiling at him. "Indeed I think it a most delightful plan, and am wholly obliged to you. Please to come through."

And she added, stepping into the other room,

"Mamma, here is Mr. Browty, who has done me so many kindnesses, and of whom you have heard me speak so often. And he is here to do yet another kindness—he wishes to take you driving again—since you enjoyed yesterday's outing so much."

Mrs. Carteret acknowledged the introduction graciously. She was employed with a pencil and numerous small pieces of paper, but she put them aside, stood up, and curtsied, and said how much obliged she had been to Mr. Browty for the loan of his carriage. Today she had on her tabby silk (which Mrs. Andrews had washed out in soapwort after its drenching on Mrs. Carteret's walk to St. Paul's, and which had come up as good as new); she looked charming, with her hair glinting through a tatted cap.

"But you are busy. I interrupt you," said Mr. Browty anxiously.

"Not at all, sir; I am merely planning the menu and the quantity of wine and flowers required for a ball of three hundred persons for my daughter's coming out," Mrs. Carteret explained placidly. "But it is of no moment if I leave off for a little; the ball is not to be held until three weeks from now."

"My mother—my mother very often amuses herself with this kind of planning," Delphie said.

Mr. Browty laughed heartily and said it was a kind of planning he greatly enjoyed himself.

"When I give a ball for my gals, Mrs. Carteret, I shall apply to you for advice. But now let us be off! I hear Miss Philadelphia's pupil in the next room, and she will be wishing me at Jericho."

Delphie, abandoning her pupil for the moment, ran down the stairs after them with a quantity of shawls, but Mr. Browty assured her there was no need for them: he had enough fur rugs in the carriage to wrap up half a dozen Esquimaux.

"I'll bring her back all right and tight in a couple of hours, Miss Philadelphia, don't you fret your head!"

She was able to wave them off with a light heart and ran up the stairs again, smiling to herself as she wondered what they would find to talk about.

Since she had an hour's free time at the end of her lesson, she was about to do some shopping, and had put on her bonnet and taken up a basket, when Jenny Baggott came panting up the stairs, big-eyed.

"Lor, Miss Delphie, you'll never guess! It's *him! Himself!* Him as I'm not to speak of! A-wishful to see you, and asking is this where you reside!" Jenny stopped to get her breath. "What shall I tell him, love? Shall I ask him to step up? Shall I say as how you're at home? Just fancy *his* coming here! I was never so surprised in my life as when I saw him come walking into the shop and say, 'Does Miss Carteret live here?' Sister was going to say yes directly, but, 'Wait a moment!' says I, 'Wait, and I'll just inquire.'"

"Do you mean that *Mr. Penistone* is here?" said Delphie, very much astonished.

"That I do! Ain't it famous! Though I will say," added Jenny, "he do look in a fair tweak about something. Let's hope as seeing you will set him to rights and put him in a better skin—that is," she added hopefully, "if you *wants* to see him, Miss Delphie?"

Delphie said that she would be pleased to see Mr. Penistone, and awaited his arrival with a fast-beating heart. She did her best to quell her agitation. After all, it was probable that he merely wished to reclaim his ring. She heard his rapid step on the stair, he knocked, and next minute was in the room with her. She felt, rather than saw that he gave a swift glance around, then his eyes were on her face.

"Good day, sir," said Delphie calmly. "I am glad that you are come, as I have been wanting to return your ring to you; you must excuse me for having forgotten to do so when we parted. I had meant, again, to give it to you at Lady Dalrymple's but—but Lady Dalrymple led you off rather suddenly. However, I have it for you safe. Here it is." And she pulled it out of her reticule, and held it toward him.

He made no move to take it. He was, as Jenny had remarked, looking decidedly put out. His black brows were drawn together with a line between them, his mouth was rigidly compressed, and a muscle twitched in his cheek.

"I am come to give you a highly awkward and unwelcome piece of news, ma'am," he said abruptly.

Delphie raised her brows.

"If it is that my uncle has recovered from his deathbed, I know it already," she said coolly. "But I can hardly regard it as unwelcome if it gives him time to make his peace with God before his final dissolution."

To her surprise, Mr. Penistone gave a slight, grim chuckle.

"Well, no, that was not the information I had in mind," he said. "Though I can hardly blame you for regarding his recovery as unwelcome, since your mother's allowance is contingent upon his death."

Delphie blushed, but, rallying, inquired,

"Has Lord Bollington changed his will again, then? Is that what you are come to tell me?"

"No, ma'am; so far as I know the will stands; no, I am afraid that my disclosure is of a more distressing nature still."

"Well, I am quite at a loss to guess what it may be, and can only wait for you to enlighten me," Delphie said, though her heart had begun to beat even more uncomfortably fast.

"It is the most damnable coil imaginable," he said. "You will have to forgive my language. It seems that the person who performed the—the—our marriage ceremony was no play-actor, but a real bishop from overseas; that the licence was a perfectly valid one; and that we are, in fact, man and wife."

"*What?*" cried Delphie. She added faintly after a moment, "I hope you are jesting, sir?"

"It is no jest, I assure you," he replied bleakly.

"That man a real bishop? We are really married?"

"So it would appear."

"But—but—" said Delphie. "But how did all this come about?"

"My cousin Fitzjohn says it is all a chapter of accidents. He had asked the bishop (who had of course come prepared to read the real marriage service over me and my cousin Elaine)—Fitzjohn had asked him to read some curtailed form of the service which would sound enough like the real one to deceive my uncle, but would not be valid. And then, not to use the real license which I had procured, but merely to write our names on a piece of paper. But, either Fitz did not make himself fully understood or—or—I do not know what! It seems that the bishop—who must either have been half-seas over or queer in his attic—did neither of the things requested, and so you and I are tied together in a legal knot."

He stopped, glaring at Delphie as if it were all her fault.

She said, coolly enough,

"Well, it does not signify, after all! I believe that in cases where —where the marriage has not been consummated, it is not at all difficult to have it dissolved again, if both the parties are in agreement. If you can make arrangements to have this done, sir, I shall be greatly obliged to you."

"Ay, but it is not so easy as that," said Mr. Penistone gloomily.

"Why not, pray? Are you quite *sure* about all this?" said Delphie. "Have you been to *see* the bishop?"

"Oh, Lord, yes. He is staying in London now, with the Dean of Westminster, before setting sail back to Bengal—from which I wish he'd never set out!" exclaimed Gareth wrathfully. "No, he said he's as sorry as could be, but it's all as tight as—as oakum. He didn't fully understand what we had to repine about—for my cousin Fitz, it seems, not wishing to shock him, had not told him of your substitution for Elaine—but merely spun him some tale about Elaine's scruples as to not being married in a proper church, and her wishing to defer the ceremony until it could be done with all the trimmings. And if that was all that worried us, the bishop said, we need have no concern at all, for we could get married again in St. George's, Hanover Square, or anywhere else, as soon as we pleased!"

"Thank you, no! Once is quite enough! Your cousin certainly seems to have mismanaged the whole affair," Delphie commented.

"Ay. He, too, said he was as sorry as could be!"

"But, after all, there is no need to fall into despair. A dissolution will solve the problem, will it not?"

"But then," said Gareth grimly, "my uncle will get wind of the matter! And he will realize that it was all a take-in! And what will his feelings be *then?* No, I fear we cannot have recourse to a dissolution."

Delphie gazed at him, silenced. After a short pause, she said, blankly,

"You mean that we are married and must remain so?"

"That is precisely what I mean! We can do nothing until my uncle dies."

Delphie began to be extremely angry.

"I never heard of anything so outrageous in my life! It may be all very well for *you*—I understand that you—that your circumstances—that you were in no particular hurry to enter the married state. But what about *me?* What about *my* circumstances?"

"Well? What about them?" inquired Mr. Penistone, giving her an annoyingly cool appraisal. "Do not tell me, Miss Carteret, that if you had had a devoted admirer waiting to drag you to the altar, you would have been quite so willing to take part in that piece of play-acting last week! Every feeling would have been offended."

"Every feeling *was* offended," snapped Delphie. "And—as it happens, sir—there *is* a gentleman whose proposals I am considering at this moment."

She glared challengingly at Mr. Penistone.

"What am I supposed to say to *him,* pray?"

"Oh, well, of course," said he after a moment or two, "that does put the case on another footing. I regret the predicament that you are in."

"You cannot regret it more than I do, sir! But what, if I may ask, are the circumstances relating to yourself, which make it so imperative that you retain your uncle's favor? At such a cost to us both?"

"I am not at liberty to discuss that aspect of the matter," he said curtly.

"In that case," remarked Delphie, in a voice shaking with indignation, "I see no purpose in continuing this discussion. I shall wish you good day, sir."

"You forget," he said, a smile of annoyance curling his lip, "that, as we are now man and wife, I have authority over you. I may remain here, if I choose—even take up residence."

"You are no gentleman if you choose to do so!" Delphie fairly blazed at him. "Let me tell you, sir, that I would sooner be married to—to that piano, than to you! Please take your departure, before I am obliged to call my friends from downstairs!"

"Calm yourself, miss—ma'am; I *am* going, directly. But I fear that it may be necessary for us to meet again at some time to discuss the—our situation," he said stiffly. "Rest assured that I *bitterly* regret the necessity—quite as much as you may, indeed! I have not the least wish to force myself into your company, I assure you. But nonetheless I think I should give you some direction to which you can apply in case you need—in case you need to talk to me."

"A most unlikely contingency, I dare say!" said Delphie as he wrote an address on a card, which he then laid on the piano.

"Oh!" she said, reading the address on it, which was in care of a bookseller's, in Shepherd's Market.

"You seemed surprised, ma'am?"

"I had thought—but it is of no consequence," said Delphie, who had recollected Lady Dalrymple saying—"Lives with his mistress in a house in Curzon Street."

He misunderstood her.

"I do spend some part of my time at Horsmonden Manor, but business affairs, at present, keep me for the most part in London."

Gaming, no doubt, thought Delphie. She remarked coldly,

"It is of no consequence to me how you pass your time, cousin. Allow me to wish you good day." She then somewhat spoiled the flow of this peroration by adding, "Oh, but what about your ring? Had you not better have it back?"

"It seems to me," he said, "that you had best keep it for the present. It was my mother's ring. I am sure it can come to no harm with you."

"I will keep it tied up in a handkerchief," said Delphie.

He bowed stiffly and took his leave. At the door he turned to say,

"By the by, I greatly enjoyed your singing the other evening, cousin. Your performance was delightful."

Then he closed the door and she heard him run down the stairs.

Delphie was divided in mind between a wish to sit down and indulge in a burst of tears, and an irrational desire to observe Mr. Penistone from the window as he walked away down Greek Street. Fortunately, she decided on the second of these alternatives, for when she looked out, she saw that Mr. Browty's carriage had returned, and her mother was just alighting, with his assistance. Reflecting how extremely awkward it would have been if the pair of them had returned to find her in a crying fit, Delphie made haste to get out the bread-cake and bottle of sherry, which was all they had to offer visitors. But when her mother came in, she was alone; Mr. Browty, with most distinguished consideration, had seen her as far as the door and then returned to the carriage.

Delphie could not but be relieved.

Mrs. Carteret was in excellent spirits, and full of chat as she returned to her fireside seat.

"A most engaging man—not *quite* a gentleman, perhaps, but so full of consideration!—most truly thoughtful and obliging! Had promised to return and take her for another outing whenever she wished it—had said *he* greatly enjoyed the drive too—full of interesting conversation—tales of his life in the East—described the house in Russell Square, also—quite a curiosity to see it, she must confess!"

After she had been settled in her chair for a little while, occupied in gazing happily at the flames rather than returning to her previous lists, she suddenly remarked,

"Philadelphia!"

"Yes, Mamma?"

"Such a curious thing! You remember the other day we were talking of my cousin Gareth Penistone, who died in the Peninsula? Well, I really believe I must have seen his ghost! But what could the ghost of my cousin Gareth have been doing walking down Greek Street?"

8

Greatly to Delphie's relief, four or five days passed without incident after Mr. Penistone's visit to Greek Street, and his shattering announcement that he and Delphie were married in good truth. Mr. Browty twice took Mrs. Carteret driving in the park, but on neither occasion did he come upstairs; and beyond repeating what a charmingly considerate man he was, and how agreeable the park had looked, Mrs. Carteret had nothing remarkable to report of these excursions; the notable result of them was in the improvement of her health and spirits. Her energy seemed to be redoubled after each airing; she began to perform small tasks about the house again, and Delphie's only anxiety was that her mother might recommence her former undesirable habits, such as spending too much time and money at the ladies' gambling saloon in Orchard Street, or placing wild lavish orders at grocers and booksellers. But so far all was well.

Delphie's own spirits, however, remained in a very considerable state of perturbation, which she did her best to conceal from her parent. She still had been unable to come to any decision as to what answer she could make to Mr. Browty. She was persuaded that she must refuse him—how could she not, since she was married already?—but what reason for doing so could she give him? She felt that he deserved the truth from her—but how could she tell it? To do so would be to give away Mr. Penistone's part in the matter. Still—she sometimes thought—what *right* had Mr. Penistone to exact such secrecy from her? He had done little enough for her, in all conscience.

And yet she felt a decided reluctance to betray him.

She could, of course, merely tell Mr. Browty, as she had done already, that she thought they would not suit. But to Delphie's scrupulous conscience this smacked of hypocrisy, not to say downright dishonesty. For in many ways, after thinking it over, she was bound to admit that they would suit very well. She was not blind to the fact that this was so. There was nothing romantic about Mr. Browty, but she felt that she could learn to love him for his unfailing kindness and good humor, for his practical abilities, even for his clumsy, but endearing sense of humor. As a father she knew him to be kind but firm; he was fond of his girls, but they were not overindulged. And he seemed disposed to take the same amiable care of Mrs. Carteret; he had shared little jokes and arranged small treats for her on their excursions; Delphie felt quite certain that her mother would receive the most kindly welcome if she should become a member of the Browty family.

It seemed almost wicked to turn her back on all this kindness and good fortune which merely awaited her acceptance!

Consequently Philadelphia gave her lessons, performed her household tasks, and attended to her mother, with a very heavy heart.

Of the fifth day she chanced to return home from giving a lesson to a pair of sisters in Westminster, just in time to see an exceedingly well-dressed young lady entering the Baggotts' millinery establishment. The lady was wearing a French cambric dress adorned with knots of blue velvet ribbon, a Zephyr cloak, Roman boots of blue Denmark satin, and a Lavinia chip hat, tied down with ribbons to match those on her dress. Even Delphie's low spirits rose a little at such an elegant vision, and at the thought of the handsome purchase that the lady must be about to make from the Baggotts—very probably she might buy as much in ten minutes as they were used to sell in the whole of a day.

What was Delphie's surprise, therefore, on entering the shop, to hear the young lady demanding, in a loud and somewhat arrogant voice, whether or not a Miss Carteret lived here. As she did so, she glanced impatiently around the shop, and her supercilious glance met that of Delphie.

"I believe I am the person you seek," Delphie said with quiet civility, moving forward. "How can I serve you, ma'am?"

Inwardly she was entertaining herself by wondering what need this haughty stranger could have of her. The young lady did not look as if she were capable of demeaning herself sufficiently to take lessons and pay deference to the bidding of a teacher; but yet she did not look old enough to possess children of an age for music lessons. Putting aside her fashionable accouterments, she was handsome in a somewhat stolid way, with round blooming cheeks, a straight nose, a full chin, china-blue eyes, which held a decidedly disparaging expression as she glanced about her, and a profusion of light brown ringlets, elaborately dressed.

"*You* are Miss Carteret?" said the young lady.

The disparaging glance swept up and down, subjecting Delphie to a complete scrutiny, from her basket willow bonnet to her sprig-muslin skirts. "Oh! How very—how very queer it all seems!"

She stared about her with apparent disgust, and said impatiently,

"Is there no place where we can be more private than this? I did not bring my maid with me, and I am not minded to stand talking in a shop!"

"Pray step upstairs, ma'am," said Delphie politely. "Allow me to lead the way."

When they reached the small, neat apartment, Delphie offered the visitor a chair.

"Thank you—I prefer to stand," she replied. "I hope my business need not take long."

And again she surveyed Delphie, in her muslin dress, dark blue jean half boots, and shabby shawl, with a kind of astonished disdain.

She said,

"I understand that you pass yourself off as Miss Carteret?"

"Pass myself off? I *am* Miss Carteret," Delphie replied, surprised, but with a dim inkling of what might be to come.

"How *can* you be?" demanded the other in an angry tone. "*I* am Miss Carteret!"

Delphie's ready sense of the absurd betrayed her into a small smile, which increased the young lady's look of indignation.

"Excuse me!" Delphie remarked. "But surely there must be room enough in the world for more than *one* Miss Carteret? Or is the breed so singular?"

"You are pleased to jest, ma'am, but it is no joke, after all! I understand that you have had the effrontery—the indecorum—the extraordinary pretension—to go through a form of marriage with *my* husband!"

"If he is your husband," Delphie pointed out, "it cannot be possible that I have married him."

"When I say *husband*," the young lady amended, "I should explain that the arrangement between us had not yet culminated in matrimony, but was of such a long-standing, binding, and thoroughly predetermined nature that its claims were equally strong! We have been promised to each other by family consent from earliest youth. I have considered him as my spouse, any time this ten years. When we met, it has been on this footing. And now—to have the arrangement overset by a nobody—by a vile pretender without respectable connections—by a vulgar *upstart*—this passes the bounds of what may be borne!"

The young lady's unconciliating manners were beginning to offend Delphie, and she was greatly tempted to reply,

"Yet it seems they must be borne, since, apparently, the gentleman has not been so decided in considering *you* as *his* spouse!"

But as this was not exactly the case, and as there would be no purpose in merely bandying words, and sending the affronted young lady further up into her high ropes, Delphie temperately answered,

"Am I to conclude that the gentleman you refer to is Mr. Gareth Penistone?"

"Who else? I have been affianced to him forever!"

"And may I inquire from what source you have the intelligence that he and I are married?"

"That is of no moment!" she irritably answered. "I have it on good authority, however. In any case, I am not here to be questioned by you, ma'am!"

"What are you here for, then?" Delphie politely inquired.

"I am here to demand that this disgraceful, improperly fadged-up arrangement be instantly annulled and set aside!"

"As to that," Delphie replied, "even should I wish to oblige you—which, in consideration of your insulting language and wholly unpropitiating demeanor, you have no right to expect to be the case—it is quite out of my power to take such a step unless the gentleman agrees. And I am informed that there are reasons why he wishes *not* to take such a step. However, it seems to me that your best recourse is to make application to him. If the bond between you is as strong as you claim, you will surely have no difficulty in persuading him?"

The young lady drew herself up even more rigidly.

"I am not accustomed to being treated in this way! You provoke me beyond all reason! In any case, *who* are you? How dare you lay claim to the name of Carteret?"

"I claim it by right," Delphie shortly answered. "My father was Captain Richard Carteret, of Barham, in Norfolk, who died in 1797 at the Battle of St. Vincent. My mother is Mrs. Elaine Iseult Carteret, daughter of Lancelot, Fifth Viscount Bollington; she married Captain Carteret in 1784."

"That *cannot* be true! That *must* be a monstrous piece of falsehood! *I* am all those things! Those were *my* parents!"

"Then there are two of us," Delphie answered, with an endeavor at calm, though her heart was beating rapidly.

"I have been brought up all my life—supported by my great-uncle Mark—in the knowledge that I was Miss Carteret!"

"Perhaps we are sisters?" suggested Delphie doubtfully, though she could see or feel no resemblance between herself and this arrogant girl. "May I inquire your age—the date of your birth?"

"I do not see what business it is of yours," she resentfully answered, "but I am twenty-three. I was born in 1793."

"Then I do not think we can be sisters—unless we are twins, which seems improbable in the highest degree," Delphie remarked thoughtfully. "For we were born in the same year."

"I must request that you instantly desist from putting yourself forward under this deceitful designation!" cried Miss Carteret. "You must immediately take some other name!"

"Come, come, ma'am! That is hardly a reasonable request, since I have worn my name all my life," Delphie replied, raising her brows. "I might ask the same of you—"

"Oh! Such impertinence!"

"—But, as it falls out, I have taken another name," Delphie

continued equably. "It seems that I am now Mrs. Penistone. You may address me as that if you so choose."

She glanced out of the window.

"I am afraid I must now bring this interview to its close, ma'am. I see one of my pupils across the street, on her way here; and also my mother, returning from an airing. My mother is but just convalescent from a severe illness, and I should most certainly not wish her to be troubled by disputes of this nature. So I will take the liberty of bidding you good day."

She held open the door in a marked manner.

"You will give me *no* satisfaction of any kind?" demanded Miss Carteret in a voice almost choked by passion.

"What can I say? I cannot cease being who I am, simply because you demand it! And as to the other matter—all I can suggest, as I have said before, is that you should apply to Mr. Penistone."

"But I do not—" began Miss Carteret. Then she pulled herself up, and said,

"Very well! I shall do that!" and ran angrily down the stairs.

Delphie, who, after a short pause, followed her down, saw with relief that she had quitted the Baggotts' establishment (both sisters gazed after her with admiring but disappointed looks) just before Mrs. Carteret entered it. They did, indeed, pass one another on the pavement, and Delphie observed the other Miss Carteret pause and check, as if taking careful stock of her rival's parent.

Then she walked swiftly away.

"Really I do not know what can be the cause," said Mrs. Carteret, upstairs, taking off her bonnet, "perhaps it is resulting from my illness—or just old age coming upon me!—but I seem to keep seeing faces that remind me of the past. Last week I thought I had seen the ghost of my cousin Gareth. And now today I observed a young lady whose face, for some reason, was an irresistible reminder of a period long gone by—though I cannot exactly call to mind *which* period, or of whom she reminded me—"

"Do you refer to the young lady in the blue and white, with the ribbons?" Delphie inquired.

"Yes—how did you guess, my dear?"

"She has just been calling here. She said that *her* name was Carteret too," Delphie cautiously divulged.

"How very curious! Some cousin of your dear father's? *Could* it be?" Mrs. Carteret was extremely perplexed. "For Richard was an only child, and so was his father—he had no Carteret cousins that I ever met. Yet stay—I believe there were some distant connections in the North—but they never came to London. What a singular occurrence! How I wish that I had been at home when the young lady was here. You should have persuaded her to stay a little longer, my child."

Delphie could not but be glad that she had not done so.

"However, perhaps she may come again; or we could wait upon her," Mrs. Carteret reflected. "Yes, that would be the civil thing to do. I wonder from what quarter she found out our direction? Perhaps from some of your great acquaintance, Philadelphia—perhaps from Lady Dalrymple. The Carterets are an exceedingly well-connected family—you have often heard me say so. They are cousins of the Cecils. If some Carteret cousins are come to town, it is *certainly* time that we gave our ball."

Delphie sighed, and suggested, "Let us postpone the ball for a few weeks yet, Mamma, until you are more completely restored to health and strength," hoping, as she said so, that the acquisition of better health would cure her mother of these grandiose fancies.

"Very well, if you think so, dear child; it is true that June is a better month for a ball . . . Where did you say Miss Carteret was residing? It will be proper to leave cards."

With some relief, Delphie was able to disclose to her mother that, unfortunately, Miss Carteret had omitted to leave her direction. Mrs. Carteret was very disappointed.

"That was not well done in you, child, not to find out. But never mind. I will ask Mr. Browty when he comes again. By the by, Philadelphia, he has invited us for dinner in Russell Square, on Thursday next. He is all kindness—full of the most delicate and pleasing attentions."

Delphie wondered, rather sadly, how soon her mother would realize that these were the attentions of a suitor for her daughter's hand; and what would her response be to them then? Would she consider Mr. Browty as an eligible parti? Or would she dismiss him as she had a chemist's assistant who four years ago had aspired to Delphie's hand, with the comment that he was "well enough in some circles—but smelt of the shop—quite unsuitable for *my* daughter," a verdict which had not perturbed Delphie, since she had heartily disliked the chemist's assistant, who had very encroaching manners, a passion for pickled onions, and a repertoire of most objectionable songs. But Mr. Bowty was in quite a different category . . .

"I shall ask him about this other Miss Carteret next Thursday," decided Delphie's mother. "He is so clever and capable that he will know how to set about finding where she lives. I daresay it will be in some rented house."

There was no need for Mrs. Carteret to take this step, however, for on the next day a note arrived, addressed to Mrs. and Miss Carteret, inviting them to take tea with Miss Carteret, who lived, it seemed, in care of a Lady Bablock-Hythe, at an address in Brook Street.

Delphie was instantly suspicious of this invitation. She felt sure that no good would come of it, and if she could have found a means of dissuading Mrs. Carteret from accepting the invitation, she would have seized on it. But Mrs. Carteret was by no means to be dissuaded; she set to work immediately, furbishing up her bonnet with a fresh piece of satin, and, with Mrs. Andrews's assistance, making herself a new sarcenet mantle.

Two days after that, a letter arrived for Delphie, in a crabbed and unfamiliar black hand.

> "*Dear Ma'am*" it said. "*Circumstances have arisen which make it urgently necessary that I should speak with you privately. If it is not inconvenient to you, I should be glad to call at your house in Greek Street at two o'clock this afternoon, to take you driving in the Park.*
>
> *Yours, &c.*
>
> *Gareth Penistone.*"

Ha! thought Delphie at once, Miss Carteret has tracked him down. (For she had had a shrewd suspicion that, at the time of her visit, Miss Carteret did not know where to find Mr. Penistone, though naturally she would not admit this.)

Now she has found him, and is constraining him to have his marriage dissolved, thought Delphie. Well, it is a very good thing. No doubt she will be able to exert a great deal of influence on him, and he will be obliged to accede to her wishes, and so he ought! I am sure *I* do not wish to be tied up in this odious, havey-cavey manner!

But she could not help feeling a little sorry for Mr. Penistone, and wondering that he should be willing to marry a lady who seemed so full of self-consequence, so lacking in kindliness or humor—particularly if he were so devoted to his poor little mistress in Curzon Street.

But it's entirely his own affair, thought Delphie; no doubt it is all because he is in need of money—and I do not know why *I* should concern myself in the matter, after all! I shall be heartily glad to come to the end of it.

Fortunately she had no pupil at two. The day was cloudy, and had not been thought suitable for one of Mrs. Carteret's excursions with Mr. Browty. Instead, Delphie's mother was sitting by the fire, carefully trimming her sarcenet mantle. Delphie found no difficulty about stepping out, on the excuse of purchasing some fastenings for the mantle, and another reel of silk.

"I shall be back in an hour's time," she promised. "Long before you have finished the silk that you have there."

"An hour? It does not take an *hour* to buy a reel of silk! Why do you not procure it from the Baggotts?"

Delphie said that she had one or two other commisions to execute, and escaped; she had seen Mr. Penistone, driving a rather old-looking curricle, pull up his horses in the street outside.

She arrived on the pavement just as he was about to give a boy a penny to hold his horses.

"Which I am very glad not to do!" he said after greeting Delphie with a slightly constrained smile, "for the horses belong to my cousin Fitzjohn, and that was a most untrustworthy-looking urchin! Why is it that the boys who offer to mind one's horses always resemble infant Dick Turpins?"

"Probably because that is what they are," suggested Delphie as he helped her to a seat beside him. She added, as he gave the horses the office to start, "Do I understand, then, that your cousin Mr. Fitzjohn has also come to town?"

"Yes," he replied, guiding the team carefully out into Oxford Street, where he allowed them to break into a collected trot; Delphie observed that he drove very well, with light but firm hands, keeping his horses well up to their bits, and managing his whip with grace and dexterity. "Yes, Fitz has come to town. Luckily for me! I cannot afford to keep a carriage in town—but he is always obliging about lending his. That is why I wished to see you. It is the most damnable thing—"

What now? thought Delphie, studying his angry, perplexed face.

"My uncle, it seems, is so much better that *he* now proposes to travel to town!" explained Mr. Penistone in tones of exasperation. "That is why Fitz is come up—he is busy opening up the town house in Hanover Square and making it ready. In two or three days, Great-uncle Mark threatens to be here!"

"Pray what have you to object to in that?" demanded Delphie. "I should rather have thought that it was cause for congratulation. He must indeed be amazingly improved in health if he dares to subject himself to the fatigue of traveling."

"Why," exclaimed Gareth irritably, "don't you see—my uncle will expect to find us living together as man and wife! Indeed I should not be surprised if that is not why he is come—because he has always suspected that my regard for my cousin Elaine was not very great! And he has been right. Which was why I was in no haste to conclude the marriage. He wishes to make sure that the marriage was not a mere formality. The very first thing he does will be to come and call at my house in Curzon Street—and he will expect to find *you* there! And he will be inviting us to dinner in Hanover Square—he will be expecting to see us at assemblies—"

"Could you not say I was gone out of town?"

"We have no idea how long he is likely to stay. Mordred talked of his being in Hanover Square until the end of July! You could hardly be absent all that time!"

"No, I suppose I could not," Delphie said reflectively. "Not supposing us so recently married—I believe newly married couples are expected to be very devoted."

Mr. Penistone gave her a sharp glance, which she returned with one of extreme innocence.

"Well, then," she said, "*you* could go out of town. My uncle will hardly wish to see me without you, considering his aversion for the female sex."

"I am quite unable to leave town at present," Gareth Penistone replied briefly. "I have many and pressing business affairs."

"Oh! Well, in that case, I do not see what is to be done!"

Delphie waited in tranquil silence while he guided his horses around the corner into Park Lane, and then, presently, through one of the entrances into Hyde Park. The team appeared to be a trifle fresh and resty, she noticed; which was odd if Mr. Fitzjohn had just brought them up to London. But perhaps he kept a stable in town as well as at Chase.

"As I see it," said Mr. Penistone in a tone of quiet decision, after he had driven some distance in the park, "As I see it, the only solution is for you to remove to my house in Curzon Street. And your mother too, of course," he added, as Delphie gazed at him in total astonishment, for once quite at a loss.

"To your *house?* in *Curzon* Street? But what—?"

What about your mistress? she had almost said, but caught herself up just short of such a breach of propriety. Doubtless the mistress, poor thing, would be bundled out, obliged to decamp, until after the end of Lord Bollington's visit. What a perfectly outrageous scheme! How could Mr. Penistone even have the gall to suggest it? Every feeling of decency and pride must be utterly exacerbated!

"It falls out very conveniently," he said, "for my tenant on the ground floor—who was a brother-officer of mine in the Peninsula—has just been ordered to join his regiment on the Continent, so the rooms are standing empty."

"I could not possibly, in *any* circumstances, agree to such an arrangement!" Delphie said.

He looked at her with evident exasperation.

"Why not, in the name of heaven? It would be altogether for your benefit—your mother's too. The rooms are large—sunny—far superior to the close little cramped quarters you occupy at present. There would even be a garden for your mother to sit in!

I have thought it all out with the greatest care. You would have—you would have undisturbed occupancy of your apartments—it goes without saying—"

"Thank you!" said Delphie, with awful civility.

"You could—you could continue giving music lessons there, if such is your wish; you could install your piano—"

He really *has* thought it all out, marveled Delphie. Who would have expected such consideration from him?

"Of course there would be no rent to pay—"

"I must repeat, sir, that it is quite out of the question." No rent! she thought. Seventeen shillings a week saved.

"*Why?*" he demanded.

"Why? If you do not immediately see why, I do not know how I am to explain it to you. There is a total want of delicacy—a lack of decorum—an absence of those nice scruples which must completely—"

"Fiddlestick!" he said, and added bluntly, "You did not appear to have so many nice scruples three weeks ago! If you can *marry* me, I do not see what there is to cavil at in living with me!"

"Sir!" uttered Delphie, inexpressibly shocked. Then she perceived that he was laughing at her.

"Come, now!" he said. "You are not so affronted as you would have me believe. Pray consider! There are so many things to be said in favor of the arrangement."

"Name them."

"Your improved situation. Curzon Street is a far pleasanter neighborhood than Soho. A better address for your pupils. Closer to the park for your mother."

"Even allowing that to be so—suppose we happen to prefer it in Greek Street?"

"It is impossible that you should!"

"*Oh!* How can you be so arbitrary—so tyrannical—so utterly unreasonable—!"

"Come, consider!" he urged again, in a milder tone. "Am I *really* being so unreasonable? What is there to object to in the arrangement? I had even thought that, through it, we might—become known to each other; become friends?"

Delphie was somewhat shaken by this argument, but said after a moment,

"Well—it is deceitful, for one thing."

"We are already embarked on a course of deceit."

"Purely for *your* benefit."

"No; not for mine," he said.

"For whose, then?"

"I should have to obtain permission before I could tell you that."

"Well," said Delphie, "I can tell you this: if you are asking me to remove myself to your house for the benefit of Miss Carteret, you are quite at fault, for I have taken her in extreme dislike! She is the most odiously insolent, overbearing, puffed-up dictatorial creature I have ever come across, and I think you two should deal extremely. Indeed, I can't imagine why you haven't been married to each other this age, so well suited as you are!"

Mr. Penistone turned a face of utter astonishment and consternation.

"*Elaine* is in town? You mean to say that you have *seen* her? But—I thought that you did not know one another!"

"We do *now*," said Delphie grimly. "And of all the—" Then she broke off, and exclaimed,

"Mind your horses, Mr. Penistone!"

For some moments, she had noticed with vague uneasiness that the team seemed to be behaving very oddly. They were tossing their heads a great deal, uttering short cries, seemingly attempting to bite and kick one another as they proceeded, and, all the time, tending to increase their pace, which had become very fast indeed. Now, at this juncture, they appeared to grow completely ungovernable, screaming, rearing, frothing at their bits, and then galloping forward at such a headlong speed that all Gareth Penistone's strength and skill were of no avail to check them.

"My God!" he exclaimed. "What has got into the brutes? They appear to have run mad!"

Women and children along the sides of the carriage-way were shrieking and running onto the grass, out of their path. Men cursed and dashed to try and stop them, thought better of it, and retreated again. Drivers of other carriages frantically whipped their horses aside, out of the way.

Delphie went rather white, but said calmly,

"I believe when horses run mad that you should blow pepper up their noses. Unfortunately I have none with me—but perhaps you carry snuff? That might prove equally efficacious?"

Holding the reins with a grip of steel, he replied,

"I do use snuff, ma'am, but unfortunately I have left my snuffbox at home! I admire your cool-headedness, however. But at the rate we are going, I am not perfectly convinced that it would, in any case, be found possible to introduce the snuff up their noses. Have you any other suggestions?"

"Only to let them run until they tire themselves out. I must say, Mr. Penistone, you certainly know how to drive to an inch," Delphie said encouragingly, as they whirled past a flimsy high-perch phaeton with less than a whisker to spare.

She could not help wondering how long he would be able to keep it up, though. The horses, in their frenzy, appeared to be tireless, and there was so much horse-drawn traffic on the carriage-way that their headlong career was like some terrifying obstacle race; every instant Mr. Penistone had to be judging, guiding, and steering his frantic team between barouches, landaulets, curricles, and phaetons; it seemed a miracle that he had so far avoided a collision, and almost inevitable that sooner or later, as he tired, there must be an error of judgment which would precipitate some terrible accident.

"Should you, perhaps, turn your horses toward the water?" suggested Delphie as the Serpentine came in sight. "If they will enter it, I cannot but feel that it would slow down their progress very considerably, and might exert a calming effect."

"A good idea, cousin. It is certainly worth a try," said Mr. Penistone, and began to turn the course of the enraged pair, by very slow and nice degrees until they had left the graveled track and were running across the grass.

"That was very well done!" approved Delphie. "I fancy you are getting the better of them, and that they are beginning to tire."

"There is plenty of go in them yet!" he commented grimly. "I believe that it will be best, cousin, if you descend to the footrest, and kneel down with your arms protecting your head. There is a considerable degree of slope at the edge of the water, and it is not inconceivable that the carriage may overturn. I wish I might assist you to move, but my arms are fully engaged at present—in fact they are nearly pulled out of their sockets!"

"Pray do not be in any anxiety about me," said Delphie. "I will do as you say, if you really think it best."

"I do think so."

Accordingly she edged herself off the seat—with no little difficulty, for the curricle was tilting and swaying wildly from side to side as the horses whirled it over the rough grass—and then knelt on the footrest as he had directed. In another moment the horses entered the water. Gareth had managed to guide the curricle safely down the bank, but when they felt the water on their legs and bellies, the horses screamed again, reared desperately, and broke apart. The curricle heeled over, and Delphie lost hold of the seat which she had been clutching. She was hurled through the air onto the bank; something struck her head, and she knew no more.

Delphie recovered consciousness, choking, as somebody endeavored to introduce a small quantity of cordial between her lips.

"Enough—thank you—I am better now." she gasped.

"She will do very well in a moment," said an unfamiliar voice. "There is no concussion, I am glad to report—merely some bruising. She should remain quietly resting for a period of time."

Delphie opened her eyes and found, to her astonishment, that she was no longer in the park, but in a large sunny room, which appeared to be absolutely full of people. Faces were staring at her—of all sizes, and from all sides, it seemed.

"Where am I?" she said faintly. "Oh—I am afraid my mother will be so anxious about me!"

A familiar voice—that of Gareth Penistone—said,

"Have no apprehensions, Miss Carteret. You have been unconscious only for a very short time. I have, however, already dispatched a boy with a note to your mother, informing her that you have been delayed, and will be returning home shortly. I thought that would be less alarming for her than tidings of an accident."

"Thank you—that was very thoughtful," she murmured, closing her eyes again.

She heard Gareth saying, "I am greatly obliged to you, Doctor, for coming with such speed. You can imagine our alarm!" and the other voice, the doctor's apparently, promising to "call in Greek Street tomorrow and see how she goes on."

Then Gareth's voice said, "Run along, children, now! You have been helpful and good, but the lady is weak and faint still; she does not want you clustering all over her until she is better. You shall see her again, I promise!—Bardwell, I think it would be a good thing if you were to make some tea."

"Certainly, sir."

"May we see her before she goes?" piped up a little voice.

"Yes, yes! You may bring her tea. Now, run and see to your mother, and let Dr. Ellworthy out of the front door."

Delphie heard the patter of what sounded like dozens of feet, the near slam of a door, and then a more distant one. Silence reigned. She opened her eyes again, and found that she was looking straight into the face of Gareth Penistone. It was decidedly pale, and he was studying her with an expression of strong anxiety in his dark eyes.

"Drink a little more of this!" he said, and held the cordial to her lips again.

"Thank you—but what of yourself—were you not injured?" she asked when she had sipped a little more, and felt its reviving warmth run through her veins.

"Not a scratch! Right as rain. I was tossed clear into the water—took no harm at all, except a ducking, like your friend Miss Baggott." Indeed she noticed that he seemed to have changed his clothes somewhat hastily. "But you, I fear, were thrown onto the bank, which was less comfortable; however, the doctor has examined you most thoroughly and found no hint of concussion, or any broken bones—which is little short of a miracle!" he said, his voice expressing the relief he felt. "When I remember my sensations—but *you* were so calm, so fearless and practical—"

"In reality I was shaking like a blancmanger, I assure you!"

said Delphie. "—But it is all over now, thank heaven. What about your cousin's horses? Did they take any hurt?"

"Very little, amazingly enough, though his curricle is in a sad state. One of the pair has a swelled fetlock. It is certainly thanks to your notion of driving them into the water that we—and they —came off so lightly. But they are still in a very queer state—wild, frothing, and sweating. Tristram—one of the boys, who is very knowledgeable about horses—has suggested that they might have been *hocused*—given some drug in their feed to make them run wild as they did."

"But how very extraordinary! Who would do such a thing?"

"I do not know!" he said grimly. "Somebody who has a grudge against my cousin, perhaps. I certainly intend to make some inquiries. How do you do now, Miss Carteret?"

The formality of this term of address made her smile a little; she said,

"You seem to forget that I am your wife, sir!"

"No, I do not forget it," said Mr. Penistone.

Delphie struggled to sit up, and looked about.

"Pray be careful," he said, and piled some cushions behind her.

"Where am I?" she said again.

"Why"—he sounded apologetic—"I am afraid you are in my house in Curzon Street! I knew your views about it—that you would not wish to be here—but really it seemed so unquestionably the closest and best harbor—Are you sure you should be sitting up?"

"Quite sure, I thank you. I am almost recovered. What a pleasant room," she observed, looking around her.

It seemed to be on the first floor, for she could see the tops of trees, at no great distance, in the park, presumably. The room was somewhat bare, very sparsely furnished, but what furnishings there were, though on the plain side, showed considerable sign of taste and elegance.

"I cannot claim credit—" Gareth said apologetically, noticing her glance. "I inherited all these things from my father."

"It is charming." She rose, with caution, from the chaise longue on which she had been reclining. He took her arm.

"Pray take care, cousin. I do not think that you should stand for long."

"Very little weakness—it will soon pass." She moved her shoulders, and said ruefully, "I shall be stiff tomorrow, though!" Then, walking to the window, she looked out, and said politely,

"You certainly have a delightful prospect here, Mr. Penistone."

A smile just touched the corners of his mouth. He said,

"I am happy that you admire it, ma'am. When you are rested, and have taken some refreshment, perhaps you would care to see the rest of the house? And, in particular, the empty rooms on the ground floor?"

She hardly knew what to reply. He *could* not, after all, have displaced his mistress so quickly. Did he intend to *introduce* her?

While she was wondering how to answer, he walked to the door, put his head through, and called to some invisible person,

"Is not the tea ready yet?"

Then he returned, led her to a chair, and said,

"I hope I have not misinterpreted your wishes?"

"Oh, no! It is what I would like of all things!"

In a moment the tea appeared—brought, much to Delphie's astonishment, by two little girls in dark gray linsey dresses and brown holland pinafores, who came slowly and carefully in, one of them carrying the cup of tea (which she bore with intense concentration, never lifting her eyes from it) and the other with a plate of bread-and-butter. These things being placed on a small table beside Delphie, the children were free to look at her, which they did with huge eyes.

"Thank you very much!" said Delphie, smiling at them both. "Tea and bread-and-butter is exactly what I long for most, after a carriage accident. What are your names, my dears?"

"I am Melilot," said one of them, the tea-bearer.

"And I am Morgan," said the one who had brought the bread-and-butter.

"Well, Melilot and Morgan, I think you have very pretty names. And do you have any brothers and sisters?" Delphie inquired. She noticed Mr. Penistone smiling somewhat wryly over their heads.

"Yes, ma'am. Eight."

"What—there are *ten* of you altogether?"

"Yes, ma'am. Tristram, Arthur, Percy, Helen, Gawaine, Iseult, Lionel, Lance, and us two."

"Good gracious," said Delphie faintly. "What a fine family."

Now she understood the inexplicable number of faces which had clustered around the couch.

"And this is your cousin Delphie," said Mr. Penistone. "You should say, 'How do you do, Cousin Delphie?' "

They said it, curtsying primly, then broke into giggles, and ran precipitately from the room.

Delphie heard their awestruck voices outside the door, which they had neglected to shut.

"Isn't she *beautiful!*"

"She looks just like a *princess!*"

Delphie raised her brows, and looked at Gareth, whose wry smile had reappeared.

"Now I fear you have been pitchforked into one of the main arguments against removing to Curzon Street! Ten children are a weighty objection, I must acknowledge."

"Ten children! It certainly is a family!" she said, thinking of the royal dukes and their large broods of illegitimate offspring. Mr. Penistone, it seemed, had outstripped all of them, even the Duke of Clarence. "Are any of them in school?" she asked.

"Why yes, most of them, except the two youngest boys, and the girls, who stay at home to look after their Mama. The boys are at the Westminster School."

He spoke absently; he seemed preoccupied, and the somber look had come back to his face.

Delphie watched him with no clue to his thoughts. Presently he said,

"Cousin—just before the horses bolted, and our drive became so dramatic—you had made a reference to—to Miss Elaine Carteret. Was I right in concluding from what you said that she has removed to London—that you have recently seen her?"

"Indeed I have," said Delphie. "And very angry she was! She told me—in the most peremptory way imaginable—that it is incumbent on me to have that marriage annulled—also that I have no right to the name of Carteret."

"That certainly sounds like Elaine," he said grimly.

"Why in the name of heaven did you ever allow yourself to become affianced to her?" Delphie wished to exclaim—but she held her peace, merely remarking, "I, of course, told her that she must apply to you in regard to such an annulment—but I was not perfectly certain that she had your direction in London."

"You did not supply her with it?" he said, raising his brows.

"She did not ask me for it," said Delphie primly.

"My cousin Mordred could have given it to her—but perhaps she is not aware of his presence in town," Gareth murmured, half to himself. "They used to be very thick at one time—practically lived in one another's pockets; but I do not know if that is any longer the case. Do you know how long Elaine remains in London?"

"I am afraid not. She is staying with Lady Bablock-Hythe in Brook Street," Delphie said in a neutral manner. He nodded as if this was to be expected. "And she has invited my mother and me to take tea one afternoon next week."

He turned around sharply at that.

"Your mother and you—are you both going?"

"Mamma plans to; yes. Have you any objections? My mother is delighted at the prospect of discovering new Carteret connections. And perhaps we shall be able to trace the source of the confusion."

He frowned, and said impatiently, "I do not trust Elaine. She has always been bone selfish—ever since I used to visit her at her school, and all she wanted was sugarplums. And she has been foolishly overindulged by Lady Bablock-Hythe, who has undertaken the care of her for the last two years, and arranged her coming out. Lady Bablock-Hythe is a real shatter-brain. There is an old nurse too, who has been with her forever, spoiling and cosseting her. She is too used to her own way."

He seemed remarkably detached in his view, Delphie thought, of the lady he was intending to marry.

"Why do you say you do not trust her? What might she do?"

"Oh—spill the beans to Uncle Mark, I suppose! Even though, by doing so, she might be lopping off her own bough—I do not trust her to look ahead far enough to consider that possibility. But perhaps Fitz may be able to talk some sense into her—he has always had more influence than I did."

"Why should she be lopping off her own bough?"

"Uncle Mark only leaves her a share of his fortune on condition she marries me. At present she would receive her legacy, were he to die—for he is under the impression that she and I are married—but who knows what turn his fancy may take if she runs to him crying telltale? It is a thousand to one that the whole will go to those moth-eaten hounds!"

"Is the money so *very* important to you?" Delphie could not help exclaiming wonderingly. For his knuckles were clenched and his lips pressed together in what seemed like acute and angry calculation. Then she thought: What a foolish question. With ten children to support, of course it is important. She could have bitten out her own tongue.

He looked at her, frowning.

"To me? No. I rub along on very little—have done these past ten years. Horsmonden would support me tolerably well. But—however, I should not waste your time talking. You must be anxious to return to your mother." He looked at her, hesitated, appeared to come to a decision, paused again, and then said,

"Come with me for a moment, however, and you will see part of what this is about."

He opened the door. The origin of a certain shuffling and rustling outside was now revealed: half a dozen children were close at hand, packed together at the head of the stairs. Morgan and Melilot, who had brought the tea, were there, besides two angelic-looking small boys with curly dark locks—also twins, it seemed—a stout, well-grown boy of around eight, and a thin freckled girl of perhaps seven.

"Gawaine, Iseult, Lionel, Lance, and the girls you have already met," said Gareth rapidly. "And this is Helen, who looks after us all." A worried-looking dark child of nine flushed pink with pleasure at this tribute and shyly extended her hand. "Here is your cousin Delphie, wishful to meet your mother. Do you think she is well enough?"

"Yes, I am sure she is," said Helen, who seemed to be the

spokesman. "She is resting, but she is awake. One of the boys is reading to her."

Gareth ran up another flight of stairs (they circled up a well in the middle of the house, under a very pretty lantern) and called gently, outside a door,

"Una? May I bring Cousin Delphie to see you?"

The response was evidently in the affirmative, for he came down again, took Delphie's arm, and carefully assisted her to mount. A door on the upper landing stood open, and they passed through.

9

The scene that met her eyes was so orderly that Delphie could have laughed at herself for her wild imaginings. She did not quite know what she *had* imagined, but it certainly had not been anything like this: a small narrow couch, with a small frail person, wrapped in shawls, lying back against a pile of pillows, taking, from time to time, a languid stitch in a pair of boy's trousers in which she was endeavoring to mend a rent; meanwhile one boy read aloud from the works of Ovid (translating as he went), another boy stirred something in a saucepan that simmered over the fire, and a third lay on his stomach on the floor, apparently repairing a very small bridle, possibly that of a pony.

Like the room downstairs, this one was very frugally furnished; beyond the bed, a chair, a small chest, and a jug and basin, it was almost bare; Delphie began to receive an impression of poverty by the side of which she and her mother seemed quite comfortably established.

It was impossible not to remark a resemblance between Gareth Penistone and the girl—for she seemed little more—on the bed; indeed, on entering the room, Delphie had only just witheld an exclamation of surprise. She felt her cheeks burning at her own stupidity, remembering how idly she had said to Jenny, "It could have been his sister?"—and yet she had not truly thought so. There could be no question but that this was Gareth's sister. Her face was small and pale, instead of dark and swarthy, but the shapes of cheek, brow, and nose, were identical; her eyes were as dark, but listless, where his were flashing; her hair, lighter in color than his, had been carelessly swept up into a knot on the top of her head. Jenny—not an acute or observant judge—must have been misled by the difference in stature, for this girl was very slight and small.

Gareth said, "Una, here is your cousin Delphie. Delphie, my sister Una," with as little ceremony as when he had introduced the children. "And these are Tristram, Arthur, and Percival."

The three boys nodded politely to Delphie. The reader stopped in the middle of a sentence. And the girl on the bed gave a faint smile as Delphie walked forward, extending her hand, and saying,

"How do you do? I am very happy to meet you."

"You will forgive my not rising, won't you?" breathed Una softly. "I have this stupid affliction in my legs. On some days it is better. Oh dear, I have heard so much about you from Gareth. You are quite a heroine in this household, I can tell you!"

Somehow, despite her tone of wistful admiration, Delphie was made to feel that to be a heroine was rather vulgar, and that Una, given her opportunities, would have made a different use of them —but this was probably her imagination.

Una said, "I never knew that we had any more Carteret cousins, apart from that odious Elaine—but you look more like a Penistone than a Carteret—how can that be? You are exactly like the portrait of great-grandmama."

"I doubt if that can be any recommendation," Delphie said, smiling. Then Gareth pulled forward the solitary chair and she sat in it, while Una—in her breathless, exhausted voice—poured out a series of questions as to Delphie's mother, about their life, about Delphie's pupils—

"You are so *clever* to be able to teach," she murmured with wistful envy. "How wonderful it would be if you were to come and live with us, as Gareth has suggested. For then you could bring your piano. Imagine having a piano in the house again, Gar! Of *course* we would not permit the children to tease you for tunes or for lessons—otherwise they would all be wishing to learn, I don't doubt—but perhaps you would not object to play a little for them sometimes—just for a treat—just if they were especially well behaved?"

This, thought Delphie, seemed to be taking a good deal for

granted. Una glanced toward Gareth, who was sitting on the end of the bed, advising the boy, Tristram, about the broken harness. "What do you think, Gar?" she said plaintively. "The children are so *fond* of music."

He said, without raising his eyes from his occupation, "That must be for Cousin Delphie to decide."

Delphie wondered if unspoken messages were passing from sister to brother. There seemed a certain constraint in the room. She said,

"I am certain that—if I were living here—I could find a little time to teach some of the older children." She noticed a look flash from Arthur to Percival, and added firmly, "Only if they were wishful to learn, mind! Nothing is more abhorrent than forcing music on those to whom it is constitutionally repugnant—and I have more than I like of that among my present pupils."

"Oh, you are so fortunate to be able to earn your living," Una sighed. "Look at me—all I can do is mend clothes. And even in *that* I cannot by any means keep up—they tear things far more quickly than I can repair them."

She smiled wanly, in pretty self-denigration.

"Never mind, Mama," said Percy, the boy at the fireside. "Helen and Isa do pretty well as it is, and I daresay the twins will learn how in a year or two. Then all your troubles will be over."

"So they will be, my dear!" said his mother with a radiant smile. But Arthur, the reader, muttered,

"Blest if *I'd* wear anything cobbled together by those little goosecaps."

Delphie now said firmly that she must return home; despite Gareth's message (which had been delivered by Tristram) Mrs. Careteret would certainly be anxious, and wondering what had befallen her daughter.

"You are so lucky to have a mother!" breathed Una.

"I shall see you home," said Gareth.

"Oh, no! There is not the least occasion for it. Pray do not trouble."

"Most certainly I shall! I would not dream of letting you go unescorted."

"Gareth is the most thoughtful creature in the world," said his sister with a wan smile, as Delphie said farewell.

On the middle floor a gray-haired man with a respectful smile handed Gareth his hat and jacket and said,

"I have managed to get the mud out of the other ones tolerably well, Mr. Gareth."

"Thanks, Bardwell! I am just going to show Miss Carteret the rooms on the ground floor."

"They are all clean and redd up, sir."

In fact the rooms on the ground floor were completely empty; they just glanced through each door in turn; and Delphie could not suppress the knowledge that they were far superior to the rooms in Greek Street. But Gareth said nothing in the way of further attempts at persuasion. He accompanied her all the way back to Greek Street, walking beside the chair which he had had one of the boys call up for her, but was silent on the way, wrapped in thought, it seemed. When they arrived at the Baggotts' shop, he said,

"Should I not come up and reassure your mother about you?"

She was a little doubtful.

"My mother is—tends to be—a trifle absentminded since her illness. Also I cannot deny that she has a decided distaste for the Penistone family, since she was cut off . . . But it is true, I believe, that her objections do not extend to your branch, Cousin Gareth. Only, please do not take offense if she should run on rather oddly!"

He promised not to take the least offense in the world, and they mounted to Mrs. Carteret's chamber. What a lot, Delphie thought, had she learned, since leaving it that afternoon!

Luckily Mrs. Carteret was in high gig, having finished the mantle (without the need of the extra silk, as she pointed out to Delphie rather caustically); she was longing for someone to admire her work.

"Mamma," said Delphie, "here is Cousin Gareth Penistone."

"How charming to see you, my dear boy," said Mrs. Carteret. "You are so like your father, my cousin Gareth, who was killed trying to jump a double oxer when out hunting with the Quorn, two years before my marriage. He was the most amiable fool in the world—thought about nothing save horses."

"Thank you, ma'am. I have been told that I am like him," said Gareth. "Only, that was my grandfather, not my father," he added politely.

"Oh, then you must be *Gateau's* son?"

He smiled a little. "Yes, I believe that my father had that nickname at one time."

"It was because he was so greedy," Mrs. Carteret said reminiscently. "He was four years younger than I, you see; and when he came to stay at Chase once, with his French governess, he stole an almond cake that she had intended for her own supper, and she was so angry! So from then on, Gateau was all that we called him."

Gareth listened with unaffected interest to this piece of family lore, assured Mrs. Carteret that she need have no anxiety about her daughter's misadventure (which Mrs. Carteret certainly showed no sign of doing; in fact it appeared doubtful whether she apprehended that any misadventure had occurred); then he took his leave.

Delphie went down to let him out through the shop, which was closed.

"You can see what Mamma is like," she said, undoing the chain. "Rather confused about present-day happenings. But when it comes to long-ago events, she is as clear as a bell."

"You and I have something in common," he said smiling a little—and, as she looked at him inquiringly, "We both have anxieties about our relations." He was silent for a moment, and then said abruptly,

"Would you be able to rise early and meet me tomorrow morning?"

"What for?" said Delphie, astonished.

"I should like—to take you somewhere. Could you meet me—at seven, say—at the corner of Piccadilly and St. James's?"

Very puzzled, Delphie said she thought she could manage to do so, provided she did not stay out too long. She had no pupils until ten. And Mrs. Carteret often slept until quite late in the morning; Mrs. Andrews could give her her breakfast when she woke.

"Very well," said Gareth. "At seven, then."

He gave her a brief bow, and walked away down the street.

Delphie was awake much earlier than seven, the next morning; her curiosity had been thoroughly aroused by Gareth's odd manner. She confessed to herself that she did not know what to make of him at all. Sometimes he seemed so stiff, abrupt, curt, and cold that she felt sure he had a strong dislike of the whole female sex—and who was to blame him for that? she thought. The two members of it that he had most to do with seemed, respectively, selfish and self-pitying. And now he was tied to Delphie by this inconvenient bond! But at other times—when he had been talking to the children, for instance, or during the brief interview with her mother—his rather hard face had relaxed, and, momentarily, he looked as if he might be capable of more kindly feelings. Also Delphie suspected that he might have a sense of humor; once or twice she had observed a lurking twinkle in his eye when he spoke of the children.

Was he now prepared to accept her as his true cousin? And if so, what difference might that make to their situation?

Silently slipping out of bed and putting on her gray stuff dress (for the morning was a cool one, although it promised to be fine later), Delphie continued to ponder about her cousin Gareth. What had he been doing, for instance, at Lady Dalrymple's party, where he seemed so bored and angry? And what were the business affairs that kept him in London?

Wrapping herself in a shawl, Delphie softly let herself out and ran down the stairs. She had left a note for her mother, giving a few early shopping errands as the excuse for her absence, but she trusted that Mrs. Carteret would not wake, and that it need not be read.

Amusing herself with many wild guesses as to what Gareth intended to show her—a puzzle as to which she had no real clue whatsoever—Delphie walked lightly and rapidly in the direction of Piccadilly, threading her way along the narrow streets, passing many small carts and barrows proceeding in the opposite direction, loaded with greenstuff, eggs, milk, and other country produce for the markets of Soho.

She arrived early at the meeting place, but stood waiting with no fear of being accosted; at this hour of day only working people were abroad, and they were too busy to trouble her.

Presently, coming eastward along Piccadilly, she saw a little procession which at first she took for more market folk. There was a donkey, its panniers loaded, several very small persons, and one very tall one. When they came closer she realized to her astonishment that these were Gareth, accompanied by several of the children, three boys and a girl. Closer still she found them to be two of the older boys, Tristram and Arthur, little curly-headed Lance, and the red-haired Iseult.

"Good morning!" Delphie greeted them, smiling, when they came up to her. The children gave her cheerful greetings in return, but Gareth looked extremely grim, as if he now greatly regretted the impulse which had caused him to issue the invitation and was wishing that he could find some means to rescind it.

Observing his mood, Delphie made no attempt to break into his evidently somber thoughts, but calmly fell into step beside the children as they proceeded down St. James's Street. She looked about this street with interest, for Mrs. Carteret had many times besought her never to go down it unescorted, since it was lined on either side with gentlemen's clubs, and any unaccompanied female who ventured through it would naturally be taken for a harlot. But at this time of day not a face looked from any of the windows; the only people to be seen were cleaners, scrubbing front steps.

"Where are we going?" Delphie inquired of little Isa, who was walking beside her, casting shy looks up into her face, while the boys squabbled as to who should lead the donkey, and Gareth strode morosely ahead. They seemed to be proceeding in the direction of Westminster.

"Going?" The child opened large pale blue eyes in her thin freckled face. "Why, we are going to give poor Papa his breakfast, of course!"

"Indeed? I did not know that."

"A different set of us go every morning," confided Isa. "At first, we all wanted to do it. Now nobody does, very much; so Uncle Gareth said it would be fair if we all take turns."

"I see. Certainly that does sound best. But why does nobody wish to go, now? Do you not want to see your Papa?"

Delphie was dying of curiosity. Where could Una's husband be? She had assumed that he must be dead. If alive, why did he live apart from his family? She did not like to interrogate the child—the more so as Gareth, striding irritably ahead, was within earshot. Why had he not previously mentioned the existence of the children's father? But then he had not mentioned his sister, either. Delphie realized that she did not even know Una's married name. And, since her husband was alive, why did he support his family so inadequately?

"Well, we want to see him *quite*," explained Isa, with scrupulous honesty. "But we should love him *more* if he ever seemed pleased to see us. He is so busy writing his poetry always, you see."

"Poetry? Your father is a poet, then, my little one?"

"Oh, yes; did you not know that? I had thought that everybody knew about papa," said Isa naïvely. "He writes such beautiful poetry that I had thought the whole *world* knew about him!"

"Very likely they may; but, you see, *I* am not certain what your father's name is," Delphie explained, as the procession wound out across Westminster Bridge. Early mist was rising from the Thames; a few barges floated on the pearl-colored water, their reflections hanging motionless below them.

"Do you not? Oh, how strange!" Isa was evidently astonished that any person should be unaware of her father's name. "Why, our father is Thomas Palgrave; Mama says he is the greatest poet of the century," she added primly.

"*Thomas Palgrave!* Upon my word," exclaimed Delphie, greatly startled. "You are certainly right in thinking that all the world knows about him; and I daresay your Mama may be right also in —in her estimate of his poetry. He is a very fine writer indeed; you may well be proud to have such a papa."

"Yes, we are," agreed Isa with a certain lack of enthusiasm, "only it is just not always very convenient having to take his breakfast and supper each day."

Having crossed the bridge, Gareth now turned eastward along Lower Marsh Street. Not very well acquainted with London south of the Thames, Delphie was soon quite lost, and had no notion where they were going; they crossed a wide, dirty thoroughfare, Blackfriars Road, and continued in an easterly direction.

"This seems a long way for you to go twice a day," Delphie remarked. "Could you not live nearer to your father? Or he to you?"

"Oh, no!" Isa sounded surprised. "We, you see, live in Uncle Gareth's house. And poor Papa is not able to move. At first we did not mind it; we thought it was quite an adventure; specially when Uncle Gareth bought the donkey to carry the things; and the boys still quarrel about who is to lead him."

"He is a very nice donkey," agreed Delphie.

"Oh, and he is so good! And it makes such a difference to carrying Papa's clean laundry, and all the books he needs!"

Some eccentric recluse, was all that Delphie could conclude; a recluse who chose to live apart from his invalid wife and his ten children.

Naturally she had heard of Thomas Palgrave. Mrs. Carteret, exceedingly addicted to poetry, made a point of procuring his works from the circulating library as soon as possible after publication; she had read *The Baron, The Lord of the Isles, The Troubadour, The Pirate, The Sultan's Bride, The Count of Castile,* and the rest of them. Delphie, who, on the whole, found that she preferred prose to poetry, had skimmed through these works, and could see their merit; certainly they had a fine and sonorous flow; yet, to her mind, they left something to be desired; she could not quite say what it was; she preferred the verses of Pope. But she was impressed by the fact that she was to meet (so it seemed) this well-known poet, and only perplexed that he seemed to live in such an insalubrious quarter of London. Now they had crossed Southwark Bridge Road, and were among even tinier and more twisting ways, where the streets were unpaved and small spotty children, very insufficiently clad, sailed chip boats in the gutter.

Delphie tried to recall what she knew about Thomas Palgrave, but found that her information was decidedly scanty. He was a younger son of a minor but respectably connected family in the West Country—Bristol? Plymouth?—he had come to London, made a great name for himself, and then—then? She did not know. He seemed to have sunk into obscurity again.

"*Now* we're nearly there," said Isa with an air of relief.

They had crossed—still continuing eastward—another wide main road, at an intersection where five roads met, presided over by a handsome but black and grimy church, whose bells were just ringing for early morning service.

"That's St. George's," said Isa, skipping joyfully. "*Now*, Papa is just across the street. And the way back *never* seems so long. Sometimes Uncle Gareth tells us stories."

Opposite St. George's church rose a high wall, intersected by a pair of iron gates. Outside these gates stood waiting a considerable crowd of nondescript-looking people, most of them carrying crumpled paper bags, or small dingy bundles, or loaves of bread, or jugs of milk. They looked shabby, resigned, yet expectant; and almost immediately Delphie realized why, as St. George's clock struck half-past seven, whereupon a person appeared inside the gates holding an enormous key, and, with a certain amount of clanking and grinding, unlocked them. Instantly the waiting crowd began to move purposefully through; this was evidently a regular and familiar pilgrimage.

Arthur and Tristram led the donkey through, while Gareth paused and said something to the man with the key, who glanced at Delphie and nodded.

"What *is* this place?" whispered Delphie, walking beside Isa down a narrow entry inside the gate. Another locked door was opened at the farther end, which admitted them to a kind of lobby, across which they passed and so through another door into a yard. Here the boys, who had preceded them, were already tying the donkey in a businesslike manner to a large iron pump, covered with green slime, which stood beside a grating.

Delphie looked around her with amazement, and some consternation. The narrow paved yard where they stood was surrounded by a high wall, spiked at the top. Despite the clearness of the spring day, this place seemed both damp and stuffy; Delphie wondered if the sun, even at midday, was able to shine down into its murky recesses. In the middle rose an oblong barrack building, which was composed of a double row of houses, built back to back, with a number of doors along each side, and a row of chimneys like baluster knobs along the top. The dejected pilgrims, with their offerings of bread and eggs and jugs of milk and clean laundry, were now disappearing with the speed of rats into the various doorways. Tristram and Arthur had unloaded a number of supplies from the donkey's panniers, and now disappeared likewise.

"What *is* this place?" repeated Delphie, this time to Gareth as he came up to her.

"This place? Why, it's the Marshalsea," he replied. "Have you never been here? Nor had I until five years ago. Now you see where the debtors of London are housed."

He spoke with a kind of angry irony, as if he would have liked to make a joke about the place, but found it impossible.

Delphie shuddered; she had, of course, heard of the Marshalsea, where people who could not pay their debts might be imprisoned for ten years—fifteen years—twenty-five years—even for their whole lifetime; people died in there, she knew, babies were sometimes born; a dreary miasma of despair seemed to hang over the prison. It was not terrifying, exactly, but dank, sad, unutterably ugly and dismal.

Little Isa had run up the stairs with Lance, the youngest boy, she carrying a loaf, he a bag of apples; Delphie found herself temporarily alone with Gareth.

"Is the children's father—is Thomas Palgrave in *here?*" she asked in a whisper—as if it mattered who heard them.

Gareth shrugged. "In here—ay, and has been ever since the birth of the younger twins. Here he remains, and who knows when he will come out? He has no talent for managing his affairs. However—come up and see him."

He turned and led the way rapidly through one of the doorways, and up a flight of narrow stairs. The smell inside was bad: stuffy, and worse than stuffy; Delphie wondered, shivering, how many generations of prisoners had each left a layer of grime as they plodded out and in.

On the second story, Gareth stooped his tall head and led Philadelphia through a doorway into a small and rather cluttered room. The children were there already, bustling about: Tristram was lighting a fire in the tiny grate; Arthur was carefully placing books in a small deal shelf that hung crookedly on the wall; the two younger ones were placing bread, milk, marmalade, a plate, a napkin, a knife, a spoon, on the small table.

"Child, child!" said a rather querulous voice. "Mind what you are about! No—no—*don't* disarrange my papers—leave them be! You had best occupy yourself by emptying the tea leaves out of the pot, and fetching my shaving water; that will keep your little fingers out of mischief! Run along with you; there is the can by the door, where some careless person left it yesterday. Tristram, my dear boy, can you contrive to make a *little* less smoke in your ministrations? We shall all be suffocated! No, boy, no! Do not fan the fire like that—you are sending great pieces of burnt paper floating all over the room. Most disagreeable! Ah, Gareth, my dear fellow, how are you? Delightful, delightful."

"Thomas," said Gareth, "may I introduce my cousin Philadelphia, who has been so kind as to accompany us this morning. Philadelphia, this is my brother-in-law, Una's husband, Thomas Palgrave."

"How do you do, sir," said Philadelphia, curtsying and holding out her hand.

The hand she received in return was so damp, limp, and chilly that, she thought, it was rather like clasping a cold cooked leek. She gazed in wonder at this person who had made such a name for himself in literature, had sired ten children, and then, apparently, had so mismanaged his affairs as to be forced into this dismal retreat.

Thomas Palgrave, wearing a faded velvet gown and nightcap, sat in a small armchair, near the hearth where his eldest son was attempting to kindle a fire. He might be in his mid-forties. His face was beardless, thin, and transparently pale, but unlined; his nose was fine and straight; his eyes were of a dim grayish blue; his hair was scanty, thin, and weak, of a pale color somewhere between white and straw. His mouth was very small; too small, it seemed, to convey any expression save a kind of weary petulance. His feet, also very small, were clad in buff-colored silk stockings and carpet slippers. He held a pen in his hand, a notebook on his knee, and only raised his eyes from the notebook long enough to remark,

"Ah: Miss Cartwright; delightful; delightful," before dipping his pen in a rusty metal inkwell which stood beside him, and adding a word or two to what he was writing.

The fire now beginning to burn brightly, Tristram found a frying pan in a box, a lump of butter somewhere else, an egg somewhere else, and began in a capable manner to fry the egg. Meanwhile Isa had returned, struggling with a heavy can of hot water and the empty teapot. Arthur poured a little of the water into a mug, found a stump of soap and a razor, and began to shave his father, who absentmindedly turned his neck and chin this way and that, allowing passage for the razor, while he continued to write in his notebook. Tristram filled a kettle with some more of the water and balanced it over the fire beside his pan, where it immediately began to sing.

Delphie, discovering that there was only one chair in the confined place, moved to the little bookshelf and studied its contents: various volumes of essays and poetry, a few works in Latin and Greek; the plays of Shakespeare.

Then she turned and inspected the somewhat airless chamber. It was small, certainly, but furnished with an eye to convenience, and with various humble comforts. There was a piece of furniture which appeared to combine being a bedstead below and a chest of drawers above (into which Isa was putting the clean laundry); the walls had been painted mustard yellow—by one of the boys? The painter had left a good many streaks, over which various prints and children's drawings had been tacked up. The window (which looked into the dismal yard) was uncurtained, since little enough light came through anyway, but a dingy piece of carpet covered the floor. However, there were cushions, and a tablecloth, and a few homemade ornaments, probably also of the children's construction; there was even a melancholy-looking canary in a cage, which, when Isa had finished attending to her father, she carefully fed and watered.

"Ah, I see, Miss—er—Cartwright is admiring my small library," Mr. Palgrave remarked in his weary voice. "Small, but choice, I flatter myself! The dear boys refresh it every few days—take away something, bring something else. Even in this unpleasing spot, you see, Miss Cartwright, the philosopher may kindle his tiny lantern. Why, indeed, should he require more than a cell? And yet," he continued, wiping his neck with a snowy towel, which Arthur offered, and then turning to the table, which now had a pot of tea, a fried egg, two nicely made pieces of toast, and a slice of ham, "and yet," he said, taking a mouthful of egg and buttered toast, "yet, Miss Cartwright, he *does* require more."

"I—I suppose so," faltered Delphie, not quite sure where this was leading.

"He longs, Miss Cartwright," said Thomas Palgrave, turning his pale eyes in her direction, "he longs for his nearest and dearest. Thank you, child," as little Lance spread another piece of toast with marmalade. Mr. Palgrave took a bite of it and heaved a martyred sigh. "*Some* prisoners, Miss Cartwright—*some* lucky prisoners have the inestimable comfort and refreshment of having their families always with them."

"Indeed?" said Delphie hesitantly. "Families living in the prison—is that allowed?"

"Oh, dear me, yes. It is more the rule than the exception. In fact I think I may say that most of the—the inmates of this place have tender, devoted families supporting them with their permanent presence. I have made the suggestion to my *own* nearest and dearest. I have made it, I think I may say, several times. But"—he heaved another sigh, taking a swallow of tea—"but it was not to be! There are those in my circle who think not as I do—who think otherwise." His pale blue eyes glanced momentarily in the direction of Gareth, who was impatiently flipping through the pages of Shakespeare.

"We do see you quite frequently, Papa," remarked Isa, taking away her father's empty cup and refilling it.

"Yes, child, yes. But that is not the same as being with me always, night and day, in darkness and in light; is it, now? Think of the weary watches of the night, when the candle burns low and the spirit mourns, uncomforted; think of the pale sorrows of dawn when the sun seems lost in hopeless travail and the hands of the clock move not. Think of that!" he said to Delphie, who could only remark, most inadequately,

"Yes—I suppose you must long for your breakfast—before they are let in!"

"But I do not repine!" remarked Mr. Palgrave languidly. "No: I accept my lot. What is to be, must be." He pushed aside his cup and plate, and received in the corner of his mouth a small cigar which Tristram had lit for him. "Thank you, my boy. Would one of you—it matters not which—polish my shoes? Would another of you—any will do—brush my coat and hat? If the day is fine, I shall presently walk in that disagreeable yard for half an hour, while meditating on my next canto."

"How is your work going, Papa?" politely inquired Arthur.

"It goes—it goes. A hard—an arduous path, my boy, is that your father follows. But I persevere; I do not despair. Gareth, my dear boy, by the by, six more cantos lie there, ready for the printer; take them with you when you go and drop them in at John Wallis, in Ludgate Street—would you, like a good fellow? Or, if you wish, you may take them direct to Gillets the printers in Salisbury Square; I leave the choice quite to you."

"I will take them to Gillets," Gareth said calmly, gathering up the bundle of paper. "Are you ready, children? Then I think we should return. Your mother will be needing your help. And your cousin Delphie has to return to *her* mother."

The remains of Mr. Palgrave's breakfast were swiftly tidied away; materials for a nuncheon were left conveniently disposed upon a shelf and Mr. Palgrave's attention was drawn to them (he acknowledged this by a nod, without raising his eyes); the polished shoes and brushed coat and hat were arranged respectively under and on the bed. Then, as Mr. Palgrave was once more absorbed in his writing, the children softly stole through the door, each murmuring, "Good-by, Papa," to which Mr. Palgrave replied merely by a sigh.

"We will take our leave, then, Thomas," Gareth said.

"Good-by, good-by, my dear fellow, you won't forget Gillets, now, will you? Your servant, Miss Cartwright, so pleased to have met you," said Mr. Palgrave, his hand with the pen still traveling over the page at a great rate.

Once out of Mr. Palgrave's room, although they were still within the dingy confines of the prison, the spirits of the whole party insensibly rose. Tristram gave vent to a shrill whistle, Arthur turned a somersault along the passage, and the two younger children went gaily clattering down the stairs.

"Have a care, Cousin Delphie; they are so steep," said Gareth, and cupped a hand under her elbow.

Down in the yard the boys were carefully loading soiled laundry and empty vessels into the donkey's panniers; then the procession retraced its steps through the lobby, the narrow entry, and the various gates.

Just as they were about to step into the street, they were arrested by a respectful cough, which seemed to come from the shadows by the turnkey's office.

"Ahem, there, young ladies and gentlemen!"

"Why!" said Isa, turning with a broad smile of pleasure, "It's Mr. Swannup! We were just thinking that we hadn't seen you, Mr. Swannup, and wondering where you were!"

Mr. Swannup was a somewhat gangling youth, whose pale face was adorned by a thick ginger-colored moustache, and whose block-shaped head ended abruptly in a very bristling quantity of bright ginger-colored hair. He was at work with a bag of tools, evidently repairing some defect in the lock of the main gate.

"Being as I'm a locksmith by trade, you see, missie," he said to Isa with a rather wan smile, "whenever there's a little job of this nature as needs doing, why, they calls for me. That's why I wasn't up there as usual a-sweeping of your Pa's floor, but it'll get done by and by, don't you worrit your pretty head. I've too great a reverence for litter-ayture to let your Pa's room go dusty, young ladies and gentlemen; so long as Samuel Swannup is in the Marshalsea, Mr. Palgrave's room will remain spic and span, there's my hand on it, and so you can tell my friend Mr. Bardwell."

"Very obliging of you, Swannup," said Gareth, stopping by him, and there was a slight clink as two palms met.

"I *would* a been happy to do it just for the service to litter-ayture," said Mr. Swannup mournfully, "but I thank you, sir, just the same."

Then he fixed his rather colorless eyes on Delphie. She, for the past minute, had been wondering why he seemed so familiar; then, as he spoke, she realized where she had seen him.

"Am I right in addressing you, ma'am, as Miss Carteret, what lives up above my intended, Miss Jenny Baggott, in Greek Street?"

"Why, of course, Mr. Swannup; I was wondering why I seemed to know you so well. I am sorry to see you here," said Delphie. "I hope it won't be for long?"

"I hope so, too, ma'am, I'm sure," he said rather dolefully. "It's all according to Providence. Sometimes she giveth, and sometimes she removeth; and she's in the removing way at the moment, so far as Sam Swannup is concerned. But, ma'am, I'd be greatly obliged if you'd just drop a word to my Jenny as how the fragrance of one of her apple turnovers wouldn't half sweeten the air of this stinking crib (asking your pardon), not to mention as how the sight of her sweet face 'ud cheer me up."

"I'll certainly tell her," promised Delphie. "Er—how much are you in for, Mr. Swannup?"

"Oh, it's only a mere tilbury sum, miss, compared with Mr. Palgrave upstairs; he's a real plummy cove," said Sam with great respect. "Mine's only a tenner, miss, I feel downright humble at being allowed to consort with gents like Mr. P."

"Only ten pounds! Oh, how dreadful!" said Delphie, wishing that she had it to spare, so that she might buy him out. But Gareth, grasping at her elbow, said,

"Come away, Cousin Delphie! I can see how your thoughts run, but if once you begin to think like *that,* in the Marshalsea, you will end up here yourself, probably before a month is out!"

"I suppose so," she said regretfully, waving good-by to Mr. Swannup, who still stood regarding them with melancholy eyes through the bars of the gate. "But it seems so sad! Such a nice young man! And all for a ten-pound debt." Then, rather tentatively, she inquired, "How—how much is your brother-in-law liable for?"

"Oh—" said Gareth with an impatient sigh, "even the *amount* is almost impossible to ascertain! His affairs were in such a sorry tangle—debtors here and creditors there, fines for offenses (quite unwitting, I am sure) against the revenue laws, and more fines for not paying those fines, bills backed by people who have since vanished away, assignments and settlements of things that ought not to have been assigned and settled in the way they were—I sometimes despair of ever getting it all sorted out. That was why you saw me at Lady Dalrymple's party—because I knew that one of his creditors would be there—but it is hopeless, I sometimes feel. Even if I get him out, what is to prevent him from plunging back into the same kind of muddle?"

He had spoken unreflectingly loud, and little Isa suddenly burst into a heartrending fit of sobs.

"Oh, *poor* Papa—*poor* Papa!" she wept. "*Why* should he have to live there, in a cage—like a poor canary?"

And she looked back at Sam Swannup, still watching them through the bars of the gate.

Overcome by compunction at having asked the question that gave rise to this outburst, Delphie knelt down on the cobbles by the sobbing child.

"Come, do not cry! Think how brave your father is, he does not cry a bit! And he keeps writing away at his poetry, and one of these days I daresay so many people will have bought his poems that he will be as rich as the King, and they will let him out of those gates, and he will come riding home in a bright red carriage! Now let me dry your eyes, and then perhaps your uncle Gareth will allow you to ride on the donkey for a very little way!"

"Yes—that *is* allowed on the way home," said Gareth, smiling faintly. "And we will go back over London Bridge, so that I can leave your father's papers at the printer, and you will be able to see the Tower of London."

"Oh yes!" Isa brightened up. "And you will tell us about the Princes in the Tower, and their wicked uncle—won't you, Uncle Gareth?"

Gareth looked amused.

"Wicked uncles are a favorite theme in this family," he told Delphie. "I do not know how it comes about! The children seem to prefer them to ogres and brigands."

The way home, therefore, was enlivened by all the tales of wicked uncles which the combined memories of Delphie and Gareth could produce.

When they reached Fleet Street, Gareth turned aside, saying he would just leave their father's manuscript at the printers in Salisbury Square; they might go on slowly and he would catch them up. The children went on, but Delphie loitered a little, waiting for Gareth, and asked him, when he rejoined her—the children being now some fifty yards ahead—

"What was Mr. Palgrave's profession before—before he was incarcerated? Or has he always been a poet?"

"Profession?" said Gareth dryly. "Why—none, to speak of. The man's an amiable sponger—always has been! He's well bred enough, and had just a little money of his own—met my sister—she fell in love with him—thought he was the most handsome, romantic man in the world—ran off with him, my mother objecting to the match, as well she might—and look at the result! Can you wonder that I think as I do on certain subjects—romantic marriages—love at first sight, woman's intuition—? Then, of course, he spent all Una's money, having already run through his own, and, in return, bestowed ten children upon her. Luckily they are as good little things as ever twanged—"

"I can see *that*," said Delphie warmly.

"But how in the world are ten children to be provided for," he said furiously, "when the father does nothing but scribble verses behind bars, and the mother lies upon a sofa and blames everybody in the world but herself? I tell you, it is enough to put one out of all patience with—"

"With what?" asked Delphie as he broke off, his eyes suddenly fixed ahead in a look of incredulous dismay.

"Good God!" he exclaimed. "I know Mordred warned me of it—but I had no real expectation that he would come quite so soon—Those are my uncle's bays, unless I am much mistaken—and that is his traveling carriage!"

"What? Where?"

"There! Yes—it is he! What's more, he sees us. He is opening the window—he is making the coachman pull up." Casting a glance ahead toward the church of St. Clement Danes, Gareth muttered, "What a piece of luck that at least I had directed the children to walk on! He may not connect them with us."

"Why? Does he not approve of them?"

"He does not *know* of them! And he would certainly not approve! By great good fortune, he did not hear of my sister's disastrous marriage—for it took place during one of the periods when he was abroad, taking the waters. Fortunately, also, his visits to town are so rare: he has no friends, and listens to no gossip. For if he did hear of my sister's marriage—we should be completely in the basket!"

"Take care!" exclaimed Philadelphia, for at this moment the carriage which had been the object of Gareth's attention pulled up close beside them, and the face which Delphie had last seen apparently *in articulo mortis* now looked peevishly down at them from the window.

Lord Bollington was grotesquely swathed in traveling capes, and had an extraordinary, countrified, wide-brimmed hat, pulled down over a series of flannel bands, which were wound and tied under his chin. Certainly he did not look quite so ill as he had at Chase, but he did not, Delphie thought, look at all well, either; there was a bright flush on his cheekbones, his mouth worked, his eyes were glazed and rheumy, and the gloved hand with which he beckoned to Gareth perceptibly shook. A faint suspicion, which Delphie had been entertaining, that Lord Bollington had feigned his deathbed scene in order to hurry his nephew into matrimony, was rapidly dispelled at sight of him; she exclaimed,

"Oh, my dear sir, you should *not* be driving about the streets in your state of health! It is *most* ill advised!"

"Shut your head, ma'am!" growled his lordship ill-temperedly. "I didn't halt the carriage to be given a lot of vaporish advice which I don't require! *I'll* be the judge of whether I'm fit to ride about the streets, and I'll thank you to remember that!"

"My—my dear wife was merely solicitous on your account, sir," Gareth remarked.

Lord Bollington gave a sudden malicious bark of laughter.

"Didn't think to see you two strolling along arm in arm like a pair of turtledoves at half-past eight in the morning, I must confess! Come about, have you? Decided to run in harness? I never thought you was sweet on your cousin Elaine," he said to Gareth. "Truth to tell, thought you detested her!"

"Why," said Gareth coolly, "I wonder what can have put such a notion into your head, sir? We are excellent friends, are we not, my dear?" he added, looking down at Delphie; the expression in his eyes filled her with an urge to burst out laughing which she had to choke back as best she could.

"Indeed we are," she agreed demurely.

"Glad to hear it! Wish it may last!"

"And what are *you* doing in the streets at this hour, sir?" inquired Gareth.

"Confounded wheeler cast a shoe at Deptford; obliged to rack up for the night at a devilish noisy drafty ill-run dirty inn called The Blue Boar; wouldn't wish such a night on my worst enemy! Glad to make an early start and get away."

"In that case, sir," said Gareth, "you must be extremely anxious to reach the comfort of your own house, which I know my cousin Mordred has ready for you, and we will detain you not a moment longer."

"Yes, sir," added Delphie, "I am persuaded you should immediately retire to bed—between *thoroughly* warmed sheets—with a tisane, a hot brick, and a sprinkling of aromatic vinegar on the pillow!"

Since this was precisely what his lordship had been proposing to do, he nearly snapped her head off.

"Hot fiddlestick, madam! Keep your nostrums to yourself! I intend to go to my club. But tomorrow evening I shall come and take my mutton with you both in Curzon Street—I trust you are dining in? Want to make sure you are settling down! Needn't fidget your cook to give me anything out of the common—Gareth knows I can't abide fancy Francayed foreign kickshaws!"

"Oh!" responded Gareth rather blankly. "Of course, sir! *Are* we dining in, tomorrow, my love?" he added, to Delphie.

"I—I believe so!" she said, rather breathless. "At wh-what time do you care to dine, great-uncle?"

"At five!" said Lord Bollington, and called to his coachman to drive on. "I shall be at your house by a quarter before five!" he called, and shut the window.

"Now look what you have done!" exclaimed Gareth as soon as the carriage was out of earshot. "You have properly landed us in the suds! What possessed you to give him that wretchedly ill-timed and meddlesome piece of advice, just when he would otherwise have gone off to bed and forgotten us?"

"I—I couldn't resist it," said Philadelphia guiltily.

"Just as I thought! You did it out of pure mischief!"

"No, no!" she defended herself. "It was *good* advice. Besides, I am persuaded it made no real difference. He was bound to insist on coming around to Curzon Street sooner or later."

"Yes," Gareth said gloomily. "And now that all our skeletons are out of the closet, I imagine that you have completely set your face against complying with my suggestion that you come and occupy my ground floor?"

"Do you?" said Delphie. "Then you are strangely mistaken! On the contrary, I intend to move myself and Mamma without delay. I shall have to, shall I not, if we are to entertain Great-uncle Mark tomorrow at five?"

10

Delphie's parting from Gareth and the children was brief and unceremonious. If she and Mrs. Carteret were to be moved into Curzon Street by tomorrow, there was much to be done; for in among the business of the move must be sandwiched other necessary operations: pupils to be notified of her change of address, lessons to be given, and, last but not least, Miss Elaine Carteret to be visited that afternoon.

On her way home, Delphie cut through Covent Garden Market, and arranged with a carter there to come and transport their belongings and pieces of furniture during the afternoon. That done, the news was to be broken to Mrs. Carteret.

Delphie delayed doing this until she had woken her mother (who fortunately proved to be still asleep on her return) and had served her a comfortable breakfast; then she informed her that they had been offered very spacious ground-floor accommodation, rent-free, near to the park, in Cousin Gareth's house in Curzon Street. Though somewhat startled at these tidings, Mrs. Carteret made no objections to this change of abode; their residence in Soho had always been a matter of expediency, not preference, because housing was cheaper in that district; she was delighted to remove to a more fashionable neighborhood.

"And there, ten to one, some eligible gentleman will see you as you pass along the street, and come to ask me if he may pay his addresses," she said happily. "Oh, I can see *many* advantages, Philadelphia! But do you think that Mrs. Andrews will be willing to remove with us?"

Delphie had been exercised in her mind on this point. Since they were saving the rent, she thought that she might be able to offer to pay Mrs. Andrews a little extra to come with them and assume the duties of a housekeeper.

The old lady, when this was put to her, was delighted to accept.

"Living in Curzon Street—lor! That's a very nice part!" she said. "What next! For sure, I'll be happy to come with you, Miss. Blood's thicker than brine, but to tell truth, I shan't weep millstones not to be quite so cheek-by-jowl with Anne and Jenny; good gals, both, as ever stepped, but I can't abear all those nasty fried onions! And they keep their kitchen in such a pickle! I'd dearly like to get my hands on it, but Anne is that twitty, and up in the stirrups at once if you venture to shift so much as a teaspoon!"

Delphie promised that, in Curzon Street, where they were to have a kitchen of their own, Mrs. Andrews should reign undisputed mistress of it.

By this time the ten o'clock pupil had arrived, and Delphie was obliged to concentrate on giving her attention to the lesson, which she endeavored to do conscientiously, though random, anxious reflections *would* break in: What were they to give Great-uncle Mark for dinner tomorrow, for instance—how could his presence in the house be kept from Mrs. Carteret—should Elaine Carteret be told of their move—how should the china be packed—and would Mrs. Andrews object to the ten children upstairs? And how in the world was the existence of this tribe to be concealed from their great-uncle when he came to the house?

Delphie was unaffectedly sorry to be moving away from the comfortable presence of the Baggott sisters, who had stood staunchly by her in many a crisis; she strongly doubted whether the languid Una Palgrave would ever become such a sympathetic friend, and was quite certain that she could never be able to render such practical assistance.

Jenny, too, was very doleful when she heard the news. "Oh, mercy, Miss Delphie! Leaving us? Me and Sis are real put about at the news! The house won't be the same without you and Missus, it won't indeed. I hope it's naught we've done or said that's given you a disgust for the place—?"

"Of course it is not, goose!" Delphie said warmly. "It is only that—that my cousin has offered us a chance of superior accommodation, close to the park; and for my mother's sake I thought it right to accept. And after all, we shall be less than a mile away! I shall be forever coming past the chop on my way to give lessons, and shall often be dropping in to find out how you all do—and your Aunt Andrews will be coming back and forth too, I've no doubt."

"Yes, *that* she will," said Jenny, drying her eyes, "and driving Sister into a twit with her fossicking ways. Well, I daresay it's for your best, Miss Delphie—but what about the lady, eh?"

"It *was* his sister all along, Jenny," said Philadelphia, not trying to pretend ignorance of what Jenny meant. "We should not have been so suspicious."

Jenny's brow cleared wonderfully.

"In *that* case, Miss Delphie, I'm *sartain* it's for your best! Why, you'll be as close as currants in no time—but just the same, we shall miss you sore!"

Delphie had already given Jenny the melancholy message from Mr. Swannup, incarcerated in the Marshalsea, and she now pulled out a little package, which she had wrapped in a scrap of silver paper, and said,

"Here, Jenny, is a small keepsake, which I wish you will accept in return for all the many, many kindnesses you have done me and Mamma—and also for your very supporting company on my journey to Kent! Now listen: I fear it is not worth a great deal, but I had it valued by Mr. Rumbold at the silversmiths in Old Compton Street, and he tells me that—if you wish—he would give you twelve pounds for it—which would be quite enough to get Mr. Swannup out of jail. So you must do as you think best about it. The decision is to be entirely yours. Some lovers are best left in jail, perhaps!"

And she folded Jenny's hand around the packet, which contained a small silver-and-pearl brooch she had had from a child, and hurried away, leaving Jenny gazing after her open-mouthed.

Soon after noon the carts arrived and the household goods were packed into them; Delphie was just superintending the careful removal of her pianoforte into the first cart when Mr. Browty's carriage pulled up farther along the street and that gentleman descended, his eyes wide with astonishment.

"Hey-dey, what's all this?" he exclaimed. "Moving house, Miss Philadelphia, and you never told Jos. Browty? That's bad, very bad! You're not shooting the moon, I trust?"

"No, no, sir, nothing like that; and we should have told you, directly," she answered, laughing. "It is just that we had the offer of some very superior accommodation in Curzon Street, which—which we had to take up immediately if it was to be secured."

"Curzon Street—ah, that's something like!" he said approvingly. "That will put more roses into your and your Mama's cheeks than this close little quarter. Well, I will not stand prosing on when you've a dozen things to do with each hand! But how would it be if I took your Mama for a drive—I came to invite her, indeed—that would take her away from all this dust and huffle-scufflement for an hour or two?"

"That, my dear sir, would be the kindest thing you could possibly do," Delphie said with real gratitude. "For I've the hardest job in the world to stop her from trying to do more than she ought. Then, sir, if you will be so kind, you could return her to our new lodgings—by which time I shall hope to have all ready for her there."

"Humph," said Mr. Browty, "I have the greatest respect for you, Miss Philadelphia, but if you can get all this sorted"—he looked at the loaded carts,—"*and* a chamber prepared for your Mama, you are even more of a wonder than I had thought! It seems to me I had best take Mrs. Carteret back for a nuncheon in Russell Square first."

"You are too kind to us—but perhaps that *would* be best," Delphie agreed thoughtfully. "Only, in that case—if it would not be too much trouble—"

"Yes?" he said encouragingly, with a twinkle in his eye, which Delphie had observed on occasions when his daughters were trying to wheedle something out of him.

"If you would not mind returning Mamma to Lady Bablock-Hythe's residence in Brook Street!" Delphie confessed. "For she and I are expected there at three."

Although Delphie would have been glad to prevent her mother from going to Brook Street, Mrs. Carteret was not to be dissuaded. Making the best of the business, Delphie could only hope that her mother's fickle memory might yield some clue as to Elaine's identity.

"Why not? Nothing could be simpler!"

So Mrs. Carteret, protesting that she had left a hundred things undone, was whisked away in Mr. Browty's carriage, and Delphie went back to work with a will, sorting their last belongings, and throwing away various odds and ends which were not worth saving. One such article, a child's picture book with rather crumpled pages, left over from her own early days, she handed to a little ragged boy, one of a group of idle spectators, who stood gazing in the roadway. He gave her a somewhat startled look, and then ducked into the crowd with his treasure. Delphie, forgetting him in an instant, walked into the shop to say good-by to the Baggotts.

"Until tomorrow!" she said cheerfully. "For I shall be walking past this way then."

Both sisters embraced her warmly, and Jenny whispered in her ear,

"I decided to pop the brooch, love! It's that pretty it nigh broke my heart to part with it—but well—Sam comes first. Mum's the word, though—Sis don't know!"

"I am *sure* you did right!" Delphie said warmly.

Then she jumped onto the tail of the last cart and went riding down to Mayfair with the furniture, delighted that Mrs. Carteret was not there to see and be scandalized by such a proceeding.

Mrs. Andrews had gone on ahead, and was already installed in the rooms at Curzon Street. With her help, it did not take too long to set out their scanty pieces in the large airy rooms. To Delphie's surprise, some other pieces of furniture were there already.

"The gentleman from upstairs come down, missie, an' I told him what you had got and what you didn't got," Mrs. Andrews explained, "and he said as how there were some bits of sticks atop as he never uses (him being but a single gent) and you mid as well have the use of them. So Mr. Bardwell, that's his gentleman's gentleman, brought them down. And I've give them a polish and they've come up real tiptop! Spare well and have to spend, I allus say. One man's dish clout is another's tablecloth. No need to buy new when old will do. That's right a nice gentleman up there,

Miss Delphie! Handsome, kindhearted, and civil-spoken as a beadle!"

Gareth had plainly made a favorable impression.

"Wh-what about the children?" Delphie said nervously. "Have you encountered them yet? They live on the *top* floor, of course!"

"Bless their little hearts! They've been *that* helpful! The boys was sweeping an' the gals was dusting, an' one o' them lit the fire in the kitchen grate, an' the others ran errands and carried things about—then I told them they'd best run back to their Ma, so as to give you a bit of peace and quiet, Miss, to settle in, and off they skipped, as biddable as doves! I never saw a set of childer that was likelier, nor better behaved."

Greatly relieved at this excellent start, Delphie helped move the last pieces of furniture into position.

They now had a commodious parlor, which housed the piano and where Delphie would give lessons, and a large bedroom for Delphie at the front; a spacious room for her mother, looking out onto the very pretty garden at the rear, a decent-sized kitchen, and a smaller but comfortable room for Mrs. Andrews.

Delphie, looking around their new quarters, could not help rejoicing in the increased amount of air, light, and space; the rooms, too, were so handsomely proportioned that they showed off the Carterets' modest furnishings to the best advantage, and these, together with the pieces lent by Gareth—an escritoire, a set of chairs, an oval loo table, and a cabinet for china—made a very pleasant impression.

Delphie wondered where Gareth was—would have liked him to see the rooms—but he did not appear. Doubtless he had gone out. His man Bardwell came down, however, and very civilly offered his assistance if Delphie found that she needed anything moved, or a stiff door eased, or a nail driven in to hang a picture. Delphie thanked him, but was able to assure him that at present his services were not required.

All was complete to a shade by the time that she must start for Brook Street. She had washed her face and replaced her crumpled gray gown by a clean muslin with a tiffany sash, and put on a bonnet which she had remodeled from one of Mrs. Carteret's—an old-fashioned Grecian helmet shape, lined with frillings of the leftover gray jaconet. Thus she was respectably, if not modishly dressed—but her Paris parasol, at least, added a touch of elegance.

The arrival in Brook Street was timed to a nicety. Just as Delphie approached from one end of the street, Mr. Browty's carriage rolled along from the other direction, and Mrs. Carteret descended, a little cross that she had not been allowed home first, to put on a more stylish dress and to rearrange her hair—but at least she had on the new sarcenet mantle.

"However, I must say they were all as kind as can be," she said. "That is a most excellent, unaffected man, Delphie, and the daughters are good little things, neither mouseish nor undesirably putting themselves forward."

The carriage departed; Mr. Browty, Mrs. Carteret explained, had regretted that an appointment in the City prevented him from escorting her to Brook Street—and they approached the doorway of Lady Bablock-Hythe's house. As they did so, the door opened, and a very fashionably dressed lady, in a violet-colored pelisse and hat trimmed with ostrich plumes, came out of it. She was about to mount into a waiting phaeton, when she paused, looking at Mrs. Carteret in a searching and puzzled manner.

"Can I be mistaken?" she then inquired. "Forgive me, ma'am, if I should seem intrusive and importunate but—can my eyes deceive me? Or do I dream? Am I run mad? Or do I perceive before me my long-lost but most deeply regretted, most sorrowfully mourned friend, cherished companion of my childhood hours, Ella Penistone?"

"Oh, madam!" cried Mrs. Carteret in turn. "Can it be so? I am all amazement, but sure I cannot mistake—none other could bear those lineaments! You must, you must be my dearly loved schoolmate, Maria Gosport!"

Both conjectures proved to be correct, and the ladies embraced with tears of joy.

"But I thought you had married Lord Enderby and departed to the West Indies!" exclaimed Mrs. Carteret.

"Alas, madam, I did so, but my dear Enderly survived only four years—too good, too excellent creature!—and on his decease, leaving me endowed with a very handsome fortune, and on my thereafter marrying the governor of the island, a truly estimable and benevolent man and a friend of long standing, and on his retiring and observing how deeply desirous I was of once again re-entering my native land, and on my admitting the truth of this, we returned hither some three years since—only to have my second husband follow my first into the tomb! Little then did I apprehend, in my lonely widowhood, that my dearest Ella was still in the land of the living, for a mistaken report had informed me of your death. My beloved friend—how glad I am that it was not so!"

The ladies embraced again and then, the clock of St. George's, Hanover Square, striking the hour and reminding the erstwhile Lady Enderby of a pressing engagement in Upper Wimpole Street for which she had been about to set out, the friends were obliged to quit one another, but not without making arrangement to meet again and hear one another's histories. Delphie very cordially invited her mother's long-lost friend to be their first guest in Curzon Street and come to breakfast on the day after the following.

"Lord, Lord," murmured Mrs. Carteret to herself as they rang the bell and were admitted by a manservant. "Only to think of my setting eyes on Maria Gosport again. She was my particular friend at the Miss Pinkertons' school; but when she married and departed from this country, I had thought never to see her more!'"

She was so absorbed and delighted in this discovery that she took very little notice of their surroundings, but kept murmuring and exclaiming to herself. Delphie, on the contrary, looked about her with great interest. She guessed that this was a furnished house, hired for the Season; but if so it was a very expensive one, fitted up with considerable magnificence, though with little true elegance of taste; the servants were arrayed in gorgeous liveries; and the whole was on so grand a scale that it seemed more like a hotel than a private residence.

Upon Delphie's giving their names to the principal manservant, with the information that Miss Carteret expected them, they were asked to step upstairs; Miss, they were informed, would receive them in her own apartments.

After this they were ushered into a suite of rooms on the second floor which, though sufficiently grand, were not on the scale of those below; and there the other Miss Carteret was waiting for them. *She*, however, was very fine; she had on the most dashing half-dress imaginable, made of sea-green Berlin silk and embellished with bugle trimming and a demi-train; by the side of it the two visiting ladies' dresses looked countrified and shabby; but Delphie could not help secretly thinking that if *she* had such a fair complexion and pale blue eyes, she would not have chosen that particular shade of green for a gown.

Delphie greeted her politely, and said, "Allow me to present my mother, Mrs. Carteret."

"Quite a coincidence, is it not?" murmured Mrs. Carteret amiably, quite unaware of the young lady's very piercing regard, for she was gazing all about her with a very absentminded expression. "I believe my dear Richard did have some very distant cousins who resided in Westmorland—or was it Wigtownshire? At all events it was in the North and began with a W—you will be from that branch of the family, I daresay? Gracious me, only imagine running into my dear Tussy again—for Tussy we would always be calling her, I wonder why? Stay, I recollect that it had something to do with an India tussore silk that she had from her grandmother—"

Plainly more than a little baffled by Mrs. Carteret's ramblings, Miss Elaine directed an inquiring and haughty look at Delphie, who calmly explained that her mother had had the good fortune to encounter an old friend in Brook Street. This appearing to be of no interest whatsoever to Miss Carteret, she begged them to be seated, and then called out,

"Durnett! Pray bring in the refreshments!"

A hard-faced woman of middle age, dressed plainly in a stuff dress, with a maid's apron and a great cap that covered her hair completely, here brought in a tray with ratafia and glasses and a plate of sweet biscuits. She wore, Delphie noticed, an extremely sour expression, and subjected both visitors to as sharp a scrutiny as her mistress had previously done. Then, having poured and handed glasses of ratafia, instead of leaving the room, she busied herself at the far end of it, first sorting slowly through a box of ribbons and laces, then tidying out the papers in a writing desk.

She appeared, Delphie thought, to be listening to their conversation.

"Now, ma'am," said Elaine, sipping her ratafia and giving Delphie a cool, businesslike stare, "we have to discuss what's to be done."

Delphie politely set her lips to the rim of her glass, but she did not drink, for she strongly disliked the almond flavor of ratafia.

"What do *you* have it in mind to do, ma'am?" she inquired, setting down her glass again.

"We cannot go on like this!" cried Miss Carteret.

"Can you perhaps make yourself a little plainer, ma'am?"

"Oh, it is all too provoking! It is quite ridiculous that there should be two of us claiming to be the same person! *I* have always been accepted as—as my uncle's great-niece; he has paid for me and supported me; I think, therefore, that *you* should write a declaration, renouncing any claim to inheritance in the event of—of my uncle's demise."

"You are of the opinion that I should do that?" inquired Delphie levelly.

"Most certainly I am! Otherwise—if he should die—how could it be known which of us—some mistake might be made—"

"I do not quite see why you are so apprehensive?" Delphie said. "Since *you* have always been accepted as Miss Carteret, surely you will continue to be so? I am making no claim for myself; all I have done is stipulate that an annuity should be paid to my mother."

She noticed Durnett, the maid, again favor Mrs. Carteret with a very searching glance. The latter, who had been following this conversation in a vague and troubled manner, gazed at the two younger ladies, wide-eyed.

"Delphie?" she said in a puzzled and perturbed voice. "What is all this about? What uncle does this young lady refer to? And why should you both assert that you are the same person? I do not perfectly comprehend what you are saying."

"Do not trouble your head about it, Mamma; I am sure it will all be straightened out," Delphie said gently.

"But," burst out Elaine, without taking the least notice of Mrs.

Carteret, "how can *I* be accepted as the *true* Miss Carteret, if *you* are married to Gareth Penistone?"

Plainly this was her chief and keenly felt cause of grievance; when she pronounced the words *Gareth Penistone* her voice took on a covetous, admiring note, as if she had said *the crown jewels*.

"Married to Gareth Penistone?" said Mrs. Carteret perplexedly. "Delphie, do you think the young lady is a little feverish? Much of what she says appears to be nonsense. Perhaps she ought to be laid down with some hartshorn or spirits of ammonia?"

Delphie said with composure, "Do not let it distress you, Mamma, it is all a kind of silly tangle, which will be unraveled in time, I am certain." And to Miss Elaine, she said, "If only you will be a little patient, ma'am, I believe it will help matters! *I* have not the least wish in the world to be married to Mr. Gareth Penistone, I assure you. But I am persuaded that nothing can be done at the moment, the more particularly since my uncle is in town—"

"*What?*" exclaimed Elaine, bounding out of her chair. "Great-uncle Mark is here? In Hanover Square? Is Mordred here too? Why did not he *tell* me?"

"Lord Bollington arrived only this morning," Delphie said.

"*You* seem to know a great deal about it. Pray, how comes it that *you* are so well informed?"

Delphie noticed that the hard-featured maid had abandoned all pretense of tidying the desk and had moved a little nearer, listening intently.

"I happened—quite by chance—to observe Lord Bollington in his coach in the Strand this morning," Delphie replied.

"Then—then there is no time to be lost! Will you write the declaration I require? Renouncing any claim to the Penistone money?"

"No. I certainly shall not," said Delphie. "I do not see that I am under any such obligation to you to do so. For my part, matters may take their course."

"Then—I consider that you are the most odious, detestable, disobliging—"

"Quiet, now, Miss!" said the maid, Durnett, sharply. "There's no sense flying up into the boughs like that. Besides, you're frightening Madam, there."

"Oh—!" Elaine stamped her foot furiously upon the floor. "If you will not accede to my request, I wonder that you stay here where you are not wanted! Why do you not begone!"

"Miss, miss!" remonstrated the maid, and then, in a sharper tone, "For shame, Miss Elaine! Hold your tongue and try for a bit of conduct!"

It was true that at Elaine's outburst, Mrs. Carteret had made a sharp little movement of distress, half rising to her feet, and upsetting her glass of ratafia, which spilt down her skirts. Then she sank back again weakly, crying in a plaintive tone,

"Delphie, I don't like it here. I don't like these angry voices and all this talk of *Bollington* and *Penistone!* I do not like it at all. Let us go! Take me away!"

"Very well, Mamma; we will go directly," said Delphie. And she added, to Miss Carteret, "I am only sorry we came. This discussion has done no good. And it has distressed my mother very much."

"Go as soon as you please!"

Delphie carefully assisted Mrs. Carteret to her feet.

"Madam's weak yet," said the maid, watching with a vigilant gray eye. "Best let her have a sniff of this," and she proffered a vinaigrette.

"Thank you, but I believe she will do," said Delphie, accepting it, however.

"Best keep it for the moment, Miss. You never know but she might come over faint outside. Miss Elaine can send around to Greek Street for it tomorrow."

Delphie thanked her again, somewhat surprised by this unexpected solicitude, and then added,

"But we are not in Greek Street any more. We have removed to Curzon Street."

Busy guiding her mother to the door, she did not see the look of consternation which appeared on Elaine's face at this news. Elaine opened her mouth to make some protest or ejaculation; as Delphie turned in the doorway to say farewell, she was astonished to see the maid, Durnett, sharply box her mistress's ears, as if this were the only way to bring her to reasonable behavior. Delphie could hardly believe her eyes. But she thought it best not to become embroiled any further, and busied herself with helping her trembling mother down the stairs.

"Can you call my mother a chair?" she civilly asked the manservant when they were down in the hall. "She has come over a little faint."

"Certainly, miss."

He stepped outside and returned in a moment to say that a chair was waiting.

Mrs. Carteret seemed relieved by the fresh air.

"I don't need that thing!" she said impatiently, pushing away the vinaigrette, which Delphie was offering. "I don't want it! Put it in your reticule."

"Very well," Delphie said, and helped her mother into the chair.

"Can you tell me, my man," Mrs. Carteret inquired of the manservant, "what was the name of the gray-haired lady who came down the steps just as we arrived?"

"In a violet silk pelisse, ma'am?" he said, looking a little surprised. "Why, that was the mistress. That was Lady Bablock-Hythe!"

Mrs. Carteret was unusually quiet and subdued all the way to Curzon Street. Delphie blamed herself bitterly for having allowed the visit to Miss Carteret. When they arrived at the new rooms, she could see that all these novelties together in one day were too much for her mother; Mrs. Carteret suffered herself to be shown around in silence, with a stunned, almost stupefied air which troubled her daughter very much.

"Very handsome!" she murmured, absently, hardly appearing to take in what she saw. "Am I dreaming, Delphie, or are we really here? And did I dream that I saw Maria Gosport and those others —or did *that* really happen? I feel very much confused—too many things have been happening to me. After such a handsome nuncheon too—cold chicken and cake and fruit in wine! Far more than I am accustomed to take at midday. It has been too much for me, Delphie; I think that I had better lie down on my bed."

Delphie, with feelings of guilt that all these things should have occurred also on the day of her impulsive change of their abode, carefully assisted her mother to bed, helping her to undress and drawing the curtains.

"Pray give me my handkerchief, dear," feebly said Mrs. Carteret when she was upon the bed, and a mild breeze from the half-open window blowing upon her.

Delphie pulled out the handkerchief, and a biscuit fell out of the reticule.

"I slipped it into my bag—for later on," confessed Mrs. Carteret. "When they offered—so full of Mr. Browty's delicious—but did not like to refuse altogether—"

"It looks rather dusty now," Delphie said.

The biscuit was covered with fluff and hairs from the bottom of the bag, and looked very uninviting. Delphie dropped it out of the window onto the paving outside, where a covey of hungry sparrows immediately pounced upon it.

"I will bring you a few of Madame Lumière's cakes, Mamma, when you are feeling a little better. Now, try to sleep a little."

"Very well, child . . . *Who* was that young lady?" Mrs. Carteret said fretfully. "And why was she saying such very strange things—that you are married to Gareth Penistone—that she and you are the same person? Is she deranged?"

"I do not think so, but I believe she may have a very turbulent temper. But do not fret about it, Mamma; it is all a stupid mistake which will be cleared up in time."

"Well, I do not like it at all. It is very uncomfortable. And I do not wish to see that disagreeable girl again. Can you shut the window, child, the wind is blowing a draught."

"Very well, Mamma." Stepping back to do so, Delphie paused, frozen to the spot with horror. For where the ring of greedy energetic sparrows had been pecking away at the biscuit, five little dead birds now lay on the flagstones.

"Mamma!" she said hoarsely after a moment.

"Yes, dear? What is it? Why do you sound so strange?"

"Those biscuits that they served us—that Miss Carteret gave us. Did you eat any of yours?"

"No child—did I not just tell you? I put it in my bag."

"The ratafia? Did you drink any of it?"

"Hardly a sip," said Mrs. Carteret regretfully. "It was spilt, unfortunately. Why? Why do you ask?"

Miss Carteret had sipped at her own ratafia, though, Delphie recollected. It must have been innocuous. But the vinaigrette! Where was that? What a merciful dispensation that her mother had not sniffed at it. She found the thing in her own reticule and walked with it toward the door—looked back, searchingly, at her mother, who now seemed more peaceful, drowsily settling toward sleep.

"You know that girl—that disagreeable girl," Mrs. Carteret murmured. "In the strangest way she reminds me of some occasion connected with *your* early life, Delphie. But I cannot call to mind what."

"Try to sleep, Mamma!" whispered Delphie. "I will come back presently to see how you do."

And, holding the vinaigrette somewhat at arm's length, she passed out of the door and climbed up the stairs toward the first floor, calling softly,

"Cousin Gareth? Are you at home?"

11

❁

Gareth's part of the house seemed to be empty. But Delphie encountered three of the children (Percy, the responsible Helen, and the stout Gawaine) at the foot of the top flight of stairs, and they shyly asked if she would be good enough to step up and pass a few moments with their mother, who was lonely for company.

"For company? With all of you?" asked Delphie, amused.

"Ah, but that's not the same as grown-up company," said Percy wisely. He was a small dark replica of his uncle Gareth, and Delphie's heart warmed to him.

Today Una was not even trying to pursue any occupation, but was lying quite flat and looking very dejected.

"Are you in pain?" Delphie asked compassionately. "Did the noise we made downstairs disturb you?"

"Yes—no—I don't know! It comes and goes. Some days I am better—I can get up and go out. But I have the wretchedest feeling of *affliction* at all times! I feel so mortified when I think of *you*—healthy—active—doing all the things that you do—the children say that already you have moved your furniture into the house, and that your rooms downstairs look as if you had always lived there."

"I can claim no great merit for that—I had the carters and Mrs. Andrews to help," Delphie said with a curiously uneasy feeling, as if Una's persistent envious harping on her strength, health, and talents might presently cast an evil spell which would suddenly deprive her of these gifts of fortune. But she tried to dismiss such a superstitious notion, and said, smiling,

"I am very sorry if thinking about *me* makes you worse! What can I do to atone? Shall I read to you?"

She glanced with envy at some new books and periodicals which lay in a shuffle, as if irritably pushed aside by the invalid.

"No—no—thank you! Just talk! Tell me what you have been doing?"

Delphie had not the least intention of telling Una about the interview with the other Miss Carteret. She therefore described the removal, and her farewell to the Baggott sisters, and her ride down from Soho on the movers' cart, at which Una shut her eyes as if in pained deprecation of such behavior, but the boys clapped their hands.

"Uncle Gareth would laugh at that," said Percy.

Una's eyes opened again. "Oh, are you children still there? I wish you will go away—this room is not big enough for so many people. In about half an hour from now you can bring me some tea and bread-and-butter—cut nice and thin, mind!"

"Very well, Mama." They went out obediently, and Delphie wondered how it could be that two such limp, ineffectual people as Thomas Palgrave and Una could have produced ten such cheerful, obliging, and capable children.

When they had gone—

"Is Gareth in the house?" Una asked, reopening her eyes, which she had closed while the footsteps pattered away.

"No; I think not," Delphie replied.

"Is it true—this extraordinary tale he tells me that you and he are *married?*" Una demanded.

"Yes—in a way; but it was all a mistake," Delphie said apologetically. "It makes me very uncomfortable, I can tell you. To be married by accident to a complete stranger is so ridiculous! I wish it might be dissolved immediately, but—but Gareth seems to think it will be wiser to wait."

But, she thought, how *long* shall we have to wait? One can hardly wish for Great-uncle Mark to die; but supposing he should live on for years and *years*. And then it occurred to Delphie—for the first time—that perhaps it had not been a very wise act to come and set up house in the same building as Gareth; might that, perhaps, make the marriage less easy to set aside?

But I have Mamma as a chaperone, she thought; after all, our living quarters are quite separate. I must not stay up here too long; I must go down again in a moment and see how Mamma does. *Could* they really have meant to *poison* her?

"You know that in reality Gareth is very well suited by this marriage?" suddenly pronounced his sister, opening her eyes very wide and giving Delphie a surprisingly sharp look.

"Indeed?" said Delphie with caution. "What makes you say that?"

Her hand found the sinister little vinaigrette, which she had tucked into her pocket. Hastily she let go of it again.

"Oh, Gareth hates all women. He has quite set his face against marriage. He swore some oath about it, I believe. He—he despises the female sex. And in particular he always thought Cousin Elaine the most odious self-willed creature, so it must give him great pleasure to have you as a defense against *her*. So as long as he has this mock marriage to you—he is quite safe! You do not love each other—and yet he is under no compulsion to marry anyone else. I should not wonder but that he would be quite content for the arrangement to stand forever."

"Oh? Do you think so?" Delphie added firmly, suppressing the somewhat hollow sensation Una's words had given her. "I do not at all think that would suit *me*."

"You will be lucky if you can persuade him to see that! Gareth has the most amazing knack of having his own way."

"But might he not, in the end, wish for an heir? I believe it is a thing that men do wish for?"

"Gareth will not," Una replied carelessly. "There are *my* children, after all. He can leave his money to them."

If he has any left after bringing them all up—and supporting *you*, Delphie thought.

"Why does Gareth hate women so?" she asked. Not that she expected to believe what Una told her, but she could not help asking.

"Oh—he was jilted long ago," said Una impatiently. "He was affianced to a girl once—Uncle Mark did not know about it, fortunately, or there would have been terrible trouble—her name was Lady Laura Trevelyan—but then when she discovered that he would have less money than she expected—she cast him off and married Teasdale, a much older man with more money. Such a common tale! It happens all the time. And Gareth, like the burnt child, dreads that it will happen again. He has grown so hard and unfeeling! He cannot believe in a marriage like mine—in a union of two souls that love one another, that cling together, despite poverty, despite separation, despite hardship and misfortune! I fear that Gareth is hard through and through—hard, and cold, and materialistic. I am persuaded, Cousin Delphie, that if *you* do not make a push to have your marriage dissolved, *he* never will! Unless, of course," Una added reflectively, "he should come across Lady Laura again. I believe her husband was very sickly—not expected to live long; perhaps he may have died already. Gareth is so uncommunicative about his own affairs!"

"Indeed?" said Delphie politely. She was beginning to conceive a strong dislike for Gareth's sister. "Now, if you will excuse me, Mrs. Palgrave, I believe I should go down again and see how my mother does; she was not feeling quite the thing when we came in."

"Oh?" said Una, disappointed. "I was in hopes that you would sing to me. Gareth says that you have a very pretty voice."

"Some other time," Delphie said, and made her escape. Her thoughts flew back to the house in Brook Street. What, she wondered, was the relationship between Miss Carteret and her maid? It had seemed a very strange one—the maid appeared to have dominion over the mistress. And yet not wholly—

As she was descending the stairs to the main hall of the house, the door opened from the street, and two men came in: Gareth, and Mr. Fitzjohn. They appeared to be engaged in a heated argument.

"I am beginning to feel certain that Elaine is the imposter," Gareth was saying. "Why, you have only to see this girl's mother—"

"What is that to the purpose? I never heard such a crack-brained scheme!" Fitzjohn burst out. His pale, freckled face wore a harassed frown, his hands were trembling; Delphie had not imagined that he could look so discomposed. "It will not answer, Gar, it really will not! What can have led you into such a piece of folly?"

Then both men looked up and saw Delphie coming down.

"Ah, Miss Carteret—" said Fitzjohn. "I am just saying to my cousin that I cannot approve of your coming to live in this house."

"Stuff!" said Gareth, walking upstairs. "It was the only possible answer. Nothing will happen, unless Elaine cries rope on us. You go and see her, Mordred—she will listen to you—persuade her that she will only cut off her own expectations if she does so."

Mr. Fitzjohn heaved an impatient sigh, and stood nibbling his thumb. He said to Delphie,

"That is always the way with Gareth! To suggest something to him—to give him any advice—is the way to make him straightway go and do the exact opposite."

"Best advise him in the contrary direction," Delphie said, smiling. Mr. Fitzjohn gave her such a sharp look that she wondered if this was, in fact, his habit. "Oh, well—if *we* are in the basket, cousin, may I hope that *you* at least are secure!"—a remark which also seemed to startle him. She added, since he was returning to the street, where his curricle waited—evidently he had driven Gareth back from somewhere—"Are your horses recovered from whatever it was that afflicted them, Mr. Fitzjohn? I see that you are driving a different pair today."

"Yes—no—the others are still in rather poor trim," he replied. "Was that not a strange mischance? And most wretchedly uncomfortable for you, I fear. I would not have had it happen for worlds! I am glad to see you none the worse for your toss. My groom thinks that perhaps some moldy ergot must have found its way into their feed—it has a very poisonous effect."

"Does it indeed? Then I hope for your sake that your groom will be more careful in future—or that you will change your feed merchant."

"Thank you. Good-by—er—ma'am," he said, and left.

Delphie went to look at her mother, who had slipped into a peaceful doze.

About ten minutes later, Gareth came down the stairs again.

"Do I disturb you?" he inquired, tapping lightly on the open door of the parlor, where Delphie was arranging books on shelves. "I will not make a practice of interrupting you, I promise—but I wondered if you had found all as it should be—if Bardwell had helped you. How pleasant you have made it look."

"Thanks to your kind loan of chairs and tables! Otherwise it would have been bare indeed. We are not used to such large rooms. Yes, Bardwell has already offered his help. We are most snugly established here, and, I believe, will be very comfortable. But—Cousin Gareth—there is a matter on which I wish your advice—quite a serious one."

"What is the trouble?" he asked as she came to a stop, suddenly feeling all the difficulty of putting what she had to tell him in such a way that it would not sound like a hysterical fancy.

"Would you be so obliging as to walk through into the garden for a moment?" she said, and led the way along a drugget-lined passage to the glass-paned door which led out into the pleasant little courtyard—it was hardly more—where wallflowers were shedding their scent and apple buds were just beginning to show pink on the boughs of two small trees. A gate led out from the back to the unused coach house, and the stable where the donkey was housed.

"I wish you to look at these birds," Delphie said, and showed him the five dead sparrows lying around the nibbled biscuit. He stared at them in bewilderment; Delphie wondered if he thought she had suddenly run mad.

Then she led him indoors again, and, producing the vinaigrette, said,

"Cousin, I fear you will think this is a piece of vaporish nonsense, but—I believe that Elaine Carteret tried to poison my mother this afternoon."

"*What?*"

She told, slowly and with care, the story of their visit to the house in Brook Street. Gareth listened, stone-faced. When she mentioned the vinaigrette he stretched out a hand, saying, "Give that to me."

She passed it to him and he took the cap off and made as if to sniff it.

"*Don't!*" said Delphie, involuntarily.

"Perhaps you are right. Wait a minute—" he said. "I am nursing a patient of Lionel's—poor little creature—I fear it will not survive in any case—"

He left the room and came back in a moment with a small box covered by a cloth. The cloth when lifted off revealed a white mouse, which lay on a truss of hay, with closed eyes and heaving sides, looking (Delphie thought) weak, frail, and remarkably like Una Palgrave.

"We will make an experiment," said Gareth grimly; he held the vinaigrette to the tip of the mouse's pointed nose. The result was instantaneous—the mouse jerked once; its tiny claws curled up tightly; and it was dead.

"I will need to buy Lionel another mouse," remarked Gareth. His tone was expressionless.

Delphie said, "Of course, what kills a mouse—or a sparrow—*need* not hurt a human being—" Her voice trailed off, as she looked at the dead animal. Gareth was silent. She went on, "Then there were the horses, you see, too—bolting like that. Poisoned by ergot, Mr. Fitzjohn said. Was that not strange? Of course there need be no connection. But it is singular."

"*You* are singular," Gareth said. "Three narrow escapes from death—and you take them with astounding calm."

"But what is to be done?"

"I will need to reflect," he said. "Mordred is already on his way to warn Elaine—perhaps that will be sufficient. She is a self-willed, headstrong girl—but I believe she minds him."

"You do not think she should be brought to book for what she has done—attempted to do?"

He said impatiently, "How can we do that without disclosing the whole? Excuse me—I will need to think about this."

And, leaving her, he began to mount the stairs.

"Shall I tell you what *I* think?" said Delphie.

"Yes—what?" He paused, turning his head, but looked as if he would rather *not* hear her thoughts.

"I think we should relate the whole history to Great-uncle Mark—make a round tale of it—and leave off all this prevarication."

"Oh, you do, do you? Well, let *me* tell *you*, my dear cousin, that you do not know your great-uncle so well as I do! The effect of that would probably be to lay him in paroxysms on the floor—next he would send for his lawyer—and then he would strike *all* his descendants out of his will, and leave his entire fortune to the upkeep of the Chase Kennels."

"Do you really believe that?" she said in a quenched tone.

"I know it."

"Oh. Is your sister Una a beneficiary under his will?"

"At present she is; yes," he replied. "And now, if you will excuse me, Cousin Delphie, I am about to be late for an appointment in the City."

"Just one thing—" said Delphie. He turned again, and now there was real exasperation in his expression.

"What now?"

"When Uncle Mark comes to dinner tomorrow—do you wish to entertain him upstairs, or down here? And shall I tell our Mrs. Andrews to prepare the meal?"

Evidently Gareth had not yet applied himself to consideration of these domestic problems. Hiw brows drew together.

"Bardwell can very well prepare a meal—or, no, let it be sent in from a chophouse—I do not wish *you* to be troubled in the matter."

"Are you out of your mind?" exclaimed Delphie, scandalized. "Chophouse meals are abominable—and abominably expensive, too! Uncle Mark would be disgusted. I am sure we can contrive to do better than that, if I may have Bardwell's assistance, and if you will tell me Lord Bollington's preferences."

"Oh—" Gareth said hastily. "I fancy he likes any kind of game—detests ragouts—does not care for creams or jellies—beyond that I fear I can tell you nothing."

"Then I must do my best with that."

Delphie walked back into her parlor and shut the door. Suddenly she felt extremely tired, and began, very much, to wish herself back in Greek Street.

It was not late, but she had been up so early, and the day had been so full of incident, that she decided to take herself off to bed. Mrs. Andrews, equally fatigued, had long ago retired. Mrs. Carteret was likewise asleep. But when Delphie went in for a last look at her mother, she found the poor lady very restless and distressed, stirring and sighing, and crying out in her sleep, "Oh! Take care of the baby! Oh! Pray don't drop it, nurse!"

Delphie laid a hand over that of her mother, which seemed to soothe her, but as soon as the hand was withdrawn she began to cry and toss about once more. Evidently the occurrences of the day had troubled some deeply buried memory; and Delphie once again blamed herself bitterly for permitting the visit to Elaine Carteret. She had hoped for something from it—she hardly knew what—some recognition, some confrontation, which had not occurred. Instead the visit had proved harassing, useless, and dangerous.

Mrs. Carteret's bed was too narrow for more than one occupant, so Delphie quietly made herself up a kind of pallet on the floor beside her mother, where she could be at hand to soothe and comfort when it was necessary; and it proved necessary many times during the hours before midnight. But presently Mrs. Carteret's sleep appeared to become deeper and less troubled by anxious dreams; Delphie herself was therefore enabled to doze off for longer periods.

During one of these she was suddenly awakened by something —she knew not what: a soft, sharp sound, that had her instantly wide awake and fixedly listening. Her mother now slept peacefully, drawing long, regular, steady breaths; it was not any motion or sound from the bed that had woken Delphie.

It came from a corner of the room, where the little writing desk stood which Gareth had lent them. The sound was not the creak of its lid, but the rustle of papers.

Delphie, lying on the farther side of her mother's bed from the window, was in deep shadow, well concealed; thus she was able cautiously to raise her head and steal a glance over her mother's sleeping form, toward the corner where the desk stood.

She observed that the sash of the window had been raised; and a dark figure stood by the desk, rapidly extracting its contents.

Delphie was almost paralyzed by astonishment and fright for a moment. Then, struck, suddenly, by the remarkable *smallness* of the figure by the desk, she rose, softly, first to her knees, then to a crouching posture: then she sprang, as fast as she could, around the end of the bed, and pounced on the figure, shouting, at the same time, very loudly indeed,

"Help! Thieves! Help! Thieves!"

The figure writhed, squirmed, and wriggled in her grasp, kicked furiously at her shins, tried to bite her wrists, and several times almost managed to pull free, but Delphie, shifting her grip on a skinny, muscular arm, was able to reproduce a hold she had once observed employed by a Bow Street runner when apprehending a thief, and pulled the intruder's arm sharply up behind his back, eliciting a shrill cry of pain.

"Lemme go! Lemme go! I'll mizzle off quietly! I won't take nothing!"

"No, I certainly shall not let you go!" replied Delphie, and continued to shout for help.

By this time her mother was awake, exclaiming confusedly,

"Delphie? Is that you? Oh, dear, what is it *now?* Oh, my gracious me! What in the world is going on?"

Next, other personages began to appear: Mrs. Andrews, with a candle and formidable castellation of curlpapers under her nightcap; Bardwell, the manservant, carrying a dark lantern and a pistol; Gareth, wearing a silk dressing gown and likewise equipped.

By the brighter light, Delphie was able to distinguish her captive.

"Good heaven!" she exclaimed. "It is you!"

For she found that she was holding the small dirty boy who, earlier in the day, had stood watching while the Carterets' belongings were packed up for removal, and to whom she had given a picture book.

"You ungrateful little brat! Was one book not enough for you?"

"The deuce!" said Gareth. "Do you *know* this boy, Cousin Delphie?"

"Not at all! I saw him in the street, merely; gave him an old book."

"It's a kinchin," pronounced Bardwell. "Gangs o' thieves uses 'em—they're better for getting in winders and climbing up awkward places, see?"

"Lemme go!" whined the boy. "I didn't take no vallybles! You can't bone me for what I done!"

"Oh, can't we! The Beak will be glad to see you in the morning—I dare say he knows you well! Until then you can spend the night in the coal cellar, tied up with the clothesline. Come along!"

So saying, Bardwell approached the boy and grabbed him roughly.

"Ay, that will teach the little varmint!" approved Mrs. Andrews.

But the boy, with an expert squirm, suddenly whipped away, as Bardwell was removing him from Delphie's grasp, and in a flash was over the windowsill and away through the garden before anybody had the presence of mind to stop him.

"Oh, well," said Delphie, chafing her hands together—for they had been almost numbed by the strength with which she had been obliged to grasp him. "He had not taken anything, after all!"

"Oh!" quavered Mrs. Carteret. "I shall never be able to sleep securely in this room, if thieves are to be always breaking in and waking me up!"

"Ay," remarked Mrs. Andrews, "a postern door do always make a thief!"

"Have no fear, ma'am," said Gareth grimly. "Tomorrow morning we put bars across the window!"

"*Bars!*" objected Mrs. Carteret. "As well live in a prison!"

"Let us discuss it in the morning," said Delphie, who found her mother's analogy unfortunate. "I do not imagine the boy will return tonight! I am obliged to you all for coming to my aid so swiftly."

"I am beyond anything vexed," said Gareth, sounding it, "that such a thing should have occurred on your first night here."

"Oh yes indeed," agreed Delphie cordially. "After a week or so here I dare say we should not have regarded it in the slightest!" which earned her an outraged look from her cousin, as he retired with Bardwell.

"In any case," said Mrs. Carteret after they had gone, "now I bethink me of it, there was nothing at all of value in that desk. Only old papers—letters, and my wedding lines, and other such stuff. I presume the boy was looking for money, but he was sadly out of luck!"

But Delphie, having returned the papers to their pigeonholes and checked that none were missing, locked the desk, and spent the rest of the night with the key under her pillow.

Next morning she encountered Gareth briefly, as she darted out on her way to give a lesson in Grosvenor Square.

"How are you, cousin?" he inquired, viewing her carefully. "And how does your mother? I fear you must be somewhat anxious and distressed after the alarums of the night?"

Delphie gave him her flashing smile, with the two dimples.

"My dear cousin—how thoughtful you are! But pray do not waste your solicitude on us—we are in the very best of health and spirits. Why, since I have encountered you, I have hardly known what it is to be dull: life in your circle offers one interest after another—deathbed ceremonies, headlong carriage rides—poison—threats—housebreakers—really I cannot imagine how I endured the tedium and languor of my existence before I met you! But if you will excuse me, I am late for my lesson. I shall see you tonight. Pray, for my sake, do not be one minute later than twenty minutes before five o'clock!"

And, leaving him looking rather blankly after her, she ran away up South Audley Street.

Great-uncle Mark arrived with terrifying punctuality, at exactly a quarter before five o'clock.

In the end it had been decided that it would be best to receive him on the ground floor: thus there would be less danger of his hearing any sound from the inmates of the top story. Furthermore, the Palgrave children had been bribed to be quiet as mice, by the offer of a trip with their uncle to Astley's circus on the following evening.

"Why not send them off tonight?" Delphie had suggested. "Then they would be out of the way altogether."

"But suppose they returned just as Uncle Mark was taking his leave?" Gareth pointed out.

Delphie chuckled. "Very true! We should have to pretend that they were total strangers who had mistaken their direction and come to the wrong house. How one piece of deceit does lead on to another."

Gareth gave an impatient sigh and walked away, leaving her to regret her lighthearted words.

Bardwell had, in the course of the morning, carried down, leaf by leaf, a handsome dining table, which he had erected in Delphie's front parlor. Then he had produced an epergne, various pieces of crested silver, and an elegant set of wineglasses.

"Lucky we just got the silver out of hock," he remarked laconically. "Mrs. Una had a lucky runner at Chester—Fly-by-Night. But don't tell the guvnor! He don't like it above half if she has a flutter!"

Delphie promised that she would not mention the matter. But her opinion of Una went down still further.

"If you care to leave the arrangement of the table to me, ma'am, I will see that all is as it should be," Bardwell said.

"Thank you, Bardwell! I am sure that you know more about such matters than I do," Delphie said gratefully.

Uncle Mark's fondness for game and dislike for ragouts and jellies had given Delphie, Mrs. Andrews, and Bardwell, who was called in to advise, very considerable need to exercise their wits, since game was far from plentiful in the month of May. The best they could achieve (Gareth having provided the necessary cash) was a goose-and-turkey pie, a capon dressed with artichokes, some buttered lobsters, and a sirloin of beef. This was followed, for a second course, by a pair of ducklings with cherries and green peas, various vegetables, a dish of apple tartlets, and some almond cakes—hardly an elegant repast, as Bardwell said, sighing, but at least a neat, plain dinner. However, since Lord Bollington spent so little time in town, was not in the habit of fashionable fare, and was known to be a frugal eater at home, Delphie hoped that the meal would do well enough. Fortunately Mrs. Andrews had proved to be a notable cook, and such dishes as they *had* managed to produce could not be faulted. Bardwell, casting his eye over the side board, announced that he thought they could all congratulate themselves.

Delphie had taken a great liking to Bardwell, a lean, spare, gray-haired personage who, she learned, had been his master's bâtman in Spain, during the two years Gareth had served in the Peninsular War before, on his father's death, he had been obliged to sell out of his regiment and return to assume the management of the manor at Horsmonden and his sister's affairs.

This was all news to Delphie. And if she had not scrupled to ask questions of a servant, and if they had not all been so busy, she would have liked to find out much more. But, glancing at the carriage-clock, she exclaimed,

"Mercy! My uncle will be here in half an hour! I had better go and dress directly!"

She put on her white crape, and borrowed a silver necklace and a Norwich shawl from her mother, who, on hearing that company was expected, had declared that she did not wish to see *anybody*. Mrs. Carteret had kept her bed all morning, quite worn out with the fatigues and excitements of the previous day and night; she did get up in the afternoon for a short time to sit in the garden, but then returned to her bed at four, announcing that she should not stir from it again.

"Mrs. Andrews can bring me a little soup when you dine; that is all I wish for. And perhaps a handful of almond cakes."

This decision was a relief to Delphie, who would have tried to persuade her mother to such a course had not Mrs. Carteret arrived at it independently. She had felt obliged, in honesty, to mention that Lord Bollington was expected, but when Mrs. Carteret said faintly,

"Oh, heaven! Not *another* of them?" in a piteous manner, Delphie thought it best to drop the matter entirely. She would have been very apprehensive as to the effect of such a confrontation upon her mother's nerves—though she could not repress some curiosity as to Lord Bollington's reactions.

Gareth came downstairs at four-thirty, dressed plainly but correctly in knee breeches, silk stockings, a white waistcoat, and a long-tailed jacket; if his apparel was plainly far from new, at least it looked in good trim.

"You are as fine as fivepence, cousin," Delphie told him politely.

"You, too!" he responded. "I am afraid all this is a dead bore for you, and much more nuisance than I had intended; I must indeed apologize. I hope that Bardwell has done most of the work?"

"Pray don't think of it," said Delphie, smilingly waving aside all the hours she had spent in rolling pastry, paring apples, podding peas, boning, stoning, stuffing, larding, basting, stirring, beating, and chopping, under Mrs. Andrews's exacting eye. "After all, think in what an excellent cause! To earn my uncle's favor must be an object with us all!"

He gave her an ironical glance, but only observed, "You have a dab of flour on your nose, cousin."

"Thank you—I must have got it when I took those wretched pies from the oven," she said, rubbing at it. "What a fortunate thing you informed me! Do I hear a carriage outside?"

"You *still* have not got it—here—" he said impatiently, and, laying a light hand on her shoulder, turned up her face with the other hand. For a moment their faces were so close that she could see his eyes were not black but a very dark brown; she had the oddest feeling that he might kiss her—he did look very intently into her eyes—but at that moment came a loud peal on the doorbell, and he gently rubbed the end of her nose with his handkerchief, before moving quickly into the hallway, bracing his shoulders as he did so.

Evidently it took some little time for Lord Bollington to be extracted from his carriage, supported across the pavement, and inducted into the house; but at last he appeared in the parlor doorway, limping heavily, assisted by a thick ebony cane. As he gave a peevish glance about him, Delphie swept him her best curtsy.

"We are delighted to welcome you, great-uncle. Pray come to the fire!"

"No need to have piled up such a bonfire on *my* account!" he snapped, allowing Gareth to shepherd him to an upright chair with arms. "Good God! There must be half a stone of coals on the hearth!" Despite which criticism he seemed glad enough to sit and warm himself. He still looked far from well, but was dressed very correctly in old-fashioned evening attire. On his right middle finger he wore an enormous ruby ring with a stone large as a pigeon's egg, which flashed dark gleams back into the flames.

It was plain that he did not wish his health referred to; he irritably turned aside any inquiries about it.

"You young ones have no idea what illness is! My afflictions are wretched—wretched! But I make nothing of them—I do not allow them to deter me from my duty, which is," he said to Delphie, "to make sure that you and your cousin are properly established together."

"I hope that your doubts on that head are now wholly resolved, Uncle Mark," she said.

"Ay, ay," he exclaimed testily. "You may smile! I dare swear it's all smiles and sherry *now*, while you are new to one another—but how will it be in five years' time, when the claws begin to show?"

"That, uncle, only time will reveal," Delphie said, beginning, as Lord Bollington grinned his disagreeably malicious grin at her, to feel very sorry for poor Prissy Privett, and to wonder what sort of a wretched life the pair of them had led together until his unkindness had killed her. Delphie could not help thinking Great-uncle Mark a dismal old wretch.

Lord Bollington then demanded of Gareth where various heirlooms were which he had expected to see and did not. Delphie wondered if Gareth would tell his great-uncle that they were at Horsmonden, but he merely replied,

"I sold them, uncle!"

"What? Sold your father's Cellini saltcellar—and the pokal—and the pineapple cup?"

"I was obliged to. Besides, the pineapple cup was hideous!"

"Would you not care to come to the table, uncle?" Delphie said hastily.

"Might as well," Lord Bollington grumbled. "I hope to heaven you haven't served up a lot of foreign fal-lals and kickshaws that I can't digest."

However, on the whole, he was pleased to approve their choice of menu and (for a confirmed invalid) ate an amazing, and, Delphie thought, a wholly injudicious quantity, particularly indulging in the buttered lobsters, the ducklings with cherries, the almond cakes, and the apple tarts. He called for cheese with the latter, which Bardwell was luckily able to produce. Delphie, too nervous to touch more than a few mouthfuls herself, watched his gastronomic prowess with startled eyes, until she chanced to meet Gareth's amused glance, when she was obliged to press her napkin to her lips for a moment or two, and stare resolutely at her plate.

"Fishbone gone down the wrong way, niece?" inquired his lordship. "Swallow a little hock and seltzer—that'll shift it."

"Thank you, Uncle Mark—I am better now."

"Brother Lance was devilish fond of hock and seltzer," Lord Bollington observed. "Said it would sober him up, be he never so concerned!" His tone was melancholy, reminiscent; absently he removed his wig in order to scratch his (perfectly bald) head, then replaced the wig again, somewhat lopsided. "Always would have hock and seltzer at the end of an evening, Lance would. If only—but there! What's the use to repine! But he was a devilish good fellow, m'brother Lance; good seat on a horse; sharp eye for a wench; it was a thousand pities that little twopenny ha'penny flibbertigibbet should ha' come betwixt us at the end. If I'd known how it would all turn out, I'd far sooner ha' dropped *her* in the moat—so spiteful and vixenish as she turned out to be!"

"And did you drop my great-uncle Lancelot in the moat?" Gareth inquired interestedly.

"No, no, boy—no! In course I didn't! We fought fair—but it was a frosty night—leads were devilish slippery—poor fellow lost his footing—wouldn't have had it happen for worlds," Lord Bollington morosely remarked, staring into his glass of burgundy as if he hoped to see his brother Lancelot swimming there. "At the time, of course, didn't expect to come into the title—Lance's son still alive—but then your crackbrained brother had to run off and join the Navy!" he said, suddenly directing a glance of indignation at Delphie. "And get himself killed!"

"I think you must mean my uncle Tristram, great-uncle," she said gently. "My mother's brother."

"Eh? What? Oh—er—yes, Elaine's brother—yes." For a moment he seemed confused, but presently inquired, "What's *your* name, then?"

"I am called Philadelphia, uncle, but my name is Elaine too, after my mother."

"*Philadelphia?* What kind of a heathen name is *that?*"

"It has been a name frequently used in the Carteret—in my father's family."

"Yes!" he said, immediately striking off at a new tangent. "Then *she* had to run off too—elope—mizzle off! As if life was insupportable at Chase! None of them would stay there! And I dare say it *was* insupportable," he added glumly, after a moment, "with that vulgar harpy at the foot of the table—not to mention her two base-born brats. They went off too," he muttered. "But then the boy came back. Put in a fair job as agent, but never did like the cut of his jib somehow: always a bit too anxious to please. They're all after me for what they can get!" he suddenly cried angrily at Gareth. "None of them love me for myself!"

How could they? thought Delphie dispassionately, gazing at him.

"It would have been different if I'd had one of my own! But that, she couldn't—wouldn't—do. Ah, the best of them all was Mary—your mother," he said to Delphie.

"I think you mean my grandmother, Uncle Mark."

"Mother, grandmother—what's the difference? Ah, *she* was a real beauty—real class, *she* had. Good enough to be the Queen of England! But Lance had to get in ahead and snabble her—Lance *always* had to get in ahead," Lord Bollington muttered moodily. "Still an' all, I'm sorry I pushed the poor fellow in the moat."

Delphie began to feel rather sorry for the poor old scarecrow, fretting away over his griefs, and sins committed so far back in the lost and ineradicable past. Whether or not he really had pushed his brother off the roof, it seemed certain enough that he had at least felt the impulse to do so. Perhaps, Delphie thought, he was one of those poor jealous souls who never crave something unless it is the property of somebody else; it seemed plain enough that he had coveted his brother's wife, his title, and his mistress.

Her eyes met those of Gareth again; now she had no impulse to laugh.

"Do you think perhaps I should retire?" she murmured in a low voice.

"I think it would be better if *he* did," Gareth responded in the same tone, and added, in a louder one,

"Are you tired, Uncle Mark? Shall I send Bardwell for your coach?"

"Eh? Eh?" Lord Bollington jerked himself out of his sad reverie, coming back, it seemed, from an immense distance. His eye fell on Delphie.

"Did they treat you well at that school in Bath?" he suddenly inquired. "Queen's Square Academy—whatever it was called? Felt at times I should have had you to Chase—but—well—t' tell you the truth—couldn't *stand* the prospect—child on her own, what could *I* do?—felt too bad about it all."

"Never mind, uncle," she said quietly. "It didn't matter. I was quite happy."

He raised sad, bloodshot eyes to her face.

"If only your mother had been alive—"

"But—uncle—my mother *was* alive! My mother *is* alive."

"Eh? How *can* she be? Midwife's letter came—saying she had died in childbed—"

"Would you not like to see her? To see for yourself—?"

Delphie was puzzled by his last statement, but all other concerns were obliterated by the knowledge that she could alleviate at least *one* of his many griefs.

"Wait!" she said. "And I will see if she is still awake—"

"Delphie, are you sure that what you are doing is wise?" Gareth said softly as she went toward the door.

"The poor old man! Surely it must ease at least *some* of his trouble, to see that Mamma is alive and well?"

"Mamma!" she called, tapping gently at her mother's door. "Are you still awake?"

"Yes, I am, dear," replied Mrs. Carteret's voice, quite briskly, from within. "And, if you have any made, I believe I will take just a taste of tea! I have had such a refreshing nap!"

The open door revealed that Mrs. Carteret was up, sitting in her armchair, very fetchingly arrayed in her cap and frilled bed jacket.

"Certainly I will bring you some tea," said Delphie. "But also—Mamma, would you mind *very* much if I brought Great-uncle Mark to see you, just for a moment? He is so very sad and sorry for all he has done wrong, that I think it would be the greatest kindness if you would do so? He is so *wretched*—about grandfather—about Uncle Tristram—about your running away—about everything!"

Mrs. Carteret looked very startled and uneasy. Her hand fluttered to her lips.

"Must I?" she asked fearfully. "Must I really, Delphie?"

"Just for one moment, Mamma!"

"Oh—very well! If you think it will really do him good."

Delphie ran back to the parlor, where Uncle Mark was now tottering in the direction of the hall door, supported by Bardwell and Gareth, as well as by his ebony cane.

"Mamma says she will see him—just for a moment."

"I still doubt if it is wise," muttered Gareth. But he continued to help the old man along the hallway toward Mrs. Carteret's door.

Lord Bollington reached the doorway, looked through, and saw Mrs. Carteret ensconced in the armchair, becomingly wrapped in her white frills.

He stared at her in silence for a long moment, his mouth ajar, his face working, his hands clenching and unclenching. Then—

"*Mary!*" he ejaculated, in a hoarse croaking tone—and suddenly sagged heavily on the arms that supported him. His head dropped forward, and his cane clattered on the floor.

"Oh lord! I knew it!" Gareth muttered. Mrs. Carteret let out a faint cry.

"What has happened? Is he ill? Oh, the poor soul!"

"Go to your mother, Delphie," said Gareth. "Shut the door."

Appalled, Delphie found voice enough to murmur,

"What is it? Has he—?"

"His heart has stopped," said Gareth.

12

To Delphie, the rest of the night seemed to go on forever. First she had Mrs. Carteret to soothe, and that was no easy task; it was finally achieved by a drop or two of laudanum in a cup of tea, for the poor lady was so overset by what had occurred that a deep and oblivious sleep seemed the only solution for her. Leaving Mrs. Andrews nodding off in an armchair by her mother's bedside, Delphie then returned to her own bedroom, at the front of the house, where Lord Bollington's corpse had, for the time being, been laid.

During the time that Delphie had spent attending to her mother, Lord Bollington's carriage had been dispatched to the house in Hanover Square, and had come back with both Mr. Fitzjohn and Dr. Bowles, Lord Bollington's own doctor, who, by great good fortune, had escorted the old man to London.

Dr. Bowles, having carefully examined his defunct patient, gave it as his unhesitating opinion that the death had been caused by failure of the heart, following a severe shock, on the top of too much lobster, hock, and duckling.

"Not a bit surprised!" Dr. Bowles said cheerfully. "Could have happened any time this past seven years! Only amazed it didn't! The old curmudgeon was such a stingy eater at home that, if ever he chanced to dine at someone else's expense, he couldn't resist overdoing it. Often and often I've warned him—haven't I, Fitz?"

"You do not think," Mr. Fitzjohn suggested gently, "that my uncle might have been er—poisoned—by any undesirable element in the food he has just consumed?"

"*Poisoned?*" said the doctor scornfully. "What kind of a totty-headed notion is that? Look at the others—ate the same food—

they're all right and tight! No *need* to poison the old feller, when he had duckling on top of lobster! No, no, old dame Nature has served him trick and tie at last, and no need to blame yourselves," he said to Gareth and Delphie, who, silent and white-faced, had been awaiting his verdict in wretched suspense, "for he made as good an end as any man need! Wouldn't mind hopping the twig myself after such a dinner as you describe!"

"And I do think," said Delphie falteringly, "that although it was such a shock for him to see my mother, he was both moved and—and happy at the sight of her. I believe he thought that she was *her* mother—my grandfather's wife—for whom he seems to have felt a—a strong passion. Do you not think so?" she inquired of Gareth.

"Yes—very likely," Gareth agreed gloomily. "He certainly shouted out *Mary* at the last."

"Eh, well," remarked the doctor, "there's one more patient gone! Come along," he said to Mordred. "We might as well return to our beds, there's naught we can do here. I'll make arrangements to have the body fetched in the morning—can't go knocking up undertakers at this hour of night. He'll be buried at Chase, I presume? Funeral in the chapel there?"

"But you can't leave the body here!" said Gareth indignantly. "It's in my cousin's room! What about—?"

He caught himself up suddenly.

Delphie, who thought she had observed Mr. Fitzjohn casting some very sharp and suspicious glances, both at her and at Gareth, here said composedly,

"Of *course* the body must remain here, Gareth! That chamber is not required, in any case. You may return upstairs, and I, naturally, shall need to spend the night in poor Mamma's room. I shall be exceedingly anxious about her until she has woken, and I can reassure myself that the tone of her mind has not been too rudely overset by such an experience."

As this was eminently reasonable, Gareth made no more objections, and the other two men took their leave.

Gareth, locking the front door after them, said,

"But shall you feel safe in that back chamber, after the burglar last night?"

"Oh yes," Delphie said tranquilly. "Bardwell—who, I must say, is the most useful creature in the world!—tells me that during the day he had a locksmith come in, who fastened the window so that it will not open more than a few inches. I shall feel perfectly secure. But thank you for your inquiry."

She added, diffidently,

"You were right and I was wrong, Cousin Gareth, about taking the poor old man to see my mother! I am sorry for all the distress and awkwardness that it has caused you."

"Oh well," he said tiredly. "Don't put yourself about. As Dr. Bowles told us, it might have happened any time during the last seven years. But it was certainly a piece of good fortune that Bowles was at hand, so no one can think it was anything but the course of nature. At least—I hope not."

"And now at least," said Delphie, "you are rid of one of your most inconvenient problems."

"What is that?"

"Why," she said, moving softly toward her mother's room, "as soon as you like—tomorrow morning, if you please!—you can set in hand the arrangements to have your marriage annulled."

And, stepping into the darkened room, she softly closed the door behind her.

She had hardly expected to be able to sleep for hours to come; after dismissing Mrs. Andrews she was still sitting with open eyes, gazing at the window, and had been doing so for about ten minutes, when she became aware of a scratching and tapping outside, and heard whispering voices:

"Cousin Delphie! Cousin Delphie! Could you please open the door and let us in!"

After yesternight's burglar, Delphie had taken the somewhat irrational precaution of carrying her wedding lines around with her in her pocket; her hand found and closed on the paper now. But then she realized that the persons outside were *not* burglars.

"Good heavens," she thought confusedly. "The children!"

Only now did it occur to her that, throughout all the excitement during the previous hours—the carriage coming and going—the doctor and Fitzjohn arriving and departing—not a sound, not a footstep, not a murmur had been heard from upstairs. Despite the promise the children had given their uncle, this seemed too good to be credible—ominously good; and here, now, was the proof of that.

They had not been in the house at all!

No doubt they had been to Astley's Amphitheatre on their own, thought Delphie tiredly, getting up out of her chair and throwing a shawl over her shoulders. And I cannot say that I blame them—I am sure they do not often have a treat, poor little things; and it is really a fortunate occurrence, for, despite his promise to them, Gareth could hardly take them now, on the day after his uncle's death.

She tiptoed swiftly to the glass door leading into the garden, and opened it. To her considerable surprise, there seemed to be several persons more than just the children clustered outside in the dark little paved yard.

"Heydey, Miss Delphie! Ain't this a prime caper then!" whispered a cheerful, familiar voice.

"Good God!" exclaimed Delphie in utter astonishment. "It's never Jenny Baggott! What in the name of heaven are *you* doing here at three o'clock in the morning?"

"Let us in, Miss Delphie, and we'll give you the whole history!" Jenny whispered. The children were already slipping past, murmuring and giggling amongst themselves—

"*Don't* go into the front room!" said Delphie hastily—not that there was any particular reason why they should take it into their heads to do such a thing. "You'd best—you had better all come into the kitchen and tell me what you have been doing," she added, with as much severity as she could muster, fastening the glass door behind the last of the shadowy figures. With stifled squeaks and exclamations, and a great deal of chuckling, they obeyed her, perching themselves on chairs and table, and squatting on the floor. Delphie, following, lit a candle and then a lamp, which she set on the dresser.

Turning from adjusting its wick—

"Good God!" she gasped. "*Mr. Palgrave!*"

For, to her utter consternation, she found the poet in the midst of his children, seated comfortably in Mrs. Andrews's rocking chair, already looking about him in a vague, absent way, as if searching for a pen, and a bit of paper to write on.

"Ain't it a prime lark!" said Jenny again, and the two smaller boys, Lance and Lionel, could no longer restrain their delight, but burst into an exuberant, capering dance, crying out,

"We rescued Papa! We rescued Papa!" while all the rest of the children broke into excited, self-congratulatory chatter.

"Don't you think it was clever of us, Cousin Delphie? We took the donkey for him to ride on—just like Jesus—hold your tongue, Lionel!—in case poor Papa couldn't walk so far after all those years in prison—and we took our supper and waited out in the park for hours and hours until it was truly dark and late at night so there would be fewer persons about—we had *such* larks dodging the constables and hiding in bushes—stop being a jaw-me-dead, Percy, let *me* tell the tale—of course it worked in very well because we *knew* Cousin Gareth would be pleased to have us out of the way while he gave his party—shut your head, Tristram! Cousin Delphie *knows* that already—and we left Helen looking after Mama because Helen's quake-spirited and don't care for larks above half—and we made ourselves masks out of newspaper and painted black, so that it would seem like a real rumpus—"

Indeed, many of them were still wearing black loo-masks, evidently homemade.

"But—good heavens!—how did you ever succeed in getting your Papa out of the prison?" said Delphie faintly.

She could not find it in her heart to reproach them—so filled with evident pride and delight as they were, so bursting with pleasure at the success of their expedition—but she did feel that the rescue of Thomas Palgrave was far from being an unmixed blessing, and must certainly be attended by unheard-of complications in the near future.

Mr. Palgrave himself seemed to be imbued with somewhat similar doubts, for he looked around the crowded kitchen with a touch of irritability, and said in a querulous tone,

"Not so loud, pray, not so loud! Lower your voices, if you please! You appear to forget that for six years I have been used to a very considerable degree of solitude, and silence, and privacy. This clamor grates on my hearing, I fear—it grates! I have need of a great deal of quiet, I do indeed! Perhaps there might be prepared for me some small, retired chamber—any will do, so it has a couch, a chair, a table, an inkstand—to which I might repair?"

"Oh, but you must have some supper, Papa!" cried Isa. "May we give him something to eat, Cousin Delphie?"

"Yes of course you may, my dear," Delphie replied absently. "Look in the larder—you will find cold duck, cold beef, cold capon, cold goose-and-turkey pie, a piece of cheese, and a few apple tartlets; pray take whatever you fancy."

The children needed no further invitation; most of them set off in the direction of the larder immediately.

"But I still do not understand how you managed to get your Papa out of the prison," Delphie went on, addressing herself to Arthur, who had remained.

A deprecating cough behind her in the corner at this point made her turn around.

"Ahem! I daresay *I* can explain that point, miss!"

Very much astonished, Delphie observed a personage whom she had hitherto overlooked among the crowd—the gangling figure of Mr. Sam Swannup, who stood in a corner beside Jenny Baggott, with a look of simple pride on his face.

"You see, miss, it was all along of your kindness in giving Miss Baggott here the wherewithal to buy me out—and indeed, ma'am, I'm *that* obliged to you—I'll be pleased to attend to any locks of yours that should chance to require mending free gratis to the end of my days—Miss Baggott come to me in the prison, all smiles, and, says she, Sam Swannup, you're a free man, for Miss has give me the dibs, and I've paid your blunt! And we can get wed next Thursday fortnit, the minute I've my wedding dress made, she says. Oh, my stars! says I. Whatever can we do to repay Miss? And she says, Sam, you're a locksmith, you can unbolt a betty as good as any man in Smithies' Road, why don't you let Miss's friend out of the buckle? Oh, says I, for sure that's a first-rate notion, and it will be a service to litter-ayture into the bargain; so then, Mr. Bardwell chancing to employ me to dub up the betty on your downstairs window—"

"Mind your language, Sam! For shame! I daresay the young

lady can't make head nor tail of what you're a-telling her!" said Jenny reprovingly.

"Beg pardon, miss, I'm sure! As I was a-saying, Mr. Bardwell (which is an old chum of mine, and he it was who passed me the word to keep an eye on His Nabs here while in the Bastile)"—here Sam cast a look of great devotion at Mr. Palgrave—"Mr. Bardwell, as I say, employing me to do this little job on the lady's window—I was able to pass the nod to the young'uns upstairs as how I'd be pleased to help them fetch their Pa out of durance vile."

"But how did you manage the escape?"

"Why," said Sam, "on account o' me being a locksmith, miss. Natural, when they gets me to do the job on the gates in the clink, I keeps a bread-cast of the locks as I mends 'em; I'd be a poor sort o' betty-faker if I didn't do that; it's only common sense to fake a screw of any lock you works over!"

"So," said Tristram, unable to keep out of the tale any longer, "all we had to do was wait till the turnkeys were all asleep—for they keep mighty poor watch at the Marshalsea!"

"And then," burst in Percy, "Mr. Swannup unbuckled the betty—I mean, picked the lock—and I went in, because I'm smaller than Tris and can go more quietly than Artie—and I sneaked past the charleys—and roused up Papa and told him the coast was clear—"

"And we fetched him back on the donkey!" chorused the children all together. "Only Isa had to go back for the canary, of course—and then Papa wanted all his books, so that made it take a good deal longer—"

"And *I* went along for the lark—we was that tickled to think we could do you a good turn, Miss Delphie," said Jenny exuberantly, taking a large bite out of a chicken leg which Percy had handed to her.

"Won't Mama be pleased! How soon may we tell her?" Lionel was beginning, when a harsh voice from the doorway froze them all where they stood.

"*What* is the meaning of this *disgraceful* pandemonium?"

Delphie, turning with a wishbone in her hand (which she had absently picked up) met the furious eyes of Gareth, who, standing on the threshold, surveyed the exultant scene before him with an expression of unmixed wrath and disapproval.

"Uncle Gareth!" Percy said happily. "We have rescued Papa!"

"So I see! And what, may I inquire, do you propose to do with him now? Is he to be hidden in the cellar? Or transported overseas? You are aware, I suppose, you bacon-brained young numbskulls, that the constables, learning of his escape, will be around here first thing in the morning—that it is an indictable offense to help a prisoner escape from jail—that you will all be liable for sentences—and I shall too, as your guardian—you sap-skulled, totty-headed, bird-witted idiotic little goosecaps!"

A ring of horrified, open-mouthed faces stared at him. None of the children said a word, until Isa began to cry.

"Oh, *poor* Papa!" she sobbed. "But we *couldn't* leave him in the pokey for*ever!*"

"I begin to wish you had, however!" said Mr. Palgrave testily. "All this commotion is having the most adverse effect upon my wretched, overstrained nerves. Indeed I think that at any moment I may be subject to a Spasm!"

"I knew that little sense could be expected from the younger ones," Gareth went on furiously, ignoring his brother-in-law, "but had you bigger boys not reflected for a *moment?* Did you not know how I have been working, week in and week out, for years now, to amass a complete list of your father's debts and liabilities, so that I could come to an agreement with his creditors? That, indeed, I had almost succeeded, and might, in another month or so, have been able to pay off his debts and arrange for his release? And now—*now*—you have to go and overset all my careful work with your cork-brained heedlessness—God knows what will happen—he will be seized and thrown back into jail—possibly some different jail, as his offense is now of a different order—you wretched, stupid little ninnyhammers!"

Others besides Isa were now in tears, and Mr. Palgrave himself was beginning to look very lugubrious at the thought of what was in store for him, while Jenny and Mr. Swannup gazed at each other in horror.

"Lawks-a-mussy!" said Jenny, aghast. "If only I'd a thought—but there! I never do, as Sister says: if she's said it once, she's said it a hundred times, Jenny, says she, if ever there was a shatter-brain, it's you, always flying off on some mad freak without giving it any thought—"

Gareth, taking cognizance of Miss Baggott for the first time, gave her a glance of bleak dislike, coupled with surprise.

"As for *you*, ma'am, I do not at all understand how you came to be embroiled in this crackbrained escapade but—remembering your behavior on our previous encounter—I am very ready to believe that you encouraged and abetted these silly children in their folly."

"I'm sorry, I'm sure!" whimpered Jenny dolefully. Mr. Swannup laid a protective arm around her shoulders, but he, too, was looking wholly subdued and crestfallen.

"What had we better do, Uncle Gareth?" said Arthur humbly.

"What must you do? Why, take him back again, to be sure!" said Gareth.

Delphie, who all this time had remained silent in gathering indignation, could now restrain herself no longer.

"How *can* you be so unkind and—and quelling—and unsympathetic, when these poor children thought they had been so clever and useful and done their Papa such a good turn!"

"It was for Uncle Gareth we did it really," said Percy, knuckling a tear out of his eye. "We *knew* he hated having to go every day with Papa's meals—"

Delphie's exclamation, however, had gone unheard by most, for the children, evidently inspired by Gareth's suggestion, were exclaiming, in chorus,

"Yes, yes! That is what we will do! That will be an even better lark! Come, Papa—finish your last bite of tart!—Tristram, make haste and get the donkey out of its shed—Percy, do you take the books—Lance and Lionel, you had best stay at home this time, you are too little to walk such a distance twice in a night—Morgan and Melilot too, your legs are not long enough to keep up, for we shall have to go *very* quickly—it will be light in two hours more—come along Papa—make haste!—and you too, Mr. Swannup—"

In another moment the kitchen was empty. The larger children had left precipitately, dragging Mr. Palgrave, and accompanied by

Jenny and Sam Swannup; while the four smaller ones, evidently anxious to escape from their uncle's disapprobation, had scurried softly away up the stairs.

"I suppose I may know whom I have to thank for the inception of this addlepated escapade!" Gareth said bitterly, finding himself left face to face with Delphie, who was beginning in an absent-minded manner to tidy away the plates of cold meat and brush up the pastry crumbs. "For five years I have accompanied the children to and from the jail without any such notion entering their heads. But as soon as *you* appear on the scene, with your nonsensical romantic notions, every kind of trouble comes upon us!"

"Who invited me here?" she began indignantly, but, ignoring her, he went on,

"Aware as I am of your previous association with that outrageously vulgar girl—who, I do not doubt, planned the hoydenish trick by means of which you gained entrance to Chase—"

"Thank you! Pray say no more!" flashed Delphie. She was trembling with rage. "Your attitude empowers me to tell you that I think Jenny Baggott has more kindness and genuine good feeling in—in her little finger than you have in every inch of your body! I was never so shocked in all my life as when I heard you berating those poor well-meaning children in such a way! How *could* you? I wonder that even you—hard, cold, and unfeeling as I know you to be—were not ashamed! You are the most odious, callous, insensitive person I have ever had the misfortune to encounter and—I am sorry I ever met you! I most heartily wish that I never *had* come to Chase!"

"You cannot wish it more than I, ma'am!" declared Gareth, rather white around the nostrils. "You seem to have brought me nothing but misfortune and disaster at every turn. If it had not been for your absurd notion of introducing Uncle Mark to your mother, he might still be alive now—instead of which his death may still be a cause of scandal, gossip, and for aught I know, criminal proceedings! I do not scruple to call you my evil genius!"

"You have said enough!" said Delphie. With shaking hands, she pulled her wedding lines from her pocket, tore the paper in half, and handed the pieces to Gareth, who received them with a very blank expression. "I am excessively glad that at least now our association may be terminated," she went on. "I shall make arrangements to return to Greek Street tomorrow!"

Then she recalled that unfortunately she could not do that, for Jenny had already rented the rooms to a gentleman in the woolen hosiery and hat buiness. A sharp decline in spirits began to replace her anger.

Gareth said, "Pray make exactly what arrangements you think best!" and, turning on his heel, left the room. Delphie heard him run up the stairs very fast, and then there came the slam of a door on the upper story.

Left alone in the untidy kitchen, she sat down, put her elbows on the table, beside the forgotten canary, and burst into a storm of tears.

13

It was not to be expected that Delphie could soon compose her spirits enough to sleep. In whichever direction she turned her thoughts, they encountered so many occasions to alarm, distress, or mortify, that her mind seemed to rebound, wretchedly, from one point to another. As soon as she tried to fix on one aspect of her troubles, to arrive at some practical resolution, some different cause for anxiety would intrude itself.

First, and worst, was her quarrel with Gareth, and her impulsive announcement that she would immediately remove herself and her mother from Curzon Street.

Certainly it was her most eager wish to do so; she felt she would die if obliged to remain for another twenty-four hours under the same roof with Gareth; yet how could she possibly subject her poor mother, after such an unprecedented series of shocks, to the distress of yet another upheaval? It could not possibly be done within twenty-four hours; Mrs. Carteret's spirits must be given a few days, at least, in which to settle.

Then there was the horrifying—but hardly to be doubted—fact that Elaine Carteret apparently hated them enough to attempt to contrive their death—or at least, that of Mrs. Carteret. True, her scheme had been a decidedly clumsy one, and said little for her intelligence—but still—suppose she tried again? Tried some other method? Poor Mrs. Carteret, still so unsettled in health, would constitute easy prey to such stratagems.

She thought next of Mr. Fitzjohn. Without quite knowing why, Delphie could not avoid a decided feeling of mistrust toward him. The original affair of the bungled marriage was, after all, due to his agency. How *could* he have made such a mistake?

Could it really have been done by accident? Or had he arranged it on purpose? And if so, with what intention? To handicap his cousin Gareth in some way? To insure Elaine's inheritance? Gareth had said that Mordred and Elaine had at one time been very close. Did he *know* that she was a false claimant? Then there was the accident with the horses—Fitzjohn's horses. Could it have been an accident—or was it deliberate? If so, was it meant to injure Gareth—or herself?

Delphie further admitted to herself that she had found Fitzjohn's attitude after the death of Lord Bollington decidedly alarming. He had seemed inclined to suggest that the old man might have been deliberately hastened to his end—with the object, presumably, of forestalling a possible change of his will. Could criminal charges be preferred against Gareth and Delphie? Might Fitzjohn inculcate some kind of action? Delphie's knowledge of criminal procedure was of the scantiest—she did not know if such a thing were possible. Could she and Gareth be accused of murder, because the death had taken place after the meal they had provided? There was, of course, the evidence of Dr. Bowles—but was Dr. Bowles himself a beneficiary under Lord Bollington's will? If so, his evidence might be inadmissible.

"I don't trust Fitzjohn," Delphie said to herself.

There had been a very strange moment, just as he and the doctor had been on the point of departure. Fitzjohn had suddenly walked back to the corpse—hesitated—and then removed from the dead finger the outrageously enormous ruby ring.

"Best not to leave *that* to get stuck on with rigor mortis," he said, "or some spry undertaker's assistant will be making off with it. Here take it—" and he had handed it to Gareth.

"What ought I to do with it?" Gareth said, looking at it doubtfully. He made as if to put it in his pocket.

"*Not* in your pocket!" exclaimed Fitzjohn with a sharp note of harshness and strain in his voice. "It could roll out—fall through a hole—get prigged by a pickpocket! Put it on, you fool! On your finger is the best place for it!"

And, as Gareth had somewhat reluctantly done so, Fitzjohn remarked, in a tone of strange, ironic satisfaction,

"There! *Now* you are all set! Dubbed up and riding high, eh?"

Then he had followed the doctor to the door.

How, Delphie wondered, turning restlessly on her pillow, trying to banish the thought of Mr. Fitzjohn—how would Lord Bollington's death affect Gareth's situation? Would Elaine Carteret, once she was satisfied with her share of the estate, cease her attempts to injure or discredit Delphie and Mrs. Carteret? Presumably she would now be more anxious than ever to marry Gareth—who must now be Lord Bollington, the Eighth Viscount. Would Gareth be relieved of his cares and anxieties—secure in his own fortune, and, it was to be hoped, free of the responsibility for his sister, who would now have money of her own?

Oh, how I wish that I could discuss some of these matters with Gareth! Delphie confessed miserably to herself. But there would be no possible chance of *that*; he had made it abundantly plain that he regretted his association with her. Every scrap of pride and self-respect now dictated that she keep entirely out of his way and make not the slightest effort to approach him. Doubtless he would now wish to marry his Lady Laura What-was-her-name—supposing her now to be rid of her elderly infirm husband? (That was, of course, if he could get away from Elaine Carteret.) Well, Lady Laura was welcome to him, thought Delphie miserably, shifting yet again on her hard pallet; probably Lady Laura was not aware what a devilish temper, what a disagreeably puritanical nature, what an atrociously hard and unsympathetic heart he had! Imagine speaking in *such* a way to children who thought they had done something useful! It was fortunate that he had none of his own.

Uncomforted by any of these considerations, Delphie at last fell into a brief deep slumber, from which, all too soon, she was abruptly aroused by Mrs. Andrews, come to tell her with gloomy relish,

"The undertakers' men is here, miss, to remove the mortal relics of the poor gentleman as died. Ah well," she went on, "*he* was one that ate of the goose that shall graze on his grave! Ain't it singular to think, miss, that at this very time yesterday—give or take half a dozen hours—we was podding the peas and buttering the lobsters that was to carry the poor soul to his rest? We mid as well ha' spared ourselves the pains! If your name be cheese, lay not your head upon the grocer's counter!" With which obscure and menacing proverb she went cheerfully away to brew Mrs. Carteret's morning chocolate.

Delphie wondered if the children had managed to smuggle their father back into jail. She had left the back door unlocked for their return, reckless of the risk of burglars; but did not know whether they had slipped in during her short period of sleep. But she did not like to go upstairs and inquire, for fear of encountering Gareth.

However, while she was assisting Bardwell to remove the last leaves of the dinner table from her parlor, Gareth came down the stairs, dressed in severe black, with a very carefully tied white neckcloth. His expression was forbidding, and Delphie made no attempt to approach him.

He, however, paused when he saw her; made as if to speak; appeared to change his mind; finally said,

"How does Mrs. Carteret do this morning?"

"Only tolerably, thank you."

"You will not—" He paused again. "You will not think of removing her today?"

"No," Delphie said reluctantly. "Her state is too low. I believe I must not."

In any case, she thought, before removing her, I need to find another lodging to remove her *to*. I will go and consult Jenny about it—and apologize, too.

Gareth said, with haughty composure,

"Do not be thinking, ma'am, that my presence here need incommode you or—or cast you into affliction—during the next few days. I am about to see my uncle's man of business; then I shall be obliged to go to Chase—very soon—if not directly—for there will be the funeral to arrange, and other tasks of a similar nature. Pray, therefore, remain here as long as you think necessary."

She curtsied in silence. Taking his hat from a chair, he went out, slamming the front door behind him.

Delphie waited, biting her lip, until the sound of his rapid footsteps had died away down the street; then she ran up to the second story to find the children.

They were all assembled in their schoolroom (a somewhat battered chamber, furnished with a kitchen table, two globes, and half a dozen broken-backed chairs). The girls were silently cutting out paper dolls, while the boys carved spinning tops from chips of wood. They seemed unusually subdued. However, they greeted Delphie with apparent pleasure, and when she asked if they had succeeded in slipping Mr. Palgrave back into prison again, they assured her that it had been as easy as pie, had all gone off like clockwork, and that Papa had seemed quite pleased to return to the peace and seclusion of his prison quarters.

"But we forgot the canary!" Isa said. "We must remember to take it with Papa's supper tonight."

"Did your Mama get to hear of all this?"

"No," Arthur said. "Uncle Gareth said it would be best not to afflict her spirits by telling her, as it would be such a disappointment that he had come and gone without even seeing her. However, he said, now Great-uncle Bollington is dead, it may only be a short time before he can get Papa out of jail; he can *borrow on his expectations*, he says."

"I hope that your uncle has apologized to you for flying out at you in such a way last night," Delphie said severely. "I was never more shocked in my life."

Tristram grinned. "He can fairly rip off when something puts him in a tweak, can't he, though? But I will say for Uncle Gareth, he don't bear a grudge. It's sharp while it lasts—but it's soon cry, soon fly, with him. In fact, he's a great gun! He has given us the money to go to Astley's, tonight, as he may have to travel to Chase and could not come with us, in any case, because of great-uncle's death, which is a great shame, it seems to me! I suppose," he added reflectively, "I suppose it *was* rather a totty-headed notion to rescue Papa. But it was prime fun while it lasted, and I'm not sorry we did it."

Relieved at this news, and feeling slightly more in charity with Gareth, Delphie was turning to go downstairs, when a faint voice from across the hall called out,

"Is that Cousin Delphie?" and she was obliged to step through and have a word with Gareth's sister.

The news of Lord Bollington's death had evidently, Delphie was interested to observe, had a most salubrious and revivifying effect upon Una. She was sitting up in an armchair, pink-cheeked, sipping at a cup of chocolate, and demanded, as soon as she saw Delphie,

"When is the funeral to be? And where?"

"At Chase, I believe," Delphie said.

"Ah, so it should be." Una nodded approvingly. "That will be much better. The country air will be good for me—and for the children too. I daresay Gareth will be arranging for carriages to take us down? I shall have to procure a new black silk; the one I wore for Mamma's funeral has become wretchedly shabby; it will not do for Lord Bollington's sister. Gloves, too, and a hat. Shall you be going into blacks, Cousin Delphie?" she added, in a tone of mild reprobation, eyeing Delphie's sprig-muslin. "You will surely wear black to the funeral?"

"I have not given the matter much thought," Delphie answered. In fact she had little expectation of attending the funeral, and certainly none of attending it uninvited. She told herself that she never wished to set foot in Chase again.

"I must leave you now," she said, moving toward the door. "Mamma is expecting a visitor."

"Pray, do, my dear Delphie, come and sit with me this evening!" begged Una. "I have hardly had a chance to converse with you yet. I long to know you better. My nerves, too, have been so much oppressed by the thought of that poor old man's death downstairs! And Gareth is going out of town—I shall feel sadly solitary."

Strongly suspecting that Una merely wished for a detailed account of the events of the previous evening, Delphie replied with civil regret that she was unable to come up that night; she and her mother had an engagement to dine in Russell Square, and, for Mrs. Carteret's sake thought it best to fulfill it if possible: her mother's spirits sadly needed the distraction of cheerful company. For this was the day of their dinner at Mr. Browty's house. How long it seemed since the invitation had been issued!

Una's eyes sparkled with curiosity at this information.

"An engagement—in Russell Square?" she cried archly. "And without your husband? Fie! La, brother Gareth's nose will be quite out of joint."

Delphie explained, rather stiffly, that the host was the parent of two of her pupils—but Una insisted on extracting every detail as to Mr. Browty's age, income, and matrimonial status, and finally gave it as her opinion (in a very rallying manner) that Delphie was a sly puss, a sad flirt, playing a deep game, cunning as a cartload of apes, all of which playfulnesses and pleasantries made Delphie feel exceedingly awkward and uncomfortable.

She was glad to make her escape from Una and run down the stairs to receive Lady Bablock-Hythe, who arrived promptly at ten in a claret-colored barouche with a very powdered coachman and two outriders, which hardly seemed necessary for the short trip from Brook Street.

A couple of hours' cheerful chat with her old friend did much to restore the tone of Mrs. Carteret's spirits. Not a word was said of yesterday's sad and frightening events. Instead, the two friends had a thoroughly enjoyable time recalling events of their schooldays, and vilifying various of their preceptresses. Delphie soon formed the opinion that Lady Bablock-Hythe was remarkably silly, though abounding in good humor.

"But tell me one thing, Ella my love," said Lady Bablock-Hythe after a number of these reminiscences. "If *this* young lady is your charming daughter—then who is the *other* young lady, who has been residing with me for the past two years, whom I have brought into polite society and introduced everywhere under the impression that she was your daughter—that she was Miss Carteret? She, I apprehend, is your niece—your husband's brother's daughter?"

"Why that, ma'am, I am sure I can't tell you!" declared Mrs. Carteret. "It has me in quite a puzzle! I met the young lady at your house yesterday, and very disagreeable I thought her! She certainly is no child of mine! I only ever had the one—my sweet Philadelphia here—for although there were two little boys before she was born, both of them died, poor little angels. So who *that* young lady is, I cannot imagine! For my dear husband had no brother."

"If this is indeed so," remarked Lady Bablock-Hythe, "it seems plain that she must be a rank imposter—and I shall turn her out of my house without delay! Passing herself off as your child, indeed! Telling me that you had died in childbirth!"

"Indeed it is very singular," said Mrs. Carteret perplexedly, as Lady Bablock-Hythe collected her reticule and parasol and rose to take her leave. "Good-by, my dearest, sweetest Maria! Pray let us see one another again very soon!"

Her dearest Maria then propounded a plan which had that instant come into her head: as soon as the false Miss Carteret and her maid had been evicted, why should not the real one, with her amiable Mama, come to Brook Street for a visit of several weeks?

"I should like it of all things, my dearest Ella! For we still have a thousand things to talk about—and I quite long to show you my collection of tropical feathers, cowrie shells, recipes for Native Foods, and a great number of sketches done by my first dear husband!"

Encouraged by the promise of these treats, Mrs. Carteret said she, too, would like the visit of all things; and Lady Bablock-Hythe promised to inform them by a note as soon as she should have rid herself of the false imposters, and propose a time for the true Carterets to come.

Delphie did not look forward to this visit with any great delight, for she found Lady Bablock-Hythe something less than sensible; but she seemed a good-natured woman enough, and genuinely fond of Mrs. Carteret, and this would certainly be a solution to the problem of their continued residence in Curzon Street. From Brook Street, Delphie could at her leisure set about the task of finding a new lodging.

"And I shall arrange no end of outings and parties for you both!" Lady Bablock-Hythe promised happily. "For outings and parties are what I like best in the world."

Delphie replied with all that was proper, but stipulated that she must continue giving lessons to her pupils—did Lady Bablock-Hythe have a pianoforte in her house, or should Delphie bring her own?

"Lessons!" said Lady Bablock-Hythe with a small shriek. "You are not to be giving *lessons*, you poor little thing! I shall take you to Vauxhall and procure you vouchers for Almacks, and fit you out with something rather more in the mode than that dowdyish sprig-muslin."

"There!" said Mrs. Carteret rejoicingly when her friend had gone. "Did I not tell you, my love, that presently our fortunes would take a turn for the better? *Now* I do not at all despair of your forming some eligible connection!"

And, betaking herself once more to her pencil and pieces of paper, Mrs. Carteret began happily planning menus for a rout party of five hundred guests, followed by a Masquerade.

Delphie knew she ought to be glad that her mother's spirits were better. But her own were very low. She dutifully gave a lesson to Miss Smith (who this time, fortunately, had remembered to practice her aria); then, seeing her pupil off the premises, remarked a hackney carriage pull up by the front door. Out of it stepped Gareth, and, to Delphie's astonishment, Mr. Palgrave. The latter appeared calm, serene, pensive, and quite unaffected by the adventures of the night. Gareth *must* have borrowed on his expectations, Delphie surmised. The two men walked upstairs without observing her, and Delphie went to assist her mother dress for the evening at the Browtys'.

Mr. Browty kept early hours, and his carriage arrived to pick them up at four o'clock. Delphie, wearing her white dress and a shawl, was just helping her mother up the carriage steps, when Gareth came out with a brow of thunder.

He said,

"You are taking your mother *out*, at this hour of the day? How *can* you think that a sensible thing to do?"

His manner was so harsh and abrupt that Mrs. Carteret paused and gazed at him wonderingly.

Delphie replied than an evening passed in pleasant, rational, tranquil intercourse with agreeable friends could not help but promote her mother's well-being, and was just what she needed. Mrs. Carteret had been looking forward to the evening all week, she added. She went on to mention that very shortly—tomorrow perhaps—she and her mother would be removing to Lady Bablock-Hythe's house in Brook Street.

Gareth's brows drew together at this information.

"What of Elaine? You can hardly be there together? When—and where—does she go?"

"I have no idea," Delphie coldly replied. "I am not cognizant of her plans."

"I shall be obliged to see you—to discuss—" he began, but Delphie, interrupting, said with finality,

"Forgive me, cousin, but we keep Mr. Browty's horses waiting. I think you should write—if you have anything to say—write to me at Lady Bablock-Hythe's direction."

And she stepped into the carriage.

The evening in Russell Square seemed very long. Mr. Browty was a kindly and attentive host, but Delphie could not help finding that the hours dragged, and the entertainment was somewhat insipid. Out of consideration for Mrs. Carteret's recent illness, no other company but themselves had been invited, and the rest consisted of Mr. Browty, his girls, and their governess, Miss Beak, a dried-up little woman whose conversation was limited to the exclamation "Well I declare!" uttered at every appropriate and inappropriate juncture.

The repast served was certainly splendid—three times as lavish as that contrived for Great-uncle Mark—but Delphie found that she was not hungry.

"You are tired, Miss Philadelphia," said Mr. Browty kindly. "I shall take the liberty of ordering the carriage for you early. You had a disturbed night of it."

Delphie had given him a brief account of Lord Bollington's death, to which he had listened with the greatest interest.

"So your cousin will be the new Viscount, eh?" He gazed at Delphie speculatively, and she, on an impulse, inquired,

"Do you know anything of my cousin's history, sir? I am very ill informed about him, since the branches of the family have always remained separate."

"I know only what I heard at the club this morning, m'dear: that he has had a hard time of it, making ends meet; that Lady Laura Trevelyan threw him over when she discovered that he was obliged to support his sister and ten nephews and nieces on the income from his manor (sister's husband dead or overseas, I understand; what happened to him did not seem to be known). And they say that your cousin was so enraged at the jilt—and at his sister's ill-judged marriage that had brought him to such a pass in the first place—that he swore a solemn oath in White's club, in front of all his friends, that *he* would never form such a foolish, imprudent alliance; that unless he could satisfy every requirement of sense, prudence, and rational moderation in his matrimonial arrangement—or some such rigmarole, I do not recollect the exact words—" said Mr. Browty, "he would never marry at all."

"Oh, indeed?" said Delphie faintly. "I have—I have certainly observed that he is not very lenient toward romance or sentiment—or toward the female sex. But indeed, his sister is enough to put anybody out of patience."

Let alone the sister's husband, she thought.

"Well, well," said Mr. Browty. "Young men make such vows! But then they think better of them. However, now he has come into a fortune there will be plenty of ladies setting their caps at him—he will be able to choose sensibly enough, I dare say."

"Yes. No doubt."

"I hope," continued Mr. Browty, "that he will be more inclined to be liberal to you and your Mama than his uncle was."

"I place no dependence on it."

"You will not have heard yet as to your Mama's annuity? I dare say the will has not been read yet?"

"Not to my knowledge," said Delphie. Then, observing that her mother was comfortably engaged in a game of whist with Miss Beak and the two girls, she said,

"Mr. Browty?"

"Ay, my dear?"

"About that matter—about the subject which you raised last week in Russell Square garden—?"

"Ay—ay—" Mr. Browty nodded hastily. "I know what you will be at, Miss Philadelphia! Mum's the word!"—glancing indulgently at the whist players. "There they are, so snugly engaged, never dreaming we are looking their way, bless them! They do not hear us. As to that other matter, my dear," he went on, very rapidly, before Delphie could speak, "I have been thinking around it, as you bade me, and I have come to the conclusion that you were quite right—quite right, my dear! We should not suit! January and

May, youth and age—no, no, you were perfectly in the right, and it would not have done. Besides, now your great-uncle's underground, I dare swear that you will be well on the way to making a fine match of it yourself! So we'll shake hands on the matter, shall we, and say no more about it?"

He held out his hand, and, rather disconcerted, Delphie laid hers in it. The interview had not gone in the least as she had planned. But, left with no alternative, she replied,

"Yes, sir; that is—no."

"Now, then," pursued Mr. Browty, "there's another thing I was wishful to say to you, Miss Philadelphia, while the gals were all busy at their cards."

"Indeed, Mr. Browty? What is that?"

"I happened to be closeted with my man of business today, who is a devilish clever follow—a lawyer named Mundwinch—looks after the affairs of half the titled snobs in the Kingdom—wonderful attorney he is—you can trust Jos. Browty to find out the best—"

"Yes, sir?" said Delphie, as he seemed to have lost his thread.

"Ah, yes, old Mundwinch; he told me a deucedly queer tale. That cousin of yours, the new Viscount, had best look out; he ain't above high-water mark yet!"

"What can you possibly mean, sir?"

"Why, Mundwinch—knowing I've an interest in Lord Bollington—told me that he had been approached (this was in strict confidence, mind, for I'm one of his best clients, and he knew I wouldn't pass it on and," said Mr. Browty robustly, "*I* know *you* won't pass it on, Miss Philadelphia—)"

"No indeed! You can have confidence in me. But who approached him, Mr. Browty?"

"Fellow by the name of Fitzjohn—seems he's some wrong-side-o'-the-blanket connection of Lord Bollington."

"Certainly; I have met him. He was my great-uncle's agent, and I am bound to say that Uncle Mark spoke highly of him."

Insofar as he was capable of it, Delphie thought.

"Hah! Well, no sooner is your uncle cold on his bed than Master Fitzjohn is around at Mundwinch's office, bringing a suit to prove that *he's* the rightful heir!" said Mr. Browty triumphantly. "So maybe you'd best wait awhile before deciding which cousin to aim for, Miss Philadelphia! Aha, you look surprised! Thought that'd have you took aback! Directly I heard that news, I thought, Miss Philadelphia would take an interest in that. So you had best warn your great-cousin to be on the lookout—naming no names, of course!"

"I will indeed, sir, and thank you! But what a strange thing! How can that possibly be?"

"Ah well, the way Mundwinch had it, this here Fitz has papers to prove that his granda was *married* to some wench that all the world thought was only his bit of frippet—if I don't offend you, Miss Philadelphia?"

"Not in the least, sir; facts must be looked in the face. But—good God! If that were the case, then not only my cousin Gareth—but also my great-uncle Mark would have been out of the succession; in which case, *whatever* will he has made would, I suppose, be invalid!"

"Ah, you've a right smart head on your shoulders, lass! I daresay you should ha' been a man," remarked Mr. Browty. "Trust you to seize the nub of the case in a twinkling!"

"Thank you, sir," she said, rather wanly. "You have given me a great deal to think about. I wonder why Mr. Fitzjohn did not bring the suit before, while great-uncle Mark was still alive?"

"Doubtless," said Mr. Browty, "if he had expectations under that Lord Bollington's will, he thought it best to secure 'em, before trying for more. Didn't want to lose his cheese for the moon! The old feller would hardly have made a bequest to someone whom he might consider a Viper in his bosom."

"Yes—I daresay," said Delphie. "But I believe they have just finished their card game and we should be thinking of returning home—to Curzon Street. It has been a most enjoyable evening, Mr. Browty."

Which polite statement was, from Delphie's point of view, very far from the truth.

14

On the following morning, early, Mrs. Carteret received a note from her friend Lady Bablock-Hythe:

My dearest Ella:

I write to inform you that I have lost no Time in Evicting that bold-fac'd Creature from my residence, together with her Odious Maid. Needless to say, she was all Innocence and Ignorance; could not Imagine how I cd believe such a Tale of her, was in Despair that she had lost my Favour, &c; Then How, Miss, said I, can it be that you told me of your Mamma's Death in childbed & now I find that it is No Such Thing, that my Sweet Freind has all this time been living but a Bowshot from Brook St? Answer me that, Miss? Alas, Ma'am, says she, I must confess that here I fell into a trifling Prevarication; the truth being that I did not wish to distress you—for Mrs. Carteret, my Mamma, has run Mad any time these 20 years & is given, at times, to fits of the most Horrid nature; not only which, but, due to her Insanity, she quite refuses to Acknowledge me, has adopted another young lady, who comes from I know not where, & in proof of the Truth of what I say, & my own Claims, I can here shew you a Certificate of my birth. Pho, pho, Miss, says I, wd you have me beleive some dirty bit of Paper sooner than the evidence of my own Eyes & ears? My dear freind Mrs C acknowledges the sweet Philadelphia as her own Daughter, & that is enough for me. Alas, Ma'am, says she, Feigning to wipe a tear from her false Eye, but this young Person that my Mamma is putting forward may indeed be a daughter of her's, but as to what kind of person was her Father, who can say? for she was born after the death of Captain Carteret (my late esteem'd Parent) and subsequent to my Mother's Madness.—You can imagine, my sweetest Ella, that I did not stand idly by & hear you thus scandalously Traduced. Out upon you, you False, Spiteful creature, I will listen to no more of your Duplicity (cried I); I must request you instantly to leave the protection of my Roof & betake yourself elsewhere. Oh, Madam, cries She, all tears, if you desert me where ever shall I go? That, says I, I neither know nor Care, so I am not subjected to your Impostures & Deceits for another half-hour, & so I turned my back on her & desired the servants to see that She and her belongings were forth from the House by nine o'clock. I believe she is now Gone & I am all impatience to welcome my Ella & her Delightful child in that Harpy's place. Do not delay, therefore, my dearest freind, but pray make haste to come today, by noon, if it may be done; if This is Convenient to you, I will have my Carriage sent shortly before that Hour in order that we may Continue the Felicities of our Sweet recollections & mutual discourse & I may have the Pleasure of introducing your dear Philadelphia to the Polite World.

I remain, Sweet Freind,

Your ever-devoted & affectionate,
Maria Bablock-Hythe.

Mrs. Carteret's gratification at this epistle was somewhat alloyed by learning of the scandalous slanders being spread about her by her pretended daughter, but Delphie did her best to make light of these, and turn her mother's thoughts in a more cheerful direction.

"After all," Delphie pointed out, "now that Lady Bablock-Hythe has withdrawn her protection and favor from the young lady, nobody will pay any regard to what she says; it will be universally assumed that *she* was the imposter, and, since no one suggests that you are not the true Mrs. Carteret, your version of the case must be believed."

"I'm sure I hope so," said Mrs. Carteret rather dolefully. "It is all very singular, Delphie, and I think it a great shame that persons should tell such lies about us!"

Delphie then easily distracted her mother by asking what garments she thought they ought to take with them to Lady Bablock-Hythe's residence, a needless question, since both their wardrobes were so small that their only possible recourse was to take everything they possessed, but it had the effect of diverting Mrs. Carteret into a discussion of what it would be suitable to wear for morning calls, card parties, an evening at Vauxhall Gardens, or an Assembly at Almacks.

Delphie listened unmoved to an account of the pleasures that were probably in store for them; her heart was heavy, and, despite her reassurances to her mother, she was in considerable anxiety as to what harm the false Miss Carteret, in her rage at being dislodged from her secure footing in Brook Street, might attempt to do to them.

When they had packed up their clothes, Delphie mounted the stairs in order to take leave of the Palgrave family.

She had imagined that, now Mr. Palgrave was returned to the bosom of his family, Una would be less anxious for her own company, but this proved not at all the case.

Mr. Palgrave, it seemed, had already appropriated one of the rooms on the top floor for his exclusive use as sanctum and study; he spent all his time there, and was hardly more to be seen than he had been during his incarceration in the Marshalsea. Indeed, the only persons who benefited from his release were the children, no longer obliged to carry his meals to Southwark twice daily; and their joy was not unalloyed, for they reported that Papa was forever putting his head out of the door to bid them make less noise; while his wife seemed to derive no pleasure from his return whatsoever, and made no secret of her resentment at his unaccommodating ways.

"He never speaks, save to complain of the children, or his room, or to ask for something," said she. "I declare he is worse than Gareth—men are odious creatures! He has no consideration whatsoever for my afflicted state of health!" And when Delphie announced their imminent departure, her distress equaled that of somebody losing a lifetime's friend.

"Oh, my dearest Delphie, are you indeed leaving us? Oh, how acutely shall I miss your sweet companionship! I trust that your removal will be of short duration, and that you will soon be returning to us?"

Delphie said that she did not think so. Her mother's spirits had been so deeply affected by the death of Lord Bollington, that the house had acquired unhappy associations for her, and nothing but a complete change of scene could restore her serenity. (This, if not the entire truth, contained such a large element of it as to be, she thought, a reasonable excuse to offer for their sudden departure.) Una, however, was by no means satisfied.

"Oh, my dear, dear cousin, pray reconsider! I shall be so lonely here!"

"What, with ten children and your husband? And your brother too?"

"But only think! Gareth will probably now reside at Chase, or at my uncle's house in Hanover Square; Thomas never comes out of his study; and the children, poor little things, are merely an exhaustion to my nerves. And if," said Una, with a conscious and somewhat guilty glance at her cousin, "if, my dear Delphie, by any chance it was some slight playful remarks I may have passed to Gareth about your dining in Russell Square—some sportive or rallying allusions to the worthy Mr. Browty—only in fun, be certain!—which may have put some little nonsense into his mind—and perhaps caused him to be somewhat brusque with you—I am indeed sorry for it! Nothing was further from my intention than to make any trouble between you, and I hope you are not at outs with me? Gareth is in such a fidgety mood at present that the least thing puts him in a tweak; I am sure I do not know what ails him!"

Delphie coolly replied that she had been quite unaware Mr. Penistone was not in spirits, and pray let his sister not concern herself with such a slight matter, when there were so many weighty affairs to be dealt with; she was sure when Lord Bollington's business cares were settled he would be in an easier frame of mind; and she hoped, also, that the settlement of Great-uncle Mark's will would soon produce more comfortable circumstances for the Palgrave family. Una's face brightened at this cheerful thought, and Delphie left her, not sorry to think that she was removing from the neighborhood of such a whining mischief-maker.

She said good-by to the children, who received the news that she was leaving with unaffected disappointment.

"For you gave us such a bang-up supper, the other night, Cousin Delphie! The little ones said there had been nothing like it since Papa went to jail! Must you really go? We was in hopes you'd come with us to Hampton Court some time."

"Well, perhaps I may be able to do that, when we are settled in our new lodging," said Delphie. "I dare say we shall not be very far away."

She could not restrain a sigh as she thought of the rooms downstairs, so sunny and spacious. Putting aside this regret, she inquired about the excursion to Astley's Amphitheatre, and was told that it had been prime, bang-up, the best lark in the world, the most amazing thing possible; they had bought two halfpennyworths of apples, had had excellent seats, and had enjoyed the evening beyond anything.

The Carterets' removal was achieved without hindrance; Gareth, evidently, was out of London, or, at least, not to be seen. Lady Bablock-Hythe greeted them most affectionately on their arrival in Brook Street, led them to luxuriously furnished apartments fitted with everything they could possibly require, and was full of a thousand plans for their entertainment.

It was plain, however, that at least some hours of quiet rest and domestic peace were what Mrs. Carteret really needed, and her good-natured hostess soon realizing this, the two friends immediately settled down to a continuation of their enjoyable chat.

Delphie, observing this with pleasure, made her excuses and mentioned that she had a lesson to give in Berkeley Square. Lady Bablock-Hythe was scandalized at the thought of a young lady going about London on her own, and offered a maid to escort her, but this Philadelphia politely declined.

"Indeed, ma'am, I am quite used to go about unescorted, and have never suffered the least annoyance, I assure you."

"Oh dear! Really it is quite Gothick, you know, and will not do at all! Fortunately at the *moment* nobody knows you, but as soon as I have introduced you at Almacks, you will really have to give over these gadabout ways, my dear—or I do not see how we shall ever succeed in securing an eligible connection for you and establishing you creditably."

Delphie laughed, and made her escape, leaving the two ladies to shake their heads and discuss plans for launching her in polite society. She felt more than a little dismayed at the prospect. In the first place, until her mother's annuity was a settled thing, it would be highly impolitic to reduce her own earnings by discontinuing the lessons she gave; the Carterets could not rely on the continued hospitality of Lady Bablock-Hythe; nor, even had she offered it, had Delphie any intention of accepting her good offices for more than a limited period. Lady Bablock-Hythe was too foolish for any dependence to be placed on her assistance.

Even more dismaying was the thought of the eligible connection they intended to arrange for her. I wonder if Gareth has done anything yet about getting our marriage annulled? thought Delphie as she walked in the direction of Berkeley Square. I wonder if there will be *very* much public notice attached to the process? Whether I shall have to appear in a court? Or make a declaration?

The whole idea was so disagreeable and lowering that she resolved to try and put it out of her mind for a few days; she imagined that Gareth, busy with the funeral arrangements at Chase, would hardly have had time to set about the annulment. However, Delphie resolved that if she did not hear from him about it within ten days or so, she would herself have recourse to a lawyer, perhaps the Mr. Mundwinch spoken of in such enthusiastic terms by Mr. Browty.

But then an even more dismaying thought struck her—if her marriage to Gareth were annulled, would that invalidate Lord Bollington's will? I must consult a lawyer without delay, she resolved.

After the lesson had been given, Delphie walked around to Greek Street to acquaint Miss Baggott of her new direction, and inform the sisters of Mr. Palgrave's second and more legal release from jail. She also wished to apologize to Jenny for Gareth's tirade after the rescue, but that volatile young lady made nothing of it.

"Lor, Miss Delphie, it was an education to hear him! I only wish Sister could ha' been there; I have been trying to recollect his language ever since, I declare! It was as good as a play, I said to Anne, I quite fancied myself in Drury Lane. And I'm as happy as can be to hear that the poor gentleman has been set free after all, for it seemed the saddest thing in the world that he must go back into the Clink after all our trouble."

Delphie thanked her again, very warmly, for her part in the operation, however misjudged, and inquired after Mr. Swannup and the wedding plans.

"La, miss, he's forever here now," said Anne, "and indeed I shall be glad when the wedding's over, for it fills my sister's head so there's room for nothing else—not that there ever was much!"

"Oh, Miss Delphie, I hope you'll do us the honor to be present!" cried Jenny. "It's to be at the church in Golden Square a fortnit on Saturday, and, indeed, if *you* can't be there I shall think it hardly worth being married at all, so kind as you've been to us."

Delphie readily promised her attendance (after all, Jenny had been at *her* wedding, she reflected); she asked where the young couple were to live, and was informed that the gentleman in the wool hosiery and hat business had been told that the rooms upstairs were not vacant after all, and the Swannups would inhabit them.

"So it's all turned out just right and tight, Miss Delphie," Jenny said happily, "and I only hope you'll be as happy as us, dearie, with *your* gentleman, when you've come to know each other a little better! For sure, what's a few words spoke in a passion? I like a man as can speak his mind far better than your mimbling mumchance glum grudge-bearers!"

Allowing this to be true, Delphie nevertheless gave Jenny to understand that there was no future in *that* connection, and that she proposed moving out of the house in Curzon Street as soon as possible. Jenny's face fell grievously at this information, and she was trying strongly to dissuade Delphie from this course of action, when Mr. Swannup entered the shop, looking very breathless and alarmed.

For some minutes, such was the speed with which he had run along the street, that he could say nothing at all, but merely gasp and gape. His face was quite scarlet from running, and his ginger hair stood up in a damp topknot.

"Mercy on us, Sam, what can be the matter?" cried Jenny in amazement, while Anne went to procure him a glass of water.

When he had drunk it down, they were not materially better informed as to the cause of his excitement, for he could only exclaim,

"Treason! Villainy! Horrible knavery! O, what nasty havey-cavey dealings!"

"What's the matter, Sam?" said Miss Anne, presently becoming impatient with this. "Do, for heaven's sake, tell us a round tale!"

At last he had quieted down enough to do so.

"I'm that pleased to find *you* here, Miss Carteret, ma'am, for it was to discover your direction I came here, having first run all the way to Curzon Street, only to discover you was removed from there, and none to tell me where you had gone! Oh, whatever shall I do now, says I to myself, and then I recollected that Miss Baggott might have your direction."

"Indeed, I am sorry you have had all this running about on my behalf, Mr. Swannup," said Delphie, "but, pray, what has put you into such a state of agitation?"

"Well, miss, here's how it all was: My friend Mr. Bardwell as looks after Mr. Penistone (now become Lord B.)—Mr. Bardwell had put me in the way of a little job of work at Lord Bollington's residence in Hanover Square, where they wanted hatchments setting up over the doors, in mourning for the old gent as died, and also some of the locks on the doors wanted mending, for indeed his old lordship had let the whole house fall into a sorry state . . ."

Here he paused to take breath.

"I am not surprised to hear it," said Delphie, remembering the shabby and moth-eaten state of the furnishings at Chase. "But go on, Mr. Swannup—what happened?"

"Well, miss—being as how my Jenny had given me two of her notable apple turnovers to take along with me by way of a nuncheon while I was working (and real tasty they was, too, my love," he added, "that smitch of clove you puts with the apples is a fair masterpiece!); as I was saying, miss, being wishful to eat my nuncheon somewhere unespied by persons who might chance to walk in and out of the room where I was working, I bethought me to take refuge in a kind of a little gallery, where I sat myself down on the floor (for there was no chair) behind a big desk, and in between that and some railings. A rug was throwed over the railings, so I was as safe and snug, miss, as if I had been in a rabbit burrow."

"Where was this, Mr. Swannup?" Delphie asked, somewhat perplexed by his description.

"It was in the library, miss, of Lord Bollington's house in Hanover Square, where I was a-mending of a lock. Well, as I chanced to sit there quietly, miss, a-munching of my Jenny's turnover and a-thinking of her beautiful black eyes, what should chance to walk into the room below me but two persons. And before I could make my presence known to 'em, miss—though not anxious to do so, if you will believe me, for Jenny's pastry is *that* flaky and I was all over turnover crumbs—what should I hear but a voice pronouncing your name, miss!"

"Oh?" said Delphie rather blankly.

"Yes, miss! You may well say oh! 'What the devil are *you* doing here, Miss Carteret?' says the voice. I knows it, for it was the voice of that Mr. Fitzjohn, who acts as bailiff and steward and so forth to Lord Bollington; it was he who had instructed me about the work I was to do. 'What the deuce are *you* doing here?' he says. Well, miss, when I hears the name *Carteret*, I lifts just a tiddy twitch o' the rug, and claps my eye to the chink, and looks down into the room below; there stands Mr. Fitz, with a young lady I never laid eyes on before in my whole life! A monstrous fashionable young lady in a sarcenet pelisse (like the one we was a-looking at for you, Jenny) and a feather in her hat—"

"What color—?" began Jenny, but Miss Anne exclaimed,

"What is *that* to the purpose? Hold your tongue, do, Jenny, and let Sam tell his tale!"

"Well," said Sam, "I was just a-thinking, This is not *my* Miss Carteret, and may be no connection at all, when the young lady breaks out in a great tweak and taking. 'Oh, Mordred,' says she, 'it is too provoking for words! That ninnyhammer of a Lady Bablock-Hythe,' says she, 'has encountered Mrs. Carteret, who has told her some tiresome tale—' 'Met Mrs. Carteret?' says he, sounding very put out, 'Pray, how in the world did *they* chance to meet?' 'In the street,' says she, 'it is the most vexatious thing! And the long and the short of it is, Mordred, that Durnett and I have been given our marching orders and told to leave Brook Street, since the odious Lady Bablock-Hythe chooses to believe *their* tale rather than *mine!* So I have come here, Mordred!' says she, 'for where else can I go? What is happening now about that wretched girl, Mordred?' says she. 'Does Gareth believe in her tale or not?' 'How should I know?' says he, sounding mightily displeased. 'Gareth does not take *me* into his confidence. But they *have* had a quarrel, I know that, for he came here in a blazing rage at her, and has now posted down to Chase, declaring that he wishes the whole of womenkind were at the devil.' 'Aha, so he will have their marriage annulled, will he?' says she, sounding as joyful as if she had just been left fifty thousand in the Funds. 'What is that to *you?*' says Mr. Fitz, as surly as a baited bear. 'You know you are promised to *me*, and have been these five years past!' 'Now, Mordred!' cries she. 'Do but be practical. Let us understand one another.' 'Yes, by all means let us,' says he. 'Our understanding only holds good,' says she, 'on condition you win your suit, and become Lord Bollington. But in the meantime,' says she, 'I must look out for myself, and my best means of doing *that* is to marry Gareth. Then—if you win your suit—it will be the easiest thing in the world to put Gareth out of the way—a dish of oysters, or a carriage accident, or an accidental drowning, or some such thing—' 'And if I should *not* win my case?' says he, surlier still. 'Then *you* will be Lady Bollington and I shall be nothing at all—then what shall you do?' 'Why,' she says, airy as a feather, 'even then, some accident may occur, and I will be the widowed Lady Bollington, with all the revenues, and can marry you, and at least we will be the better for that!' 'And what about Mrs. Carteret and Miss Philadelphia, now Lady Bablock-Hythe believes their tale?' says he. 'Oh,' says she, 'we can soon find some means to rid ourselves of *them*—I do not regard them at all! Indeed it is only by sheer unlucky mischance that they are not already disposed of. We might discredit them easily enough, could I possess myself of their papers. (If I had not employed that stupid boy I should have them by now,' she said.) 'Or we might have it put about that she poisoned Lord Bollington.' 'That cock won't fight,' says he, 'for the Crowner's Quest this morning has brought in a verdict of Accidental Death. I do not trust you, Elaine,' says he. 'I do not believe you intend to marry me at all! I believe you have always loved Gareth Penistone—ever since you met him in Bath—I believe if you could secure him you would sacrifice me without a single scruple!' 'It is no such thing!' cries she. 'I love you, Elaine,' says he, 'and what is more I know the truth about you, and if *that* comes to Gareth's ears, you are properly dished, and may toss your hopes of him into the gutter. So you had best pay more heed to my wishes.' And then they begin to quarrel, going at one another like cat and dog, and all the time I was in a fair quake, lest someone should come in and discover me, and they therefore learn I had heard all they said."

"Great heaven!" cried Delphie, aghast. "What hideous revelations of duplicity! What outrageous monsters are these! How can such things be?"

In point of fact she was not quite so surprised as her words suggested, for she had never reposed full confidence in Mr. Fitzjohn, while Miss Carteret had from the outset made it plain that she was her open enemy. But Mr. Swannup had told his tale with such emphasis, such flashing eyes, and such a wealth of dramatic gesture, that she felt he was entitled to a fair meed of astonishment in return.

"Ah, but wait, miss—there's more yet!" he said triumphantly. "And even blacker deceit! Just you listen while I tell you. After they had quarreled for a number of minutes, she says, 'Well, if you do not want me here, I shall go down to Chase; it will be proper for me to attend the funeral in any case,' she says. 'And while I am there, ten to one I can fix my interest with Gareth, if he has quarreled with *Miss Philadelphia*.' Oh, the nasty way she said those words, miss—it fair made my blood boil! 'And once I have fixed my interest with Gareth,' says she, 'you can sing him any song you like—he will not listen!' 'You may go to the devil, with my leave,' says he. 'You are a hard-hearted selfish Vixen and I wish I had never known you and that you had never been born!' 'You are just as selfish!' cries she. 'If you had not written to me in Bath saying that the old Cull was not seriously indisposed, I should have come to Chase when he summoned me, and been married to Gareth by now. That affair was *your* doing, and I believe you wrote the letter to prevent my marrying Gareth.' 'I warn you,' says he, 'if you persist in going to Chase, I shall do what I can to queer your pitch—and there is much I can do!' 'Take heed to *yourself*, Cousin Mordred!' says she. 'For I can be an ill foe too —I could tell Cousin Gareth tales of your embezzling from the old cove that would land you properly in the basket!'

"At that Mr. Fitzjohn goes stamping out of the room. Then, to my great alarm, Miss calls out, 'Nurse! Nurse! Durnett, where are you?' Whereupon I think I am wholly in the suds, for I find there is a little old woman all the time a-listening, right there in the gallery! But after all, she has not seen me, where I am crouched behind the desk, and Miss calls out, 'Come down here, nurse, for I wish to talk to you.' So the old woman goes down and says to t'other Miss Carteret, 'You did not really intend to marry that Fitzjohn, did you, dearie?' And Miss says, 'No, I mean to marry Gareth, and always have. Mordred would be just as clutch-fisted as old Lord B. I pretended to fall in with his plans, so that he would help me; but it is Gareth I love, and I will have him somehow!' 'He don't love you,' says the old woman. 'He loves no one,' says Miss, 'but I will have him for all that, and when I have got him fast, I will teach him a thing or two!' 'You know that it is dangerous for you to go to Chase?' says the old girl. 'Why?' says she. But that question the old woman would not answer, only said again that it was dangerous. 'Well, it is a risk I will have to run,' says she. 'I do not care what danger there may be, so I can fix my interest with Gareth. He *must* marry me! I shall threaten him with the lawyers—if he won't wed me I shall tell how he deceived the old man.' 'That might be cutting off your nose to spite your face!' 'Hush your croaking!' says Miss. 'Do you go and hire a carriage and we will be off.'

"So then they quitted the chamber—and I made all haste to finish my last bite of turnover and come to find you, miss! Now, isn't that a shocking tale of wickedness and double-dealing for you!"

"It is indeed!" said Delphie. "And I am amazed that you can recall it all so clearly, Mr. Swannup! Your account was as good as a play—I could quite picture myself at the scene."

Mr. Swannup blushed with simple pride, and Jenny looked admiringly at her lover.

"Oh," he said, "that is because of my fondness for litter-ayture, miss. I have always been used to read a great quantity of poetry and plays, and also to get as much of what I read by heart as I can contrive to. In consequence I am what (on the boards) they call a *quick study*. Indeed," he said, sighing, "I have often wished that I *could* be on the boards, but Pa had me apprenticed to a locksmith."

"And look how useful that proved!" cried Jenny. "Though for sure it is a thousand pities you shouldn't have been an actor—my blood quite froze when you was a-rendering the words of those wicked murderers and all their horrid designs. But isn't it the most fiendish nasty thing you ever heard in the whole of your life, Miss Delphie? It makes my blood boil to think that Trollop is on her way to Chase, to tell all manner of wicked lies to your cousin! And, doubtless, that Mr. Fitz (who I never liked more than half, for I can't abear a freckle-faced chap) going after her! Don't you think we had best hire a chaise and pursue them, for Mr. Swannup could bowl them out by telling what he heard? We should be happy to do so, Miss Delphie!"

Delphie was rather inclined to agree, but said that she must reflect on the matter. In the meantime she urged the strictest discretion.

"Ay, never fear, miss! Mum's the word!" said Sam Swannup. "But should you wish me go get up in court, miss, and swear to all I heard, I shall be glad to oblige, Miss Delphie! I have always wished to give evidence in a Court of Law!"

Delphie walked home toward Brook Street, meditating much on what she had heard. She took her way through Hanover Square, and as she did so, she observed a curricle dash past her, drawn by two horses who were being lashed up to a dangerous pace by their driver. As he passed, she recognized him. It was Mr. Fitzjohn, driving at a breakneck speed, and with the face of a demon.

15

When Delphie re-entered the house in Brook Street she found, to her considerable surprise, that her mother and Lady Bablock-Hythe were gone out. A note from Mrs. Carteret explained this.

Dearest Child,

Mr Browty is come to take us driving in the Park. We had intended to pass the day Indoors, but his kind offer and the usually Fine Warm Weather has tempted us forth. Mr B has also suggested that we might care to share his Box at Covent Garden tonight, & invited us to dine at his house first—so it is possible Lady B & I shall not be returned until quite late. Mr B was excessively sad to miss you, but, Lord, says he, now Miss has so many Great freinds, no doubt she is occupied with some lively amusement every hour of the day & has little time left for such an old stick as I. Oh, my dear Delphie, he is the most estimable man! Such true delicacy of mind! Air and address all that it should be. He has brought me a Parasol to shade me from the heat of the sun! By the by, my dearest child, my sweet Maria had in a few freinds this morning to play at loo for 10s. points, and, only think! I was lucky enough to win 100 guineas, so here are 50 of them for you. I am very happy to be able to return to you a very small part of all you have expended on me in the last Years: pray use it for Pin Money; I shall hope to win more, as I find we shall need a considerable deal of cash at Lady B-H's house—she lives in such a fine way, & she says with truth that all our garments are sadly dowdy. It is so fortunate that I have ever enjoyed the greatest good luck at cards.

Yr. affec. Mama.

Delphie almost groaned aloud at the latter part of this letter, which filled her with consternation. Only too well did she know how far from lucky at cards Mrs. Carteret had always been, and more particularly during the period when she had attended Duvivier's Salon, when she had lost a terrifyingly large part of their scanty income. If she were to fall into the habit of deep play at Lady Bablock-Hythe's, the results would almost certainly be disastrous. Suppose that, instead of winning that hundred guineas, she had lost it! The idea was terrifying. Lady Bablock-Hythe had so little sense that Delphie did not at all depend on her protecting her simple friend from the temptations of gambling. Delphie resolved that they must remove from Brook Street as soon as might be.

She now espied another letter, which had lain under her mother's note. This one was franked from Chase, and was addressed in Gareth Penistone's small black hand.

My dear Miss Carteret:
This is to inform you that my uncle's funeral obsequies will be conducted in the Chapel here on Monday next. Should you wish to attend, a bedchamber will, of course, be prepared for you at Chase. I shd also inform you that I have instructed my Man of Business to commence Nullity proceedings; knowing your invincible Dislike of me, I was sure that you would wish no time to be lost. Though I may say that this gives me no satisfaction, as I have learned to regard you with the greatest esteem & am most sincerely sorry for any hasty words to the contrary I may have let fall the other Night.

Yr. cousin & sincere Well-Wisher,
G.P.

This letter astonished Delphie as much as the other had frightened her. She read and reread it six times at least, and was, indeed, so reluctant to lay it down that she kept it in her hand as she walked about the apartment and reflected.

What ought she to do? Absently folding the letter into a small square, she held it tightly pressed into the palm of her hand.

The thought of Mordred Fitzjohn's savagely angry face came

back into her mind. Had he been driving to Chase? She thought it very probable. The horses' heads had been turned to the east. He had looked really mad with rage—capable of any crime.

Suddenly Delphie pulled out the small carpetbag which she had taken with her on her previous excursion to Chase, and began stuffing it with a few necessities. She tugged at the bellpull and instructed the servant who appeared to procure a post chaise to take her into Kent. What a fortunate thing it was—a least in the present moment—that she had had this money from her mother!

Then she sat down and dashed off a note to Mrs. Carteret.

My dearest Mamma:
I have hired a Chaise & am about to post down to Chase on urgent business, for I have learned that the false Miss Carteret is gone there to make trouble, and also that the steward, Mr. Fitzjohn, is plotting Evil Designs against poor Mr. Penistone—Lord Bollington, I should say—and may also have gone there to do him harm. I hope somehow to put a spoke in their Wheel. I may remain for Great-uncle Mark's funeral, which is on Monday. It would be a mark of respect. Please, dearest Mamma, do not be playing at cards too much, for you know that your luck is not always to be depended upon, and almost all our savings are gone. Pray give my kindest regards to Mr. Browty, and also to Lady Bablock-Hythe.

Your loving Daughter.

And she wrote one to Jenny:

My dear Jenny:
Acting on Mr. Swannup's very kind and prompt apprisal of Mr F's wickedness and Miss C's perfidy, I have decided to go to Chase and warn my Cousin.

In haste,
P.C.

Now the servant came to tell Miss that the chaise she had bespoken was at the door, and carried down her bag for her. How quickly I am become used to having such services performed for me, she reflected as she tipped him, and handed him the two notes to deliver.

The door slammed and the chaise whirled off. It was then five o'clock.

"How long will it take you to get to Chase, in Kent?" she asked the driver. "If you go at your top speed?"

He gave it as his opinion that with luck and rapid changes of post-horses, the journey might be accomplished in something over four hours.

"I will give you double your fee if you can do it in less," Delphie told him.

"Very good, missie; we'll see what we can manage!" he said, cracking his whip.

Fortunately he had an excellent team, decidedly better than the usual run of hired horses, and Delphie was a light passenger. They made good time along the first stages of the turnpike road, though Delphie chafed at the inevitable delays when they were halted at tollgates, where, sometimes, the dilatory tollkeepers appeared to take forever to come yawning out and collect their fee.

Meanwhile Delphie had an abundance of time in which to think, and think she did, so deeply that her brain at times seemed to be in a ferment. So Mr. Fitzjohn and Miss Carteret *were* in league—or no, not precisely in league, for their schemes seemed now to run counter to one another, but evidently at some time they had been in league. But who *was* the false Miss Carteret? And how had she come by Delphie's birth certificate, which she had proffered so glibly to Lady Bablock-Hythe? Was this alone the basis of all her pretensions and claims to recognition? Then it occured to Delphie that, according to Gareth, Lord Bollington had been paying for Miss Carteret's education for the last twenty years—therefore somebody else must have perpetrated the scheme long before either Elaine or Mr. Fitzjohn were of an age to plan such villainy. Perhaps Fitzjohn had discovered her imposture and threatened disclosure? It seemed plain that he loved her, in his strange way—possibly marriage was the price he demanded for his silence. So perhaps, Delphie thought, *that* was why my first application, written during the winter, received so rude a rebuff. It probably never reached Lord Bollington at all! Mr. Fitzjohn received it, and instantly realized that the Miss Carteret in Bath was the false claimant. But she, it seemed, loved Gareth—or was she merely determined to have him for his rank and position and the money that went with it? Delphie was sure that, married to Gareth, she would give him a wretched time; at worst, it seemed, she was calmly prepared to murder him and return to Fitzjohn! If *he* could make good his claim to the title. And on what could this claim rest? Could it possibly be that Delphie's grandfather had, in fact, married Prissey Privett in time for his two children by her to be legitimate? This could not be ascertained without recourse to documents, for Delphie was not certain when Mary, Lady Bollington, had died, or when Priss Privett's son, the first Mordred, had been born. But if he was legitimate, why had *he* never put forward a claim to the title? It was all mysterious and inexplicable, thought Delphie, looking out with an absent eye at the green fields of Kent, and the lambs, now bigger and livelier than on her first journey past them. How long ago that now seemed! How disagreeable she had thought Gareth Penistone! And so he had been, in truth, she reflected, but now that she knew the cause, there were extenuating factors. She had not known then about the querulous Una, or the hapless Thomas, or the ten Palgrave children he was obliged to support; she had not known of his jilt by Lady Laura Trevelyan.

At Maidstone the driver requested a ten-minute stop, so that he might have a rest, and a bite to eat. This seemed only reasonable, and Delphie readily granted his request; she herself felt the need of a little sustenance, for she had eaten a hasty, early breakfast before packing her own and her mother's clothes in Curzon Street, and had taken no food since then.

In a small side parlor she was accommodated with such cold meat as an inn larder usually affords, bread-and-butter, and a most welcome cup of tea. Looking from the window, as she sipped her second cup, and amusing herself by watching the white-smocked postboys bringing out the fresh horses and taking the tired ones off, she suddenly stiffened at seeing a familiar face—two! There was Miss Carteret, in the sarcenet pelisse and plumed hat described by Mr. Swannup, and there, with her was the dour-faced old nurse, Durnett.

"We have no time to stop!" Delphie heard Miss Carteret declare in her loud, arrogant voice. "For all I know, Mordred may be on our traces already. We have been too much delayed by that wretched animal's casting a shoe. Put-to the fresh horses directly."

"Is there a side way out from this inn?" Delphie asked the potboy who brought her reckoning.

"Sure, miss; down that pair o' steps will take you into the lane as goes around to the stables."

"I am very much obliged to you!"

In two minutes, Delphie had rejoined her driver, and warily slipped into the chaise on its far side, unobserved by Miss Carteret, who stood by a yellow carriage at the front of the inn-yard, impatiently waiting for her fresh horses. Delphie leaned well back as they passed Miss Carteret and hoped that her face could not be seen. Then she had a moment's alarm.

"Can you tell me which road we should take for Chase?" the arrogant voice demanded of Delphie's driver.

"Tell her the Hastings Road!" Delphie whispered.

He did so.

"But 'twas a larmentable bit o' misdirection, missie!" he remarked, grinning, as they left the streets of Maidstone behind them and were out in open country once more. "I dunnamany miles out o' their way that'll lead 'em!"

"I have my reasons for wishing to arrive at Chase ahead of that young lady," Delphie said primly.

"That were what I reckoned!"

The new horses were not quite such fast goers as the previous team, but still they kept up a good steady speed, and, looking from time to time through the tiny back window, Delphie could see no sign of the yellow carriage coming after them.

But where was Mordred? Had he, driving his much lighter curricle, and with only one person in it, already far outdistanced them, perhaps even arrived at Chase? Mordred was far more to be dreaded than Elaine; if he were really set on marrying her, to what lengths might he not be driven, in order to make sure that Gareth was out of the way?

Dusk was beginning to fall. It was already eight o'clock and, after an unusually hot and brilliant day, more like July than May, a wrack of large pinkish-black clouds had arisen, covering half the sky, and, with the close and sultry temperature, promising thunder later. Indeed, one or two faint growling mutters could already be heard, far off, and presently there came a resounding crack, right overhead, which made the horses start and whinny.

"Looks like 'tis farin' to be a bad night, missie!" called the driver. "Lucky we ain't so far off now."

"You had better spend the night at Cow Green!" she called back. "I believe the inn there is quite tolerable."

"Hallo! Looks like there's a cove on ahead as has come to grief," he said after a few minutes. "There's some kind of a hurley-bulloo up yonder, and I can hear a horse a-screaming something cruel."

As they came closer, the hurley-bulloo resolved itself into a shattered curricle, half in the ditch, and a desperately writhing horse among the tangle of wreckage. No wonder the poor beast screamed—part of the splintered shaft was sticking into its side.

"I'll have to put the poor nag out of pain, missie," said the driver, slowing as he passed it. "I can't abear to leave it like that."

"Of course you must not," she agreed. "But how?"

"With one o' my brace of barkers," he explained. "I allus carries 'em loaded, case o' tobymen, you know." And, bringing his own team to a halt, he pulled a pistol from under the box, and stepped down into the road. "Reckon it were that clap o' thunder caused this little upset," he called back. "Made the nags shy, mebbe. There's only one—likely the driver rid off on the other to get help."

Delphie, leaning from the window, wondered whether this shattered curricle was Mordred's. The horse was a bay, as his had been.

"I don't like to trouble you, miss," called the driver, "but would you mind holding the heads o' my pair while I do this job? I'm afeared the shot may cause 'em to bolt."

"Certainly I will," said Delphie, dismounting. The task was no easy one, for the horses were already scared and sweating at the screams of their wounded companion; it was all she could do to keep them still as the driver held his pistol to the head of the hurt horse and discharged it.

"Poor creature—how heartless of its driver to go off and leave it—" Delphie was beginning, when a voice from behind her said,

"Well met, cousin!"

She whirled around—and discovered with a shock of terror that Mordred had appeared—where *from?* He must have come out of a field gate—and had climbed onto the box of her carriage, where, possessed of the driver's other pistol, he was now holding it in a negligent manner.

"What a fortunate thing that you came along!" he remarked coolly. "I was expecting my cousin Elaine but not, I must confess, your estimable self. You have quite a genius for turning up in the nick of time, have you not? Having failed to recapture my other horse, which had bolted, I was resigning myself to a long walk."

"What are you doing there—with that thing?" she cried indignantly.

"Going to settle accounts with my cousin Gareth. He has stood in my way too long."

"What can you mean?" she said, trembling.

"Oh, I shall not murder him! I am not such a flat as that! His death will be the result of a misguided wager—dear Gareth never could resist a wager!"

"'Ere! What's going on?" demanded the outraged driver, who, walking back from the wrecked carriage, only now observed that his place had been usurped. "You come down off of there!"

But Mordred, pointing the pistol at Delphie, said, "Stand away from their heads, cousin, or I shall be obliged to wing you in the arm—and it will not be an easy shot, with the horses so restive; I might mistake!"

He held the reins in his left hand, and now swung their ends sharply over the horses' backs, making them bound forward; Delphie was obliged to jump aside, or she would have been trampled.

The driver let out a stream of the most lurid language Delphie had ever heard, and started to run after the chaise—but it was hopeless to try and catch it; in a few moments he desisted and came back to Delphie, panting and furious.

"Was that cove *known* to you, missus?" he asked Delphie.

"Oh, yes! He is a very wicked man! I would give anything for this not to have happened," she said wretchedly.

"So would I! It's barefaced highway robbery! Where's he taking my rig?"

"Oh, to Chase, I am sure. You will probably find it in the stables when we get there."

"I had better! We got a five-mile walk afore that," he said grimly, "and we're a-going to be soused, for any minute now it's a-going to pelt!"

He was right. Huge drops of rain as large as crown pieces were beginning to plop heavily onto the dusty road, and the great black cloud had crept right across the sky. Another clap of thunder, much louder this time, pealed in the heavens as they set off walking along the road.

All the driver's good nature had vanished. He was hardly to be blamed, certainly, for his bad temper, but Delphie could have wished that he had a more stoic nature, for he grumbled incessantly all the way along the road to Chase, as the rain sluiced down on them and the thunder fulminated overhead. The storm, having apparently settled in the Chase valley, seemed to circle around and around without ever moving off; it was still thundering and lightning just as violently at the end of their walk, which took upward of an hour and a half, as it had been when they began.

By the time they reached Chase darkness had fallen, but they were able to pick their way well enough by the lightning flashes, which followed one another with startling rapidity. Delphie thought she had never been so wet in her life. The water ran out of the tops of her boots, her pelisse was sodden, and her soaked cambric dress clung to her like a flypaper.

"One thing," she thought, thumping with her clenched fist on the oak door, and remembering her previous unwelcomed reception, "*nobody* could be turned away on a night like this!"

"Let me take a hand at that!" offered the driver, hammering lustily with the handle of his whip, " 'Tis likely with all the ruckus overhead, those inside can't hear us!" as another shattering peal of thunder seemed to explode on the very rooftop.

At last the door was pulled open and Delphie saw the amazed face of Fidd peering out at them.

"Oh, Fidd, I am so glad to see you!" she exclaimed in relief.

"You remember me—Miss Carteret? My—my carriage has had an accident—the driver and I have been obliged to walk the last five miles. We are excessively wet!"

"Lor bless my soul, yes, miss, I can see that. Come in, miss," he said, pulling the door wider. "And we'll see about getting you dried off!"

"Never mind me, for the moment! But perhaps you can take this poor fellow to a fire. Did—has Mr. Mordred arrived, in a post chaise? And Miss Elaine Carteret?"

"Mr. Mordred come, miss; best part of an hour agone *he* got here, afore the storm grew so swallocky, an' his cattle's in the stable."

Delphie's driver sighed with relief at this news.

"But I dunno about no *other* Miss Carteret, miss; I never heard tell o' none; nor Mr. Fitz ever said *you* was expected."

"Well, no matter! Where—where is Mr. Gareth?"

"He and Mr. Fitz is in the library, miss. Shan't I tell 'em you're here—or take you where you can change—"

"No, first lead this good man to a fire—I can announce myself! And then if you could have somebody fetch my bag, which—which is in Mr. Mordred's carriage—"

Looking somewhat bemused at these odd directions, Fidd hobbled off, followed by the driver.

Delphie walked without hesitation to the library door, and opened it.

She walked into what seemed like a scene of debauch. Gareth and Mordred were seated, facing one another, at the center table. Both looked decidedly the worse for drink. They were in shirt sleeves, and Gareth's dark locks were much disarranged. Between them were upward of half a dozen bottles, mostly empty, some lying on their sides. More bottles lay on the floor. By the light of several guttering candles, Delphie could see that Gareth's face was unusually flushed, his eyes bloodshot. Mordred, on the contrary, was very pale, and his eyes seemed to glitter unnaturally in the flickering light. He looked, thought Delphie, quite as evil as she had for some time believed him to be: evil and rapacious. He had been staring down at the great flashing ring on Gareth's right hand. His expression did not change when Delphie opened the door, though he pressed his lips tight together. Then, ignoring Delphie completely, he said to Gareth,

"Make haste! Finish that bottle! It's time for our wager!"

But Gareth had turned and was gazing at Delphie in bewilderment. It was plain that he was very drunk indeed.

"My God!" he said, gripping Mordred's arm across the table, and pointing with his other hand. "She's come again! Or is it her ghost? She's all wet and dripping—like last time—only then it was t'other one—fell—fell in moat—like Great-uncle Lancelot!"

"Stuff!" said Mordred briskly—it was apparent to Delphie that he was not nearly so drunk as Gareth, perhaps not drunk at all. "You are fancying things—seeing visions, my boy! Nothing is there. Come along—let's go up!"

"Gareth!" said Delphie, but Gareth, looking at his cousin in a puzzled manner, inquired,

"Up? Up where?"

"Do you not remember? Our wager?"

"Gareth!" exclaimed Delphie again, but Gareth, urged by Mordred, had risen shakily to his feet.

"Wager—yes, wager," he mumbled. "Never refuse—honorable wager. Can't quite—quite remember—terms of it though—"

"Gareth!" cried Delphie, quite desperately now, for his cousin was guiding his rather staggering progress toward the far end of the library. She moved after them, and said, "Gareth, can you hear me? Can you understand me?"

"Did she not speak?" Gareth said in a troubled voice. "Are you certain you don't see her, Fitz? She did look devilish like Cousin Delphie. Only wet—wet as a herring!"

"You're a trifle foxed, old fellow, that's all," said Mordred.

"Drunk—drunk as a wheelbarrow," agreed Gareth, swaying.

"*You* did this to him!" said Delphie furiously to Mordred. And to Gareth she cried,

"Don't trust Mordred, Gareth! He means harm to you—I am sure of it! I am sure of it! Do not be taking part in his wager!"

"Can't refuse honorable wager," said Gareth stubbornly.

"Of course you cannot," said Mordred. "Come along, old fellow—up the stairs—when you start talking to your visions it means you're a bit bosky and it's time for bed."

Running forward, Delphie tried to reach for Gareth's hand, but Mordred pushed a table in her way and then half pulled, half hoisted Gareth up a short flight of stairs that led to an upper gallery in the library. The stair had a gate at the foot, which he locked after passing through it, pocketing the key, so that Delphie was cut off from them.

"Gareth! Don't go with Mordred!" she called. "He means mischief."

But they had passed through a door above, and disappeared from view.

She was sure from the expression on Mordred's face that he had no intention of seeing Gareth tamely to his bed. But where *were* they going? She shook the gate at the foot of the library stair. It rattled, but held against her. Foiled, Delphie ran out of the library and up the main stairs to the hall above. Turning right, in the same direction as that in which the library lay downstairs, she ran along a passage, groping her way in the meager light cast from behind her by a lamp on a table near the stair head. She opened a succession of doors, but all, from the darkness and enclosed smell within, seemed to lead into disused bedrooms. At last she achieved her object and found herself in the gallery, looking down at the dying candles and flickering fire of the library below. There was the stair with the locked gate. But this was where the two men had *been*. Where were they now?

Returning to the corridor, Delphie heard the great front door slam, and voices in the hall. Was that Elaine arriving? But she ignored the voices. This was no time to worry about Elaine.

She sniffed the air like a bloodhound, and then turned to her right, following the faint flavor of brandy which hung in the stuffy passage behind the departed pair. Listening intently she thought she could just distinguish the faint sound of a door slamming somewhere ahead. A lightning flash momentarily illuminated the whole length of the corridor ahead: it was empty, but the slam had been a long way off. Delphie picked up her sopping skirts and ran to the end. She opened a door, and, by another flash, discovered that it gave onto a flight of stairs, again leading up. Here, too, she thought, she could faintly discern the aroma of brandy.

Where could they be *going*? To the servants' quarters? The attics? At the top of the stairs she stopped, casting about. A passage ran both ways. And then, in the distance, glinting in the lightning flash, she saw something that lay on the floor. Through the velvet dark that followed the flash, blanketing her eyes, she made her way along until her foot struck the object. Stooping, she picked it up. Its outline was familiar; after a moment's concentration she recognized it: a little curved, gold-inlaid tortoiseshell snuffbox belonging to Gareth. She had often seen him use it. So they *had* passed this way. Now where? She paused, uncertain, for there were several more doors here, and no whiff of brandy to guide her. Then a cold damp touch of air on her cheek gave her a lead; in the next flash of lightning she noticed a small door which stood a crack ajar as if, when recently closed, the latch had failed to hold. She opened it, and instantly smelt the wet air above, heavy with the rank, acid smell of rain-soaked leads and old roofing tiles. Another short flight of steps led up to a kind of parapet, where she stopped, nervously gripping the stone balustrade, afraid of where she might be, until the next flash of lightning should come to guide her.

When it came, she could see that the aged mansion's roof was like a moonworld all around her. The slates flashed almost white in the electric glare from above—towers and battlements stood up like rocks, with their crenellations etching a jagged line across her eyeballs against the livid blue of the luminous sky beyond. When the dark fell again, the ridges of different roof sections lay across her remembered vision in a series of broken parallels. What a strange, huge region! How would she ever dare explore it, in this intermittent light? But the two men were out there somewhere. She knew it—had known it all along, she felt now; somehow she had understood in her bones that when Mordred referred to *the wager*, he had a scheme in his mind related to that other affair of long ago, the duel on the roof between Lancelot and Mark.

But where had they gone? Another flash helped her to memorize the contours of the area close to where she stood: the small door through which she had emerged had brought her into a kind of flat, leaded valley, between four rising ridges. Nervously she began to climb the pent of a ridge, and, as she had hooked her fingers over its angle, another flash suddenly revealed the two men, about fifteen yards away from her, moving behind a great outcrop of twisted, sloped, bent, crow-stepped, intricately piled chimney stacks. Somehow Delphie managed to scramble over the peak of her ridge; then she waited, afraid to venture farther until she was certain that the ravine of an inner courtyard did not lie between her and her quarry.

Another flash came, and again she followed, surmounting yet another ridge—yet another—skirting around a gable, feeling her way among a jumble of slate and stone. Now she saw the men again—rather nearer; they seemed to have come to a stop, on a flat open place with nothing beyond it but darkness. She caught a voice—Mordred's—saying:

"Best take *that* off—wouldn't wish any accident to overtake the family ruby—!"

Now the two men were standing close together, comparing, it seemed, the lengths of objects which they held; then they turned and walked apart, pacing, measuring. Gareth still swayed drunkenly, as if blown by the wind—it seemed incredible that he had managed to stagger so far through this wilderness. He must have been buoyed up by the irrational sense of balance that sometimes carries drunkards along paths narrow as tightropes and beside the verge of precipices.

"Stop!" shouted Delphie. "Gareth, come back! Mordred, I can see you! *Don't shoot!*"

But they were ignoring her, they were on the other side of a drop filled with crisscrossing walls, exhibited like actors on a stage. They stood braced, each in the same attitude, one leg forward, one back, in the posture of archers, each pointing a pistol.

The light went suddenly, and then came back again, a huge leaden glare, throwing every shadow as distinct and sharp as if it had that instant been traced out in wet black paint. The lightning seemed to hover in the sky for a dreamlike spell of time—perhaps ten seconds in reality; the crack of the pistols was drowned by a huge roll of thunder which followed, but Delphie saw the red flash from one of them—Mordred's. Another blaze of light an instant later showed Gareth fallen and rolling toward an edge of blackness—and it showed Delphie something else, too: Elaine

Carteret, white-faced, glaring at Mordred, half a dozen paces away from him.

She heard Mordred exclaim:

"How the devil did you get up here? I expected t'other one—not you!"

"Nurse Durnett told me the way up—she guessed what you would be at. You murderer! You vile murderer!"

"Well, really, m'dear, it is only what you yourself intended. You said so! Now, where the devil did I lay that ring?" He stooped, searching about; by the light of the next flash, Delphie saw Elaine violently strike his head with the pistol butt. He staggered and fell backward over the edge into darkness, and she flung the pistol after him. Then, stooping also, she snatched up something and ran away, climbing the roof ridges with the speed of a lizard, vanishing over a distant series of sierras.

But Delphie began with slow and careful labor making her way in the opposite direction, toward where she had seen Gareth last. Four—five lightning flashes—and she must be nearly there; now she was on the wide flat expanse of lead roof where they had stood, and could see that beyond a low parapet, only an inch or two high, there lay nothing but black space. Trembling, she levered a bit of rubble out from between the bricks of a chimney stack and tossed it away into the dark; she thought she heard a splash. Did the moat lie down there?

By the next flash she confirmed that it did: she could see the outer bank, and a few heads of water lilies, closed for the night into black spearheads, outlined against the silvered water. The lightning had shown her something else—a pistol, Gareth's, it must be—lying farther back from the edge than she had expected, in a dark pool of some liquid. Blood?

She waited for another flash and then ran to where the pistol lay. Surely, she thought, if Gareth fell backward—*that* way—then he might *not* have gone into the moat? Dropping to her hands and knees she crawled gingerly to the parapet, which here described a right angle; felt it with her fingers, and waited for the next flash to come. When it came, she looked down, and found that she was overlooking a kind of gulley—vertical on one side, sloping on the other, where a narrow peak of roof was contained between two square towers. And below her, not six feet away, jammed in the acute angle between roof and wall, lay Gareth's body. It was about six inches back from the drop to the moat—if he had fallen sideways, rather than backward, he must certainly have gone over the edge.

In the next lightning flash, Delphie stared about her with agonized speed, trying to learn everything that she could of the geography around her—the angles, verticles, and horizontals of her situation in relation to that of Gareth.

Yes—there! If she went back, and then to her right, quite soon came a point at which the roof peak below her was not so very far down from her own level. She could climb down to it, and then make her way diagonally across its slope to the crack where Gareth's body had been caught.

She began to move in the dark, feeling her way around the shallow parapet—found where it turned to the right, followed that—presently another flash showed her that she had already come too far and passed the highest point of the roof peak. Patiently she crawled back, scrambled on hands and knees over the parapet, and let herself backward down the four feet or so onto the ridge below. This, in darkness, was frightening; she hoped she had not mistaken the spot. No, here was the ridge—now down the slope . . . and presently, she felt the vertical wall with her right hand. Now, forward again—inch by inch, this time, for Gareth's body must be within a few feet and she must not risk jolting or nudging it; there! She had found his hand with hers, groping; she grasped his wrist. Bracing herself with one foot on the slope and one pressed against the wall, she exerted all her strength to pull him backward; began to despair; pulled again, and felt his body move a little.

Dragging, panting, and gasping, she presently had him as far back from the edge as it was possible to move him, on this level, right against the back wall of the gulley. Would it be feasible to pull him up the slope of the roof, and then hoist him from its peak onto the level above? Looking up, the next brilliant flash, Delphie thought not. The roof itself was a steep slope, five or six feet high; then there would be the vertical lift of another three feet; and Gareth was a tall, muscular man. He was too heavy. She did not think she could manage it. But at least he was away from that awful edge!

Now, with trembling, eager hands, she felt for his pulse—and found it, to her amazement, solid, firm, steady as the tick of her metronome. He was alive, at least! Perhaps not even badly hurt? In her astonished relief at this almost unlooked-for good fortune, Delphie burst into tears.

"Oh my dear, mad, crazy creature!" she sobbed. "How could you have been such an *idiot* as to let him entice you up here?"

Gingerly, carefully, when the next flash of lightning came, she began looking over him to find, if possible, where he was wounded. Where had all that blood come from? But to her perplexity she could find no trace of blood on him; his clothes seemed intact—so far as she could make out, there was no bullet hole anywhere to be found.

After a while she began to conclude that he must have staggered and fallen backward into the gully just at the instant when Mordred's pistol was discharged. What a strange piece of good fortune! For if Gareth had not fallen so, and Elaine therefore supposed him dead, she would not have taken her revenge by striking Mordred; since the latter had fallen outward Delphie felt certain that he must have gone straight down into the moat. He must have been killed, and she was disposed to think that the world was very well rid of him. As to Elaine—she was of small importance; Delphie's entire concern at present was to see that Gareth should be prevented from rolling or falling until he should have recovered consciousness.

It was possible, she concluded, ruefully, that he was merely in a drunken stupor; no doubt when he did come to he would have the most atrocious headache, and would believe himself at death's door. In the meantime, all she could hope to do was keep him warm, which she did by edging him into the angle of roof and wall, and huddling herself against him. (Any slight awkwardness she might have felt as to this necessary precaution was dispelled by the fact that she herself, in her soaked velvet and damp cambric, was excessively cold, and needed all the warmth she could find.)

An hour or two went by. Slowly, the storm began to abate. The intervals between the lightning flashes grew greater. The thunder was no longer a deafening crack overhead, but had dwindled to a gentle mumble, far away in the distance. Then the clouds began to drift apart; at last, a half moon was revealed, gently illuminating the strange, angular world in which they were perched.

Delphie looked at Gareth and confirmed again, with infinite relief, that he was not dead, not even fainted, she thought, but just heavily asleep, in a kind of brandy-soaked coma.

She began to wonder if she could wake him. For it was decidedly cramped and uncomfortable in their triangular niche. Perhaps she could go off to summon help—but no, it would be too dangerous to leave him unguarded. He might wake, or half wake, and make some incautious movement.

"Gareth!" she said hopefully. "Gareth, you odious wretch! Wake up! *Pray* wake up! It is too cold to be perching here like a pair of swallows!"

But Gareth slept obstinately on, snoring somewhat. Since he must be quite as cold as she, besides suffering from the effects of a heavy fall and God knows how much brandy, Delphie with difficulty removed her damp pelisse and spread it over both of them. Then she began waiting for dawn: at least five hours more, she reckoned dejectedly.

By slow, insensible degrees, her eyes closed. Then she, too, was asleep.

16

Delphie opened her eyes to a blaze of sunshine. She felt quite warm, but cramped and damp; like some creature hatching out of an egg, she thought confusedly. Then she saw Gareth's face, close to hers, looking down at her in a puzzled manner.

"I daresay I am dreaming still?" he confided. "I have certainly had some very singular dreams during the night. If I am *not* dreaming—what the devil are *you* doing here?"

Now Delphie realized that his arm was around her, and that her head was, in fact, pillowed on his shoulder. She blushed slightly, and said,

"Well, it is perfectly easy to give you an account of it all, Cousin Gareth—"

"Naturally! I am quite sure of that! The stupidity was mine, first of all, in not realizing that you were a witch! You touched me with your wand—gave me a worse headache than I have ever suffered in my life before—and then popped me onto your broomstick and transported me—us—here. Where *are* we, by the by? It is exceedingly uncomfortable!"

"It is not only uncomfortable, but exceedingly dangerous! We are on the roof at Chase, and, if you are able to do so, I believe we should move from this spot directly." She added in a scolding tone, "The stupidity was certainly yours, in allowing your cousin Mordred to make you so inebriated!"

"Oh, I was inebriated, was I?"

"Disgracefully so!"

"Did I say or do anything foolish?" he inquired with interest.

"Oh dear me, no," said Delphie with awful irony. "Only allowed Fitzjohn to entice you up to this perilous spot and then shoot his pistol at you, under the pretext of some silly wager!"

"Oh—yes," he said slowly, frowning. "Deuce take it—my poor head! It feels as if the thunderstorm were still inside it. There *was* a thunderstorm, was there not?"

"One of the worst I have ever experienced. It was quite terrifying."

"Yes—it all begins to come back to me. Mordred arrived—said he had something of importance to divulge to me. I'd been feeling low-spirited—had had a drink or two—nothing much. Then we had a drink or two more."

"Indeed you *had*," she said with asperity. "From the look of the room, you had each imbibed about four bottles of brandy. It is not to be wondered at that your head aches."

"No—no—dash it, my dearest girl! Most of those were wine bottles."

"Mr. Penistone," she said, ignoring his appellation. "I think we should try to climb up on the roof above."

"You should properly address me as Lord Bollington."

"I think we should try to move."

"No, why?" He tightened the arm around her.

"Just now you said it was uncomfortable here."

"I have changed my mind. I think we are delightfully situated. The sun shines on us, the swallows are twittering—why must you be forever carping and finding fault? It is true that, as usual, you have a certain amount of grime on your nose"—he removed it, with a careful finger—"but otherwise I have no complaint to make regarding my position—not the least in the world."

"Oh," she said, laughing, "you absurd creature! Come along—we *must* bestir ourselves!"

"Both my arm and my foot have gone to sleep. I am quite unable to move them!"

"Then you should shift without delay—they are probably frostbitten, and will presently fall off!"

Moving herself out of his grip with considerable difficulty, she scrambled up the sloping roof against which they had been reclining, and turned, when she was seated on its peak, to reach a hand down to him. He was looking up at her with a good deal of amusement on his face.

"Cousin Delphie, what *have* you been doing? Every stitch you have on appears to be both wet and filthy—your boots are covered in mud—your hair is in rat's tails—and your face looks as if you have been climbing chimneys!"

"I have been climbing chimneys," said Delphie. "Come along!"

He caught hold of the hand she reached down, and allowed himself to be pulled up, wincing as he moved his head. Seated beside her on the roof ridge, he held her hand to steady her, while she clambered up and over the parapet onto the wide expanse of flat roof beyond. When she turned around she saw that he was swaying and looking rather pale.

"Gareth! Quick, take my hand!"

"Thank you; it was but a passing touch of vertigo," he said as she assisted him to follow her. "Ah, this is certainly better"—as they stood on the flat leads, a safe distance from the edge. "Most refreshing, in fact—a charming prospect!"

From this eminence they could see a considerable distance over the surrounding countryside, and the green sheep-studded pastures near at hand. The sound of bleating came faintly through the sun-warmed air.

"What the deuce is *that* doing up here?" said Gareth, frowning. He had just caught sight of his pistol, which was lying in a puddle at no great distance. He crossed to it and picked it up.

"What is that? How strange—it is not water, but oil," Delphie said, observing the rainbow hues of the damp patch where the pistol had lain.

"Neats'-foot oil!" said Gareth, suddenly and blankly. "What was that you were saying about a duel?"

"I told you! You and Mordred were fighting a duel."

"A fine sort of duel!" he said, inspecting the pistol. "It is not loaded."

"How strange! I am sure his was—I saw the red spark when he fired it. You are *sure* you are not wounded?"

"I suppose, come to think, this graze on my arm must be from a bullet."

She exclaimed as he bared a red, furrowed graze, which, under his shirt sleeve, she had missed the night before.

"But what is that oil?"

"Uncle Mark used to say—when he was in his cups—that he had oiled the spot where Lancelot was to stand on the roof. I think Mordred must have taken a leaf out of his book—slipped up here beforehand and done the same thing." He looked about and said, frowning, "Where *is* Mordred, then?"

"Elaine Carteret somehow followed him onto the roof. She—she thought he had killed you. When he was stooping—searching for something—she pushed him off the edge—"

Without answering, Gareth walked to the edge and looked over.

"Gareth! *Pray* take care!"

Anxiously she followed him and looked down. Among the close-set pattern of the lily pads they could see a larger clear space; something appeared to have disturbed them and pushed them apart.

"Come away from the edge!" Delphie said, shivering.

He did so, and then put his hands on her shoulders, looking down at her gravely.

"And where were *you*, when all this was going on? How come you to have arrived at Chase in the midst of all this?"

"Oh, well, it—it is a long story! But I chanced to learn that both Mordred and Elaine had plots against you—and that they had quarreled—I believed it possible that he might wish to get rid of you—murder you, perhaps—as *she* wished to marry you—and indeed I saw him setting out for Chase looking exactly like a Fiend! So I—so I followed. And when I arrived, I found you both in the library—he was urging you to some wager—"

"Yes, I remember now. He told me that he had a valid claim to the title. His father, he said, was after all a legitimate son of Grandfather Lancelot, who had married Prissy Privett. I said in that case he was *welcome* to the title—I wanted nothing that did not come to me by right. But that did not suit him—he said, why not fight for it, fight a duel like grandfather and Uncle Mark—?"

"*That* does not sound as if he were very sure of his claim," said Delphie.

"So we came up onto the roof—I remember his telling me to take off my ring. Where is it?" he said, staring around.

"I think Elaine took it down."

"Oh—well, it does not signify. After that, I remember nothing. I do not remember *your* arrival at all."

"I am not surprised!"

"Was I uncivil?"

"Oh, no—not in the least. I believe you thought I was an apparition."

"And then you followed us up here—"

"—Hoping to dissuade or somehow prevent you from fighting. But I was too far off. So then—so then I looked to see if I could find where you had fallen—"

Her voice trembled a little as she remembered how she had felt at that point. "And then I saw your body—"

Moving his hands down from her shoulders, Gareth took her into a close embrace. She put her own arms tightly around him, and thought, How natural this feels!

"And then you spent the night beside me, making sure that I did not fall off," he said, resting his cheek on the top of her head. He added, and there was a smile in his voice, "I wish I had been awake, after all!"

Her chuckle was muffled against his shoulder.

"So did I! You were snoring horribly! Now I know the worst about you!"

"You have known *that* any time this last six weeks! I am uncivil, misogynistic, overbearing—" He held her at arms' length, looking her in the eyes, and said seriously,

"I love you. You know that?"

"I—I believe that I do."

"But do *you* love *me*?"

"Oh, good gracious! How can you *conceive* of such a notion? Why, I came to Chase—walking five miles through a downpour, I may say, because that odious Mordred made off with my carriage—followed you up onto the roof—clambered over I do not know how many obstacles—dragged your lifeless corpse back from the chasm's brink—all from motives of the calmest—most phlegmatic—neutrality—and altruism—"

The last words came out of her in jerks, for he was shaking her.

"Oh, you little wretch! How often have I not longed to wring your neck! Or at the very least to do this—"

And he set his lips on hers.

After some time, Delphie said,

"Gareth?"

"Yes, my angel?"

"Do you not think we ought to get down off the roof?"

"Why? I should be happy to spend the rest of my life up here!"

"*You* might be so, but *I* should like some breakfast. Besides, I can hear horses down below—I believe a carriage is arriving."

From where they stood, it was not possible to see the drawbridge or the main court, so, with some difficulty and several false starts, they retraced their way back to the original door from which they had come out.

"How we ever found our path through this maze in the dark—and in a thunderstorm to boot!" said Gareth. "But Mordred was brought up at Chase. I suppose he knew the roofs from a child."

However, when they tried the door, their plans received a check. It appeared to be locked; no amount of shaking, banging, or rattling would shift it.

"I suppose Elaine did that," Delphie said thoughtfully. "Hoping perhaps that I should fall off the roof in the dark—or die of starvation—or some such thing."

"The puzzle is," said Gareth, "how *she* found her way up here. For she has never been to Chase."

"She said her nurse told her—I wonder where they are now."

"Downstairs, perhaps, asserting her claim to be the true Miss Carteret."

Delphie then bethought herself to tell Gareth about Lady Bablock-Hythe's expulsion of Elaine, and how this had led to the quarrel with Mordred.

"It is all most singular," he said. "I had long since decided she was the false pretendant, but we still have no clue at all as to *who* she is, or why my uncle Mark should have supported her from infancy."

Delphie was visited by inspiration.

"Could she not be a child of his?"

He burst out laughing.

"Begotten in his fifties—not if I know my uncle Mark! Besides, who could the mother have been?"

"Oh—well—how should I know?"

"A most improper suggestion, Lady Bollington!"

"Good gracious," she said, blushing. "How strange it sounds. I had forgotten."

"That we are married? I had not, however; in spite of your tearing up your marriage lines—spitfire that you are!"

Rather shyly avoiding his glance, Delphie moved away around a gable, and made her way to a parapet, which, being three feet high, offered reasonable security.

"Oh!" she cried, looking down. "I can see into the main courtyard. And—good gracious—there is my mother walking across the grass! With Mr. Browty! And Lady Bablock-Hythe. How very singular. "*Mamma!*" she shouted down. "Mamma! I am here on the roof with Cousin Gareth, and we are locked out. Can you send somebody to release us?"

Whether Mrs. Carteret, so far below, fully understood the purport of her daughter's request seemed doubtful, but at least the people in the yard were now aware of the fact that the roof was inhabited, and presently they heard the rattle of bolts inside the door, and it was opened by one of the footmen, panting and apologetic.

"Lor bless me, sir—my lord—can't think how it came about—very sorry indeed, I'm sure—if we'd a had any idea—we've been hunting high and low for you, sir—my lord, and Miss, too—Mr. Fidd was *that* put about, wondering what had become of you, and Mr. Mordred too—"

"Never mind that now, Cowley," said Gareth. "We were shut out by accident. All we need now is dry clothes and some breakfast."

"Yes, sir—right away, my lord! The young lady's valise has been taken to the Blue Chamber and—and there's company below, sir, arrived unexpected."

"So I apprehend. But we are in no condition to receive them immediately. Let them be taken to the dining room—or wherever is convenient—and served with some refreshment."

They descended the narrow stairs. At the foot a flustered housemaid—Meg—led Delphie away to a chamber: not the one she had shared with Jenny; this was in better trim. Here, at last, she was able to remove her damp and draggled clothes, wash her face, and brush out her untidy hair. After swallowing a cup of chocolate and a roll (brought by Jill) she put on her sprig-muslin, which was the only other dress she had brought, and, feeling decidedly more the thing, ran down the stairs and into the dining room, from where she heard voices issuing.

What was her astonishment, on entering this room, to find a considerable party assembled: not only her mother, Mr. Browty, and Lady Bablock-Hythe, but also Jenny Baggott, Mr. Swannup, and Una Palgrave with all her children.

Fidd was moving about, serving the adults of the party with glasses of sherry, and the children with lemonade and sweet biscuits.

"Good heaven!" said Delphie, pausing on the threshold in amazement. "How can this be?"

"Oh, my dearest child!" exclaimed Mrs. Carteret, coming swiftly to embrace her. "Such *tales* as we have been hearing from Miss Baggott. If I had had the least notion that you were in danger—Miss Baggott told us all about Mr. Fitzjohn and that wicked creature—I declare, it is just like *The Orphan of the Wilderness!*"

"And it has all ended just as well, Mamma! Gareth and I are alive and hearty. But I am afraid you must have found it a dreadfully tiring journey?"

"Oh, dear no! We stayed the night at the Angel, in Maidstone—a most comfortable inn. It was Mr. Browty's idea."

"When we got back to Brook Street, you see, and found Miss Baggott and Mr. Swannup there," began Mr. Browty—

"—So worried and anxious as we was about you, Miss Delphie!" cried Jenny. "We couldn't abear to think what might be happening with them Hyenas—"

"So Mr. Browty kindly said, 'Why not let us all go down and see,' " said Lady Bablock-Hythe.

"And he axed me and Sam to come along in case Sam was needed as a witness—"

Gareth came into the room, dressed with propriety and elegance. He, too, paused in the doorway, looking rather startled. Delphie hastily made the necessary introductions.

"But where *is* that nasty Mr. Fitzjohn?" cried Jenny, looking around disappointedly.

"We—er—fear he may have fallen into the moat, Miss—Baggott," said Gareth.

Jenny turned slightly pink.

Meeting Delphie's eye, Gareth added in a murmur, "I have given orders to have it dragged. There seems to be no sign of Elaine."

"And her—t'other Miss Carteret?" said Sam Swannup.

"Oh dear—we certainly do not want that disagreeable girl," said Mrs. Carteret plaintively.

Una's children had surrounded Delphie and were giving her joyful greetings.

"Hallo, Cousin Delphie! Isn't this famous! Mamma said we might as well all come down for the funeral—Papa is coming later, in a separate carriage—do you think Uncle Gareth will allow us to row on the moat? May we explore the house?"

"I am sure you may!" said Delphie warmly. "Go wherever you please! Only—excuse me a moment—I wish to hear what Fidd is saying!"

Fidd, coughing politely, had remarked in an apologetic manner,

"Er—ahem—I can perhaps provide the answer as to the whereabouts of the young lady as called herself Miss Elaine Carteret. Chancing to encounter the young lady and her Ma in the upper floors of this house, I very soon sent them to the right-about. Of course if I had known that they had incarcerated you, miss, and Mr. Gareth, upon the roof all night long, I should not have been so lenient; as it was, since they were anxious to depart, I paid off the driver of the hired carriage and allowed them to make use of it and him; I believe they set out in the direction of Dover, Mr. Gareth."

"And a good riddance," said Gareth briefly. "If they have the ring, they may keep it!"

A chorus of questions and exclamations broke out from other quarters of the room.

"*You* sent them away, Fidd? But why? Who *were* they? You said the young lady and her *Mamma?* Pray explain yourself!"

Fidd coughed again, deprecatingly.

"Why—as to that, Mrs. Carteret, ma'am—the young lady was certainly Mr. Mordred's cousin, that was true enough. Perhaps, ma'am, you remember a wet nurse you had, at the time Miss Delphie was born, named Lucy?"

"Good heavens—yes, I do," said Mrs. Carteret faintly.

"That Lucy, ma'am, was the younger child of Prissy Privett—er—by an unknown father. Mr. Mordred's father's half sister, that is. She was brought up at Chase but—er—at a youthful age she contracted an unfortunate alliance with a sergeant of fusiliers called Durnett, and run off to London after him. On his abandoning her, which happened almost at once, I understand, being left unprovided for, she applied for the position of wet nurse in your establishment, ma'am, and then, I apprehend, rewarded you for taking her in by pinching Miss Delphie's birth certificate. She then wrote a lying tale to Mr. Mark, saying as how *her* child was Miss Delphie & as how you had died in childbed. She knew she was safe enough to do that, acos she'd often enough heard you say, ma'am, that you'd never have anything further to do with your family!"

"Oh, what a tale of wickedness and depravity! But how do you come to know so much about all this, Fidd?"

"Well, ma'am," he replied, "I take an interest in Lucy—I've a reason to—so I got the story out of her. You'll have no more trouble from *them*, ma'am—Miss Philadelphia—my lady—I reckon they were glad enough to get away without being taken up for fraud."

"I should just about say so!" struck in Mr. Browty. "The designing harpies! It puts me in such a passion—to think of all the years they have been drawing off the funds that should have been at *your* disposal, ma'am"—addressing Mrs. Carteret.

Then, clasping the hand of Mrs. Carteret in his, he said to Delphie,

"I must now tell you something, Miss Delphie, that—ahem!—may surprise you a little, but, knowing me as I hope you do—knowing that I'm a plain man but an honest one, whose word is as good as his bond, who likes things straightforward—and likes all about him to be happy and comfortable—er—where was I?"

"You were going to tell me something, Mr. Browty!" said Delphie, smiling at him with considerable affection. She had already guessed what it was.

"Ah, that's right, Miss Delphie! What a head on your shoulders you always have! I was about to tell you that I have asked your dear Mamma to marry me, and she has said yes! And that has made me a very happy man," said Mr. Browty simply, "for I know she'll love my gals, and I shall do my possible to make *her* happy for the rest of her life. Won't I, my dear?"

It was plain from Mrs. Carteret's smile that this programme was already under way.

Delphie ran forward and embraced them both.

"You could not have done anything which would make *me* happier, sir!" she said. "I know you will get on together famously! Mamma will be forever making plans for parties, and *you* will be giving them!"

"Just so!" he said, delighted. "And I hope you'll be coming to every one of 'em, Miss Delphie! But there's one thing *I* should like to be clear about—relative to what you and I was saying the other day, Miss Delphie—"

"Yes, Mr. Browty?" said Delphie, casting an anxious glance at two gardeners, who had come in through a back door and were conferring with Gareth in low voices. She caught the words "Moat—body—Mr. Fitzjohn—" Then Gareth gave them some directions, they saluted, and went out again.

"Well," said Mr. Browty, "we just heard that the young lady as was pretending to be *you*, Miss Delphie, has been sent packing—and a hem good thing too!—but what about that Mr. Fitzjohn? And the suit that he had a mind to bring, proving that he was the rightful lord?"

"I do not think that would have borne investigation," said Gareth, returning from his conference with the two men. "It seems to have been based on the fact that my grandfather did, apparently, marry Prissy Privett—Mordred was able to show me a certificate of marriage, which he had recently discovered, tucked into a Bible in the library—but the date of the wedding, regrettably, came eighteen months after the birth of Mordred's father and six months after that of Lucy, so there would still be no question of their being legitimate."

"Ahem!" came the deferential voice of Fidd. "As to that, sir—!"

Everybody turned and looked at him.

"As to that," said Fidd modestly, "even Lord Bollington's marriage to Prissy Privett wouldn't ha' made no difference—whether the children was born in wedlock or out of it—for the marriage was what I'd call a bit of a spong-up; Prissy Privett was married already! She was married afore she ever took up with his lordship. *Either* of their lordships!"

"Good gracious!" exclaimed Mrs. Carteret. "Was anyone ever so *much* married as that Prissy Privett?"

"She must have had considerable appeal," said Gareth, turning thoughtfully to gaze up at the portrait of his great-aunt by marriage, who stood leaning against a tree and laughing down at them all.

"First she married the Fifth Viscount—and then she married the Seventh Viscount. But who was she married to first of all, then, Mr. Fidd?" inquired Delphie.

"Why," said Fidd calmly, "she were married to me!" He added, sighing "A proper flighty piece she were; you couldn't hold her down, no more than thistle-blow."

A stunned silence filled the room for some moments, and then, glancing thoughtfully about at the company, Fidd remarked,

"Would you be wishing me to serve a nuncheon, then, Miss Delphie?"

"Yes, Fidd, thank you," she replied. "We shall be twenty, for Mrs. Palgrave's husband is arriving separately, and Lord Bollington has also sent for Mr. Wylye."

"Thank you, ma'am," said Fidd, and bowed himself from the room.

"Well—what a thing!" declared Una, who had been silent so far. "Only imagine—*bigamy!*"

"If not *trigamy*, my dear sister!" said Gareth.

"What an outrageous scandal! It is a good thing it was all a long time ago."

"Talking of scandal," said Lady Bablock-Hythe, who had obviously experienced some difficulty in following the involved and shocking ramifications of the Penistone family's previous generations, but had now chosen ground she understood, "Talking of *scandal*, Lord Bollington, did my ears inform me correctly—can it be possible that what Fidd gave us to understand just now is actually the case—?"

"I am afraid I do not quite follow you, ma'am?"

"Why, that you and Miss Philadelphia Carteret spent the whole *night* together up on the *roof*—quite alone—quite unchaperoned?"

Delphie blushed, and met Gareth's eyes, which were full of laughter.

He said, "Well, yes, that is certainly true, ma'am—and devilish wet and uncomfortable it was, I can assure you! Quite the most disagreeable night I can ever recall having passed."

"But what are you going to *do* about it?"

"Well I don't know about Delphie, ma'am—but *I* plan to retire *very* early tonight, into a mustard bath, and I shall also take a stiff dose of paregoric. And I strongly advise Delphie to do the same."

"That is not in the least what I mean—do not pretend to misunderstand me, sir—are you going to offer for her hand?"

"Certainly not," said Gareth, taking it. "What would be the point? Delphie and I have been married these six weeks past—and very wearing it has been. However, I am in hopes that matters may now begin to improve. Honeymoons, you know, madam, are inclined to be trying! Now, if you will all excuse us, my wife and I have one or two things of a domestic nature to discuss together. We shall see you again around the luncheon table."

And he firmly whisked Delphie into the next room, a very pretty parlor with a french window, and out through the window into a paved rose garden.

"Why, this is charming!" said Delphie, sniffing the budding flowers. "I had no idea there was anything so pretty at Chase. Just a minute, Lord Bollington"—for he was about to take her in his arms again.

"Well, what is it *now?*" he demanded impatiently, for she was digging in her reticule and produced an envelope.

"Knowing that you have vowed not to conclude any matrimonial alliance that does not satisfy every dictate of sense, prudence, and rational—"

He snatched the paper from her. "*What* is all this? It can't be your marriage lines—you've already torn 'em up. *Lord Bollington?* What has this to say for itself?"

"It is just," said Delphie, "that I thought we should not begin our married life without a proper introduction!"

He read:

> *My dear Lord Bollington . . . This is to introduce to your Notise a young Connection of yours, Miss Carteret. Miss Carteret is the best, most scrupulously honest young Lady of my acquaintance . . . Her Morals are Unblemish'd, her Character direct & Sinsere, her Mind of a Purity the most Unecsepshionable & Limpid. . . .*